H

"The knockout first entry in Kageyama's detective series starring Kats Takemoto... Arresting plotting and suspense, Hunters Point becomes a vital vessel to illuminate the past and those who lived there. This stellar San Francisco noir novel boasts rich characterization and a vital connection to the past."
Editors Pick, Booklife by Publishers Weekly

"Well researched... immersive setting... striking cameos. A fun and captivating historical noir."
Kirkus Reviews

"City politics rules in Peter Kageyama's debut mystery featuring a fully realized Japanese American detective, Kats Takemoto, during the height of the Cold War era. San Francisco, the center of the arts, naval history, and Asian American communities, is the perfect setting for P.I. Takemoto to encounter sharp turns and dangerous inclines in his investigations. A very intriguing beginning of a promising series."
Naomi Hirahara, author of the 2022 Mary Higgins Clark Award winner, *Clark and Division*, a Japantown Mystery

---

"Well-crafted, carefully researched, and written with insight and understanding of the lives of the people and the world they live in, this is a strong debut novel."
Judy Alter, award-winning author, Kelly O'Connell Mysteries

Published by St. Petersburg Press
St. Petersburg, FL
www.stpetersburgpress.com

Design and composition by St. Petersburg Press
Cover design by Justin Groom
Illustrations by Lisa Wannemacher

Print ISBN 978-1-940300-81-8
Ebook ISBN 978-1-940300-82-5

First Edition

MIDNIGHT CLIMAX

A KATS TAKEMOTO NOVEL

BY PETER KAGEYAMA

For Lisa, my first reader in all things.

Acknowledgments

I am very happy to return to the world of Kats, Molly and Shig. The first book made me even more excited to return to these characters and their world and as I write this, book three is well underway. I am most grateful to all the love and support my family and friends have shown me in this ongoing process. Writing is solitary but being a writer is being part of a larger community than I ever realized. Special thanks to Dr. Dominique Thuriere who gave me incredible insight into the mental health issues several of these characters face. She also inspired a character in the book and I bet you can guess which one. Thanks to Rodney Paul, my San Francisco & Bay Area sherpa. His knowledge of the city and willingness to share it with me and others is a true gift. Thank you to San Francisco City Guides (sfcityguides.org), in particular Kay & Harry Rabin for their insight into Chinatown. Thanks to Mark Andrews for being an early reader. Big thanks to the St. Petersburg Press family – fellow traveler Paul Wilborn, Justin Groom for yet another great cover and Amy Cianci who makes the whole thing work.

And to my wife Lisa. I couldn't write a better life than the one we share.

ILLUSTRATIONS

BY LISA WANNEMACHER

similar to a mace or a flail.

End – Caffe Trieste, where Shig had many a coffee with the likes of Allen Ginsberg, Lawrence Ferlinghetti, Bob Kaufman and Ken Rexroth. Still there, cash only.

CHAPTER 1

"It's OK, baby, come on inside," she said as she pulled him by the hand into the dimly lit bedroom. The man followed, almost reluctantly, like he didn't fully understand what was about to happen. She laughed and grabbed his hand to pull him close. Her hands ran up his sides, and she nuzzled his neck. "You got the cash, baby? You said you had cash."

Slowly, like a man remembering something, he reached into his jacket pocket and drew forth a wallet. He pulled out two twenties, and she smiled. "We're gonna have a good time. I'm going to slip into something naughty," she said, while rising up on tiptoes to kiss him. She didn't usually like to kiss her clients, but this one was different because he was handsome. Six feet tall with strong shoulders, close-cropped brown hair, and dark eyes. He had sharp cheekbones and a full mouth. So much better looking than the ones who usually approached her. She'd seen him several times before. Working the same corners had that effect. She noticed him because he was quiet and would never quite look her in the eye. Tonight he'd finally talked to her, and within minutes they were walking the short way to her 'apartment.'

"Make yourself comfortable. I'll just be a minute," she said as she crossed the room to the bathroom. Before she entered, she turned on a floor lamp with a red shade. "Mood lighting, baby." She closed the door behind her.

The man stood there, hands at his sides as he slowly scanned the room. He took off his jacket, laid it across the back of a chair, and sat on the bed. After a moment, he began to untie his boots.

"Suzie looks good tonight," said the younger man, whose name was Billings. He sat in front of a glass window, a one-way mirror, that looked into the bedroom. The darkened room was illuminated by the window. He raised a camera and took several photos of the subject and a couple of Suzie that he'd add to the special file. A second man was busy in the corner, his back to Billings. As he turned, he carried two martini glasses and a full cocktail shaker. The other man, named Stiles, slightly older and more experienced, sat and shook the container before pouring two drinks. He took a small sip, nodded approvingly, and handed the other glass to Billings. "To Suzie," he said, and they clinked glasses. They both laughed at their own joke, referring to the bestselling book and hit Broadway play, *The World of Suzie Wong*, about a Chinese prostitute. Tonight they knew the girl they called Suzie was performing for them.

They watched as Suzie re-entered the room. She wore a short black negligee that clung to her tiny frame. The man sat on the bed, seemingly frozen. As she walked toward the bed, she did a pirouette, stopping before him. The man's hands reached out and cupped her tiny buttocks. "I love Suzie's ass," Billings said with a snort. The older man smiled but said nothing. In his mind, he would have preferred a White woman, blond, with bigger breasts. *Next time*, he thought.

Inside the bedroom, things had progressed. Suzie's negligee slid over her head and revealed her lean torso. The man pulled her close to him, his head pressed against her small breasts. He held her there for several moments, like a child in his mother's embrace. Suzie looked a bit confused as to what to do. She stroked his hair and stole a furtive glance back toward the mirror. She made a tiny shrug of her shoulders and continued to hold him. She managed to push him away from her breasts as she lay down on her back. She maneuvered him toward her and between her legs. As he moved on top of her, the men in the viewing room caught sight of the john's torso. He had several scars crisscrossing his chest and back. A ragged scar circled his neck, like he'd once escaped a hangman's rope, which in fact he had. The men also quietly, and somewhat enviously, noted his rippling muscles.

Suzie wrapped her legs around the man as he thrust inside her. Most johns only lasted a few thrusts, but she was surprised and pleased that he didn't. "This guy's a stallion," said Billings with a laugh. The older man nodded and refilled their glasses.

Inside, the man had flipped Suzie onto her hands and knees as he entered her from behind. This gave the men behind the glass a perfect view of her splayed sex, and they clinked glasses again. The man thrust faster and faster into her as she writhed on the bed. With a groan that they heard even through the soundproofed walls, the man arched his back, muscles corded in exquisite tension, and then fell to the side in release.

Billings lit a cigarette and shifted on his chair, trying to ignore the hard-on that threatened to form a tent pole in his pants. "Good show tonight," he said nonchalantly.

Stiles stood, downing the last of his drink. "The things we do for King and country," he said. He set his empty glass on the counter and walked toward the rear door. "You have the second act. I need to get to the office."

"Yes, sir," Billings said, and in a moment he was alone.

Suzie, whose real name was Mai, lay on the bed next to the prone man. His eyes were closed, and he was breathing heavily. Despite the fact that this was work, she looked at him appreciatively. She raised a hand and placed it on his shoulder in an almost collegial gesture. Now to work. She rose and walked to the cabinet. Opening the double doors, she revealed a hidden bar that was well stocked. "Baby, let me get you a drink," she said. "What do you want?"

The man, still on his back, his eyes coming back into focus said, "Just water."

"Whatever you want, baby." She carefully pulled two tumblers from the top shelf. One was clear, the other a pale blue. There was a carafe of water that she poured into the two glasses and returned to the bed. She handed him the blue tumbler. "Cheers, baby," and she drank from hers. He gave her a small smile and took the glass. The cool water went down easily. Despite the paid-for affection, for the first time in a long time, he felt relaxed. The girl snuggled up next to him, and he closed his eyes.

"Touchdown," Billings said inside the warm room. He took out his watch and made a notation on a clipboard. Then he walked to the movie camera on the tripod and switched it to record. Standard procedure was to let the subjects fuck first and then dose them. They told the girls that the doctors insisted on that procedure. The reality was that they got a free show. He'd been doing this for the past six months, and each time had followed a similar pattern. The drug would take about thirty minutes to kick in, and it was the girl's job to keep the subject in the room. If that meant another go-round, so be it, but they had to keep the subjects in place. Suzie was well experienced in all of this, and he saw that she had already started phase two by slowly stroking the subject's cock. In a few moments, it rose to full attention, and Suzie knew she had him. Billings watched as Suzie lowered her head and took the man's cock into her mouth. Thinking he had time and the room to himself, Billings pulled out his own member and began to stroke it, thinking about the last time Suzie had gone down on him.

The man, whose name was Epps, felt the warm heat of the girl's mouth on him and lay back. It had been so long since he'd been with a woman, and when she'd approached him earlier that evening, he finally let his guard down enough to talk to her. Once they'd begun to chat, she was so friendly and so beautiful that it had been almost easy to end up here. Now all he could feel was ...

First there was a twitch on his face, then a tickle, like a feather in the back of his brain. Then it was a point of light that filled his vision even though he knew his eyes were closed. From somewhere he heard a low rumble that got louder and louder until it burst forth in an explosion of sound. It was then he realized he was screaming.

In the adjacent room, Billings was nearing his own orgasm when he noticed the man on the bed twitch violently, his head shaking back and forth. *No way. Too soon.* It had barely been five minutes, yet the man was showing signs—extreme signs—already. As Billings pulled up his trousers, he saw and then began to hear the man emitting a blood-curdling scream. Suzie rolled off him and was cowering next to the bed. The man clutched at his head, violently pulling at his short hair and his ears. Billings watched, again noted the time, and made a quick note on the clipboard. Inside, Suzie moved to the mirror and was frantically tapping on the glass.

The man jumped from the bed and seemed to land right behind Suzie, pinning her to the glass. *No way he could make that leap*, thought Billings, yet he'd just seen it. The man pushed Suzie's terrified face to the glass and moved his own face next to hers, almost as if he were whispering to her. Even through the glass, Billings could see that the man's pupils were completely dilated, making his eyes look like black holes in his twisted face. Suzie was crying, and Billings was thinking he might need to help her, but his standing orders were to avoid interference once the experiment started.

The man pressed Suzie's face into the glass. Then he grabbed her hair, pulling her terrified face back and then forward, slamming her head into the glass, which cracked the surface. "Shit," said Billings, now thinking he had to do something. If the girl was hurt or killed, there'd be hell to pay. He watched in dismay as the man picked the slumped form of the girl off the floor, raised her up with one hand by the neck, and pinned her to the wall as she kicked and twisted in his grasp. Billings turned and went to the desk in the back of the room. He rifled through the lower drawer and pulled forth a .38 revolver that he knew was loaded. He rushed to the concealed door that opened to the bathroom inside. In a moment, he was in the bedroom.

His training had shown him how to strike a man with the butt of a gun to disable him, so he approached the man from the back, and with a savage downward blow, struck him across the back of the head. To Billings' horror, the man spun around, dropping the girl, and now faced him like a feral wolf. The naked man twisted his face and let out a guttural noise and stepped forward. Billings' hand shook, and he took a step backward, firing twice as the man stalked toward him.

The first bullet grazed the man's rib cage, twisting him around. The second missed him entirely, instead finding the center of the unconscious girl's chest behind him as she slumped against the wall. Her eyes momentarily went wide and then closed forever.

Epps had no rational thought. The drug pulsed through him, and he seethed with energy. Then this man emerged before him. *Gun. Threat.* His hands moved without conscious thought. In rapid succession, he knocked the gun to the side and struck into the man's soft throat, causing him to gasp and fall to his knees. His larynx crushed, Billings collapsed to his knees, already dead but not knowing it. As Billings clutched at his throat, his eyes widened in horror because he couldn't draw any air. The thirty seconds of life he had remaining were cut mercifully short as Epps stepped behind him and, with clinical precision, like a reaper cutting wheat, twisted Billings' head backward, severing his spinal cord in one swift move.

The naked Epps stood in the center of the carnage, barely breathing heavy. In the stillness that emerged, he brought his energy under a semblance of control, and instinct took over again. *Get out.* Moving deliberately, he retrieved his clothes, pulling on his pants and boots. He walked to the door and stepped outside into the far end of the hallway. Next to the door, a window was open. The cool night air filled his nose, and his chest rose and fell like a bellows. He tasted and felt every breath with exquisite sharpness for a dozen heartbeats before he ran down the stairs and into the night.

Chapter 2

Molly Hayes felt the sweat running down her face, her breathing heavy. She pulled the sinewy Japanese American man closer and saw that sweat covered him too. Katsuhiro Takemoto, her boyfriend for over a year now, smiled back at her. *We're getting good at this,* she thought. She felt him move his hips and, instinctually, she dropped her own hips lower, twisted, and pulled him into her orbit. With a grunt, Kats flipped over her hip and landed on the mat with what Molly thought was a satisfying "thunk."

"Very good," he said, smiling, while on his back. "Your *randori* is getting much better. You felt that weight shift I tried and reacted perfectly."

She smiled down at him, thinking that many things had gotten better with them. She sat astride him on the thick mat that covered the *tatami* room in the back of Kats' office on the lower floor of the three-story home on Post Street. Her red hair was pulled back in a ponytail, and the thick cotton uniform, a *dogi*, was drenched in sweat. She leaned forward and kissed him, the training over for today. She pulled open her *dogi*, and their *randori* took a decidedly more sensual turn.

Later, they lay naked in the sunlight from the window, Molly nestled into the hollow of Kats' arm, her head on his lean shoulder. He slowly stroked her hair, and eventually she said, "I need to go in early today. We have a big show coming in next week, and the boss is nervous about marketing." Ann's 440, formerly known as Mona's 440, was a nightclub that had initially been famous for catering to a largely lesbian clientele, but the audience had expanded, and now Ann's was known for booking hot musical acts. The club was packed every weekend.

"I can take you," he said. "Nice day to take the bike. And I can grab lunch with Shig."

"Will he be at City Lights?"

"He's always at City Lights," Kats laughed.

Just after 2 pm, they rode the Harley Davidson Sportster up Kearny and into the North Beach neighborhood. Molly had gotten used to riding on the back of the bike after Kats had modified the seat to better allow for a passenger. Roaring up and down the hills of San Francisco had become a pleasure, and she loved the closeness that riding together brought. They turned onto Broadway, and Kats swung the bike around to stop in front of Ann's 440. To Molly's surprise, several of the girls were standing outside on the sidewalk, apparently talking and smoking.

"Something's going on," Molly said to Kats as she eyed

the conclave.

"I'll wait," he said, turning the bike off. Molly crossed the sidewalk and approached the three women, who appeared, in Kats' estimation, to be upset. As a private detective, he was paid to be observant. Today he was just concerned. The girls gestured emphatically as they spoke, though Kats couldn't make out what they were saying. Molly gave one girl, a short-haired blond, a hug and held her for several seconds as the girl appeared to be sobbing. Molly stroked her hair, and eventually the girl seemed to calm a bit, and they turned to go back inside. Molly walked back to Kats with a grim face.

"One of the girls who used to work here was killed last night," she said, and Kats took her hand. "Do you remember Mai, the pretty, young Chinese girl who worked as a cocktail waitress?"

"I do. What happened?"

"Some crazy shit. She was shot in an apartment in the Tenderloin. The cops found a dead guy there, too, and a bunch of drugs." Kats shook his head as Molly continued. "They think Mai was turning tricks on the side, and something went very bad."

"Was she a prostitute?"

"Some of the girls here supplement their income, and I know she had been in the past, but I thought she'd stopped last year."

"I'm sorry," he said.

"She wasn't into drugs when she worked here, but she left several months ago, and the girls think she got mixed up in some bad stuff. Apparently there was a lot of that LSD in this apartment over on O'Farrell."

"In the Tenderloin?"

"Yeah."

"Not the kind of drugs I'd have expected in the Tenderloin. I have a contact over at police HQ. You want me to ask
around?"

"The girls here are pretty upset, so yeah, anything would
help," she said and gave him a kiss. "Pick me up around 11
pm?"

"See you then," he said and started the bike.

Five minutes later, Kats walked into City Lights Bookstore on Columbus. Sitting behind the counter, on the perch
that served as both office and de facto throne, Shigeyoshi
Murao, the irascible store manager, was yelling into the
phone. Kats smiled at the furious bluster Shig often por-
trayed to the world. He was smart, passionate, and demanding when it came to 'his' store, and God help the vendor,
writer, or publisher who got on his bad side. In the midst
of the expletive-laced takedown he was exacting on some
unfortunate soul on the other end of the line, Shig, seeing
Kats, broke character and gave his friend a big grin and a
thumbs up before returning to the phone. Kats wandered the
store, noting the mix of tourists, scruffy young Beats, and
graying academics who filled the tight confines of the shop.

City Lights had become the psychic center of the North
Beach artistic and intellectual movement that most simply
called Beatniks. The store had become nationally famous
two years ago when federal obscenity charges over a book
of poetry were brought against the owner, Lawrence Ferlinghetti, and Shig, who had the distinction of selling the
copy of Allen Ginsberg's *Howl* to the undercover cop. Shig
had laughed and joked about it, but it was a scary time and
showed that people were still uncomfortable with new ideas
and with change. Charges were dropped against Shig, and

Ferlinghetti won at trial. Now the bookstore, Ferlinghetti, and Shig had become local icons for free speech and cultural change. Kats knew Shig loved it. As Kats thumbed through a copy of the bestseller *Doctor Zhivago*, a familiar voice came over his shoulder.

"That's a loaded weapon," Shig said as he pointed to the book in Kats' hands. Kats looked skeptically at the book and then at his friend. "I'm not kidding. The Soviets hate that book, and the fact that it won the Nobel Prize for Literature last year embarrassed the hell out of them."

"Another book that got people all riled up," Kats said, "You operate in a dangerous world, Shig."

"Bookselling's not for pussies," he said with a grin.

"Got time for lunch?" Kats asked.

"Sure."

They sat in Caffe Trieste, a North Beach gathering spot and one of Shig's usual haunts. The sun streamed in the window, and as they ate, Kats told Shig about the girl from Ann's. He, too, was shocked. "I remember her," Shig said. "Kind of a party girl, which for a Chinese girl was a bit different."

"Apparently there was a large amount of LSD on-site. You know anything about that stuff?" Kats asked.

"The latest drug of choice for a bunch of folks. Supposed to open up your mind and expand your consciousness."

"And it's not even illegal," Kats said.

"Not yet," Shig replied. "Marijuana and cocaine weren't illegal at first either. Did you know that Coca-Cola once had coca, the basis for cocaine, in it?"

"That explains why you're hooked on it," Kats laughed. Shig raised his bottle of Coke with a smile.

"I was talking to a guy about LSD last week," Shig said.

"This writer is doing a book about North Beach and the scene there. He came into the shop, and we started talking."

"As you do."

"Yeah. So he was extolling the mind-altering benefits of LSD and mescaline and some other stuff. Talked about how it had fueled his writing."

"That sounds a bit crazy."

"Here's the crazy part. He said the government was actually doing tests on people at the hospital in Menlo Park where he worked. He'd volunteered for the testing and had been taking all kinds of psychedelic stuff for months."

"Wow. We know the government has done some shady stuff ..."

"This isn't even shady. It's right out in the open."

"Well, I know someone over at the police headquarters. I'm going to see if I can find anything out for the girls over at Ann's. They seemed pretty shaken by the murder."

Kats walked the short distance to the corner of Kearny and Washington where the headquarters of the San Francisco Police Department was located. The Hall of Justice, built after the 1906 earthquake, was known for its arched windows and classical façade. Its upper floors served as the city jail. Five square stories of stone and glass, it looked both beautiful and imposing. Entering the main doors, Kats walked to the front desk, operated by a young woman in a crisp, blue uniform. *That's progress*, he thought, though he did think it would be a while before the department had her patrolling the Embarcadero.

"How can I help you, sir?" she asked.

"I was hoping to see Officer Blackstone if he's available."

"Let me check." She picked up a phone beside her, dialed

a single digit, and waited. "Yes, connect me with Blackstone." They waited.

"Yes, there's a man requesting to see you ..." she looked at Kats.

"Takemoto. Kats Takemoto."

"Takemoto." She nodded and said, "I'll let him know. Officer Blackstone said he'd be down shortly. Please have a seat over there," she gestured to the bench.

"Thank you," Kats said and took a seat. As he waited, he thought about Elliot Blackstone, the officer he was here to see.

As a private investigator, Kats often worked with minority communities, including the increasingly visible homosexual community of San Francisco. In 1955 he'd been working on his least favorite type of case: a marriage gone bad. An Italian woman hired him to follow her husband, a man named Sal. She was convinced he was having an affair and insisted on knowing. Kats reluctantly agreed and followed the man for several ordinary and boring nights. There was nothing that even remotely suggested marital impropriety in the man's routine. Until the last night. That's when Kats followed Sal to a hotel in the Tenderloin. Kats knew the hotel by its illicit reputation and realized to his chagrin that he'd have to share this information with his client. As he waited outside, he saw a group of San Francisco police officers round the corner and look toward the hotel. Two patrol cars edged into the intersections, and a paddy wagon parked down the street. *Raid*, thought Kats. From his vantage point across the street, Kats could see the police setting up their net over the next ten minutes but suspected that no one in the hotel could see the coming onslaught.

Like a military operation, the raid began with simultaneous movement at the front of the hotel and men entering the rear door and covering the fire escapes. Within minutes, the police started dragging people out of the hotel in handcuffs and lining them up on the street. Kats noted that most of them were men in various stages of dress. Some had on nothing but their underwear, while others wore a suit and tie. A couple of women were, to his surprise, being particularly roughed up by the police officers. Then, after a violent shove by one officer, the woman's wig fell off, revealing short, dark hair, and Kats realized the "woman" was a man in drag. Even more troubling for Kats was the realization that he was the husband, Sal, whom he'd been following for the past several days.

Kats walked across the street to join the crowd of gawkers and hecklers who were gathering for the evening's entertainment, not sure what he should do. He heard people yelling "faggot" and "fucking queers" and laughing when the police tossed another embarrassed and frightened man outside. Homosexuality was a crime. So was cross-dressing, and the cops were continuing to rough up the husband, seeing him as an even more extreme version of the queers they hated and secretly feared. One officer grabbed the fallen wig and twisted it on Sal's head. Another officer came forward and kicked Sal to the ground. Kats felt his stomach twist, and he wondered what he could possibly do, when another officer came forward and pushed his comrade back. "That's enough!" the officer said. He then proceeded to walk up and down the line of terrified men, pulling the officers back and trying to calm the situation. As the paddy wagon rolled up, the officer ordered the gawkers back and threatened several of them with arrest if they tried to do anything to the men.

Kats watched as the officer walked over to Sal, helped him up, and almost politely led him to the paddy wagon.

Kats observed a second paddy wagon pull up and slowly fill. As the numbers of the arrested dwindled, so did the spectators, who moved on to their own nighttime haunts. Kats lingered, watching the one officer. As things were finishing up, Kats stepped forward and caught his attention.

"Excuse me, officer," Kats began. "Would you mind answering a couple of questions for me?"

The officer, a White man with square, blunt features and dark hair, turned toward him. Kats would have guessed him a few years older than him, mid to late thirties, though he found out later that the two were the same age. He looked Kats over for a moment, let out a long breath, and wiped a hand across his brow. "What can I do for you, sir?" he asked.

"What's going to happen to those men?"

"They'll be processed down at the Hall of Justice, but that will take most of the night. Nobody's getting bailed out tonight, so they'll all be spending the night in jail."

"And the charges?"

"Well, homosexual activity and cross-dressing are 'deviant acts' according to the municipal code," he said in a formal tone. "There will be some fines, some possible jail time, but mostly just a lot of embarrassment and hurt for those men and their families."

Kats wasn't expecting such a compassionate response. "I saw what you did to help some of those men. That was commendable, but I'm curious why you did it."

"My religion teaches me to love everyone—saints and sinners alike. We're all God's children. And as a police officer I should be protecting people. All people. The community needs to trust us, to see us not just as enforcers, but as partners in making better, safer places."

"That's a remarkable perspective, Officer ...?"

"Blackstone. Elliot Blackstone."[1]

"Thank you, Officer Blackstone."

Blackstone nodded and turned back toward the final clean-up efforts.

Since that night in 1955, Kats and Blackstone had become friends. The police officer was initially hesitant to engage with Kats once he found out he was a private detective. But Kats never asked for favors or anything that would compromise Blackstone's moral and ethical standards. He became a reliable source for information once he realized that Kats was also an ethical man. They shared conversations over coffee and lunches that covered their respective military careers—Blackstone served in the navy in the Pacific—local politics, and ideas on how to make neighborhoods safer. Today he hoped that Elliot would be able to provide some information that the newspapers couldn't.

Blackstone, blocky in his dark blue uniform, approached the lobby and waved Kats through the waist-high swinging gate. The two men shook hands. "Officer Blackstone," Kats said with a smile.

"Mr. Takemoto," replied Blackstone with a wink. "Come on in."

The two walked across the lower level, took the center stairs up one flight, and turned into the section marked "Vice." Blackstone sat down behind his cluttered desk.

"I still think it's odd that they have you working in vice, Elliot," Kats said.

Blackstone smiled, "I look at it as God's way of testing me. Sending me among those in need of his grace. What can I help you with today, Kats?"

"I was hoping you might have some more information about the double murder in the Tenderloin."

"You already working a case?"

"No, but some folks I care about knew the girl who was killed, and they were hoping for some answers. They're shocked."

"Yeah, it was a mess over there. We got a call last night after a neighbor heard gunshots and then saw a half-naked man running from the building."

"Who was the other victim?"

"Male, thirtyish, named Howard Billings. We think it may have been a blackmail operation gone bad."

"How so?"

"The apartment where we found the bodies had a one-way mirror installed to look into the bedroom. Movie camera set up too. We think the john found out what was going on and killed the girl and the pimp."

"How were they killed?"

"That's a strange one. The girl was shot, and the man had his neck broken. Really broken. His head was nearly twisted off his body."

"Did you recover a weapon?"

"There was a revolver lying right by the man. We're running tests for fingerprints and powder residue, but it seems likely it was the murder weapon."

"Anything on the film?" Kats asked.

"The lab boys have all that stuff. There may be evidence there."

Kats nodded, taking it all in.

"My turn to ask some questions,"

Blackstone said, and Kats nodded. "What can you tell me about the girl?" Blackstone asked as he opened a notebook and grabbed a pencil.

"Mai Su Han, or May to her friends. She worked as a cocktail waitress at Ann's 440. Her friends think she might have been working as a prostitute a while back, but they thought she'd quit last year."

"Apparently not," Blackstone said.

"The other girls at Ann's said she was a bit of a party girl, but they didn't think she was into drugs."

Blackstone made a face and sat back. "There were definitely drugs at the scene." Kats waited for him to continue. "It wasn't the usual party stuff, though. There were pharmaceutical vials of LSD, mescaline, and some other stuff that our guys had never even heard of."

"Seems like you're involved in the investigation," Kats said.

"Not really. Because of the prostitution angle, vice was brought up to speed, but homicide is leading this."

"Can you keep me updated on any developments?" Kats asked hopefully.

"Only if you agree to share any additional information about the girl."

"Deal."

"Tell your friends at Ann's that they'll probably get a visit from the detectives in the next day or so."

"Will do. Thanks, Elliot."

CHAPTER 3

The man called Stiles walked across the campus of the hospital toward the main administrative building. He entered the double doors and walked up two flights of stairs in the central atrium to the third-floor office, his destination. The door read 'Research Administrator.' He knocked twice before turning the handle and entering the room.

Inside the windowless office, behind a large desk, sat a thickset man, mid-forties, with short, thinning brown hair. The man was writing something, and without looking up, said, "Sit." Stiles sat in the straight-backed wooden chair and waited for the storm he knew was coming.

Conrad Hauser, research administrator for the Menlo Park VA Hospital, set down his pen, straightened the papers in front of him, and glared at Stiles, who shifted uncomfortably under the gaze. "Report," demanded Hauser.

"Sir, Billings and I observed our civilian asset retrieve a subject last night and bring him to the safe house." Hauser stared, and Stiles continued. "We observed her dose him at approximately 10:30 pm. At that point, I left Billings to record the remainder of the session and went back to the station."

"Nothing unusual about this subject?"

"No, sir. He seemed fitter and stronger than most. Also had some scars that suggested he might have been ex-military."

"Did you document him?"

"Yes, sir. We took some photos. Not sure if Billings had

the camera running after I left."

"And those photos?"

"Apparently in police custody as evidence along with all our supplies, including the new LSD-psilocybin compound we recently received."

"Was that the protocol used on the subject last night?"

"Yes, sir."

Hauser drew a deep breath and sat back in his chair. "This is quite the fuck-up, Stiles. My safe house is compromised and crawling with police. A civilian asset is dead. So is Billings. The press is writing about this, and the police have impounded our materiel. Does that accurately sum up the situation?"

Not sure if the question was rhetorical or not, Stiles gave a curt nod, "Yes, sir."

Hauser glared at the man, letting him stew. He continued. "Our supplier in Chinatown has already reached out and offered to help."

"What kind of help, sir?" Stiles asked.

"Use of their club, protection of their men, and a steady supply of their women."

Stiles nodded, his thoughts churning and his face pinched with worry. "Something you wish to say, Stiles?"

Stiles looked surprised to be asked but cleared his throat and said, "Sir, shouldn't we lay low for a while? Let the heat blow over?"

"Why? Do you think the Chinese or Soviets are lying low? Hell no! They don't even have to hide their work. They just order some poor bastards to show up, and bam! Human guinea pigs. They're fucking animals, but you have to admire their efficiency. No, we reset as soon as possible. Contact Wen at the Hong Kong Club and get things moving again."

Stiles sat wide-eyed for a moment, not sure how to respond. Then Hauser gave him a nod, "Dismissed." Stiles rose and silently left the room. Hauser's eyes followed the man out the door and he sat silently, inwardly seething and gathering his thoughts before he made the next necessary phone call.

He dialed a number that few knew and even fewer ever used. It rang once and was answered by a woman's voice. "Identify," she said.

"Hauser, AIC MKUltra, California," he replied.

"Hold." Twenty seconds later, the line connected and a male voice spoke.

"Dulles," said the familiar voice of his boss, Allen Dulles, the director of the Central Intelligence Agency in Washington, DC.

"Sir, I have an update on Project MKUltra[2] and the shadow op for your ears only."

"Proceed."

"Two nights ago, we had an incident at the primary safe house in San Francisco. A test subject got out of control, and a civilian asset and an agent were killed before the subject escaped into the city. The police were summoned by neighbors, and they compromised the site before we could clean it. The story made the press."

"Will the cover hold?"

"Yes, sir. The dead agent had a full background in place, and the civilian was a prostitute. It will look like a blackmail operation gone bad, and the press has already posited that angle."

"And?" said Dulles, knowing where the conversation was going.

"Sir, I need authorization to use our assets in the local police department to retrieve evidence on-site and to redirect any overzealous investigation."

There was a long pause, and Hauser shifted uncomfortably in his chair.

"Granted. But Conrad, no more mistakes. Burn it all down if you have to, but you can't let this get out." The line clicked off.

Hauser noted the use of his first name and knew it wasn't a collegial gesture. He'd worked with Dulles since 1944 in the Switzerland station of the Office of Strategic Services, the OSS, which preceded the CIA. But Hauser knew the two weren't friends. The intimacy was Dulles' way of telling him that it was their shared history that gave Hauser another chance.

MKUltra was Dulles' operation that had started in 1953 as "brain warfare" and had evolved into experiments in mind control, truth serums, and induced insanity. Dulles had sold the operations to President Eisenhower by saying the Soviets and the Chinese had already started down the path, which was nominally true. There had been evidence of Chinese experiments on captured soldiers during the Korean War, but those efforts were primitive compared to where MKUltra had taken the science. Using a host of experimental drugs, including LSD, mescaline, DMT, and other psychotropic agents, the CIA sponsored doctors and researchers in institutions across the country to run experiments on "volunteers" who were never given the full story of what they were taking. More insidiously, they also experimented on those unable to give consent, such as prisoners, suspected criminals, and the mentally impaired.

As the 'research administrator' at the Menlo Park VA Hospital, Hauser was coordinating the new voluntary experiments the hospital was running. Officially part of the research into drug treatment for various afflictions, almost no one knew of the connection back to the CIA. It was Hauser's job to keep it that way and to get results, which Dulles demanded. It was also his job to run the so-called "shadow operation" that even fewer knew about. That project, known as Midnight Climax,[3] allowed the CIA to test the drugs on unwilling and unwitting subjects. They set up operations in New York and San Francisco, using prostitutes to lure men into their safe houses and secretly dose them with the experimental drugs. Results had been mixed, but the agency felt that the unwilling subjects were a good control group to counter the results they were getting from volunteers. For four years, Hauser had been Agent In Charge, the AIC, clandestinely gathering data and keeping the operation secret from even those with top-secret clearance. This fuck-up had put the whole operation in jeopardy.

Hauser looked through a small address book, picked up his phone, and dialed. The line connected, "San Francisco Police Department. How may I direct your call?"

CHAPTER 4

Kats sat in his Japantown office, finishing up a simple report for a client on Nob Hill, when his phone rang. "Takemoto," he said into the handset.

"Kats, hey. It's Elliott."

"Elliott, hi. Thanks for the call. Got something for me?"

"No, and that's why I'm calling." There was a pause. "We just got closed down on the investigation into the blackmail house case. That's what we've been calling it, but apparently word came down from upstairs, and the case has been moved."

"Moved? Moved where?" Kats asked.

"There were some federal guys in here yesterday. They took the evidence we collected and all the written reports."

"How is this a federal crime?"

"It's not. That's what I wanted to tell you. There must be some connection we don't know about to warrant this type of federal intervention." Elliott was quiet on the other end of the line. "It feels like a cover-up," he said quietly.

"Elliott, is there any way ..."

"Sorry, Kats. I can't say any more. I thought you should know, but it doesn't look like SFPD can do anything."

"I appreciate that. Thanks for the call, Elliott." The line clicked closed. Molly and the girls at Ann's weren't going to be happy. Kats' mind was spinning over the implications of what had seemed to be a simple blackmail operation gone bad when his front door opened, and two young Asian men walked in.

Chinese, thought Kats. Dressed in black *hanfu*, the traditional Chinese men's coat and loose-fitting pants, their cuffs were embellished with emerald-green silk. *Tong*, thought Kats. *Hop Sing Tong.* They stood just inside the door, looking the room over. Kats sat back, keeping his hands in front of him. A moment later, a powerfully built Chinese man dressed in a well-tailored Western suit entered. Close-cropped black hair framed a large forehead and deep-set eyes. The man was Kats' age, thirty-four. He knew this because he'd celebrated the man's birthday years ago.

"Hello, John," Kats said calmly.

"Hello, Kats," said the man as he waved his men out the door. He walked toward the desk and extended his hand. Kats rose and shook the man's calloused hand.

Lin Tai Lo, "John" to his western associates, was the second in command of the Hop Sing Tong in Chinatown. According to the city and police department, the Tong no longer officially existed, but these shadowy Chinese societies had survived the Tong Wars of the late nineteenth and early twentieth centuries. There were at least half a dozen groups, with many more splinter factions, and they'd effectively carved up the illicit trade and activities of Chinatown. The Hop Sing Tong specialized in gambling, but these groups overlapped enough that they needed soldiers and enforcers to protect their business and their turf. Lin had proven himself as an exceptionally competent and occasionally brutal soldier, which had moved him into the role of 'Red Pole,' or enforcer of the group. Though younger than most who had held that post, Lin proved to be tough and relentless. And he was surprisingly smart for a man who used his fists for a living. Kats knew all this because they'd attended the University of San Francisco at the same time, taking several classes together, along with Lin's cousin Gracie, whom Kats dated at the time.

Lin took a seat across from Kats and glanced around the office. "So, this is how you use your business degree?" he asked, no trace of an accent in his deep voice.

Kats shrugged, "You sound like my father," he replied.

"Asian parents," said Lin, and both men nodded.

"What can I do for you, John? I'm assuming this isn't a social call."

"No. I'm here about Mai Su Han, the girl who was killed in the Tenderloin." He paused. "She was my cousin."

"Oh, I'm sorry. I had no idea."

Lin nodded. "Yes, she was the youngest daughter of my mother's sister. By far the most 'American' of my cousins, and that includes Gracie."

Kats smiled wryly, "That's saying something," and he thought about Gracie, his college girlfriend and the new 'Tiger Lady' of Chinatown. She ran a black-market operation that Kats had called upon for help the prior year. "Lots of cousins in Chinatown," Kats concluded.

"I want to hire you to investigate what happened to Mai. I've heard that the police are doing nothing on the case."

Kats was impressed with Lin's network that already had that information passed down. The reach of the Tong was clearly growing beyond Chinatown.

"Why me? You clearly have information resources and the Hop Sing Tong at your command."

"There are things that we do well, and things that I know you do well. At investigation and surveillance, no one is better than you."

Kats nodded gratefully but had to ask the hard question, "And if I find something or someone? The Tong will take revenge?"

"Would that be wrong? One of ours is dead, and no one seems to care outside of Chinatown."

"Perhaps not," Kats said and then paused. "But is that the Christian thing to do?"

Lin's eyes narrowed, and his lips pressed into a thin line. Kats wondered if he'd crossed the line with this dangerous man, who once was a friend. Kats knew Lin's secret, the one he kept hidden from most in the Chinese community and certainly from the Tong. Lin was a Christian. He'd converted in high school and was quietly quite devout by the time he reached college. The violence he was occasionally compelled to visit upon others in his role as enforcer for the Hop Sing Tong caused him great angst, but in a Chinese manner, he separated his personal beliefs from the collective necessity of his group. After the violence, Lin would find himself in church, asking for guidance and forgiveness, yet he would dutifully show up for whatever the Tong required him to do. Kats had often wondered how it was possible to reconcile both halves of such a life, and it was this very argument that had driven the men apart years ago.

"My beliefs are mine alone," Lin said formally. "My obligation is to my family and to the Tong. I can live with both, Katsuhiro. I have to."

Kats looked at the face of his old friend and knew the inner strength that it took to hold so much inside. He nodded, "OK, I'm in."

Lin gave a short, forward bow of his head, and the deal was done.

"I should tell you right now that I just talked with a contact over at the police department, and some federal agents have taken over the case. This may be difficult."

"Our sources had told us this as well. That's why I came

to you."

"OK. My fee is ..."

"I know what your fee is. Double it. We want your full attention." Kats made a slight bow from his chair, sealing the terms.

"What can you tell me about your cousin?"

John made a grim face and momentarily looked down. "She was estranged from her parents. Mai was always rebellious, but things became worse last year. She was arrested for prostitution, and I had to bail her out of jail. The family was most upset." Kats nodded, knowing the importance Asian families place on propriety.

"I tried to intervene on behalf of my aunt and uncle, but she was most defiant. And then I found out she was involved with drugs."

"What kind of drugs?" Kats asked pointedly.

"Opium," John said grimly. It was the drug that had destroyed far too many Chinese families.

"Hmmm," Kats replied. "Was LSD ever a thing for her?"

"Not as far as I know."

"There was a large amount of LSD and some other psychotropic drugs found at the scene."

"Psychotropic?"

"Mind altering, not just the kind that get people high."

John shook his head, "No, the last time I saw her, maybe three months ago, was at a club in Chinatown. A friend called me to say she was there, so I came to collect her. She was clearly on opium. We argued, and I tried to get her to come home, but to no avail."

"Which club?"

"She was at the Hong Kong Club, which is a Hei Long operation," he said tightly. Kats nodded, knowing the Hei

Long, the Black Dragon Tong, were known for drugs and human trafficking. They usually used girls from mainland China for their brothels. Kats also knew that the Hei Long and the Hop Sing were blood enemies.

"Do you think the Hei Long were using Mai for their ... operation?" Kats said cautiously.

With apparent effort, John replied in a steady voice, "I can't say for sure. She was lost, and the drugs had certainly affected her decision-making. The Hei Long may have taken advantage of that weakness."

"But you can't take the Hop Sing to war over a hunch," Kats said, holding John's gaze.

"No, I cannot. The peace has held for many years in Chinatown and kept us all out of the press, but should it be shown they did anything to my family, there will be blood." Kats let the thought sink in, knowing that the enmity between the rival Tong was deep already, and if there was a war in Chinatown, many innocents would be caught up in it.

"All right, I'll start on this immediately, but please tell your men to stand down. I don't want any incidents."

"Very well, but their patience and mine is finite." John rose, preparing to leave. "If you require anything—men, weapons, equipment ..."

"I'll call," Kats said. "Just like Chinese takeout."

CHAPTER 5

T he man jerked awake, looking for the enemy. He took a deep breath as his eyes wildly looked around him. *Where am I?* Gasping, he realized he'd been sleeping under a thicket in what appeared to be a forest. Rising slowly, he looked around to see that he was atop a wooded hill that overlooked the city. Yerba Buena Park. When he first escaped to San Francisco, he'd spent many days walking around the steep hills and sitting quietly on the benches. The park was close to the massive Golden Gate Park, but because it was so hilly and steep, it kept many from ascending its heights. He liked the solitude, which was hard to find in San Francisco.

He quickly did a self-survey as he'd been taught. There was an abrasion on his rib cage that had bled and then crusted over. His arms and legs had scrapes and a few bruises, but no damage that would limit him. He felt in his front pants pocket and was relieved to find the roll of cash there. He began to try to piece together how he'd gotten there. He remembered a girl. A pretty Asian girl. And a man ... with a gun. Something had turned him red. Something had brought that horrible heat behind his eyes. He shook his head as if he could dislodge the memory.

He found a water fountain and rinsed himself off as best he could, straightened his shirt, and walked out of the park toward the room he rented in the Tenderloin.

Kats sat with Molly at the bar of Vesuvio, the local watering hole across the alley from City Lights Bookstore. A favorite of the Beat writers, artists, and, increasingly, tourists,

Vesuvio was still cool enough to keep the locals coming in. As the evening slowly turned toward night, Molly sipped an iced tea because she had to work at Ann's later, and Kats nursed a beer. "So you're really going to investigate this case?" she asked.

"I told John I'd try but made no promises, especially if there really is a cover-up of some kind going down. I need to talk to the girls at Ann's, especially the ones who were close to Mai."

"I can think of one who seemed to be her friend. It's Friday, so she should be working tonight. We can talk to her before the club opens."

"Are you sure 'we' is a good idea? I can ..."

"People know you're my boyfriend, but I'm not sure they'll open up unless I'm there with you." Kats nodded, and she added, "Besides, I'm your partner now!"

"Sam Spade doesn't have a partner."

"You're smarter than Sam Spade, which is why you should have a partner. Let's go."

Kats left cash on the bar, and they stepped outside and began the short walk to Ann's 440. Kats mused on the idea of Molly as his partner. They'd grown close very quickly after the events at Hunters Point, and Kats had worried that maybe things were going too fast. But time together proved comfortable and much easier than he'd initially thought. They still got sideways looks from some people who were surprised to see an Asian man with a beautiful, redheaded White woman. But Kats found that he really didn't care anymore, and Molly, always tough and fearless, had more than once gotten into gawkers' faces, challenging them—"You got something you want to say?" They wisely did not.

They entered Ann's, and several people said hi to Molly.

She'd become the entertainment coordinator, and whenever she was there, she was the on-site manager. They were prepping for a swing band from Los Angeles that was starting a two-night stand at Ann's that evening. Molly, with a surprisingly good eye for talent and trends, had booked them, but she was starting to see a shift away from jazz and more interest in rhythm and blues and the emerging rock and roll. She'd suggested a change in booking strategy, but Ann, the owner and a jazz performer in her own right, wouldn't hear of it. It was Ann's club, so Molly left it at that. Approaching the bar, Kats and Molly saw a pretty blond woman setting up glasses and moving bottles from below the bar to the shelves behind it. "Evening, Lola," Molly said, and they sat down at the bar.

"Hi, Molly. Hi, Kats," said the deep-voiced Lola. When she was working with customers, Lola put on a more feminine voice, but among friends, she let the natural baritone of her voice come out. Hearing a deep voice from her pretty face was sometimes surprising, but Kats had become used to it over the past year. The 440 was home to many outliers, which was part of its charm.

"Lola, we need to talk to you," Molly began. Lola smiled and continued to stock the bar shelves.

"You want to give me a raise?" She smiled, saying, "I'll take it."

"Actually, we want to talk about Mai." Lola stopped at the mention of that name. "Kats is doing a bit of investigating into what happened to her, and I know you were a friend of hers. Could we ask you some questions?"

Lola looked back and forth at their faces, "You're not working for the police?" she asked hesitantly. "I can't talk to the police."

"Far from it," Kats said. "Some of her family want to know what happened to her, and the police have apparently dropped the case. We might be the only ones looking for some justice for Mai." He let that thought hang there for a moment.

Lola grabbed a bottle of Jack Daniels and put three shot glasses onto the bar. "It's not a conversation I want to have without a drink first." She poured three shots for them. "To Mai," she said, downing the glass. Molly looked at Kats, who nodded, and they each followed, "To Mai." Lola poured herself another.

"The initial story was that there was some kind of blackmail operation going on at the apartment where they found Mai. They said she was a prostitute. Do you know anything about that?" Molly asked.

Lola leaned forward onto the bar and quietly said, "Yeah, I knew exactly what she was into."

Molly lowered her voice as well, "She told you this?"

"She didn't have to. I was doing it too," Lola said grimly.

Molly and Kats looked at each other, and Kats said, "Can you please explain?"

Lola took a sip of her drink. "She and I both had turned tricks in the past. Hell, half the girls here have done the same."

Molly nodded, "I'd heard that. I don't judge."

"Mai was popular because she was an exotic Oriental beauty. And me ... well, some guys like their girls a little different, ya know? About a year and a half ago, this guy approaches me and Mai over at the Hong Kong Club in Chinatown. We're dressed to the nines, and he offers us a wad of cash to listen to a proposal. We think the guy wants a three-way, so no problem, we take the cash. Turns out he had something else in mind." Lola took another sip.

"This guy—older guy, kind of big and a little intimidating—starts talking about a special project he's working on. He says he needs girls like us to make the project work. That they're using some experimental drugs to try to help people. They need test subjects, and he says the government won't let them help people. Sounded like a drug company of some kind was doing it. Said all we had to do was pick up our clients and bring them back to their house. Sounded easy." Lola looked around the club, which was getting busier as they prepared to open later that night.

"What kind of drugs were they using?" Molly asked.

"They didn't officially tell us, but they did say LSD and some other stuff that I'd never heard of. We were just the bait for their project. We got to keep all our money, plus they paid us an extra $25 per session. They maintained the house and promised us immunity from any kind of hassles with the police. They even offered us some other drugs, ya know? Speed, cocaine, marijuana. They had it all."

"This guy even says he can help with my 'situation,' he called it. Doctors that could help me with the surgery, ya know? I've thought about it, and I can't afford to go to Sweden to have it done. They said they had a surgeon in LA who could work with me. After I helped them, though. And I remember what he said. He said after my 'tour of duty.'" She shook her head.

"Were there other girls?" Kats asked.

"Oh, yeah. There must have been over a dozen. They had a whole procedure we had to go through before we could start. We had to be checked out by their doctors. Full physical. Checked for VD and all that."

"Their doctors? Where was this?" Kats said.

"That was a bit of a pain. We had to go down to this hospital near Palo Alto. They said it was the only place they could really trust. It was a big VA hospital too. Menlo Park."

Kats tilted his head to the side at the mention of Menlo Park. That was the hospital that Shig's contact had said was doing experiments with LSD. Something to follow up.

"I did it for a couple of months. The money was good, and they ran a precision operation. The drugs we gave these guys mostly seemed harmless. They would get all dreamy and stare at their hands moving or at the lights. Some just went into what seemed like a coma. But a couple of them kind of went crazy."

"Crazy? Like how?" Kats asked.

"Like scary crazy. One guy started to scream and bang his head against the wall, saying his brain was crawling with ants. He cracked his head open, and I thought they'd come in and stop it, but they just let this poor bastard wail until he knocked himself out. He laid on the ground talking gibberish for an hour before they let me out of the room."

"But that's not the one who made me quit." She paused and looked down at her drink. "It was this one guy I picked up. Apparently, he didn't realize I was ... different."

Kats nodded, and Molly squeezed Lola's hand.

"But once we got started, he was into it, and I thought we had a good time. After I slipped him the dose, we lay there, cuddled, ya know. It was actually kind of sweet. I could tell the drug had started kicking in after some time had passed. There were the usual signs: breathing becomes heavy, they start staring at things, they'd often smile and start talking. But Jim—his name was Jim. Funny how I remember that— started to cry and curled up into a ball. He was swaying back and forth, talking about something, and I put my hand on his shoulder. He looked at me with the most hate-filled eyes. He was screaming something about a priest and penance and that the devil was in my cock. And then he ... he attacked me."

Lola stood straight behind the bar, and in a controlled, matter-of-fact voice, described the vicious attack that put her in the hospital. "I screamed and yelled for help, but no one came. He broke my collarbone," she pulled the right lapel of her shirt back to reveal a slightly crooked clavicle, "and eventually knocked me out. I woke up in the hospital the next day with a concussion, a battered face, and a security guard at my door."

"Wait, was that like a year ago?" Molly asked. Lola nodded. "You told us you were in a car crash!"

"I couldn't tell you the truth. They wouldn't let me. They paid me off on the condition that I keep everything quiet. They said they'd help me with the surgery, too, but I'm not sure about that, and I sure as hell don't trust those guys."

"Mai knew about the attack?" Molly asked. Lola nodded.

"She was scared, too, but she liked the money, and I think they treated her a little better than me. Lots of people think I'm a freak."

They sat quietly for a few moments. Molly spoke first. "Thank you for sharing that with us. I know how difficult it must be."

"Yes," Kats continued, "thank you for being brave," he said with a slight bow. "I need to ask something, though," he said. Lola nodded.

"Do you think you'd recognize these men if you saw them again? The ones who were running the program?"

"I think so. There were several guys, but one guy I met early on and saw a couple times after that was clearly in charge. The other guy, his name was Stiles. He seemed to be running these sessions." She started looking antsy, checking her watch. "Look, I gotta get ready for tonight."

"Of course. Thank you, Lola," Molly said.

"Yes, this has been very helpful. Thank you," reiterated Kats.

As Lola returned to work, Molly looked expectantly at Kats. "Did you get something? I thought I sensed that you got something?" she asked.

"Just the Menlo Park thing. Shig was just telling me about how he'd heard about some drug experiments that the government was running down there. Maybe just a coincidence …"

"But?" Molly asked with a mischievous smile.

"But it might be worth a trip down there to check it out."

CHAPTER 6

The slender, athletic man ran up the last hill of the day. Though nearing fifty, he still moved with a fluid grace. His heart pounded and his legs burned with the effort of the last hill. Cresting the summit, he eased up and allowed himself to slowly jog down the trail toward his office at the hospital. Dr. Dominic Turier had been in California for nearly a year and still didn't fit in. Turier was French, but as the son of a French man and an Algerian woman, he didn't look like a traditional Gaul. His black hair and dusky complexion marked him as North African and, to many in his native land, less than French. He'd thought that being in America might change that feeling of being different, but to his American colleagues he was a foreigner with a funny accent. So, he used his daily runs as a form of meditation and stress management. Especially when he knew he had a meeting with Hauser at the end of the day.

Turier showered and changed at the hospital and walked into his office at 8:55 am, a full five minutes before his first session. He was an acclaimed doctor of psychiatry, doing groundbreaking work with soldiers after they returned home. *Shell shock* or *battle fatigue* were the layman's terms for it, but Turier had been studying the effects of battlefield trauma on men for most of his life. After his own father came back from the Battle of the Somme during the First World War, Turier saw firsthand how damaging and lasting those battlefield wounds to the mind could be. His once happy and playful father came back a changed and haunted man. During his psychiatric residency at the Sorbonne, Turier learned of his father's suicide and vowed to help men like his father overcome those wounds and find themselves again. The Americans had recruited him to head up the work they were doing with vets from the Korean War. The opportunity to work in the States making a generous salary was an offer Turier couldn't pass up. But today he wondered about the wisdom of that decision.

Kats picked Shig up at City Lights, and by midafternoon they were driving south toward Palo Alto and the VA Hospital located just outside the city. After Kats relayed to Shig the story Lola had told, Shig was more than happy to contact the young writer who worked there. He found the man's contact info, and a couple days later he arranged to meet one Ken Kesey at the hospital during one of the man's evening shifts.

"What did you tell him when he asked why we wanted to meet?" Kats asked Shig.

"He didn't ask. Just said 'Cool' and to come down." Now they found themselves on their way to meet this young writer and volunteer for human experiments. Both men had trouble understanding the latter.

Kesey had told Shig he'd be working the swing shift that day, from 4 pm to midnight. They arrived at the sprawling hospital complex, parked, and walked toward the building marked Sanitarium. The building was a large, two-storied Spanish-style design that enclosed a courtyard. If not for the visible bars on many of the windows, it presented as an ordinary building. As instructed, Kats and Shig entered and told the front desk they were there to see Kesey. Ten minutes later the door opened and a tall, blond man walked into the waiting room. Smiling at Shig, he approached him and shook hands. "Hey, man," Kesey said to Shig. "I was surprised you called. But happy to see you." This large, soft-spoken man wasn't what Kats had expected. Kesey wore green tinted scrubs that strained to contain his chest and shoulders. The man was thick like an athlete. *Not your typical writer*, thought Kats.

"Thanks, Ken," Shig said and turned to Kats. "This is my friend Kats, the one I told you about." Kesey smiled easily at Kats and shook his hand. Kats noted Kesey's receding blond hair, large, leonine features, and pale blue eyes.

"You're the private investigator," he said.

"Yes."

"Very cool," Kesey said. Kats relaxed inwardly. Often his profession made people nervous, and he wanted this man's help. Kesey turned to the front desk, "Get me a couple of visitor badges for my friends, would ya?" Moments later, they followed the blond into the sanitarium.

Kats had agreed to let Shig handle most of the conversation with Kesey. Shig held a respected position with the literary community in the Bay Area, and Kats was the outsider. Shig began with a few background questions. "How long have you been working here, Ken?"

"I started my graduate writing fellowship at Stanford last year, and after a few months of just teaching and writing, I needed something to break up the day, ya know? The hospital was hiring, and a friend told me that if I worked the late shift, it was quiet and I could write, so I signed up."[4]

"What kind of work do you do here?"

"I've been working in the mental ward. Lots of former soldiers who have all kinds of issues. Schizophrenia, depression, paranoia, battle fatigue. You name it, we got it."

"Battle fatigue?" Kats interjected.

"Yeah, it's surprising how many of the guys here are affected by that in some way. I mean, Korea was over five years ago, and World War II was almost fifteen years ago. Yet they're still suffering from those traumas."

"Some wounds take a long time to heal," Kats said quietly, and Shig looked at his friend. Kats noted the concern.

They continued to walk through the halls, moving toward the inner courtyard. "I've also been working on the disturbed ward. The violent and dangerous patients. The administration likes the fact that I was a wrestler when I was younger and can handle some of the troublemakers."

"Do you get much of that kind of trouble?" Shig asked.

"Well, most of the staff call that ward the 'cuckoo's nest' and won't go near it. I haven't had much trouble, except one night early on. Almost made me quit after it happened."

"What happened?"

"There was this one guy who had been brought in a year or so ago, before I signed on. This guy got a lot of attention and special protocols—who could interact with him, who could take him food or even clean his room. So one night I'm working the cuckoo's nest and an alarm sounds, and me and three other orderlies are told to get to the special psych ward where this guy was kept. We get there and this guy ..." Kesey paused and looked like he was struggling with the memories. "This guy had killed a doctor and orderly with his bare hands. Broke them like rag dolls. There was another doctor there trying to talk him back into his cell, and two more orderlies had tranquilizer shots ready to go, but no one could get close to the guy. He was talking to someone in his head and pacing back and forth. Like manic energy, man. The guy's eyes were truly terrifying. They were like black saucers, his pupils were so dilated. This guy was on some kind of bad trip. Then this admin shows up and starts yelling at us to tackle the guy, and the doctor is arguing with him, still trying to reason with the guy. But four of us go in together to restrain him." Kesey stopped walking then. "Me and three other guys, my size or bigger, go in. And it's like we tackled a raging bull. This guy was unbelievably strong, and I was scared. I've never felt that powerless. I did manage to get a scissor lock around the guy, and the other orderlies hit him with shots of Thorazine. Like enough to knock out a gorilla, and still this guy kept fighting for almost a minute."

"Wow," said Kats. "That's really terrible. Yet you didn't quit."

"No, but I thought about it. I didn't go back for a couple weeks. When I did, they offered me a little perk to make up for the incident."

"What kind of perk?" Shig asked.

"Well, remember how I told you about the government-run LSD experiments?" Shig nodded. "They let me participate in that."

Kats was about to follow up, but Kesey turned and walked out into the sunlit inner courtyard. The place was active with doctors, nurses, and staff crossing the open space. There were also clusters of men who appeared to be patients involved in some kind of group therapy sessions.

"So, these experiments," Kats asked cautiously, "they're done here?"

"Not in this building, but nearby, yeah. I know you think I'm crazy to volunteer for something like this, but man, LSD has opened the gateways of the universe to me. It's freed my mind and really helped my writing."

Shig nodded, "Lots of artists have used external stimuli to aid their creative journeys. Oscar Wilde, Samuel Coleridge …"

"Who knows about these experiments?" Kats continued.

"Pretty much everybody. It's not a big secret. But they're careful about who can be part of the program."

"That's kind of crazy," Kats said.

"Nah, man. You want to know what's crazy?" Kesey asked conspiratorially.

Kats and Shig looked at Kesey and leaned in to hear the secret.

"That guy who went wild and killed those people," Kesey looked around to make sure no one else was listening, "he fucking escaped."

Hauser headed to the sanitarium for his meeting with Turier and quietly mulled over how to get rid of the man. He had brought Turier in almost a year ago, specifically to work with Steven Epps, but now that Epps was gone, Hauser found Turier an impediment to his larger work.

Epps had been a special case. For two years following his return from the North Korean prison camp in 1955, Epps had been at the military hospital in Tokyo undergoing a long "debrief" by the CIA and military intelligence. He'd been subjected to a long series of chemical interrogations and brainwashing while in Chinese custody. They'd hoped to turn him into a weapon that could be used against his own side, and in some ways they succeeded. If Epps had been an ordinary soldier, the CIA would have declared him "Missing, presumed killed in action" and quietly disposed of him. But Epps was unique. He'd been a twice-decorated combat veteran and received special training from the army and the South Korean military. Epps was a lethal weapon who'd shown exceptional talent in the field. But it was what the North Koreans and the Chinese had done to him while in their custody that excited the military.

Epps had been subjected to an intense barrage of psycho-active chemicals and brainwashing in an attempt to turn him into a sleeper agent who could be triggered at the appropriate time by his Chinese handlers. The drugs had interacted with each other and possibly with Epps' own unique body chemistry to change him in startling ways. When he became excited or stressed, the drugs triggered a massive hormonal reaction that made him freakishly strong, fast, and seemingly immune to pain. It also put him into a psychotic state that he wouldn't remember once he calmed down. The military believed Epps might be the key to unlocking a real-life super soldier formula. He would be the textbook they'd learn from, but Epps proved to be a complex cocktail of drugs, trauma, mental issues, and physical danger. They'd needed a team of specialists in multiple disciplines to work with the man, and when they'd searched for the leading authority in combat-induced trauma and battle fatigue, they'd found Dominic Turier, working at a NATO hospital in Paris.

Despite Turier's credentials and clear knowledge, Hauser hadn't liked him from the beginning. Too smart, too independent, and too principled to go along with the greater program. Turier knew he was working for the military but likely would have objected to any CIA connection. *Maybe that's how I get him to leave*, thought Hauser. Approaching the special psych ward, he found Turier engaged with a patient, a longtime resident, who'd been at the Battle of the Bulge during World War II. Clearly, the doctor cared about those under his care, and that irritated Hauser.

"Good afternoon, doctor," Hauser said, and Turier looked up from his patient. He nodded, patted the old soldier on the arm, and left him with the paper and crayons they'd been using. *Fucking crayons*, thought Hauser.

"We're making progress with Williams here. The creative therapy has opened up some memories for him, and I think these will prove to be very therapeutic."

Hauser merely nodded, "Can we go someplace to talk?"

"I want to finish my rounds. Walk with me and we can talk," Turier said, hoping the open spaces might make the interaction more tolerable. He didn't wait for Hauser to answer as he rose and walked across the ward.

"There's been a development that you need to be aware of," began Hauser. "It involves Epps." At that, Turier stopped and turned.

"Have you found him?" he asked.

"No, but we've had a sighting of him in the city."

"*Très bien.* Good news!"

"No, just the opposite," Hauser said, and Turier frowned. "Do you recall hearing about those murders a few days ago in the Tenderloin? A man and a prostitute were killed?"

"*Oui.* I read they thought it might have been some kind of blackmail operation."

Hauser shook his head and opened a large folder he'd been carrying and handed an 8×10 photograph to the doctor. "This was taken from the camera they recovered from the crime scene."

"*Mon Dieu.* That's Epps!" The photo showed Epps, fully dressed in a bedroom of some sort. Hauser handed him another photo. This one was Epps, naked standing over a slender Asian girl. The last photo showed Epps holding her aloft by the neck. "How did you get these? Was it really some kind of blackmail operation?"

Hauser evaded the question, "I don't know the specifics of what was going on there, but I pulled some Department of Defense strings to get this evidence and move the investigation from the San Francisco Police." *Let Turier think it was a recovery operation. By the time he realized it wasn't, it would be too late.*

"So, Epps is in the city. He must be blending in these past several months." *That would be a good sign*, Turier thought. He was able to function in a normal environment. But then something happened. "Something triggered him," he said to Hauser.

"That seems to be the case," Hauser replied. "Now we need to find him before something else triggers him. If he's caught by civilian forces, they might piece together what we've been doing here, doctor."

"But we're only trying to help these men, Mr. Hauser. What's wrong with that?"

"I don't think the public would be too happy with the experimental drugs and the other therapies we've been using on our patients."

Turier paused at that. He'd been reluctant at first to approve the treatment protocols that used LSD to help the psychotic patients, but some of their results had been promising. Turier knew as well that many of the men involved in these trials had few options, and he preferred the experimental drugs to lobotomies. "So, how are you going to find Epps?"

"I have some additional evidence that I'd like you to review, and then you're going to tell me how a man like Epps might survive in modern San Francisco all this time and where he might be hiding. We have to contain this asset."

"Contain an asset? He's a man who ..."

Hauser interrupted him. "He's an animal, experimented upon and turned into a truly dangerous weapon. Before the experiments the Chinese did on him, he was already a trained killer. The drugs made him stronger, faster, and more unpredictable than anyone else would believe. You saw firsthand how dangerous he is. We'll be lucky to contain him."

Turier shook his head. "If Steven has been living in the city for these past several months, then the work we did was productive. We can bring him back to himself."

Hauser grimaced but held back his initial response. "We can't do any of that unless we reacquire him. That's the first objective."

"Agreed," said Turier as the two men walked out the double doors into the late afternoon sunshine in the courtyard.

Kats' sharp eyes, always attuned to movement, saw the two men enter the other side of the courtyard. One, probably a doctor, wore a long, white lab coat. The other wore a dark business suit. Kats was about to return to the conversation with Kesey when his eyes returned to the doctor. Black hair, dark skin, and something about the way he carried himself. At this distance it was hard to make out his features, but he appeared to be about the right height and the right age. Kats, still looking at the doctor, said to Shig and Kesey, "I'll be back in a minute."

Kats walked across the busy courtyard, watching the two men who appeared to be arguing. He wasn't sure it was the man he knew until the doctor made a two-handed gesture of exasperation and then ran his hands through his dark hair. Kats had seen that gesture many times, and he knew the man who made it.

"You can't take me off my rotations, Hauser!" Turier said with frustration in his voice. "These men need me."

"Don't give me that Hippocratic Oath bullshit. We need

you to focus on Epps right now. And doctor, you don't work for the hospital. You work for me," Hauser said firmly.

"*Merde*," was all Turier could say as he raised his hands and then ran them through his thick hair. He was about to tell Hauser to go to hell when a voice from his past sang out.

"Hello, Dominic."

Turier turned toward the courtyard and there, walking toward him, was a man he hadn't seen in many, many years.

"*C'est pas possible*," Turier said, with a surprised look.

"*Ça va, docteur?*" Kats asked in passable French.

"*Oui*. Yes, I'm well. What are you doing here?"

"Oh, I live in San Francisco and am here on a bit of work. But you're rather far from home."

"Yes, I've been here almost a year," Turier said, "working with soldiers recovering from war." He glanced at Hauser, who glowered at the interruption. "*Pardon*, sorry," he said to both men. "Mr. Hauser, this is Katsuhiro Takemoto, an old friend from the war. Kats, this is Mr. Hauser, one of the hospital administrators and my boss."

"Hello," said Kats, and Hauser gave a short nod. *Not exactly the friendly type*, he thought.

"You said you're here on work. What is it you do now?"

Kats looked a bit embarrassed and said, "Well, I'm actually a private investigator." Turier made a surprised look, and Hauser's eyes narrowed.

"I'm sure there's a story to that," Turier said, "and I'd love to hear it. Perhaps we can get together for dinner or a drink?"

"Or a run," Kats smiled, and Turier laughed. Kats handed him his business card. "Call me, and we'll set up something." He smiled at the doctor and extended his hand. Turier shook it.

"I really am pleased to see you, Kats," he said, and both

men nodded. Kats turned and walked back across the court-yard. Turier watched him.

"So, how do you know this private detective?" Hauser asked.

"I can't really say," Turier replied.

"Why the hell not?"

"Doctor-patient confidentiality."

Kats rejoined Shig and Kesey, who were talking in the shady side of the courtyard. "Sorry," he said, "an old friend."

Shig quietly nodded, noting a future conversation with his friend. But Kesey was clearly agitated. "Man, those two guys ..." he began, then stopped. He turned and walked back inside with Kats and Shig following.

"Ken ... Ken!" Shig said and trotted to catch up to the big man. "What's wrong?"

Kesey stopped and looked back at the doorway, almost as if he were afraid of being followed.

"It's OK, man," Shig consoled him, and they waited for Kesey to gather himself.

"That incident I told you guys about ..." he said quietly, "that was the doctor and the admin guy at the scene!"

"That was the doctor?" Kats said slowly. "Dominic Turier?"

"I don't know their names. I've seen them around a bit but they're not in my area. After that night in the ward, I didn't want to know them. But yeah, those were the guys."

"Holy shit," Shig said and looked at Kats. "And you know that doctor?"

"I knew him fifteen years ago. He's a good man."

"But a lot can change in fifteen years," Shig continued. "He may not be the same guy you knew." Kats nodded but said nothing. They walked back through the building.

"Hey, guys. I should get back to work," Kesey said.

"Of course. Thanks, Ken," Shig said.

"Quick question before you get back at it," Kats asked. "Have you ever seen young civilian women being brought in for medical care? Young, pretty women?"

"No, can't say I have, but this is a big place, and I mostly work nights here. The routine medical stuff is in other buildings."

Kats nodded, "Thank you, Ken. We appreciate your help."

"Sure, sure, man. Shig, you're going to introduce me to Ginsberg, right?"

Shig gave a short bow, "Of course!"

"Cool. And hey, just a word of warning. That administrator guy in the courtyard," he said with a thumb jerked back in that direction, "folks in here stay clear of that guy. You might want to follow suit." He turned and was gone.

As they drove back from the hospital, Kats was quiet and lost in thought. Finally, Shig couldn't stand it any longer, "So, what the fuck was all that?" Kats smiled and eased the car onto the highway.

"Yeah, I know that doctor. Dominic Turier, a Frenchman. He's a psychiatrist. I worked with him during the war."

"Worked with him?" Shig asked. "Why would you be working with a psychiatrist during the war?"

Kats looked over at his friend in the passenger seat. "I worked with him as in he was my doctor." Shig looked confused and started to say something, stopped, then frowned.

"Remember I was wounded in the Vosges. They treated me in a field hospital at first and then sent me to a hospital in Besançon to recover. That's where I met Dominic."

"But why would you need a psychiatrist?"

"My body wasn't the only thing messed up. My head was … it was bad."

"Like battle fatigue? You're the toughest guy I know."

"Tough has nothing to do with it. There are things that happen, things you see, that you can't unsee, you can't undo.

"It was war, man."

"People use that excuse all the time. I don't think it exonerates you of your sins."

"Sins? C'mon man. You're not religious."

"You don't have to be religious to know that some things are wrong. I was having nightmares, I was barely eating, barely talking. If the war wasn't still raging, I might have ended up in Ken's psych ward. But they needed men. They needed me to get back in the fight."

"And this psychiatrist helped you?" Shig said.

"He really did. I'd say I owe him my life." Kats was quiet for a while. "I think I need to ask him what's going on there."

"Man, you saw that he's working for the government now. Can you trust him?"

"I guess we'll find out."

CHAPTER 7

S teven Epps closed the door to his one-room flat in the Jefferson Hotel on Eddy Street in the heart of the Tenderloin. He set his bag of hamburgers down on the small table next to the window and began to remove his work boots. The foreman at the Mission District jobsite wasn't happy that Epps had gone missing for several days, but he also knew that Epps was strong and got his work done. He wasn't union, and they paid him in cash at half the rate of the other workers, so they begrudgingly welcomed him back. Still, he thought he should look for another job.

As he sat next to the window eating his burgers and drinking a Coca-Cola, he could hear two men arguing through the thin ceiling. He focused on his breathing as he'd been taught and was mostly successful in blocking out the conflict. He stared out the window at the early evening sky and the still busy streets. He wasn't sure why, but he liked it here. The sights and smells of the city agreed with him. The fog, when it rolled across the bay, was particularly comforting. Tonight would be clear and cool, and he was thinking ahead to his walk.

"*C'est pas vrai*. This can't be true," exclaimed Turier as he sat with the folder open in front of him on Hauser's desk. He looked across at Hauser, who merely raised an eyebrow and waited for the storm of emotion to pass. "I'm a doctor! I ..." Turier trailed off as words failed him. He looked up from the photos and reports that covered Hauser's desk. Images of Steven Epps, an Asian girl, and a male victim filled his vision. There were reports of the drugs found on the scene and a ballistics report on the gun recovered on-site. He was still processing what Hauser had just revealed to him.

"Midnight Climax?" Turier said incredulously. "Sounds like something from a Beat poetry reading. And this has been going on for how long?"

Hauser calmly sat back in his chair across the desk, "About three years. Here and in New York City."

"This isn't what I signed up for!"

"Doctor, you're not involved in this project, so spare me any personal outrage. The only reason you're involved in this now is because *your* patient escaped and got caught up in this net."

"You're experimenting on people without their consent! How is that right?"

"We do what we must because the Soviets and the Chinese are doing it too. To keep up with them we sometimes get our hands dirty. The volunteers aren't enough, and my orders are to get results."

"This can't be a VA operation," Turier said. Hauser was silent. "This seems like an intelligence operation. Military intelligence? Perhaps even your CIA?" Turier shook his head.

"Doctor, you signed on to this project, including the human trials ..."

"Those men are volunteers!"

"Yes, they are, but volunteers alone aren't going to win this war. I'll do my best to keep your hands clean in this, but you need to help me. You need to help me capture Epps." The doctor looked down, shaking his head. Then he looked up to meet Hauser's eyes.

"I'll help you find Steven. But you must promise to let me treat him, preferably away from here and your other work."

"You'll get to treat him, doctor," Hauser lied, "but I need to know how we can find him. How is he surviving in the city?"

Turier ran his hands through his hair and tried to focus. "We'd made progress over the past several months, and he was normalizing. So long as he wasn't stressed, he was good. In that state, he may have gotten a job and rented a room. It wouldn't be that hard. Lots of places pay cash for a strong back. Maybe the docks? Maybe a construction site? Epps was trained to survive for months on his own in the jungle or in the mountains. He can certainly survive in San Francisco."

"But I thought he was psychotic?"

"He has behavioral episodes that are triggered by some specific things. There's a difference. He may have found a way to control himself. More likely, he's avoiding the things that distress him. That is typical behavior—avoidance of the thing that triggers you."

"So when we dosed him again, the drugs triggered him?" Hauser asked.

"That would seem to be the case. What was he given?"

"A new mixture of LSD, DMT, and mescaline. The lab called it CS4030."

Turier shook his head. "*Mon Dieu*, there's no telling what that would do to him. We were only guessing at all the drugs the Chinese used on him. So many of them left traces in his system, which is why he had all those episodes when he became agitated or stressed."

"I remember," Hauser said grimly. "We can show his photo around to some of the worksites, some of the SROs. But quietly. I have enough men to do the groundwork. But once we find him, how should we approach him, doctor?"

"I don't think you or your men should, *Monsieur* Hauser. You should let me approach him. I think he trusts me, or at least feels something close to trust."

Hauser looked skeptical but was thinking through the situation. "All right, doctor, but we'll be on-site as backup. And I have a team on the way to ensure his recapture."

Kats walked into the Chinatown headquarters of the Hop Sing Tong at 137 Waverly Place. The four-story building, painted in their color of green, had a double-door entrance on the bottom floor, and above, offices carried out much of the legitimate work the Tong provided the Chinese community. They had classrooms for teaching English, meeting spaces for businesses, a private bank, and even a lawyer to help the local community in times of need. All the various Tong organizations provided much needed community support services alongside their illegal, moneymaking operations such as gambling, prostitution, drugs, and black-market trade. Those activities didn't occur in their headquarters, but Kats' arrival at their front door had sent several young men scrambling, even though he was expected.

As he crossed the lobby and approached the main staircase, a young, powerfully built man stepped calmly away from the group, blocking the stairs. He held his hands inside the sleeves of his *hanfu*, but Kats knew those same hands could be moving toward him in an instant. The young man wore his long hair in a braided ponytail that looped over his shoulder, bound by a red-and-green scarf. This marked him as the 'Red Pole' or chief enforcer of the Tong. It was the position John had previously held. Kats stopped short of the man and gave a small, respectful bow. The man's eyes narrowed slightly, and he inclined his head, ever so slightly. *So much for a warm welcome*, thought Kats.

"Please tell Lin Tai Lo that I'm here to see him." Kats turned and casually looked around the hallway, admiring many of the antique scrolls that lined the walls. With a short jerk of his head, the Red Pole sent his men scurrying for Lin's office, leaving him alone with Kats.

"You're the investigator," he said with a thick accent. "The Japanese," he said coldly.

Kats turned and looked the man over. "American actually," Kats said with a smile, "but I can see how you might be confused."

"They say you're a good fighter," the man grunted. Kats shrugged his shoulders and subtly shifted his stance to bring the man into his forward position.

"He is a good fighter, Shan. A very good fighter," said Lin Tai Lo from the top of the stairs. "And far too smart to be goaded into meaningless displays with young bulls like you."

Shan's face flushed with the rebuke from his leader, but he continued to eye Kats coldly. Lin waved Kats up the stairs, and they walked toward his office.

"Your replacement, John?" Kats asked.

"Shan. His family came here from Hong Kong just after the war. He grew up here and took to the violence at a young age. Follows orders, gets things done."

"A hammer," Kats said.

"Many problems can be solved with a hammer, Katsuhiro."

The exchange reminded Kats of the many philosophical arguments he and John had back in college. Those were interesting, sometimes even fun. Today he didn't feel like the game, and they walked in silence to John's office.

As they sat, the two men looked across John's dark, wooden desk. Lin spoke first.

"I spoke with Gracie the other day. I asked her about you." Kats merely nodded. "She said something about a case you were on and a large barrel of snakes." Lin actually smiled at that.

"I needed a diversion," Kats said. "Seemed to work out."

"Yes, I heard it did. You took out Jimmy Lanza and his waterfront operation."

Kats nodded at the mention of Jimmy 'The Hat' Lanza, the head of the San Francisco mafia family. John's information network was impressive. "I think 'took out' is too strong a description," Kats said. "I temporarily disrupted his business. But you didn't ask me here to talk about old cases."

"No, I didn't," he replied. Opening his top desk drawer, he pulled out a manila folder and handed it across to Kats. "My people secured these before SFPD removed the files."

Kats opened the folder, and an 8×10 photo, in grainy black and white, stared at him. In it, a young Asian woman, presumably John's cousin Mai, was cowering on the floor as a naked White man stood over her. In the next photo, the man's face was blown up to portray his wide-eyed countenance. His eyes looked wild and feral.

"That is the man who killed my cousin," he said.

"Well, that's the man who's in the photo with your cousin, but beyond that, how can you tell he killed her?"

"Always the logical one, Takemoto."

"Not logic, John. I just don't want to jump to a conclusion. If you do that, you start finding facts and notions that support your conclusion. A good detective shouldn't be married to one idea during an investigation." Kats picked up the photo again, holding it close to his face and peering intently at it.

"Fine, but we agree that we need to find that man," Lin said, and his finger pointed to the photo.

"Agreed," Kats said, looking up from the photo.

"I'll have my men searching the city."

"Please, John, no violence. If they find him, let me handle the contact with this man."

"I'll let them know," John said, "but they're hungry for revenge. Don't expect them or me to wait forever."

CHAPTER 8

Kats and Molly sat at his desk, looking at the photo John had provided with a magnifying glass. "What am I looking for?" she asked as she scanned the horrific photo.

"You want to be an investigator?" he coaxed her gently. "Look deeply." She let out a sigh and continued to examine the black-and-white image.

"OK. I see several scars on the man. They kind of look like yours," she said, knowing Kats had earned his in combat.

"Good. I saw that too. I think you're correct that this man has been in combat."

"He looks strong too. Very fit."

"What does that suggest?" Kats asked her.

"He was an athlete, or he trains hard like you do. But not many people train like you do," she said, looking at him.

"So ...?"

"So maybe he has a physical job."

"Very good. He's a construction worker."

She lowered the magnifying glass and looked at him. "How the hell can you know that?" she asked with a smile.

"Look at his shoes. His boots."

Molly raised the glass again and looked closely at the boots placed next to the bed. Heavy steel-toed workman's boots squarely placed. "I'll be damned," she said, and looked at Kats with admiration. "OK, I'll go one better," she said, "and say he's ex-military."

Kats nodded, "That's probably how he got the scars."

"Yes, but that's not why I know he's ex-military. Look

again."

Kats furrowed his brow, took the magnifying glass, and peered at the photo, wondering how he missed something. Molly laughed at his serious face.

"You store your shoes the same way. Perfectly square to the bed or the *tatami* when you take them off."

"Very good, detective," he said and kissed her.

Over the next two days, Kats and Molly assembled a list of construction companies working in the city. She'd thought they'd include the SROs, the single-room occupancy hotels, in the city as well since the murder had occurred at a notorious hotel in the Tenderloin. Kats told her, "Those places rely on anonymity. If word got out that they were sharing information about their clients, there'd be economic consequences. The only way to get information out of those guys is to flash a badge, a gun, or a large roll of cash."

"None of which we have," nodded Molly. "OK, then we go the day labor route and check in with the construction offices." She looked over the list again. "I know several of these companies from working at Harry's, and there's even one site for Charles Construction over by the wharf. I think they'll talk to me."

"They'd better if they know what's good for them," joked Kats. But he also meant it. Molly had been the office manager at Charles Construction when they'd met over a year ago. Harry Charles and his men had ultimately proven to be allies against the local mob, but Kats knew that Harry was an operator who walked the line between hero and rogue, often on a daily basis. Kats also was sure that Molly knew how to handle him and his men. "I can come with you."

"We'll cover a lot more ground if we split up. Relax. I can

handle this. I'll even take Shig with me if that makes you feel better. He's been itching to get out of the store. I think he likes the idea of being a private detective."

"He does at that," Kats said. "OK. We'll split up the list and start tomorrow."

"This is so boring!" Shig lamented as they trudged uphill toward the Financial District. The late-morning sun was hot, contributing to Shig's misery. They'd visited four construction sites, showing the cropped photo of the wild-eyed man to the worksite bosses. None had seen him, and all said they hoped not to meet him.

"This is what being a private detective is mostly about. Boring legwork. Literally, leg work," she said, feeling the burn in her thighs as they walked. "C'mon, one more, and then we can go to lunch."

The idea of lunch perked Shig up a bit, and he asked, "OK. Which one is next?"

"The one I've been looking forward to and dreading at the same time. Charles Construction is working on Folsom near the Embarcadero."

"Shit."

"Yeah, maybe. Come on, soldier," she said, and put her arm around Shig's shoulder as they walked. Ten minutes later they arrived at the busy construction site on Folsom. They spotted two trucks with 'Charles Construction' stenciled on their sides. At least a dozen men were visible on-site for a big renovation job of an older four-story commercial space. Molly looked around for a familiar face but found none. One guy looked at her and Shig, so she stopped him, asking, "Where can I find the foreman?"

The man eyed her a bit suspiciously but pointed a thumb

over his shoulder toward what looked like the main entrance. "Just inside there. But you need ..."

"A hard hat. Thanks. I know the drill," Molly said, walking past him and taking a beat-up hard hat from a worktable near the gate. She tossed it to Shig and grabbed another for herself. They entered the main doors, and it took a moment for their eyes to adjust to the darkened hallway. Ahead, below a lit alcove, they saw two men, their backs to them, engaged in some kind of debate about a blueprint in front of them.

"I know that's what the blueprint says, but it's stupid," said the middle-aged man, who had glasses and bushy mustache.

"Now you're an architect?" jabbed the bald man, also with glasses and a surprisingly modish goatee.

"No, but I know a stupid design when I see one," Heckman responded to his longtime friend Baker, who held the blueprint in front of him.

"You guys arguing. Some things never change," Molly said, as the two men spun around and, seeing Molly and Shig, smiled.

"Molly!" they said together, embracing her and shaking hands with Shig. "Good to see you, too, snake man!" Heckman said, causing Shig to smile and Baker to grimace and make a face. "What brings you guys to our little worksite?"

"Well, we're on another case and looking for a man who may have been working here or at some other construction company over the past few weeks." Molly pulled the photo of their man out of her purse.

"Jesus Christ," Baker said, "this guy again."

"What?" Molly said.

"There was two guys in here yesterday with another photo, but looking for the same guy," Heckman said.

"The same guy? You're sure?" Molly asked.

Heckman and Baker both nodded.

"Police?" Shig asked.

"Nah, they looked like stiffs in suits," Baker said.

"Like they might have been government?" Molly asked.

"Yeah, stiffs in suits," snorted Baker.

Heckman looked at the photo too. "Who is this guy? Is he dangerous?"

Molly and Shig exchanged a look, he nodded to her, and she said, "I can't lie to you guys. He's probably dangerous. But you haven't seen him?"

"No, and that's what we told those guys yesterday too," Heckman said. "And we've been here for the past several months working on this renovation."

"Yeah, I'm surprised you guys aren't on the new stadium project," Molly said, referring to the massive contract Charles Construction had received to build the new sports stadium down in Bayview Heights.

"Well, Harry felt a special need to get this project when it came up," Baker said with a mischievous grin.

"Yeah, it appealed to his sense of irony," Heckman laughed.

"What are you guys talking about?" Shig asked, genuinely confused.

Heckman and Baker looked at each other and then around to make sure no one else was in earshot. "Remember that night at Pier 23?" Heckman asked.

"How could we forget?" Shig said sarcastically as Molly nodded and unconsciously touched her left shoulder, feeling the scar underneath her shirt.

"Well, remember we had to create a diversion for the local fire station to respond to? So that we could 'borrow' their fireboat?" Heckman asked. They nodded. "This ..." he waved his arms about, "was the diversion."

Molly and Shig looked at the two of them, brows furrowed, as they wrapped their heads around the lunacy of the situation.

"So, you guys started the fire that damaged this building ..." Molly began.

"And we got the contract to fix it!" Baker laughed, clapping his hands together. Shig howled with laughter as Molly and Heckman joined in.

"That is so fucking Harry," she said.

Lunchtime found them at the edge of Chinatown, and after a round of dim sum at a local favorite, they had one more construction site to check over on Stockton. They showed the photo around to the foreman with no luck, and with very little patience, they were shooed off the site. As they exited, four young men, dressed in black with green cuffed sleeves, stood on the sidewalk eyeing them.

"Tong," Shig said quietly to Molly. "Hop Sing Tong. The ones who hired Kats." She nodded.

Their apparent leader, a young man with a scar on his right eyebrow and a bit taller than Molly, spoke, "What are you doing asking around Chinatown?"

"We're following up on some leads. Your boss hired us to investigate the death of his cousin."

"Lin Tai Lo hired the Japanese, not some ... woman," he said dismissively. The others snorted with laughter.

"*Baka yo,*" Shig exclaimed. "We're working for your boss!"

The leader spun toward Shig, "Don't get smart, book man!"

"That's both ironic and idiotic. Well done." Shig stared defiantly and began to pull Molly away from the boys. The leader put his hand on Shig's chest and gave him a shove.

"If Lin Tai Lo hired you, you work for us!" he laughed. The youngest looking one, though they all looked young to Molly, eyed her like a tiny peacock. She towered over him by a good six inches, yet he continued to look at her like a tree he'd like to climb.

"*Think she has red hair all over?*" he said in Chinese. The others grunted with laughter. "*You'll never know.*"

"*No, I think she'd show me. All these gwaipo women are whores at heart,*" he said, winking at her.

Gwaipo was a term Molly recognized. White devil woman. She'd been called that before, and the first time she found it funny. This time it annoyed her.

The little cockerel sauntered over to her, and with his right hand he patted her bottom, smiling the whole time. Shig tried to step forward, but the others held him back.

Molly cocked her head sideways, gave a closed-mouth grimace of a smile, and fired the heel of her open right hand into the little man's chin. His teeth snapped together with a loud clack, and he immediately pulled away, holding his mouth. He looked back at her with furious, pained eyes as blood poured from his mouth where he'd bitten his tongue.

Molly shifted into her combat stance, left foot slightly forward and hands raised, as she prepared for him to come at her. It never happened.

Coming up the alley, a powerfully built Chinese man shouted, "*Tingzhi!*" which is Stop in Chinese. The men froze, and Molly and Shig were backfooted by the force of the order.

The young Tong eyed Shan as he approached, and they all quickly bowed as he stopped in front of them.

"*Red Pole,*" said the tallest of them. Shan approached the short, bleeding Tong. Reaching out with his right hand, he cupped the boy's face and turned it over, looking at the blood. He eyed Molly with a cold stare and then turned to his man and slapped him on the side of the head.

"*Serves you right, Haoyu. We show respect, especially when someone's trying to help us.*" The boy nodded and bowed deeply to Shan.

"*My apologies, Red Pole.*"

"*Not me,*" Shan said. "*To her.*"

The boy stood, wiping the blood from his mouth on his sleeve so that the red blood mixed with the green of his cuff. He stepped up to Molly and Shig, bowing, and said in passable English, "My apologies for the insult."

Molly looked at the boy, then at Shig who, with wide eyes, shrugged his shoulders. She turned to the boy and said formally, "I accept your apology."

The boy bowed again and turned away to join the other soldiers. Shan turned to Molly and Shig. She noted his long ponytail, like a knotted, black rope over his shoulder. "These young men are all ..." Shan began, and seemed to struggle to find the words in English.

"Cock and balls," said Molly with a wry smile.

Shan responded with a wide smile of his own. "Yes, cock and balls!" he laughed. Molly laughed as well, thinking Shan not much older than these other 'young' men, but his authority and presence made him seem much older. He made a gesture for them to walk with him toward the heart of Chinatown.

As they walked in silence, Molly noticed that the local residents of Chinatown either scurried away from Shan's approach or made polite bows to him as he passed. Shan barely acknowledged the attention. Molly broke the silence.

"They all seem afraid of you," she said cautiously.

"It is respect they show. Not to me, but to the Hop Sing Tong."

"Looks like fear to me," Shig noted.

"No, not fear. These are our people," Shan said as he gestured around him. "The Tong serves them, protects them, provides things that the White world does not." From her conversations with Kats, Molly knew this was true. The Tong had emerged as a community support organization in a time when the Chinese were being persecuted and even murdered by the established powers in the city. Law enforcement provided no protection, so the able-bodied Chinese formed these groups based upon the secret societies of traditional China. Benevolence only went so far, and these organizations needed ways to fund themselves, so they turned to gambling and prostitution and later drugs. Molly didn't doubt that Shan and his men thought of themselves as heroes to the Chinese community, but she didn't envy those men and especially the women caught up in their business. She chose her next words carefully.

"I know that you and your men are looking for this man," she raised the folder containing the photos of their quarry. "What will you do if you find him?"

Shan stopped and looked at her with intense, dark eyes. It took courage to hold his gaze, but she did. "Lin Tai Lo has instructed us to observe and report back to him. That your man will make the initial approach." Molly nodded, knowing this was the official plan. "But if he engages my men or if he runs, then ..." Shan let the thought hang there.

"You hope he fights, don't you?"

"I am the Red Pole of the Hop Sing Tong. I always hope they fight."

CHAPTER 9

In the back of the unmarked black car, Dominic Turier sat deep in thought. Hauser had shown up at his office that morning and told him to pack some clothes and whatever else he needed for a few days and to meet back at the VA garage for transport that evening. "Where are we going?"

"Temporary housing at the Presidio while we search for Epps." Turier nodded and said nothing more. That afternoon he went home, packed a single suitcase, and returned to the hospital at 7 pm. The car was waiting for him alone. He sat in the back seat as it rolled north toward the city. The Presidio had been a military base since the Spanish established it in the late eighteenth century and was now home to the army's 30th Regiment. It also housed Crissy Field, an old airbase that had served the army since the end of World War I. It was the car's destination.

An hour later at the Presidio gates, the driver spoke to the soldier, who consulted a clipboard and briskly waved them through. Turier looked out the window at the winding, tree-lined streets that seemed more like a residential neighborhood than a military base. This must be where the officers live, he thought. As the car approached the bay, a wide expanse of airfield revealed itself. There were a series of barracks, hangars, and office buildings at the edge of the field. The car glided to a halt in front of the main tower, where Turier emerged into the warm evening air.

A uniformed man approached him. He was a lieutenant if Turier remembered his insignia correctly. "Are you Dr. Toorear?" he asked. Inwardly grimacing, Turier nodded. "I'm Lieutenant Duffy. Colonel Hauser asked me to get you settled. Please follow me."

Turier followed him across the walk toward a two-story building that looked like a small hangar next to the control tower. They walked up the stairs to a sparse room that contained a single bed, a desk, a chair, and a large footlocker. "You have your own privy, sir," Duffy nodded toward the closed door at the side of the room.

"This will be fine," Turier said, dropping his suitcase on the hard bed.

"Colonel Hauser said to meet him outside on the field at 2100 hours."

"Understood."

At 9 pm Turier walked toward the airfield. He felt the warm breeze on his face and could smell the bay. Hauser stood with his broad back to him, his large head looking skyward. As Turier quietly approached, Hauser said, "Good evening, doctor."

"*Salut,*" Turier replied. "What are we waiting for?"

"Special team being brought in from Europe. They are the ones who will help us secure Epps. I need you to brief them tomorrow morning, 0800."

"*D'accord.*" OK.

Hauser turned to face the Frenchman. "I need you for this operation, doctor. I know you want to save Steven Epps. I know you don't like this project. I know you don't like me. But I need you onboard to make this work."

"And if I have reservations about this work, director?"

"You keep them to yourself, doctor. You do your job. The mission is what matters. If you can't get behind that idea, I can have you back in Paris faster than you can say 'Charles de Gaulle.'"

"I am, as you say, 'on board' for the mission because I want to get Steven back. I want to help him. I will be a good teammate to make that happen."

Hauser looked the doctor over, made a slight nod, and looked to the sky and then to his watch. "This is them."

Turier could see twin lights on an approaching aircraft that was coming in from the direction of the city toward the airstrip. The lights touched down and glided toward the tower and the adjoining hangars. The plane was a Douglas C-47, a twin-engine workhorse cargo plane used since the Second World War. Turier noted that the plane had no military markings and was, in fact, painted a matte gray-green that made it seem almost invisible. It edged sideways, and the propellors sputtered off. A moment later, the hatch behind the wing opened, and a ladder dropped from the plane. The first off the plane was a lean blond man who easily jumped down from the hatch. Three more men followed. They moved to the waist of the plane as that hatch opened and crewmen started offloading bags and other gear. Hauser walked forward and Turier followed.

"Who are these men?" Turier asked Hauser.

"Detachment from the 10th Special Forces unit in West Germany. These men are the best."

"The best what?" Hauser didn't answer.

As they approached, the blond-haired man turned and saluted Hauser, who saluted back. "Captain Thorne, welcome to San Francisco."

"Thank you, sir," Thorne replied, with a slightly odd accent. *Not American*, Turier noted. And a bit older than he first thought. Late thirties, maybe forties. Still very fit and trim, but his face showed experience. The other men also radiated the confidence of veteran warriors. Turier noted that all wore fatigues, but none bore an insignia of rank or even nationality. He realized this was a shadow team that officially didn't exist. Turier stood at a distance, not sure he wanted to know anything more about these men. He noticed another man come up from behind and stand next to him. It was Stiles, the other man who worked for Hauser.

"So, that's Thorne," Stiles said out loud as he stared at the fair-haired soldier talking to Hauser.

Turier shrugged, "Apparently. Who is he?"

Stiles raised his eyebrows and made an odd face. "Larry Thorne. AKA Lauri Törni.[5] Finnish national and former Waffen SS officer."

"*Pardon?*" Turier asked, turning to the man beside him. "That man," he pointed toward Thorne, "was in the German SS?"

"Yep. An officer. Remember the Finns weren't on the Allied side. They were fighting the Russians, which made them kind of allies with the Germans. Thorne there was such a prolific Commie killer that the Nazis recruited him into the SS. He fought for them on the Eastern Front. After the war, our guys recognized his talent and recruited him to our side."

"How is that possible?"

"Congress actually signed an act that authorized re-cruiting foreign nationals into our military. They would be granted citizenship after serving out their term. A talent like Thorne was too useful to put into prison." Turier shook his head, wondering how he could extricate himself from this ever-worsening situation.

Thorne introduced Hauser to his men. Esteban was a short Hispanic man with dark skin and a red bandana tied around his head. Zapek was a Frenchman who Turier sus-pected had been a Foreign Legionnaire at some point. He clearly looked the part. The last man was a squarely built Black man named Collins. His fatigues strained to fit his chest and shoulders, and he hefted bags and boxes like they were empty.

"Get your team settled, captain," Hauser said. "Mission briefing tomorrow morning with my staff," he gestured toward Turier and Stiles. Thorne fired a brisk salute, and he and his men hefted their gear and walked toward the barracks that had been cleared for them. Hauser turned to Turier and Stiles. "0800."

There was a knock at the door at 0730, and Duffy, the fresh-faced lieutenant, entered the doctor's room. "Good morning, Dr. Toorear," he said, again butchering his name. "I was told to assist you this morning."

"Good morning, and my name is Turier. Two-ree-ay," he said. "*S'il vous plaît.*"

"Umm, sorry, doctor," Duffy replied. "I never took French in school."

Turier nodded, gathered his notebook into his briefcase, and turned to follow the man. They crossed over into the hangar that was busy with maintenance personnel moving about. Duffy led him across the space to a row of glass-walled offices at the periphery of the structure. One had blinders half drawn, and a large table surrounded by chairs was visible as they approached.

Duffy held the door open for Turier. "The others will be here after their meeting," he said, looking at his watch. Turier looked confused. "The team is in another briefing with Colonel Hauser."

Turier made a pained face that was not unnoticed by the young officer. "Is there anything you need, sir?"

"*Si vous plaît*, perhaps some hot coffee."

"Right away, sir." Duffy turned and headed toward the open hangar doors, and Turier turned and examined the room. There was a long table, with ten chairs, a blackboard, and chalk. He took a seat at the end of the table near the blackboard and began organizing his notes for the coming meeting.

Twenty minutes and two cups of coffee later, Hauser strode through the doors, followed by the four men who'd arrived the previous night. Hauser's man Stiles completed the retinue. The soldiers sat and looked Turier over. He noted they were dressed in army-issue fatigues but again didn't have insignia or nameplates on their jackets. *Not officially here,* thought Turier. Hauser stood at the front of the room.

"Gentlemen, this is Dr. Dominic Turier," Hauser said as he gestured toward the seated doctor. "He's our civilian expert on the missing man, and he's here to brief you on the situation and how we can effectuate this retrieval mission. Doctor, these men are highly trained operatives, much like Sergeant Epps. They know his type. They are his type."

Turier made an audible snort that caused Hauser to look sharply in his direction. "*Monsieur* Hauser, I mean no disrespect to these men. I'm sure they're all experts in their field and highly accomplished soldiers. But they're nothing like what Steven has become." Turier noted that the men smiled and laughed a bit at the seemingly hyperbolic Frenchman. Well, all of them except Thorne, the older blond man who was clearly their leader. Thorne stared intently at Turier with sharp, blue eyes. He made a curt gesture to his team, and they stopped their chatter.

"Please explain, doctor," Thorne said in that slight, eastern European accent. He continued to stare intently at Turier.

Despite the unsettling intensity of the man's gaze, Turier found his thoughts. "Steven Epps was once as all of you are. A highly trained soldier. Special Forces. He was deployed in Korea and led over a dozen guerrilla missions behind enemy lines with exceptional results. In 1952, the Chinese captured him during a mission deep into North Korea. We believe he was betrayed by a Korean double agent and walked into a trap. Regardless, he was taken north to a base near the Yalu River. Except this wasn't an ordinary prison camp. This was a special operation: part prison camp, part medical facility. It was the center of the Chinese brainwashing operation. You may have heard rumors about it." Turier paused, looking around the table. The grins were gone. They'd heard about this facility. He continued.

"As best we understand, the Chinese used a combination of psychotropic drugs, electroshock, sensory deprivation, and old-fashioned torture on Sergeant Epps. The results were catastrophic. When a UN special operation recovered Sergeant Epps in the last days of the war, he was locked in an isolation cell and in a catatonic state. They airlifted him to Seoul, where American doctors examined him. At first they couldn't get any response from him, so they tried different methods to bring him back. When they attempted a stimulant, Epps emerged from his state and attacked everyone in the room. It took six men to restrain him and enough tranquilizers to knock out a horse." Turier took a drink of water from his glass at the table.

"Something happened to Epps that was triggered by the combination of drugs, stimuli, and his own unique body chemistry. When he becomes stimulated, his body floods with a combination of hormones and adrenaline. He becomes stronger, faster, more pain resistant, and very, very dangerous."

Thorne's eyes narrowed, "Does he remember his training? Or is he a raging beast?" *A good question*, Turier thought.

"The instances of Steven's aggression initially suggested more of the raging beast as you say."

"Initially?" Thorne followed up.

"Yes, as we treated him and began to better understand the stimuli that triggered him, we saw a new pattern emerge. When he had these psychotic episodes later, they were less barbaric and more ..." Turier struggled to find the correct words.

"Precise," Hauser said from the back of the room. "It became evident that Epps remembered his training or somehow those instincts were able to come through."

"Making him one dangerous motherfucker," said the man identified as Collins.

"Were you treating him then, doctor?" Thorne asked.

"No, I was brought in just last year once Steven was returned to the United States."

"What exactly triggers him, doctor? Is it simply a question of aggression and perceived threat?" Thorne pressed.

Turier paused, looking at the man. Thorne seemed far more thoughtful than he'd expected. *He's a very dangerous man*, Turier thought. He answered carefully. "With patients who have experienced trauma, things that recall that trauma are typical triggers. For example, a dog attacks a child. When that child sees another dog, he may flinch. When a dog barks, he may cry. He will also likely try to avoid dogs in the future."

"So, what's Epps trying to avoid?" Thorne asked.

"We know he was tortured. His body is marked and scarred. He has a strong aversion to loud noises, especially the sound of a gunshot. He also doesn't like knives and sharp objects. He reacts badly to needles."

Hauser stepped forward, "He also appears to trust Dr. Turier here, which is why we're going to let him make the initial approach to Epps. He will move Epps into position, and your team," he looked at Thorne, "will be ready to capture him and take him out with tranquilizer guns."

Thorne nodded but looked impassive. "All this sounds fine, but when? Do you have any lead on this man's whereabouts?"

Hauser answered, "We have men on the street, following some insight from the doctor here. It remains our best option at the moment."

Thorne rolled his eyes. *Clearly, sitting idle wasn't Thorne's strong suit*, Turier thought.

"Your team needs to stand ready," Hauser concluded. "Dismissed."

As the men exited the room, Hauser approached Turier. "Doctor, we're up against a running clock. My orders are very specific about any loose ends such as Sergeant Epps. If he can't be contained, the entire operation back at the hospital and the other side project will need to be shuttered."

"But we're actually seeing some progress with drug treatments on the men," Turier protested.

"Not the priority, doctor. If we can recover Epps with minimal attention, we may be able to salvage the other work. That should be your priority."

Hauser turned and exited the room. Turier's eyes followed him. *He's not talking about the men at the hospital. He's talking about his prostitution ring.* At that moment, he felt very alone and far from home. *How can I make this right? I have no friends, no allies ...* He paused, thinking. Then he opened his notebook and removed a business card that was tucked discretely inside.

CHAPTER 10

Kats had just sat down at his desk that morning when the phone rang. "Takemoto," he said into the handset.

"*Bonjour*, Kats. Did I catch you at a good time?"

"Hey, Dominic. Yes, absolutely. I'm glad you called. I was wondering if I needed to track you down," Kats said.

"*Non, non.* There has been much to do with my work, but I'm going to be in San Francisco for a few days and was hoping we could catch up."

"That would be great," Kats said as he pulled his date book from his desk. "I'm free the next couple of evenings. Does that work?"

Turier thought, "Perhaps tonight then? Do you have a recommendation for your city?"

Kats was quiet for a moment. Then he laughed into the phone, "I know a place you need to try. Meet me at Blum's on Union Square. Say 7 pm?"

"*Ce soir.*" This evening.

"So, dinner with an old friend," Molly said as she watched Kats change his shirt for the third time.

"Yes, an important old friend," he said as he pulled on a dark blue shirt. He turned toward her, "I want you to meet him ..."

"Just not tonight. I get it. Boys' night out."

"No, nothing like that. We just have a lot to catch up on, and I need to ask him some potentially uncomfortable questions about the hospital he's working at."

"He's a psychiatric doctor, right?"

"Yes, a very good one. He works with soldiers who are affected by battlefield trauma and the long-term impacts of war."

Molly looked carefully at Kats, the man she cared deeply about. Part of her wanted to press and ask for more information, but she hesitated to pry into what was clearly a sensitive past. She neutrally added, "He helped you during the war."

Kats shrugged and nodded silently, finding it difficult to express himself with Molly at that moment. "He got me through a tough time," he said, holding her gaze.

She pressed her lips together, swallowing her questions, and stepped forward and hugged him. He embraced her back fiercely, gratefully. They held the moment and then stepped back. "I have some work to do anyway. Go meet your friend. I'll see you later." A quick kiss, and he was out the door.

Kats rode his motorcycle into the cooling evening air toward Union Square. He parked in the alley near Blum's, the beloved family restaurant next to the I. Magnin & Company Department Store. It certainly wasn't the fanciest restaurant in town, but Kats had chosen it for another reason. It was famous for its Coffee Crunch Cake.[6] The dessert was a bit too sweet for Kats' taste, but he had to admit it was delicious. He wanted Dominic to try it because his friend had a sweet tooth and had repeatedly extolled the virtues of French pastry during their time together in Besançon. He was a little early and took a seat at a table by the window facing the entrance.

He glanced at the menu, both excited and a little nervous to see his ... *his what*, he thought. Dominic was his friend, he knew that, but he'd also been his doctor, treating him during his recovery after being wounded in battle at the Vosges. *Once you're a patient, are you always a patient?* he wondered. Now Turier may be involved in something that impacted his professional life. How far away Besançon seemed now.

During the Battle of the Vosges in late October 1944, the all-nisei 442nd Regiment had spearheaded the rescue of a lost Texas battalion. Kats, along with most of his unit, had been wounded in combat. He'd taken two bullets in action but had singlehandedly cleared a German machine gun nest. He was initially treated at a field hospital, but once he stabilized, he was moved to a hospital in the recently liberated city of Besançon, in eastern France, for his recovery. As his wounds healed, the doctors became increasingly concerned about the nightmares Kats was having. He was waking up screaming and often thrashed about in his sleep. Once he even struck a nurse who was trying to restrain him during an episode. The doctors began to sedate him at night, and within a week, the nightmares seemed to pass, and the doctors proclaimed him well on the way to recovery.

What the doctors and nurses didn't see was the nightly ritual Kats had begun where he meditated, slowing his breathing and his heart rate. He attempted to clear his mind as his father had taught him. It helped, as did the sedatives, but during the day, he found himself flinching at loud noises. And occasionally as a nurse would change a dressing, the smell of blood would fill his nose, he'd begin to sweat, and his once-steady hands would shake. For a man who'd been taught from childhood that control was the ultimate goal of training, this terrified him. His sense of self came from that control, and Kats didn't recognize himself.

It was at that time that a young French doctor started coming into the ward, talking with the men. Dr. Dominic Turier was dark haired, with a swarthy complexion and an easy smile. Kats initially shrugged off his invitation to talk. Pride and fear kept him from sharing what was going on inside his head. He was used to being tough and able to endure most anything, so he approached this new situation with his usual mindset. His body was nearly healed, and he realized that he was terrified to go back into battle.

On a cold but sunny day in November of 1944, Kats sat outside in the hospital courtyard. He was drinking a cup of coffee when he heard footsteps approach. Turning, he saw the concerned face of the French doctor. "May I join you, corporal?" Kats gave a curt nod and sipped his coffee.

"I wanted to share some news with you," Turier began. "I just saw a message from your commanding officer informing you that you've been nominated for the Silver Star for your bravery in the Vosges." Kats grunted and looked into his coffee cup. Turier smiled gently and added, "I was wondering how that makes you feel."

Kats wasn't sure how to answer that question. He wasn't used to the army asking how he felt about anything, and his father, his other main teacher, had never suggested that feelings were of any importance. There was honor, duty, and discipline. He shrugged his shoulders. "It doesn't matter how I feel," he said quietly.

Turier nodded patiently. "The message was also asking when you were able to return to your unit." Kats clenched his jaw, felt his stomach tighten, and said nothing. Turier decided to take another approach. "I saw somewhere in your file that you were an athlete. A baseball player, yes?" Kats nodded. "I don't know much about your baseball, but I played football as a boy. You call it soccer, I believe. I wasn't very skilled, but I was a good runner. What about you?"

Kats thought back to high school, before the war and then in the internment camp, where he played shortstop and could be counted on to stretch a single into a double because of his speed. A flicker of a smile crossed his face at the memory. "I was pretty good. Faster than most."

Turier smiled at him. "Perhaps we can try something new. Would you like to go for a run with me? I find it invigorating, and there are some beautiful trails along the river and in the hills. I can get you some proper shoes. Tomorrow morning?"

Kats realized he hadn't been outside the hospital in weeks, and the thought of that freedom was appealing. "OK," was all he said.

The next morning Turier appeared carrying a pair of sneakers. "Try these on," he said. They were a pair of slightly used Dasslers,[7] the German athletic shoe from the company that supplied German athletes and Jesse Owens with track shoes during the 1936 Olympics. They fit perfectly. Still unsure of why the doctor invited him to run, he was nonetheless curious.

As they walked toward the river, Turier said, "Let's take it easy today. You're still recovering," and he set off at an easy pace. Kats paused for a moment, looking back and forth, and then lurched somewhat stiffly forward. At first his body didn't want to exert itself, but then it remembered all its training, and he fell into an easy run beside the Frenchman.

That day they ran about five kilometers. The three miles felt like a marathon after Kats got back to his room. He was, by his standards, out of shape, but he welcomed the pain and stiffness. That night he fell asleep easily and couldn't remember any nightmares. The next morning they met again, and within a week, their daily ritual had expanded to more than ten kilometers, and the pace had increased. Their runs became increasingly difficult. Into the hills, through the forest, on trails, on paved roads, they ran. Mostly they ran in silence. The only sounds were their feet tapping out the rhythm of the road and their controlled breathing.

Kats had always been among the fastest guys on his teams, but it was endurance over distance, the ability to run for miles, that had separated him from his peers and made him into a ranger for his unit. So Kats had been surprised that Turier had kept pace with him, even charging up hills at a blistering pace that Kats fought to match. When they did speak, Turier did most of the talking. He explained that he came to be a psychiatrist because of the experience his father had with so-called battle fatigue. He shared his experience of being an outsider in his own country because of his mixed parentage. His openness and candor coaxed Kats into talking about his own family and his experiences. Kats found himself sharing feelings about his parents and about internment that he'd never shared with anyone. Kats also felt his strength returning along with his sense of self.

On a cold, gray morning in early December, Kats and

Dominic raced up Mount Saint-Étienne, one of the seven hills that surrounded the city and the location of the Citadel de Besançon, the seventeenth century fortress that overlooked the entire valley. As they reached the top, Turier slowed and walked to the fortress walls, surveying the valley below. "It's beautiful, *non?*"

Kats inhaled the cold, crisp air. "It is," he said, looking at the amazing architecture and the idyllic valley below. It was hard to believe that mere months ago, the Germans had held this city.

Turier turned to him, "You know they want you back at your unit," he said matter of factly.

"I know."

"Are you ready to go back?"

"It's my duty."

"That's not what I asked you." Kats looked out over the valley. "You know, it's all right to be afraid. Even for Silver Star recipients," Turier said, referring to the recent news of Kats' commendation for valor at the Vosges.

"I'm not afraid, at least not like that anymore," Kats said. "These past few weeks have really helped. Finding my strength again, healing my body." He paused. "I haven't had a nightmare in weeks."

"*Très bien,*" Turier said.

"What I'm afraid of is ... is difficult to say."

"*Mon ami,* you can say anything you need to say to me."

"I know, but it's difficult to say that the thing I'm afraid of ... is myself." Turier looked puzzled but gestured for Kats to continue. "I told you about my *budo* training with my father," Kats began.

"Yes, the Japanese martial arts."

"At the core of that training is control. Precise physical,

mental, and even emotional control. My father drilled that into me. The army drilled that into me as well. But I lost that control in that last fight. I became something completely out of control, something savage, something I never thought I could become."

"You were in the midst of what some call *battle fury*. It's not uncommon for men to almost black out and not remember what they did during combat."

Kats shook his head, "No, I remember everything. That's the problem."

"What is it that you remember that hurts so much?"

There was the question at the heart of it all. It had taken many weeks and many miles to get here, but there it was, confronting Kats like an approaching storm.

"I remember the blood. I remember the white-hot anger I felt at the time. It was ... cathartic. It was satisfying. Doc, I'm afraid I enjoyed killing those men."

Turier nodded, taking in the words. "Katsuhiro, I've come to know you over these past weeks. I'm certain, as your doctor, that you're not one to enjoy killing. I believe you're mistaking the human nature of survival as something else. Since humans have picked up rocks and sticks to protect and defend themselves, survival has been a biological fact that's part of our existence. To survive, we must sometimes kill, and that survival is exhilarating. It might feel like joy in the moment, but it's only the release of chemicals in our brains and the relief of stress."

Kats still looked pained. "There's something that I didn't tell anyone after the battle," he exhaled deeply. "At the end of the fight in the bunker, some of the Germans tried to surrender. They threw their weapons down. I couldn't stop," Kats began to shake, and tears welled up in his eyes. "I killed them!"

Turier stepped forward, breaking a rule of practice but not caring and put his arms around Kats, who cried into his shoulder. "It's not your fault, Kats. It was a terrible moment, and in the heat of battle, tragic things happen. Do you think that the bomber pilots drop their bombs only on the soldiers? Do the shells fired from artillery never land on innocents? *Non*, this is war. This is the worst of what we as a people do to each other. But it isn't who we are. Listen to me," he grabbed Kats with both hands, looking him in the eyes. "War is a disease that we'll likely suffer from for many, many generations until we finally find a cure for it. Until then, it's upon us, upon men like you who have faced war and not surrendered their humanity to war, to be the example for others. Be a good man. Be a strong man who has faced the worst of war and survived it. The fact that you feel guilt and remorse is good. Without it, you could have become that monster that you fear."

Kats looked at him and dried his eyes on the back of hand. "What if that killer comes back?"

"That killer is a part of you. If he ... you ... need that side again, it will be with good cause. I'm sure of it."

They stood in the crisp morning air, their breath visible as they looked over the serene valley. "Thank you," Kats finally said.

Turier shrugged and then smiled.

"No, really. Thank you. I don't know what I would've done if I'd not met you. What you do for soldiers ... is life-saving."

Turier nodded and said, "I must also thank you. You've helped me in my own thinking about what I do. My colleagues think it's foolish of me to go on runs with you. They believe in the old-school approaches to treatment."

"So, you don't go running with your other patients?" Kats said with a wry smile.

"You're the first."

"Glad I could help you out there, doc," Kats laughed.

It was Turier's turn to blush and nod his head. "Come. You've earned something special. I must show you the best bakery in town." He turned and ran easily down the mountain. Kats followed him to a little pâtisserie in the heart of the town. There they ordered profiterole, the cream-filled pastry the French love so much. Kats had two.

It was after 6:30 pm, and Molly heard the phone in Kats' office ring. Molly walked down from the second-floor kitchen into the ground-level office. She sat down at Kats' desk and answered the phone, "Takemoto Investigations."

"Molly! Hey! It's Baker over at the Folsom construction site."

"Hey, hi! What's up?"

"That guy you and Shig were in here the other day asking about ... he was just here!"

"What?!" she shouted into the phone as she unconsciously stood up.

"Yeah. He came in asking about work, and Heckman, cool as could be, talked him up. He told him to come back tomorrow morning to talk to the foreman. He's gonna be back here at 8 am. How about that for private investigating!"

"That's amazing! Well done. I owe you guys a couple beers!"

"OK, so what should we do about tomorrow morning?" he asked.

"Kats isn't here right now, but plan on us coming there

early, maybe 7 am, to get set up to confront this guy."

"Roger that. I'll let Heckman know. Do you want us to bring any, you know, reinforcements?"

"I'm pretty sure Kats can handle one guy, but we may have your men positioned in case he tries to run. Thanks. See you tomorrow!" She hung up the phone, thinking, *Kats is going to be very happy.*

Haoyu stood across the street from the construction site. Tonight he was wearing blue jeans and a sweater instead of his green-trimmed *hanfu*. His legs were stiff, and his mouth still hurt from the blow he'd received days ago. He'd been almost ready to head back to Chinatown when he saw a tall, powerfully built man enter the Folsom construction site. From across the street he didn't have the best vantage point, but he thought it possible that the man who'd just entered was the man in the photograph they'd been told to look out for. But he needed to be sure. He edged closer and hoped that this was the only exit from the site. Fifteen minutes later, his patience was rewarded.

The man exited the construction site and headed up the street to Market and turned west. Haoyu followed at a distance, wondering how he could stop and contact his elder Tong brothers. He didn't want to lose the man while he found a telephone. The man stopped in a sandwich shop, and Haoyu looked about for a pay phone. Finding none, he swore to himself but continued to wait for the man to emerge. *Just relax,* he told himself. *He'll stop somewhere, and then I can call Shan. I'll redeem myself!*

CHAPTER 11

Turier entered the restaurant a few minutes late. He saw Kats wave him over, and he approached his friend. Kats rose and embraced him. "Good to see you, Dominic," he said, patting him on the back.

"And you, *mon ami*, so far from France and the war." He took off his coat and sat down. Looking around the restaurant, which was perfectly fine but more like a lunch place, he said, "Interesting choice. A favorite of yours?"

Kats smiled, "Not exactly. The food here is good, but I wanted you to try their famous Coffee Crunch Cake. I know you have a sweet tooth, and though it may not be French pastry, it's pretty damn good."

"Ha! I'm here for the company. The cake will be a bonus." They sat and ordered drinks and dinner, easing into each other's presence after many years.

Their food arrived, and by the time their plates were mostly empty, they had in typical French fashion made pleasant small talk, catching each other up on the years apart. Turier was happy to hear that Kats had someone in his life. "Yes, Molly's amazing. I really want you to meet her."

Turier smiled, knowing from his own family the challenges of a mixed relationship. His Algerian mother had struggled for acceptance in France her whole life, and that had made for difficult times for them and their mixed child. "So, you're happy?" he asked, and Kats was reminded of another friend who had asked the same, un-Japanese-like question.

"Yes, I am."

"Truly, you've come a long way since Besançon."

"We both have. You're working at an American military hospital. Hopefully helping so many soldiers in need of your skills." Turier nodded, but his face was neutral.

"I fear that my work isn't exactly what it seems," he replied.

"Well, that's kind of what I wanted to talk to you about," Kats said and slid forward in his chair. Just then, the waiter brought them a large slice of the Coffee Crunch Cake and set it between them. He poured two cups of coffee and set out two forks.

"But first you really need to try this," Kats beckoned. Turier smiled, taking a fork and looking at the extravagant dessert, frosted and covered in crunchy coffee flakes. He filled his fork and cautiously tasted it. A moment later, his face lit up.

"*Mon Dieu*, that's delicious!" He eagerly took another bite, and Kats joined him. For a few moments they attacked the massive piece of cake, the serious conversation set aside.

Sipping his coffee, Kats started cautiously. "So, I'm working on a case, and I need to ask about your hospital. My client has asked me to investigate the death of a young woman. She was killed in the Tenderloin about ten days ago. I've discovered that she was involved in some kind of drug operation, part of experiments being done on unsuspecting men." Turier sat rigidly in his chair as Kats continued. "Your hospital is doing drug experiments using LSD and other drugs, correct?"

Turier nodded slowly. "Yes, the veteran's hospital is using new drug protocols to treat trauma and mental illness. The work is promising."

"Well, the woman who was killed ... she was recruited by

a man who sent her to your hospital for screening. Another source has confirmed the same experience. I'm hoping you might know something."

Turier shifted uncomfortably in his chair, the coffee cake now forgotten. "You put me in a difficult position," he began. "I'm working for the US military, for your government, you understand." Kats simply held his gaze. Turier was clearly wrestling with many issues. Finally, he let out a deep sigh and said, "Yes, the government is conducting drug experiments. Some at the hospital, and some ... some at other locations."

"What other locations?"

"Truthfully, I don't know, but somewhere in the city."

"And there are young women involved in this process. As ... bait?" Kats said harshly.

"*Oui.* I only just learned of this myself."

"Are they still doing it?"

"I believe so." Kats clenched his fist on the table, his eyes looking furiously at Turier. "It makes me angry as well, but I don't know where the operation is located. And the man who runs it doesn't give a damn about what I think."

"Was that the man I met at the hospital?"

Turier paused to consider the ramifications of his answer. Then, deciding it needed to be told, answered, "*Oui.* Hauser."

"This operation of his got a young woman killed. My client wants to know who's responsible and why."

Epps, thought Turier. *He's looking for Steven!* Now he truly had a dilemma. "What will this client of yours do? Go to the police?"

"The girl who was killed was family to him. He's a dangerous man with a powerful organization behind him. I hope he'll let the proper authorities handle things, but I'm not certain."

Turier could feel the pressure building behind his eyes as these pieces came crashing together. *How to walk this highwire*, he thought. "But what will you do? Allow your client to take their vengeance?"

It was Kats' turn to shift uncomfortably in his seat. "He has all but told me so," Kats said with a sigh. "I'd hoped to find the answer once I found out who was responsible."

"Responsible. Yes. Who's responsible? Who can be responsible?" Turier asked pointedly.

"I'm not sure I follow you."

"What if the person you're looking for wasn't truly responsible? Perhaps not mentally competent?"

"Like insane?" Kats asked.

"An oversimplified term, but yes. Insane. Does that make this person responsible?"

"I'm not a lawyer, Dominic, but I'd certainly say that complicates the matter. What are you getting at?"

Turier knew he was about to cross a line, one that might cost him his position and compromise a top-secret government project, but his own moral compass couldn't let this one pass.

"This man you seek, the man who killed the girl, he was a patient of mine." It was Kats' turn to be at a loss for words. "He was a soldier, like you. He served in Korea and was captured by the Chinese. They ... they experimented on him."

"This patient of yours," Kats asked, "did he escape from Menlo Park?" Turier looked shocked.

"How did you know that?"

"It doesn't matter, but I do, and this case just got much more complicated," Kats sighed and took a deep breath. "Cards on the table, Dominic. We can't help each other if we don't really know what's going on."

Turier nodded, knowing he was likely finished with the Department of Defense but not caring at the moment. "His name is Steven Epps. He was a specially trained soldier in Korea who was rescued near the end of the war. But the Chinese used experimental drugs and techniques on him. They turned him into something ... something truly frightening."

"Frightening how?"

"The drugs did something to his mind and body. When he's stressed or triggered by something, he becomes stronger, faster ... almost superhuman. And he couldn't control it, at least when he first was brought to me."

"You were trying to help him control these episodes?"

"I was trying to help him not have them at all. To manage his stress and his trauma so that the event wouldn't happen."

Kats nodded. "Cards on the table," he said. "Didn't Epps kill a couple of your staff members at Menlo Park?"

"*Oui,* but I don't believe it was his intention to do so. He was ..."

Kats cut him off. "Intentional or not, he did kill those people, right?"

Turier sighed. "Yes, he did."

"And he killed my client's cousin and the other man in the Tenderloin?"

"Yes, but he'd been dosed with a powerful psychotropic. I believe Steven had begun to manage his trauma, and it was only the introduction of the drugs again that triggered him."

"As part of this secret program to study the effects of these drugs," Kats said pointedly.

"Yes," Turier said. "But I have some questions for you as well." Kats nodded, and Turier pressed on. "Who's your client?" Normally Kats would never reveal a client, but they were far beyond the usual rules.

"I'm working for one of the leaders of the local Tong. Do you know who the Tong are?"

Turier nodded, "Like a criminal gang," he said.

"An oversimplification, but yes, they operate outside the law at times. They're well organized, highly disciplined, and utterly ruthless if need be. The girl who was killed was family to this Tong leader."

The two men sat across the table in silence, each trying to process these revelations. Kats broke the silence. "Do you still think you can help this man, Epps?"

"I do. You know I don't give up on my patients," he said with a wry smile. Kats did know, and that made all this even harder.

"There's something that I still don't fully understand," Kats said. "The two who were killed at the apartment in the Tenderloin ... the man had his neck broken, which seems consistent with what you've told me about Epps." Turier nodded, and Kats continued. "The girl, Mai ... she was shot. Why would Epps shoot her?"

"Perhaps Epps had a weapon with him?"

"Maybe, but a hundred-pound woman isn't much of a threat to a man like him. Why shoot her and not shoot the man, who was a government agent?"

"Could she have had the gun and Steven disarmed her? Turned the weapon back upon her?" Turier suggested. Kats twisted his mouth into a grimace, clearly not buying the idea but not having anything else to offer.

"Doesn't seem likely. But if I can tell the Tong that the man responsible has been taken into custody by the federal government, they may be willing to accept that result."

Turier nodded, "There's a special team already assembled to capture Steven. They're awaiting a location for us to move out."

"A special team? What kind of specialists?"

"They're special forces. Highly trained soldiers brought in from Europe."

"That sounds like a kill team, Dominic."

"They assured me that I'd approach Steven and we'd capture him, not kill him."

"And you trust these people?"

Turier was quiet for a moment, then shook his head. "*Non*, I don't. I want to believe them, but that's not the same thing."

"Well, maybe we can use them and their resources and turn this around."

"How?"

"They're searching for him. The Tong are searching for him. They have me and my friends looking for him. Someone is going to find him, and then it's a race to get to him. You think he'll respond to you?"

"I think I'm the only one he may respond to, but I'm not certain."

"Then we'll need to be ready with a backup plan." Kats sat thinking for a moment. "You said he reacts to these psychotropic drugs ..."

"*Oui*, dangerously so."

"But other drugs, like a tranquilizer, would work on him like anyone else?"

"That's what the army plans to do once I make the approach. High-powered tranquilizer rifles with expert marksmen."

"I may be able to come up with a similar solution. Give me a couple days."

"I hope we have a couple of days," Turier grimaced.

"Meanwhile, we need to find out where he's hiding in the city."

Haoyu had patiently followed the man across the darkening San Francisco streets for over an hour. He thought he'd lost the man twice, but the luck of his ancestors guided him forward, and he was able to spot the slow-moving man in the dwindling light. He turned onto Eddy Street and made his way into the Jefferson Hotel in the middle of the block. Recognizing the hotel as a single-room occupancy boarding house, Haoyu knew his man had returned home. He found a phone in the drugstore across the street and, twenty minutes later, Shan, along with eight other Tong soldiers, had arrived. Haoyu bowed deeply to the Red Pole.

"*You've done well*," Shan said to the much smaller man, causing his cheeks to blush.

"*Thank you, Red Pole*," he said, as he bowed again.

The others gathered in the alleyway around the corner, awaiting orders. Shan quickly took charge, ordering a team to the back and another to the front. Two more were to take positions in the lobby, but not to act.

"What about the Japanese investigator?" asked one of his seasoned soldiers, remembering the orders from Lin Tai Lo.

"We're instructed to call him. You may do so. If he arrives, we'll determine the next steps. In the meantime, we won't let this man escape us." They all nodded and moved into position.

Molly stepped out of the bathroom, her hair wrapped in a towel, when the phone in Kats' office rang again. Immediately, she thought it might be Heckman or Baker with more information about the operation in the morning, so she hurried down the stairs. Picking up the receiver, she said, "Takemoto Hayes Investigations," with a smile.

There was a moment's hesitation on the other end. Then a male voice in thickly accented English said, "I was told to call Takemoto." *Tong*, she thought.

"He's my partner, but he's not here right now. Can I help you?"

"Ahh, you're the *gwaipo* from the other day!"

Molly rolled her eyes, "Yes, that's me. The *gwaipo*. What do you need?"

"I was told to tell Takemoto that we've spotted the man in the photograph. We tracked him back to the boarding house he lives at on Eddy Street. The Jefferson Hotel. Our men have the place covered."

"Wow, OK. I'll get a message to him and have him meet your men there as soon as possible." The line clicked dead, and Molly immediately grabbed the phone book from Kats' desk drawer, searching for the listing for Blum's.

"You good on the plan?" Kats asked again.

"Yes, I'll play along with them and try to alert you if they locate Steven first. You can then shadow us and perhaps act as a witness to prevent them from simply erasing him."

"You have my number there as well as the number for City Lights. My friend Shig is almost always there, and you can leave any message with him." Turier nodded and closed his small notebook. "And if you can find out anything further about the prostitution ring they're running, I think we need to look into that," Kats said with a fierce look in his eye.

Just then, a waiter approached the table. "Excuse me, but are you Mr. Takemoto?" he asked.

"Yes."

"There was an urgent call for you. The message said for you to call home." Kats nodded, and Turier rose as well.

"I should go before I'm missed. We'll talk again soon." Turier extended his hand, and Kats shook it firmly.

"Good to be working with you, Dominic," Kats said, and Turier headed toward the door as he walked to the phone booth in the back of the restaurant.

He dug change out of his pocket and made the call. Molly answered on the first ring.

"Kats!" she exclaimed into the phone. "The Tong called. They found the killer!"

CHAPTER 12

I t had been a good day for Steven Epps. His visit to the Charles Construction jobsite seemed to go well, and he thought about the meeting he had the next morning with the foreman. The jobsite was closer, and he was ready for a change. Still, he had several hours until then, so he pulled on his jacket for an evening walk to calm his mind and burn away his excess energy. He closed the door to his fourth-floor room and headed down the stairs. As he stepped into the lobby, he detected the eyes of two Chinese men shift his way. Years of training had taught Epps to notice when he was being watched, and these two amateurs all but stared.

He crossed the lobby to the front desk and asked the manager if he had any mail. He knew he didn't but used the mirror on the wall behind the front desk to assess the room. *They probably aren't alone,* he thought. Turning, he casually walked toward the front doors and out into the night. As he emerged, he caught movement across the street. Three men, and two more at the corner to his left. He zipped up his jacket and turned to his right, walking down the street.

So began the slow-speed chase.

Epps turned right at the next block and then left at the following corner. He was using the streets to determine how many men were pursuing him. He began to move quickly but avoided running. There was no need to run—yet. The men were herding him, trying to cut him off and isolate him somewhere less public, less visible. He scanned the street, looking down alleyways and around corners as he passed them. He, too, was looking for the right terrain. In the field he would have sought high ground and made them come to him. In the city, it was much the same, but this time he needed the high ground and ways to limit their access to him. He needed ... there!

Rounding the corner, Epps spotted a new five-story parking garage on Van Ness. During the day it would be filled with the cars of workers in the surrounding office buildings and shops. At night, there would be far fewer cars, but it would still be a labyrinth of ramps, columns, and stairwells. As he approached the front entrance with its small office and closed gate, he saw more of the Chinese appear at the far end of the block, entering the lit street. Thinking they had him cornered, they slowed and spread out over the sidewalk. Epps knew his pursuit from behind was closing in as well, but he took it all in with practiced ease. Most people being pursued by a small mob of attackers would have felt panic, but he'd faced far worse on the battlefield and knew that panic led to mistakes, and mistakes left you dead. He also knew that if he got too emotional or stressed, he'd lose himself, and that might be worse than death.

He ducked under the closed arm of the gate and ran up the ramp into the dimly lit garage. He noted the stairwells to the north and south sides of the structure but followed the ramp upward. On the third level he stopped, quieted his breathing and his mind, and looked carefully about. A dozen cars were in this section, dark and waiting for their owners to finish their work or after-work revels. He moved quickly from car to car, testing doors to see if one was open. His fourth attempt found a late-model Buick with a back door unlocked, and he slid into the rear bench seat and lowered himself down as he heard footsteps approach. Using the glass and the side mirrors, he noted several men who were dressed in dark

Chinese clothing. They spread out across the floor as they inspected dark corners and looked beneath the parked cars.

"You two, stay here in case he circles back. The rest of you come with me," said the voice. Epps could hear footsteps echo as the men seemed to recede into the distance. He slowly raised his eye level over the door rim and could see two men on the other side of the garage smoking cigarettes. They were at a forty-five-degree angle from him to his right. If he exited the opposite side of the car, he would be in shadows and out of their line of sight. A nearby siren provided enough background noise as he slowly opened the rear door and slid to the ground. He could hear the men quietly speaking in Chinese. In the tight confines of the garage he could even smell their cigarettes. Epps rolled on the ground between the cars and lay there assessing the battlefield. Most of the men seemed to have moved further up the garage, so he could slip past this rear guard and out into the city. But he had to dispatch these two first.

Epps looked under the cars and could see their feet two cars down to his right. He raised his arms over his head like a swimmer and rolled silently under the car. He continued to roll until he was underneath the car behind the two men. They stood, shifting back and forth, hoping their comrades would return with the man in tow. Epps rolled out from under the car and into the shadows between the parked vehicles. The men had their backs to him as they eyed the expanse of the garage in front of them, not knowing that their prey now eyed them from behind like the lethal predator he was.

Two long, silent strides, and Epps was upon them. The first man crumpled when an elbow smashed into the back of his skull. The second man had a moment to recoil in surprise, but Epps was on top of him in an instant, driving him backward into the wall. All the air exploded out of the man's lungs as he hit the wall with a thud. He crumpled forward, gasping for air as he met the uppercut from Epps' left hand. Epps actually caught the unconscious man and lowered him quietly to the ground. He stopped, listening. Nothing. He turned and moved toward the ramp that led back down toward the street. He'd taken a dozen steps when the stairway door ahead of him cracked open with light. He dove into the shadows between a Ford and the low concrete wall at the end of the ramp. As the door swung open, he saw three more men emerge from the lit stairwell. They moved onto the level, and in a moment one of them yelled, "Shit!" as they saw their two fallen comrades. Epps saw them run past him, and he surged toward the stairwell, pulling the door open, and entered the landing. Behind him he heard a voice, "There he is!"

Rather than running, Epps stopped behind the door and listened. He could hear the footsteps rapidly approaching the door. He took a step back and waited calmly. He heard the voices and the steps. Then, just as the metal door started to open, he stepped forward and delivered a stomp kick to the door, which rocketed it into the oncoming man's face. He heard a grunt of pain followed by falling bodies. He turned and headed down the stairs. As he reached the second-floor landing, he reached up and broke the light fixture, sending the stairwell into near darkness. From above and below he could hear voices. He pushed the door open onto the second floor of the garage, quickly looking around and not seeing anyone. Behind him in the stairwell he could hear them coming. He took a step back from the door and waited again. *It worked once before*, he thought. Again, as the door began to open, he stepped forward delivering a stomp kick that smashed it back into the pursuing men. The lead man crumbled, his nose and arm broken. He fell back into the others, creating a tangle of bodies in the darkened landing.

Epps gathered himself and turned to run down the ramp when two beams of light suddenly crossed the floor in front of him. He turned to see a tall, powerfully built Chinese man standing next to the open window of a car. He'd just turned on the car's headlights, creating a bright pool of light. Epps stopped. He heard the door behind him crack open and saw three men come down the ramp. *Cornered*, he thought.

Shan stepped forward, and the five other Tong spread out behind the *gweilo*. His men were now prepared, and they had the man surrounded. Lin Tai Lo wanted him alive, but Shan knew his men were hot for blood. They'd seen several of their brothers taken down by this man in front of them. Shan thought he might be able to pull them off of him in time to spare his life, but he wasn't particularly troubled if it didn't happen. His men now drew their weapons from their jackets. Hatchets, the preferred weapon of all the Tong. The fifth man, Leong, one of Shan's most experienced fighters, pulled what appeared to be a metal rope from his belt. The chain knife, six feet long with linked steel sections topped with a bright metal spike, glittered malevolently in the lights.

Epps allowed his eyes to defocus on the men around him. Not looking at anything in particular, he was able to take it all in. These men were amateurs, not used to fighting together as a unit. Their hatchets looked fearsome, designed more for their elicitation of fear than for their practicality. He saw that five men circled him with another, their apparent leader, hanging back by the car. He breathed in and out, waiting for them to come to him. To his left, one of the men yelled something primal and stepped forward, swinging the small ax with his right hand. Epps took barely half a step back, allowing the hatchet to swish past his face, missing by several inches. As the man's momentum carried him forward, Epps took a small step forward, pushing the man's passing shoulder. The movement was so small and subtle, to the untrained eye it looked like Epps had tapped the man on the back. But the move had Epps' body weight and leverage behind it. The "tap" sent the man sprawling forward into his circling compatriot with the chain knife. Both men went down in a heap.

From behind him, Epps felt the attack coming. He dropped to his left shoulder, rolling out of the way of the strike. From his ground position, Epps kicked out at the man's knee, causing it to buckle with an audible crack and scream of pain. The other two were now bearing down on him as he crouched low. They expected him to retreat in the face of their onslaught and were shocked when Epps dove forward at their approaching legs, bringing them down. Epps rolled to the side of them and was rising when he felt a sharp stab of pain in his left thigh. Looking down, he saw the metal spike protruding from the back of his leg. A moment later, the metal chain ripped the spike backward, and pain flared across his eyes. A surge of adrenaline followed, and Epps fought for control as the man with the chain knife circled behind him, spinning the spike like a propellor.

Shan took all of this in. The man was his prey, but the fighter in him respected Epps' ability and skill. He knew Leong was deadly with the chain knife. His other men were back on their feet, wary and prepared against the wounded man. Leong flicked the spike forward again, and the man dodged to the side but into the range of a soldier named

Han, who swung his hatchet downward in a murderous arc. Incredibly, the man blocked the blow, and he stood grappling momentarily with Han. As the others moved in to strike, the man quickly pivoted, taking Han off his feet and throwing him into the others. Just as they collapsed, the chain knife flicked again, and the metal spike seemed to appear like magic in the man's upper back. For the first time, Shan heard the man grunt in pain and thought, *now we have him.*

Kats threw open the door to the Jefferson Hotel, racing inside. Two old men sat playing cards, and the night manager shouted, "Hey! Easy on the damn door." Kats raced over to the desk.

"Was a group of Chinese men here? And a White man, about thirty years old with brown hair?"

The night manager made a face, not wanting to inform on his residents. "Yeah, there was some guys here about fifteen minutes ago, but they cleared out."

"Together or separate?"

"Hey, man. I don't want any trouble ..."

"Together or separate?" Kats demanded in his best drill sergeant voice. The man flinched.

"The Chinese guys followed the other guy out the door."

"Which way did they go?"

"How should I know?"

Kats turned, realizing the guy probably didn't have a view of the street. *What to do now?*

"I seen 'em," said one of the old men playing cards. "They went out the door then up the street toward Van Ness." Kats ran toward the street and his motorcycle.

Epps felt the metal spike rip the flesh from his back as it

flew back to its master. With that flash of pain, he felt his hold on himself waver and then melt away like water circling a drain. He knew the feeling, and he hated it. He could feel the world turn red before him and felt the surge of power from deep inside. He spun back toward the men, his face now seething with a grimace that made him look demonic. Momentarily startled by the transformation, they hesitated, and Epps struck.

With an impossibly fast leap, he reached the front man, who raised his hatchet sideways to defend himself. Epps struck downward, through the ax handle, breaking it in two. The man had barely a moment to think *impossible* before Epps' hand was striking upward into his side. The man's lower ribcage buckled and cracked, sending bone into his organs and collapsing his lung. He fell heavily and lay still. Epps pivoted as a hatchet swung at his head. He grabbed the hand holding the weapon and twisted it backward, violently breaking the arm that had held it as the man screamed in pain. Useless fingers dropped the ax, and it appeared in Epps' hand. In one fluid motion, he spun and threw the hatchet at the next man, burying its head deep in his chest. That left only Leong and the chain knife.

Shan was moving forward now. He had to intervene because this was quickly becoming a disaster. As he approached, he saw Leong flick the chain knife toward the man's face. In one lightning-fast motion, the man caught the lethal spike from midair and yanked the chain, pulling Leong forward, off balance. In one motion, the man launched himself upward, his knee rising as Leong stumbled forward. At the precise apex of the arc, knee met chin with neck-shattering effect. Leong crumpled bonelessly to the ground. *Five men were down*, Shan thought. *I must end this.*

The man crouched low as Shan approached. He didn't seem tired despite dispatching five men. His chest rose and fell like a bellows. Shan wouldn't make the same mistake as the others, having seen how deadly the man was. "I am the Red Pole of the Hop Sing Tong," he said to the man as he approached, tossing his long braid over his shoulder, "and you are dead." Shan fitted the brass knuckle duster to his right fist. The metal covered his large hand, and three metal spikes protruded angrily forward. Shan circled carefully to his right. Behind him he heard the groans of pain from his men. *Some are still alive,* he thought.

Shan advanced, left side leading, his deadly right fist ready at his side. He looked into the man's face and was shocked to see his eyes, pupils dilated and looking like holes in his skull. *What is he on?* As the man circled with Shan, he came within range of the felled body of Leong. With a quick step, he grabbed the body with both hands and launched it at Shan, like he was throwing a beach ball, not a full-grown man. Shan tried to sidestep the mass, but the effort threw him off balance, and the man was on him impossibly fast. Nearly face to face, Shan fired his iron-clad right hand toward the man's head, but the blow never fell. His wrist was caught in the man's left hand, and when he tried to pull back, he found himself caught in a viselike grip. Instinctively, Shan fired his head forward, connecting in a glancing blow against the man's head and momentarily distracting him. Shan pivoted inside the man's grasp, getting his hips underneath him and flipping him over to the ground.

When Shan took someone to the ground like this, usually the fight was over. His strength and his technique were superior, and he sought to find an arm bar to force the man into submission. Grasping the man's left arm, Shan used his full body weight to push down, feeling the beginning of a tactical advantage. To his surprise, the man's right hand reached upward, finding Shan's braid, and he began to pull. Shan's bull-like neck sought to resist, but in moments his head was being pulled backward, and he was forced to relinquish his hold on the man's arm. Shan attempted to roll out of the way, but as he did so, he felt himself jerked back by the length of his rope-thick hair. The man was upon him, looping the braid around Shan's neck and pulling him down from behind. *No!* his mind shouted, and he struggled frantically as the air that was left in his lungs started to burn. He tried to reach the man's face with grasping hands. The metal spikes on his right hand could find no target, and his vision began to fade. As the world went dark, his eyes saw a bright white light coming toward him.

"Damn," Kats swore as he looked back and forth for the men he pursued. He'd spotted the *hanfu*-clad men as he sped up Eddy Street, so he circled around the block hoping to get ahead of them on Van Ness. Instead, he saw a quiet street. *They must have gone inside somewhere*, he thought. He accelerated the bike forward, eyeing the buildings on both sides of the road, looking for a sign. He stopped midway down the block and peered into a dim alley. No one. As he slowly rolled forward, his eyes searched for movement or a sign. Suddenly Kats realized how loud the Harley Davidson's motor was beneath him. Switching the bike off, the city's sounds came back into his consciousness. Cars, the rumble of a cable car the next block over ... the sounds filled his ears. He took a deep, slow breath to find the stillness that had so often served him well. Another breath, and then he heard it. A blood-curdling scream of pain from above. Looking up, he could see the parking garage across the street and light coming from the second level. Kats stomped on the kick-starter, and the bike roared back to life. He gunned the throttle and raced into the parking garage.

As he roared up the second-floor ramp, he suddenly saw two prone men in the cone of the headlight. Turning the bike onto its right side, Kats slid to a stop and rolled off onto his feet. He saw the young Tong soldier, Shan, lying prone with the other man on top of him, holding his dark braid around his neck. *Epps*, thought Kats. He could see several other men on the ground. A couple moved, a couple did not. Epps looked at Kats but held the chokehold on Shan. The man's eyes looked wild and feral. Kats raised his hands in a calming gesture, "Please, I'm not going to hurt you," he said. "Epps, please let him go."

At the mention of his name, there was a flicker of recognition in Epps' face. His hold on Shan relaxed, and he dropped the man forward onto his face. Then he eyed this newcomer like a wolf eyeing another predator.

Kats moved slowly toward Epps. "I'm not with them," he gestured to the men scattered on the ground. "I'm a friend of Dr. Turier. Do you remember Dr. Turier?" he said in his most calming voice. "I want to take you to him. We can make everything OK." Kats wasn't sure if the words were even registering, but the man didn't move to attack or retreat. He was about to take another step forward when he heard a siren echo from up the street.

At the sound, Epps' face twisted, and he surged forward toward Kats. Even though he was ready, Kats was shocked at how fast the man was. He pivoted to the side, like a matador with a charging bull, and as Epps passed by, Kats fired a fist into the man's lower back, straight into the kidney. The strike should have disabled the man, but Epps barely grunted and whipped around with such speed and ferocity that Kats was immediately on the defensive. Epps shot his right fist toward Kat's head. Instinctively, he raised his left arm to block the blow, saving himself at the cost of his arm. He rocked back, feeling like he'd been hit with a baseball bat, and his arm fell to the side, numb and lifeless. Kats had fought men who were stronger than he was. He'd also fought men who were faster. But he'd never fought someone stronger *and* faster. He dropped to one knee trying to gather himself as Epps turned again and charged.

As the wild-eyed man came at him, Kats knew his only chance was to redirect that savage energy, so as Epps raced forward, he welcomed him in and rolled backward, using his good arm to pull the man over him, actually accelerating his charge into the concrete wall behind him. The man met the wall with an audible grunt, and Kats had a moment to gather himself, but only a moment. Within seconds, Epps was again on his feet, facing Kats, seeming to seethe with power. Then from the garage entrance a flashing red light appeared, and a siren echoed up the walls. Epps spun toward the light and, seeing the approaching police car, bolted toward the open wall. Reaching the second-floor wall, he leaped over it in one smooth motion. Kats raced forward in time to see that Epps had landed safely and was already running down the alley toward a chain-link fence. Reaching the ten-foot fence, he appeared to run up the barrier in one long step and then was over and gone in one swift, near superhuman move. As Kats stood there, his chest heaving and his arm throbbing and hanging uselessly at his side, he wondered how he could possibly stop this living science experiment.

CHAPTER 13

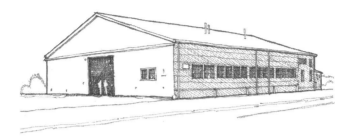

Turier sat drinking his black coffee in the small commissary. The morning paper was open before him with the headline 'Tong War' in bold print. The story recounted the deaths of three young Chinese men and several others in the hospital following what the paper described as a territory battle between rival factions. Several arrests were made, but apparently no one knew the origins of the conflict. The paper speculated that it was some secret conflict that harkened back to their mainland Chinese origins. All of it was great for circulation.

He wanted to call Kats and find out if these Tong were the same ones who were searching for Epps, but he knew he had to be careful. He was rereading the story when Hauser approached, carrying a cup of coffee.

"Doctor, we have a lead," Hauser said, and Turier lowered the paper. "Your idea about the construction sites panned out. We have a site in the Mission District where they said a man matching the photo of Epps was working until a couple weeks ago. I want you to go and talk to them. Captain Thorne will go with you." He handed Turier a small piece of paper with an address written on it.

Turier nodded and began folding the newspaper when Hauser said, "I hear you went out into the city last night."

"*Oui*, I was restless," was all he offered.

Hauser said nothing for a long moment, then, "You need to stay close, doctor. We may have to move quickly. Meet Thorne out front in thirty." He turned and moved away, leaving Turier to wonder if his boss suspected something.

Kats rubbed the stubble on his face with his right hand as he walked out of the Hall of Justice into the morning sunlight. His left arm hung from a sling, and the huge bruise there was already turning purple. Molly stood at the bottom of the stairs with a wry smile on her lips. "When was the last time you spent the night in jail?" she asked.

He smiled, "I wasn't in jail. I was giving my statement to the detectives in the police station. If I were in jail, I at least could have gotten a couple hours of sleep."

"Coffee?"

"Absolutely." They headed up Kearny into North Beach and made their way to Caffe Trieste. As they were entering, they saw Shig sitting in the corner. He waved the two over when he spotted them.

"You look like hell, man," he said, noting the sling. "What happened?"

"Coffee first," Kats said.

Shortly after 10 am Turier walked into the motor pool toward a lime-green Chevy Bel Air. Thorne stood by the driver side door, wearing civilian clothes but still looking like a soldier. He eyed Turier, nodded once, and said nothing as he started the engine and they rolled out of the Presidio into the city.

The construction site was located on 16th Street just west of Mission and occupied half the block. As they parked, Thorne turned to Turier and said, "Let me do the talking." It was late morning, and the site was busy. Thorne paused, looking around the site, eyeing several trailers and a large Quonset hut structure that had workers moving in and out. Noting the trailer office, they walked over and into the open door. Three men were gathered around a cluttered desk looking at a construction plan as they entered.

"Can I help you?" said the man in the middle, apparently the foreman.

"Yes," Thorne said brightly, in a twangy exaggeration of a Southern accent. "We're searching for a man, and our colleagues said he'd been working here."

"Yeah, those guys from yesterday. We told them he worked here for a few weeks, but we ain't seen him in a while. What is this about anyways? Stevens was a good worker. What did he do?" the foreman asked.

Turier was about to speak when Thorne put a hand on his arm, stopping him. Thorne then reached into his jacket and pulled out a badge and an ID. "Military police," he said, "We're searching for a deserter. We think the man you knew as Stevens is our deserter."

The men's attitude visibly shifted. Good worker or not, the idea of a deserter was anathema to them. "Shit," said the foreman. "You never know, do you?"

"No, you don't," Thorne said collegially. "I noticed your men going in and out of that Quonset hut over there. Is that a locker room of some kind?"

"Yeah, that's where our guys store their gear and change of clothes."

"Would 'Stevens' have had a locker?" Thorne asked.

"Yeah. Probably still some stuff over there," said one of the other men.

"Show us, please?" Thorne smiled.

Five minutes later they were searching through the work clothes that "Stevens" had left behind. Thorne pulled a business card from a heavy flannel jacket, looked at it, and smiled at Turier. "Jackpot." The card read *Jefferson Hotel, 440 Eddy Street.* "Let's go take a look."

Fifteen minutes later, Turier and Thorne stood across the street, casually observing the low-rent hotel. The Frenchman shifted back and forth and nervously looked up and down the street. "Shouldn't we call your team?" he asked. Thorne continued to slowly scan the area as he'd been doing for the past five minutes. Turier waited. Finally, Thorne looked at him.

"In due time, doctor. Reconnaissance first." He turned and walked toward the hotel. Turier followed him into the lobby, and they approached the front desk. A young man with a bad complexion and a cigarette tucked behind his ear made a face as they approached.

"Yeah?" he said, already judging that they weren't customers looking for a room.

Thorne reached into his breast pocket and pulled out the official photo of Epps from his army file. "We're looking for this man," he said, placing the image on the counter. "Have you seen him?"

"Does this look like the fucking Fairmont Hotel? They don't pay me to keep tabs on these assholes. Piss off."

"Please, this is a serious matter. You've seen him?" Turier asked. The manager just shook his head.

"My memory ain't what it used ta be," he smirked, "Ya get me?" Turier looked confused, but Thorne smiled. He reached into his front breast pocket and in one swift movement pulled out his Colt .45 pistol and backhanded the young man across the face with it. Thorne grabbed the shocked man and pressed his face into the desk, holding the gun to his temple.

"My colleague has much more patience than I do," he said to the squirming man. "Now, please look at the photo and tell us if this man has been here."

"Yeah, yeah, yeah! Stevens. His name is Stevens. He's staying here. Been here for a few weeks. But I ain't seen him since those Chinese guys came for him last night!"

Thorne released his hold on the man, who pulled back, whining and rubbing his face.

"Tell us about these Chinese men," he said in an almost friendly voice.

"These guys, these Chinese guys, were in here last night. It looked like they were after Stevens. They followed him out onto the street and down the block."

Turier looked at Thorne. "The Tong," he said quietly. "From the newspaper this morning." Thorne nodded, taking in this new information.

"Show us his room." The manager looked pained, but eyeing Thorne's casually held gun, he reached for a ring of keys and came out from behind the counter.

They walked up the stairs to the fourth floor. The manager huffed and puffed as he labored up the last steps. Neither Turier nor Thorne was breathing heavily as they approached the door marked 409. Thorne raised a finger to his lips, calling for silence as he gestured toward the manager and the keys in his hand. He then raised the pistol and held it ready.

The manager found the key he was looking for and quietly opened the door. Thorne pushed him aside and stepped into the room, gun at the ready. A moment later he called, "Clear," and Turier followed him inside as the manager retreated to his desk. His eyes quickly took in the spartan, empty room.

"There's nothing here," Thorne said. "We missed him."

Kats sipped his second cup of coffee as he recounted the evening's events starting with his meeting with Turier and culminating with his encounter with the doctor's patient, the man known as Epps. "Everything Dominic told me about this guy was true. He took out a group of Tong enforcers, including their Red Pole."

"The young one with the braid?" Molly asked, concern on her face.

"Yes. Shan is his name. You're worried?"

"He was helpful the other day, and we talked a bit."

Kats nodded. "He's in the hospital but will live."

"That guy is like their main enforcer, right?" Shig asked. "And he ends up in the hospital? That can't be good."

"Three of the Tong are dead. Another will never walk without a limp. This man Epps is ..." Kats looked for the word, "Something else."

"Please tell me you're not going to go up against this guy again," Molly implored. "The next time it could be more than your arm."

"I have no intention of taking him on like that again. But I do need to find him before the army or the Tong does." Kats could see that both Molly and Shig thought him crazy. "Look, I don't think Epps is a monster. Neither does Dominic. He has been experimented on and is really messed up. Dominic thinks he can help him, and he asked me to help find him. I owe Dominic that."

Shig pointed to the newspaper on the table, its headline 'Tong War' in large print. "This is going to send the Hop Sing over the edge. They'll be out for blood."

"They already were," Kats sighed. "But maybe we can turn that anger in our favor."

"How so?" Molly asked.

"Through that government operation Dominic told me about, the one using prostitutes here in the city. They were recruiting at the Hong Kong Club. That's a Hei Long operation. They may be supplying the girls. I need to share this information with John. He already hates the Hei Long, and they're blood enemies of the Hop Sing. Maybe we can focus that anger in their direction while we try to find Epps." Molly and Shig nodded in agreement.

"When are you going to see John?" Molly asked.

"I need a shave, a shower, a change of clothes, and a handful of aspirin first. Then I'll go see John."

Hauser shifted behind his desk, staring at the headline in the morning paper when a knock came at his makeshift office door. "Come," he said, and his man Stiles opened the door, looking sheepish. Hauser motioned him inside.

"Sir," Stiles began, "we're having a problem at the new safe house." Hauser said nothing but glared at the man. "We're having trouble with the Black Dragons. I've tried to work with them, but their leader wants to renegotiate our deal."

"So negotiate with him and get this done," Hauser said like he was talking to a child.

"I tried that, sir," Stiles replied. "Wen insists on speaking directly to you before he'll do anything." Stiles placed a slip of paper with a phone number written across it on Hauser's desk. Hauser took the paper and waved Stiles away. As the door closed, Hauser turned the phone toward him and dialed the local number. After the second ring, it picked up.

"*Wei*," said the thickly accented voice on the other end that Hauser immediately recognized. Wen Tsui Shen, more commonly known at Dragon Eye Wen, was the leader of the Hei Long Tong, a position he assumed following the mysterious death of the previous and much older leader. Now in his forties, Wen was aggressive, smart, and known for his personal use of the Tong hatchet. He was feared by most and admired by a select few—the few being the younger Chinese whose aspirations of money and power weren't limited by their parent's and grandparent's reluctance to make waves. This new generation of westernized Chinese youth had flocked to his banner and his refusal to take the scraps left at the White man's table. Hauser knew he needed him, so he prepared to stroke the man's immense ego.

"You wanted to speak with me?" he asked neutrally.

"Yes, Hauser," came the reply. "We're getting things ready for you here."

Hauser made a face, glad he wasn't sitting across from the man, and replied, "Yes, a temporary situation, and we need more of your girls."

"Of course, of course. The Hei Long is most happy to assist." Hauser waited for the 'but.'

"But we must revisit our terms. We need some things in addition to the money."

"The money is considerable," Hauser said, knowing he had to at least pretend to negotiate with the man. Hauser had more resources at his command than Wen, or most, could even imagine, but the pretense was part of his cover.

"You see the newspaper today?" Wen asked. "They talk about a Tong war. There's no war yet, but I've heard from my sources that the Hop Sing Tong are out for blood. We need weapons for the coming fight. We fight, we take over all of Chinatown." *Fucking blood feuds*, Hauser thought. *Let them kill each other.*

"I can arrange for weapons."

"Good. Very good. You come to the club tomorrow tonight. We discuss details and celebrate our partnership."

"I'm not in much of a celebratory mood," Hauser deadpanned.

"It's not a request," Wen said as the line clicked off.

CHAPTER 14

Kats entered the small teahouse off Grant and Pacific. When he'd called John, he expected to go to the Hop Sing headquarters, but John insisted on meeting here. He scanned the dimly lit room and saw John sitting alone in the back. Kats sat down as John eyed him, noting the sling. He said nothing, only poured both of them tea in small porcelain cups. He raised his cup to Kats, who returned the polite gesture, and both drank. Kats waited for John to begin.

"Three of my men are dead. More are in the hospital, including Shan. I'm told you saved him." Kats gave a small nod. John raised his cup again, "My thanks."

"Your men were supposed to contact me and let me approach the man. They're not trained for this type of work, and you see the results," Kats said, knowing that John was in pain but needing him to understand the situation. "There could have been more deaths," Kats said.

"I know what was to have happened, but I also understand that the man was on the move, and my men had to prevent his escape." *Not exactly true*, thought Kats, but he let the thought go.

"I have some information about Mai that may shift your anger," Kats said, and John sat back, listening. "I met with someone who knows the man you're seeking." John sat forward and brought his fist down on the table with a thud.

"You know who this man is?" Kats nodded. "Tell me," John said through clenched teeth.

"He's a former soldier who has some," Kats hesitated,

"mental issues. It seems likely he didn't intend to kill your cousin." John snorted.

"So, he's insane?" John asked. "A rabid dog?"

"Perhaps oversimplified, but essentially yes."

"You put down rabid dogs. We'll put this one down too."

"That may be difficult because the army is looking for him. They want to treat him. He's a valuable asset to them."

"He killed my family."

"Perhaps, but you need to understand who's more responsible for putting your cousin in that room with him. I've learned that she was recruited last year at the Hong Kong Club." At the mention of that place, John's eyes blazed.

"The damn Hei Long," John said quietly. "That's their operation, and they supply women to the brothels of Chinatown. That also explains her use of drugs. The Hei Long use opium to control their women." Kats nodded, letting John process this information. He could see John's fists clenching, squeezing unseen throats.

"There's more," Kats continued. "The government was running that blackmail operation as some kind of experiment using mind-altering drugs like LSD. They're working with the Hei Long. That's also why the army and the government are trying to find the soldier. He's an experiment gone wrong."

John looked at his hands and then laid them flat upon the table. "If it were my decision, we'd go to war with the Hei Long. I hate what they do to our people. But the peace that was negotiated during the war has held. Father Sun insists that we hold the peace."

'Father' Sun, the long-time leader of the Hop Sing Tong, was a revered elder whose credentials dated back to his membership in the Righteous and Harmonious Fists, the so-called 'Boxers' in his youth in China. He fled the failed Boxer Rebellion as a teen, landing in Hong Kong where he joined the Triads. He eventually emigrated to America as a 'merchant' under one of the exceptions to the Chinese Exclusionary Act. Restauranteurs were considered merchants under the act. Now in his mid-seventies, Father Sun had become Great Grandfather Sun, and his appetite for conflict was gone. John both loved and respected the man, but his passivity in the face of outside change and aggression made it a challenge for his number two.

"I'm not thinking war either," Kats replied. "But I could use your help in taking down the Black Dragon operation. This blackmail operation needs to end, and it may lead us to the men behind your cousin's death."

John poured them both more tea and contemplated his options. His face was a mask that Kats couldn't read, so he sipped his tea and waited. Finally, John spoke. "This is a matter of family honor. I'll have my family's justice but can't directly involve the Hop Sing. But I'll help you."

Kats and Molly walked through Japantown, taking in the afternoon sunshine. His arm ached despite the sling and the painkilling aspirin, but his brain was racing with the plan he and John had plotted. He needed Molly and probably Shig and some others to make it work, but it felt unusual for him to ask for outside help. As an advance scout in the army, he'd most often been on his own, making life and death decisions with only himself and his training to rely upon. That training, keen instincts, and occasionally blind luck had served him well. But today it was hard to ask. Molly walked along in companionable silence, knowing he needed some time to speak.

"So, John and I have the beginnings of a plan," he said as they passed Benkyodo, the Japanese bakery he loved so much. Molly nodded. "We need to see what the Hei Long are doing at the Hong Kong Club." The Hong Kong Club was a well-established nightclub, part of the so-called Chop Suey circuit. Prior to the war, Chinese Americans established their own nightclubs that catered to Asian and White audiences the way that Harlem jazz clubs established themselves in New York City. The clubs became immensely popular during the war but had seen their prominence fade as newer clubs with fresher content, like Ann's 440, now catered to the current trends. Still, the Hong Kong Club was known for its 'exotic' floorshow, food, and drinks. It was also a competitor of Ann's, so naturally Molly was curious about it.

"You want to go check out the nightclub?" she asked neutrally.

"The club is a front operation by the Hei Long, the Black Dragon Tong. They recruited Mai and Lola, remember? They seem to be the front for the drug operation. I think we can use them to lead us to the safe house, and then we can end it. John has made it a personal vendetta, a way to get back at the Black Dragons and the ones who set up his cousin."

"So, how can I help?"

"We need to do some reconnaissance," he said, and she smiled remembering the last time they were on a recon mission. It was on the docks as they walked through Pier 23 looking at the headquarters of the Lanza crime family. That had ended well enough, though she did get shot in the final play.

"You want to take me on a date to the Hong Kong Club?" she smiled.

He laughed and took her hand, "Yes, I do, and perhaps

we can make it a double date."

"A double date? Who's coming with us?"

"Shig and our friend Lola."

The unmarked car rolled slowly to a stop at the corner of Jackson Street and Wentworth Place in the heart of Chinatown. It was night, but the neon lights of the street made the scene a kaleidoscope of color and Chinese signage. The Hong Kong Club was a gaudy four-story building with the bottom two floors comprising the club. The upper floors were reserved for more illicit and profitable ventures if one believed the rumors that surrounded the club. Hauser sat in the back of the car with Stiles. He was dressed in a simple dark suit but didn't look festive. He said to the driver, "Stay close. I don't intend to be here long." He exited the car, and Stiles followed. There was a line out the front door, but he strode directly to the entrance, and the doorman bowed and waved them through.

They entered the main ballroom, awash with music from the twenty-piece band on the stage. Dozens of couples danced on the floor surrounded by tables. Above in the mezzanine level were what looked like opera boxes where the truly wealthy could sit and partake in relative privacy. Moving between the tables, serving drinks, were exotically made-up Chinese women in the traditional high-necked *cheongsam* dresses, tightly fit and cut high on the thigh. Hauser stood and panned his gaze across the room. Beside him, Stiles stood smiling until his boss's gaze fell on his grinning face, which quickly turned serious. A slender Chinese woman, beautiful and clad in an off-the-shoulder cocktail dress, approached the two men. In a slightly accented, lilting voice, she said, "Welcome, Mr. Hauser. Please come with me." She made a small bow, turned, and walked through the crowd. Hauser and Stiles followed.

She led them up a back staircase that led to the mezzanine level above the club, looking down on the ballroom from above. It was a small throne room for the one and only king in the club. As they approached, a man wearing a black silk suit detached himself from a conversation and smiled as Hauser approached.

"Conrad!" said Wen Tsui Shen, the leader of the Hei Long Tong. Unconsciously, Hauser found his gaze drawn to the man's left eye, an eerie bright blue pupil with a tiny black dot in the center. Wen had been in a fight as a youth, and a blow to his eye had permanently dilated the pupil and made the color change. Wen learned to use the oddity to his advantage, cocking his head and staring pointedly at people to make them nervous. The hatchet he often held also contributed to the effect, but he soon became known as 'Dragon Eye' Wen to friend and foe alike. Tonight, he put on his most officious face and greeted Hauser like an old friend, which he was not.

"Good evening, Wen," Hauser said, taking the glass of champagne that a waiter offered him. Stiles knew better than to take the offered drink and stood toward the entrance trying to look confident. Wen gestured for Hauser to sit.

"It's been a long time since you've come to see me," Wen said, still smiling, but a subtle reproach in his tone.

"Well, I'd thought our business was settled and, like you, I'm a busy man." Hauser sipped the champagne, which was excellent.

"So, you need my services again," Wen nodded, "and of course the Hei Long are most happy to assist." Hauser tipped his glass and gave a small smile. *Here it comes*, he thought.

"But we must talk of new terms, Conrad. The world has

changed in the past two years."

Hauser scanned the room, watching Wen from the corner of his eye. "Yes, you mentioned weapons," he said. "But war is bad for business, isn't it?"

Wen smiled an oily smile and nodded. "Normally, yes, bad for business. But the other Tong are weak and divided, especially the Hop Sing. They're led by a fearful old man. They're ready to fall. I just need to make the push."

"So you want to rule Chinatown. Fine. We can get you some guns."

"Not just Chinatown, Conrad. We want more. There's been a shift of power in the city. Last year the Lanza family was almost put out of business. You saw the fire at their pier. They still haven't recovered. First we take out the hated Hop Sing, and the others will fall in line with my leadership. Then we'll go after the organized crime throughout the city. Lanza and the other Italian crime families are in the past. The future is Chinese!" he said triumphantly.

Hauser's mind was racing with this new information. He knew that the Hei Long, though large, were nowhere near large enough to take on the Italians and the rest of the city. But the Hei Long, with all the other Tong under their banner ... that was another case. He spoke carefully. "Why should we want to crown you as the head of the west coast underworld? I'm just another cog trying to do my work—work that could be of major importance to this country."

Wen looked sharply at him with his dragon eye leading, all pretense of friendliness now gone. "You may think I'm another ignorant Chinaman, a chink, a coolie. But make no mistake. I'm not your fool or anyone else's. You ask why you should support me? Because you and your agency already are."

"What do you mean 'agency,' Wen?" Hauser backpedaled.

"You're CIA," Wen said, leering in with his wild eye. Hauser held the man's gaze, his mind reaching for an answer. "Don't bother to deny it. I'm already dealing with other CIA elements overseas. You see, the Hei Long here are allied with the Black Dragon Triad in Hong Kong. They're our brothers, and our brothers have been dealing with you for years. Since 1954 when the French ran from Viet Nam and your government stepped into their mess, we've been moving drugs for your CIA, providing cash for you to fight communism in Asia."

Hauser knew the truth of the words even if he hadn't known the specifics. Asia was the coming fight with the Communists. They all knew that. But the revelation of using drugs to fund it was both brilliant and frightening. Korea had been a trap that the US barely escaped, and any coming conflict might prove to be even worse. Still, he fell back on his years of training and obfuscation. "That's an interesting idea, Wen. You give me too much credit," he said nonchalantly, sipping his champagne.

"If denying makes you feel better, Conrad, so be it. I allow you to save face," Wen said smugly. "But we must have weapons. Machine guns, explosives, and radios."

"I'm not an ammo dump," Hauser said coldly.

"But you're my partner," Wen said brightly, "and I know you can get these things for me with a phone call."

Hauser sat back. His eyes moved across the ballroom, not really seeing, but buying him time to think. "When can we get the girls back to work?"

"When do you need them? We have many lovely ladies for your operation. They'll follow orders. We have the space in the brothels upstairs. We control them. No police, no interference." Wen smiled broadly. "So, we have deal?"

"We do. Give Stiles here a list of what you need. He'll coordinate the delivery of the weapons. He has my authorization on whatever you need." Stiles stepped forward and made a slight bow to Wen, inwardly smiling that his boss had entrusted him with the work.

"Excellent. We celebrate tonight!" Wen proclaimed as Hauser waved his hands and stood.

"Stiles will stay and arrange for the next steps. I have to get back to my work. Other loose ends demand my attention."

Wen pretended to frown in sympathy. He expected as much from the *gweilo* barbarian. No manners.

"Stiles, a word," he said as he exited the opulent box. Outside he looked around for prying ears but knew the music from downstairs covered their conversation. Stiles leaned in. "Get the rotation of girls moving again. Don't worry about prescreening; we don't have time. If some asshole gets the clap, so be it." Stiles nodded. "Then find out what supplies he wants. I don't really care if they all kill each other in Chinatown, so give him what he asks for."

"Anything?" Stiles asked cautiously.

"Well, not a fucking Nike missile, but other than that, use your judgment." *Idiot*, Hauser thought.

"Yes, sir. I'm on it." The man practically saluted, but Hauser turned and found a waiter.

"Where's the damn back exit?" The waiter gestured toward stairs down the hall. Hauser left without another word.

As Hauser left through the back alley to find his driver, Kats, Molly, Shig, and Lola finally made it to the front of the line at the club where the doorman, a young Chinese man dressed in a tuxedo, looked them up and down. The girls smiled and primped while Kats and Shig both beamed like lucky bastards who'd somehow managed to get White dates. The doorman wondered how much the girls were charging. He motioned them through.

They entered the busy club, looking about for a table. As they turned to the left, a couple stood and made their way toward the exit. Shig moved in and grabbed the small table, stealing two more chairs from nearby locations. The four of them huddled close. "OK," smiled Shig, "what are we drinking?"

"We're working, Shig," Kats said with a fatherly tone.

"Yeah, but it would look suspicious if we didn't drink, right?" The girls nodded, and Kats did see a certain logic to his point.

"One drink, and pace yourselves. We're looking for signs of their illegal operation," Kats said. The girls smiled, and he had to admit the club was lively and the music good. Molly looked around, admiring the interiors and the bandstand.

"This place is much bigger than Ann's, and what a great stage!"

"Band is good, too," Lola added. Kats regarded her, knowing it had taken some convincing by Molly to get her to come along. Still, she and Molly had decked themselves out in their best party dresses and come along to provide the necessary cover for their mission. He admired Lola's courage.

A waitress came by, they ordered drinks, and Shig started to twitch in his chair. Kats looked at him, and he smiled. "I like this kind of music!" He stood and offered his hand to Lola. "Shall we dance?" She smiled, took his hand, and they entered the busy dance floor. Kats watched as Shig cut a very fine rug as they did a cha-cha.

Molly was scanning the room as well. "What exactly am I looking for?" she asked as her eyes moved about.

"That's a good question. No one puts up a sign that says *Illegal Activity Here.*" He shifted in his seat to pull her closer and look over her shoulder. "I guess look for something out of place." He breathed in her scent. Tonight she was wearing perfume, something she rarely did, and it was intoxicating. His hands moved up her back, and he thought about asking her to dance.

"Hey!" she said a bit too loudly in his ear. "Those guys look out of place." She pivoted Kats around to where she'd been looking toward the staircase under the mezzanine. There he saw two tough-looking young Chinese men, standing on both sides of the staircase. Normally he would have brushed them off as security, but these two weren't wearing tuxedos like every other man working the club. They wore all black *hanfu* except for the bright red at their cuffs and on the collars of their jackets. That marked them as Hei Long Tong. Kats continued to survey the stairs as he played with Molly's hair. A minute later Shig and Lola returned to the table, smiling and out of breath.

"He's a good dancer," Lola said as she took a sip of her drink. Shig blushed.

"You're a good partner!" He noticed Kats staring across the room. "What are you looking at?" Shig asked as his eyes followed Kats' gaze.

"Looks like Black Dragon Tong soldiers. Seems a bit open and obvious even for them."

Lola's eyes followed theirs and just then they saw a tall, angular White man wearing a suit come walking down the stairs. Lola jumped and put a hand over her mouth.

"What's wrong?" Shig asked as he wrapped his arm

around her. Kats and Molly turned to look at the visibly shaking Lola. Molly spoke.

"Lola, honey, what's going on?"

Lola took a ragged breath and said, "That man over there. The one who just came down. I know him."

Kats looked over at the man and then back to Lola. "Know him how?"

"He was one of the guys at the house! He was one of the controllers."

"Holy shit," Molly said, turning to watch him stroll over to the bar. Lola kept her head down. "He's talking to a couple of girls now. Do you think he's recruiting again for the operation? Like how you and Mai were recruited?"

"Maybe," Lola said. "It was another guy, an older guy, bigger, seemed in charge when I was here with Mai. But that's definitely one of the guys running that operation. His name is Stiles."

"What should we do?" Shig asked. "Can we go, you know ..." Shig balled his fist and made a punching gesture.

"No, we're not punching anyone," Kats said emphatically.

"I'd punch him," Molly said, looking at Shig with a smile.

"Let's see what he does. He may just be here for a drink. But if something happens, maybe I can follow him out of here."

"Sounds a bit thin," Molly said.

"You have an idea?" Kats asked.

"Well, if he's here recruiting," she said as she reached into her dress, adjusting her breasts into a more aggressive-forward stance, "let's see if he likes redheads."

Kats was about to object when Lola spoke, "I'll go with you." They all looked at her, knowing what she'd gone through with this man and his work before.

"You don't have to do this," Molly said.

"I know. But my therapist says I should face my fears."

Kats smiled at her and said, "Mine too." Lola smiled and nodded back. Molly reached over and squeezed her hand. They rose, and as they did, Kats noticed Molly adjust her dress, raising it a couple of inches, revealing more of her long legs. *She is beautiful*, he thought as the women walked across the bar.

Lola caught up to Molly and touched her arm, "Follow my lead," she said, and Molly fell in step beside her. As they approached Stiles, he was leaning over a pretty young Chinese girl and saying something in her ear. The girl made a face, turned, and stalked off with her friend. *The man's a charmer*, Molly thought.

"Hey, sailor. Buy a girl a drink?" Lola said haughtily as they saddled up to the bar next to Stiles, who turned and with a surprised smile greeted her.

"Lola! Hey there. You look good," he said, offering a bar stool. "Yeah, happy to buy you a drink. And your friend, too."

Lola made an exaggerated hair flip and turned toward Molly. "John, this is my friend ..."

Molly stuck out a hand, "Jenny," she said. "Jenny Hazen."

"Hi, Jenny. I'm John. What are you two doing here tonight?"

"Oh, just out with a couple of nice boys," Lola said with a nod of her head back toward the table where they came from.

"Your dates or clients?" Stiles asked with a leer.

"Bit of both. A couple of Oriental boys with White fever," Lola said, and Stiles laughed. "The question is, what are *you* doing here?"

"Oh, I'm just scouting talent," he said, laughing at his own joke.

"Don't bullshit us, honey. She knows what's what," Lola said with a nod toward Molly.

"My friend here just got into town from Ohio and is looking for a bit of side work." Molly smiled and threw out her hip in her best impression of a provocative stance. Stiles nodded appreciatively.

"Very nice," he said, and Molly felt her skin crawl but continued to smile. "You vouch for her?"

"Of course, honey."

Stiles was thinking now. Hauser had wanted the Hei Long girls because they were compliant, but he thought having a bit of variety might be good for the project. And he knew that Lola had been solid until that crazy guy attacked her. Thinking Hauser would appreciate the initiative, he smiled and said, "That sounds promising. She just has to pass the audition," and he reached toward Molly. Lola reacted immediately.

"Don't pull that shit, John," she said fiercely. "You want some? You pay like the rest of them." Stiles frowned, but Lola quickly smiled and said, "Besides, I'm more your taste anyway," and she threw her arm over his shoulder. "By the way, my price has gone up. Hers too."

Across the room, Kats and Shig made their best efforts not to stare over in the direction of the girls. Kats had Shig shift positions at the table so that he could look over his shoulder at the bar and keep an eye on the girls. He sipped his drink and pretended to make small talk with Shig.

"What's going on?" Shig asked.

"Looks like he's taking the bait."

"That's good, right?" Kats moved his head from side to side, weighing the thought. "C'mon, man. You know Molly can take care of herself. And you've been training her for like a year now."

"I know, I know. But I can still be worried about someone I ..." Kats trailed off.

"Someone you what?" Shig asked, now interested in the actual conversation. "Someone you love?" he smiled.

Kats felt his face flush, and it wasn't due to the drink. "Yeah. I mean, I've felt like this for a long time now."

"So, does she feel the same way?"

"I can't say for sure. We've never actually said it."

"What?" Shig said incredulously. "*Baka yo.*" Stupid.

"I know, I know." Kats paused. "My father wasn't very demonstrative with his emotions."

"Our parents' generation wasn't known for its outpouring of emotion, but your old man was more formal than most," Shig said, and Kats knew it was true.

"You know, when I came back from Europe after the war, my parents met me at the train station. My mom hugged me. She was crying and smiling at the same time. My dad," Kats paused at the memory, "my dad shook my hand."

Shig put a hand on his friend's shoulder, "Well, then don't be like that man. Tell her how you feel."

Kats felt the initial urge to explain himself, to tell Shig that it wasn't that easy, but he knew what his friend said was right. He made a small nod and simply said, "Thanks." Shig smiled back.

"Now get your head back in the game," Shig laughed. "We're on a mission." Just then the girls strolled through the crowd and approached the table. Kats and Shig rose to meet them. "How'd it go?" Shig asked.

Lola smiled and Molly said, "We got the job."

CHAPTER 15

Turier had risen early and gone for a run through the Presidio and out toward Golden Gate Park. The hills and the many trees were very different from most urban areas, and he found the exercise calming. As he circled back through Golden Gate Park, he eyed the high hills to the south and thought perhaps he should give them a try in the future. He also thought of Steven Epps but wasn't sure why. He made a mental note for future reference as he returned to the hangar that had become the center of the operation. There he saw one of Thorne's men, Collins, the thickly muscled Black man, sitting at a table, the pieces of a rifle spread before him. Turier approached, watching the man's hands move across each piece, cleaning, oiling, and reassembling the rifle with practiced ease. Collins looked up and gave a friendly nod to the doctor.

"You're very good at that," Turier said appreciatively. Collins smiled.

"Take care of your weapon, and your weapon will take care of you." Turier suspected that Collins spoke from experience. He turned and began heading toward his room and a shower.

"Hey, Doc," Collins said, putting the freshly oiled carbine on the table, "I was wondering if you had any other thoughts about our friend Epps." Turier stopped and looked at the man, not sure how to respond. Collins continued, "I saw that movie and was thinking there must be some weakness, some vulnerability, to him. He can't really be Superman." Turier looked confused.

"Movie? What movie?"

"The surveillance footage from the murder." Turier felt his heart hammer in his chest, but he kept his face neutral.

"*Non*, I'm sorry, *Monsieur* Collins. I still believe the best way to approach Steven is to keep him calm and try to incapacitate him from a distance."

Collins smiled, running his hand up the side of the modified M1 carbine that now fired darts. "This old girl should do just fine. All I need is a clear shot."

"Hauser!" Turier shouted as he pushed open the man's door. Hauser stood in front of a map of San Francisco, his desk cluttered with reports.

"What now, doctor? I really don't have time for this," he said calmly.

"If you want my help, you'll make the time!" Hauser glowered at the man but said nothing. "There's a movie of the events at your safe house. With Steven," Turier said pointedly.

Hauser put down the file he was holding and slowly answered, "There is."

"Why did you not show it to me?"

"Because it's inconsequential to your role in the mission and on a need-to-know basis."

"You showed your team!" Turier exclaimed.

"They needed to know what they're up against."

"What's on that film?" Hauser sat down, saying nothing. "If you want to use me to approach Steven, I'll see that film."

Hauser let out a sigh and relented, "Very well."

Fifteen minutes later, Hauser turned on the lights to the conference room that contained the projector and screen. He saw that Turier sat forward in his chair, his hands steepled in front of his face, as if he were in prayer.

"Steven didn't kill the girl."

"I never said he did, doctor."

"You certainly led me to believe that was the case."

"He was there, he killed a government officer, and he caused the death of the girl. The details are inconsequential."

"Inconsequential?" Turier mouthed, his mind filling with impotent fury at this government man. He wanted to stand and smash Hauser, but he knew he didn't have the skill.

Hauser saw that Turier was about to respond, but he held up his hand for the man to stop. "Doctor, you saw that story yesterday about a so-called 'Tong War,' did you not?" Turier nodded, and Hauser continued. "There is no Tong war. That was speculation by the police and the newspaper. That group of Tong soldiers wasn't taken out by a rival gang. They tried to confront Epps and paid the price for it."

Turier's mouth moved, but no sound came out. He didn't trust Hauser, but this seemed all too plausible. Finally, he found his voice, "How do you know?"

"We have connections in the police department, and they've agreed to keep the story quiet for now, but that won't last. The story of a lunatic killer running around the city is far too salacious to remain secret for long. That's why we must find Epps before the whole goddamned city is looking for him. So I need your head in the game. If you can't help me find Epps, I'll have no choice but to start shaking some trees," Hauser said ominously.

"What do you mean?" Turier asked.

"I mean that the imperative of bringing Epps in alive goes out the window. We'll release the information that he's a murderer, wanted for multiple deaths, and get the entire city looking for him. Someone will turn him in, especially once we offer some reward money."

"But if he's confronted like that by the police, he'll fight. There will be bloodshed."

"There will be a resolution, doctor. I need to finish this one way or another. Help me find him, and we can still try your way. If not ..." he trailed off, holding Turier's gaze for a moment before returning to his report.

The Frenchman headed back to his room, his mind racing and knowing he needed to get in contact with Kats as soon as possible. But he also knew that Hauser was watching him. He was probably having all his calls from the base monitored. Then he remembered what Kats had told him. City Lights. He could leave a message there for Kats. He quickly showered and dressed and then went to the motor pool to request a car for a small errand. The sergeant nodded but left Turier to make a phone call. Several minutes later, he returned saying, "Sir, I'm told that your driver will be here shortly and that you're to wait for him." *Driver?* thought Turier. Hauser was keeping him under watch.

The sergeant pulled an unmarked sedan out front of the motor pool and left it sitting with the motor running. Turier looked around, wondering if he should just take the car, when he saw Thorne, dressed in blue jeans and a leather jacket, come walking up. "You requested a driver, doctor?" he said with a wry smile.

"Someone requested a driver," Turier replied. "It seems a bit much for a simple errand."

"I'm happy to get off the base," Thorne said as he climbed into the driver's seat. Turier followed. "Where to?"

"I'm in need of some research material. We're going to a

bookstore in North Beach on Columbus." Thorne opened a city map and quickly assessed the general location and sped off confidently. Ten minutes later they parked on Columbus and walked up the block to City Lights Bookstore. It was midmorning, but the shop was already busy. Turier made his way to the science section, and Thorne went on to the history shelves.

As Turier pretended to look through the books, he was eyeing the front of the store where a thirtysomething Asian man had sat down behind the front counter. He sported a wispy beard and mustache, just as Kats had described him. The man appeared to be reading a magazine as he sipped a Coke from a glass bottle. Turier grabbed two books that looked marginally interesting and checked to see that Thorne was engrossed in his own aisle. He walked to the front counter and placed the books down. The man reached for them without looking up when Turier said in a whisper, "Are you Shig?" Shig looked up suspiciously and was about to reply when the Frenchman continued. "Katsuhiro said I could contact him through you. I'm Turier."

Shig's eyes went wide, and he smiled, "So you're the doctor ..." he said, and Turier gestured for him to lower his voice. He indicated over his shoulder.

"That man is my escort. Please act normally." Shig nodded and proceeded to ring up the books. "You must tell Kats to meet me tomorrow morning at dawn. I'll be running through Golden Gate Park. Have him meet me at the eastern edge of the Panhandle. It's important."

Shig nodded and said, "That'll be $12.50." Turier pulled some cash out of his pocket and paid for the books. Shig was smiling at Turier and bagging the purchase when he caught sight of the angular blond man approaching the counter.

Thorne was carrying a copy of *Doctor Zhivago*.

"Doctor, I've not had a chance to get any cash. Would you please purchase this for me?" Turier looked surprised, a look that Thorne noticed with a smile. "You're surprised that I read such books, doctor? Have you read it?" Turier shook his head.

"It's amazing," Shig volunteered. "A Nobel prize-winning book."

Thorne smiled, "Yes. You see, doctor? And the fucking Communists hate it."

Shig's face lit up with a huge smile. "I told that to a friend of mine just recently too," he said as he rang up the novel. Turier paid, and Thorne tucked the book under his arm with a smile as he turned to the door. Turier's eyes met those of Shig, who gave a small nod. *Tomorrow.*

As Turier followed Thorne out of the bookstore, he was surprised that the man didn't walk toward the car parked down the street. Instead, he turned north and ambled toward the park at Washington Square. As he caught up to the soldier, he noted that Thorne was smiling, looking around like he was a tourist. They walked a couple of blocks in silence, taking in the summer sun. Finally, Turier spoke.

"It's a lovely day, *Monsieur* Thorne, but should we not be getting back?" Thorne gave a short tilt of his head as if considering the idea but continued to walk on into the park. There, old men sat on park benches, children played, and mothers pushed their babies in strollers. *An idyllic setting to be sharing with this most dangerous man,* thought Turier. Thorne strolled through the park and turned down Grant Avenue.

As they approached the corner of Green Street, Thorne turned to the Frenchman and said, "We need to go in here."

Turier looked at the café sign, which said 'Co-Existence Bagels.' They entered the tiny café lined with small tables. Its walls were covered in handmade bills for jazz shows, poetry readings, and art shows. Smoke filled the room even at midday. Thorne laughed out loud, "Look at this place! Magnificent." He turned to Turier, "Two espressos, doctor," and he sat down at a table by the window. Turier ordered the two drinks and returned to the table where Thorne was perusing his new book.

Turier sipped his espresso, eyeing the man across the table. "You're a strange one, *Monsieur* Thorne," he said, and Thorne looked up.

"Why's that?" he said with a wry smile.

"I wouldn't think that this avant-garde café with its leftist leanings would be something you'd approve of."

"They're young," he said, looking around. "They're artists and fools. We all were like this once. Even me."

Turier hesitated, but curiosity got the better of him, and he asked, "So it's true that you were in the German SS?" Thorne looked at him with unwavering eyes.

"Yes. It was just a uniform I wore."

"But not all uniforms are equal. The Nazis were monsters."

"I was never a Nazi, doctor. The Germans offered me the chance to kill Communists. I took it. To do that they bade me wear their uniform. Seemed like a small thing at the time."

Turier seemed to be processing that information when Thorne continued, "Have you not heard the expression, 'the enemy of my enemy is my friend'? The Germans were that for me. But I don't condone what they did during the war. Even in war, there are lines that aren't to be crossed."

Turier nodded and raised his small cup, "Yes, you're a

strange one, *Monsieur* Thorne," he said with a smile.

"I am what the world made me, doctor," he said with a tip of his cup. "Let's go."

"So, we should probably talk about last night," Kats said as he poured Molly her second cup of coffee. They sat at his kitchen table. Molly had spent the night as she usually did. Her small apartment in Hayes Valley seemed more like an extended closet and storeroom than a place to live, but it gave them the illusion of having separate residences. She added a splash of cream and sugar, took a sip, and smiled.

"I'm not really planning on becoming a prostitute if that's what you're worried about," she said with a grin.

"Not what I'm worried about. But I do think we have to talk about sending you back into the Black Dragon's head-quarters tomorrow night." Molly had told them the night before that the government man, Stiles, wanted her and Lola to come back to the club tomorrow evening by 8 pm for what he called 'training.'

"Lola says it's just going to be instructions on how to give the drugs to the men."

He was about to say something, but she continued. "This is a way to get inside their club, look around, and find out how they're operating. We can use that information to take them down, right?" He nodded reluctantly. "Let me go in for the training and see what I can find. Just the one time. The next day I can back out. Tell 'em I got cold feet."

Kats was trying to find a counterpoint other than his own concern for her safety. He knew how smart and tough she was. She'd also become a surprisingly adept student of the martial arts over the past year. He sipped his black coffee and slowly nodded his head. "OK. In and out," he said seriously.

She looked at him wide-eyed for a moment and then burst out laughing at his unintended pun. It took a moment, but he joined in her laughter.

CHAPTER 16

Kats stood quietly at the eastern edge of Golden Gate Park in an area known as the Panhandle. The sky was growing lighter by the minute, and the fog that hung over the hilltops seemed far away. He stretched, loosening his muscles, especially the bruised and aching shoulder. He could smell the pungent Chinese balm through his sweatshirt but was thankful for the relief it was providing. The park was already busy with early morning activity. People walked their dogs and strode the pathways as the city rose to a new day.

Appearing from the north, along the sidewalk, Kats saw the familiar gait of his friend Dominic. He appeared to be alone, but Kats knew Turier would be worried about being seen. As the Frenchman approached, Kats turned into the park and began a slow jog along the path. In a short span, he heard Turier's footfalls coming behind him, and in moments the two matched a comfortable pace, running side by side. Neither spoke nor directly acknowledged the other. They ran like that for nearly a mile. The only sound was their feet and their controlled breathing. As they ran past the Botanical Gardens, Turier led them on a southerly pathway that took them to the edge of the park along Lincoln Way. There he turned back along the pathway that followed the road and headed east.

"There's something I must tell you," Turier said in a low voice. "Steven didn't kill that girl." Kats looked sideways at his friend, who momentarily made eye contact and nodded.

"You're sure?" Kats replied.

"There's a film of the incident. They showed it to me, but I'm also sure they'll never let the police or anyone else see it."

They continued east, still looking straight ahead at their path. "And I have an idea where Steven might be hiding," Turier said. He made a gesture to their right, pointing toward the high wooded hills to the south, their tops still covered in fog. "He's a *Montagnard*, a mountain soldier, much like you. He knows how to live off the land and would be almost invisible to most up in those hills."

Kats' eyes followed the contours of the hills. "That's Mount Sutro closest to us. Twin Peaks and Mount Davidson beyond that. There are trails, but not too many people go up there."

"You were a ranger like him. Would that not make sense?"

"I'm pretty sure he wouldn't go back to another SRO after what happened at the Jefferson. If he hasn't completely left town, then yeah, it seems like a good location for a ranger. He can certainly see and hear most anyone coming." Kats scanned the southern horizon as they padded onward. "And, you can see, it's often covered in fog. Good thinking, Dominic."

"Well, don't be too pleased with me yet. I'm going to have to share this with Hauser and his team, or they'll remove me from the operation and turn it over to police."

"The police?" Kats asked.

"Yes, they'll name Steven as the one responsible for multiple murders and turn the whole city after him. They'll burn it all down if I can't assist them."

Kats thought for a moment. "Can you buy me a couple of days to explore these hills? Once I see it's clear, you can give them the go-ahead to investigate."

"I can probably get you a day or two. But you must hurry, or they'll have me back at Menlo Park, and I fear the end will be tragic for many people."

"OK. Then let's plan on giving them a diversion."

"You have something in mind?" Turier asked. Kats pointed straight ahead of them, to a small, green mountain rising up from the city.

"That's Buena Vista Park. I wouldn't use it, and I don't think Epps would either. Too many people there, but it's really steep and covered in thick trees. Let's take a look there just to make sure, but you could tell them you thought it a likely spot for Epps to hide. Then later we can let them start investigating the bigger hills to the south."

"*Très bien*," Turier said, and they increased their pace toward the park. Over the next forty-five minutes they charged up the steep trails, hearts pounding, breathing heavily, sweating, and thoroughly enjoying themselves. It was like their days in Besançon. Kats stopped several times at crossroads on the trail and walked them back into the woods at places he thought might be used as a campsite. They made their way to the top of the hill and stopped to catch their breath and to survey the city from the amazing vantage point.

"Your city is beautiful," Turier said. "So different from most every other American city." Kats nodded appreciatively. He turned to Dominic.

"Have you thought about what you'll do if you find Epps? Do you really think the government will allow you to treat him?"

"I've struggled with this for a while now, Kats. I fear they'll try to use him as a weapon or, worse, as a way to make more weapons. I've thought about going to the press if they don't let me help Steven. He is, after all, an American soldier. A hero even. And that might force them to do the right thing."

"Maybe," Kats said. "But let's try to keep our options open." Kats checked his watch. "We should probably head back down. They'll worry that you're late."

"*Oui*, but I'll explain that I went for a run and explored this lovely park. In a couple of days I'll tell them that the park made me think of Steven and that we should investigate it."

"Which means I need to get started on those other mountains," Kats said flatly.

"Is that a problem?"

"Just lots of things in motion," he said. "I'll manage."

How am I going to manage all this? Kats thought as he returned to his car, parked in the Lower Haight. The hilltops looked relatively small, but he knew they were a labyrinth of trails and hidden meadows. Running or hiking those trails would take weeks, not the few days he knew he had. He needed his secret weapon. He got in the car and headed toward City Center.

Kats walked into the stately entrance to the San Francisco Library, turned with familiar ease toward the information desk, and searched for his secret weapon. He saw her, talking with a customer across the high desk. The silver-haired woman caught his eye for a moment and then returned to helping the customer. Kats leaned casually on the high counter and looked around. He'd often told people who questioned him about his 'glamorous' work as a private detective that he spent more time in the library than in seedy bars, and today he hoped that proved to be fruitful. The older woman wrapped up with the man at the end of the desk and strolled over to Kats, a half-smile on her lips. "Just coming from the gym, Katsuhiro?" she said, noting his gym clothes.

"A case literally has me running, Gladys," he said with a smile. "I'm hoping you can help me."

She made a sweeping gesture with her arms, "This world of information is at your disposal. What do you need?"

"I need maps of the hills of San Francisco. Twin Peaks, Mount Davidson, Mount Sutro in particular. Maps that show the topography and hopefully any roads and trails that exist up there. Do you have anything like that?"

"Hmm, not your usual road map for sure. Follow me," she said and came out from behind the desk and walked toward the rear corner of the first floor. They entered the map room which, unlike the main stacks, was composed of broad drawers, stacked from floor to above his head. "Sounds like you might need to look at the geographical survey maps of the areas. The parks department catalogs those areas, and I believe they keep fairly accurate records of their trail systems. But this gentleman would know." As they rounded an aisle, there stood a small older man who was wearing a tweed jacket that looked as dusty as the books in the stacks. His nearly bald head was focused on a small map that was on top of an open drawer. "Hello, Cyril," Gladys said.

"Good morning, Gladys," the man replied without looking up. *Traces of an English accent*, thought Kats. The man made a small bob of his head, seemingly satisfied with some hidden knowledge, and closed the drawer. He turned and looked at Kats above a pair of pince-nez glasses that sat atop his thin nose. Bushy eyebrows and an elongated face would have made for a caricature of an eccentric academic except for the blue eyes that were sharp and clear as a cloudless sky. "How may I help you?"

"This is my friend Katsuhiro. He has need of a particular type of map. Katsuhiro, please meet Cyril, our director of antiquities and maps."

"Good morning, sir," Kats said. Then he noticed that Cyril's left jacket sleeve was pinned up at the elbow.

Cyril felt Kats' eyes on his missing left hand and said, "Lost in the Great War. The first Great War," he said with a wry smile.

"Katsuhiro served in the other Great War," Gladys said with a grin. "Perhaps you two can swap war stories after he finds what he needs. I'll leave you to it." She gave Kats a wink and headed back toward her office.

"So, what are you looking for, young man?" Cyril asked.

"I need to see the maps of the major hills of the city. Mount Sutro, Davidson, and Twin Peaks. I'm looking for the trails and pathways that are up there. Gladys said that maybe the geological survey maps would have the information?"

Cyril shook his head, "I know Gladys thinks she knows everything, but those maps wouldn't have what you're looking for. What you need are the Sanborn maps."

"Sanborn maps?" Kats asked.

Cyril began walking down the aisle, with Kats following.

"Yes, Sanborn maps started nearly a hundred years ago to detail cities for the fire insurance companies. They're large scale, highly detailed, and constantly being updated to reflect changes in cities." He paused in front of a stack of drawers and ran his finger over the small nameplates. "Here, I believe," he said as he opened the drawer. The smell of old print wafted up, and Cyril began to sort through the stack of large, flat books. "Start with these," he said, pulling a stack of books from the drawer. Kats grabbed the stack and moved to a large table in the center of the room. He thumbed through them and found one that said Mount Sutro in the table of contents. He spread it out on the table. There was a large topographic map of the two hills, marked with service roads, electrical boxes, water, and sewage connections. Kats peered intently at the small pathways that were indicated on the map.

"I think this is it," he said excitedly.

Cyril nodded. "Let me see about the other hills," he said, turning back toward the stacks. Fifteen minutes later he returned with a short stack of the books under his right arm. Kats had been studying the map intently, looking at the trail system that meandered through the hilltop. Cyril noted the intensity that Kats was studying the map as he stood at his shoulder. "You're looking for something that's not on this map, eh? Something the map might tell you?"

Kats looked at the man, "How did you know that?"

Cyril gave a sage nod of his head, "During the war, I was with the 2nd Lovat Scouts. We were the forward eyes of the army. I had to learn to read beyond what was on the map itself. Saved my life many times. My unit's as well."

"That's exactly what I did for the 442nd," Kats said quietly. The two looked at each other as if recognizing the other for the first time.

Cyril set down the other maps. "What are you looking for?" he asked Kats.

"Not a what, a who. Another soldier. A soldier like us. We think he may be hiding in these hills, and I'm trying to figure out where to look because I don't have time to search all of them." Kats stood up and pointed to the map of Mount Sutro in front of him. "If you were trying to avoid people, to set up a campsite where you could see someone coming for you, where you could get in and out if needed and also be able to leave your campsite and go into the city," he gestured toward the map to Cyril, "where would you go?"

Cyril leaned forward, his hawklike eyes focused on the lines of the map. After a few moments, he pointed to an area that showed several switchbacks on a fairly steep hill. "The high ground above these switchbacks would give you lots of visibility on anyone coming from that side of the hill."

"Yeah, but it also seems too busy. The switches mean people move back and forth at a slower pace. If he wanted to attack them, then yeah, that would be a good location. But he won't want to engage them."

Cyril pondered the map again. "Then maybe here," he pointed further up the trail. "See how the ground is still high, but from there you can see down the trail that comes up from the north side? And from this service road," he pointed to the west of the trails, "you can see people and vehicles going up and down those tight switchbacks."

Kats nodded, "Possible. Can we look at the other hilltops?" Cyril spread the other maps onto the table, and for the next hour they examined them and gave tactical assessments to each other, as if trying to convince each other of something. Finally, they came back to the first map of Mount Sutro, and Cyril gave a smile and said, "Give me a few minutes to locate something." Kats nodded as he departed and continued to look at the Mount Sutro map. His finger glided across the map and, when it stopped, he smiled and laughed out loud. He stood up and hurried out of the room, leaving the maps spread out on the table. Five minutes later both returned, Cyril carrying what looked to be a very old map.

"I think this may help," he said and gently unrolled the yellowed paper. "This is a map from 1879, and it was done for Adolph Sutro, the silver magnate who bought up the land that became Mount Sutro, Sutro Baths, and Sutro Heights. I recall cataloging it a couple of years ago. Look here," he said, pointing to the hilltop. "The map's eighty years old, but you can see the outlines and contours are the same today." Kats nodded. "This is also before the roads and trails were put in, but see here," his right hand pointed to a series of thin, wavy lines on the map, "these represent Indian[8] trails dating back to when the Spanish came to San Francisco."

Kats stood and looked at the old map and then across to the new one and said, "That puts the Indian trail," he ran his hand across the map, "right about here!" He smiled at Cyril. "That's interesting because it bisects the new trail and gives a pathway up even higher, and look, down toward the southern edge of the park as well."

"If the trail is still there," cautioned Cyril.

"Our man wouldn't need much in the way of a trail. In fact, if it were mostly overgrown, it would be invisible to casual observers. Very interesting." Kats smiled and pulled a folded piece of paper from his back pocket to show Cyril.

"What is that?"

"Another map that I think makes the case," Kats said, smiling. He opened a San Francisco city streetcar map for the route that stopped at the Laguna Honda station at the end of the Twin Peaks Tunnel. He pointed to a stop at the south end of the park, close to the hidden Indian trail. "That stop would allow someone to catch the streetcar down the hill to Market, and from Market you can get anywhere in the city."

"Nice work there," Cyril said with a grin.

"And you as well. This has been incredibly helpful."

"Happy to help you and this other soldier as well. I hope you can find him." Kats nodded and extended his hand, which Cyril shook. "Now, off you go. I'll make sure all these maps get back to their proper places. You can keep the streetcar map, though!"

CHAPTER 17

Kats returned to his Japantown Victorian home. Molly was already at Ann's 440, but she'd left him a club sandwich in the fridge. He wolfed that down and then showered and changed. He was about to head out when his office phone rang.

"Takemoto here."

"Hey, man," came Shig's voice through the line. "How did your meetup with the doc go?" Kats sat down behind the desk and gave Shig the rundown on the events. "We have an idea of where Epps might be hiding out."

"Where?" Shig pressed.

"He's an alpine soldier, trained for mountain warfare. He'd be very at home up one of the mountains here in town. In fact, some research at the library leads me to believe it's probably Mount Sutro."

"Sutro? Wow. I've never been up there. Half the time it's covered in fog."

"Which makes it an ideal spot to hide out."

"Hey, that reminds me," Shig said. "I just read something weird about Sutro."

"Weird how?" Kats asked.

"Apparently there's a missile command building up there. Not exactly top-secret stuff since there's a radar dish in plain sight. The *Examiner* was writing about how it's being upgraded."

"Interesting," Kats said. "Usually activity like that isn't good for hiding out, but lots of activity provides great cover. Thanks, Shig."

"Need some backup?" Shig asked, and Kats could hear the grin through the line. He appreciated the unconditional support from his friend, but he demurred.

"Not yet. I'm just going to do some recon."

"OK, but what if you run into that guy again?" Shig's voice had turned serious. "I mean, I know you can handle yourself, but look at what happened the last time."

"Thanks for the pep talk. You should have been a coach."

"Sorry, man."

"I'm going to Chinatown tomorrow for something that might level the playing field."

"What, a dragon?" Shig said, not entirely kidding.

"I'm going to see Dr. Han," Kats said.

"The wizard! Tell him I said hi!" Shig laughed.

Ross Alley, between Jackson and Washington Streets, was known for its many gambling dens. Along the alley, houses run by half a dozen different Tong co-existed in a mutually agreed upon peace. They all had reinforced doors that could slow down potential police raids just long enough to get the money out a back door or through one of many tunnels that crisscrossed Chinatown. The other shops along the way accepted the influx of gambling madmen who were mostly Chinese, but not exclusively so. The smart ones found ways to cater to those men. Money lenders and even a bank that seemingly was open all night were part of the fabric of the street. That made Dr. Han's small shop all the more unique. The dark, narrow door would be easy to overlook unless you knew to search for it. The first time Kats had come there, he'd almost missed it.

In late 1940, a little over a year before the war would find America and his family, Kats had accompanied his mother

Yaeko to the shop in Chinatown. She'd begun to suffer from early signs of arthritis in her hands, and everyone—Japanese, Chinese, and even the savvy *hakujin*[9]—went to see Dr. Han. He was called "doctor," yet no American medical organization would recognize his credentials. To the thousands of people he'd helped, though, the title meant nothing save for the polite honorific. Entering the small shop, halfway up Ross Alley, Kats had been fascinated by the dusty shelves and the containers that seemed to hold the most arcane potions imaginable. His mother gave a formal bow upon entering, while Kats stared openly. Dr. Han had long, wispy hair and a silvery beard that came to a point several inches below his chin. He also had long, pointed fingernails, and Kats wondered how he managed something as simple as brushing his teeth. He seemed old, but in an indeterminant way that said he could be fifty or ninety. You just couldn't tell.

While his mother sat, Dr. Han confidently examined her hands and then touched several points up her arms and then into her shoulders and her neck. Kats recognized these as pressure points from his training but had no idea how they could be used to treat aching joints. Han opened a small case that revealed a bundle of two-inch-long steel needles. He proceeded to place a dozen needles along those same points he'd traced before. His mother held perfectly still, looking strangely content despite the quills. The worry must have been evident on Kats' face, for Dr. Han smiled at him and said, "No fear, young man. Acupuncture has been used for a thousand years in the Middle Kingdom." He turned to his counter and began retrieving vials and containers.

Kats watched as Dr. Han mixed several kinds of powders together with casually measured ease and then poured them into a small wooden box. He then returned to Yaeko and quickly removed the pins. She smiled as he handed her the box. "A pinch with your tea in the morning and again at night," he said to my mother with a sage nod.

Kats asked, trying hard to keep the skepticism out of his voice, "What's in it?"

Han looked at him with a serious face, "Dragon seeds and ground tiger penis," he said. Kats' eyes went wide, and the doctor laughed. "Nothing so exotic, young man. Mostly white turmeric and a few other herbs to promote blood flow." Kats nodded, though he was still unsure about the whole process. What changed his mind was the effect that the powder had on his mother. Within a week, she was marveling at how much better her hands felt, and she swore it was the medicine from Dr. Han. Kats never forgot. Over the years he'd ventured back to the small shop in Chinatown, often on behalf of friends or clients, but once after he contracted a bad case of poison ivy on a case in South San Francisco. The man was known in the community, and many used the term *wizard* for him. He was that good.

Entering the shop today, Kats marveled at how the shop looked just as it had nearly twenty years before. There behind the counter, smoking a long, thin pipe, was Dr. Han. His hair was perhaps a bit whiter than the last time he'd visited, but otherwise the doctor was unchanged. *What potion does he take for that?* Kats wondered.

Kats made a bow as he entered and smiled at the doctor. "Good afternoon, *sifu*," he said, using the broad term that meant teacher as well as honored elder, similar to the Japanese term *sensei.* The doctor had just puffed his pipe and gave a small nod of his head as he placed his pipe on the counter.

"Takemoto-san," he said politely. "*Shibaraku desita ne.*"

It has been a long time. *His Japanese is much better than my Chinese,* Kats thought.

"Yes, *sifu,* it has been a while. I hope you are very well," Kats said, knowing the polite chitchat was a prerequisite to any meaningful conversation.

Han nodded, stroking his beard. "The years lay a bit heavier perhaps. The cold creeps easier into my bones. But I persevere." Kats nodded. "And how is your mother?"

"I received a letter from her just last week. She is well, as is my father. They're enjoying the early summer in Japan. I believe they're planning a trip to the healing baths at Hakone later this year."

Han gave a soft smile and a small bow of his head. *Now to business,* the gesture said. "What happened to your shoulder?" Kats was surprised by the question, not realizing that he was carrying his injured arm differently, but the keen eyes of the healer couldn't be fooled.

"I had a little accident," Kats said discretely.

"Let me see." Kats shrugged, knowing that Han was both capable and relentless. He carefully peeled off his shirt and showed his heavily bruised left shoulder and upper arm to him.

"Yes, an accident," Han said, shaking his head. "Sit." He beckoned to the chair beside the counter. He sniffed Kats' arm. "Tiger balm. Good for simple aches and pains. You need something stronger."

From behind the counter he produced a ceramic jar with a large cork top. He twisted it open and took a flat piece of bamboo from the countertop and swirled it in the jar. He pulled out the stick that was now covered in a thick, black tar-like substance that hit Kats' nose like three-day old fish. Han ignored the face Kats was making and placed the dollop on Kats' shoulder. Then he used the stick like a palette to spread the liniment across the purple bruise. Next he took out a small steel case that opened to reveal the acupuncture needles he wielded with such skill. Kats took a centering breath and willed his muscles to relax. Han methodically inserted needle after needle up his arm, then into his shoulder, and finally into Kats' left ear and temple. He then lit a small candle, which he held to the ends of select needles, warming them. Kats continued to breathe deeply and rhythmically. Several minutes passed without a word, and then Han blew out the candle and removed the needles. Kats opened his eyes and slowly raised his left arm. To his great pleasure, the pain was almost entirely gone. A bit of stiffness remained, but the ache he'd felt for the past several days was a distant echo. The dark liniment was likewise gone, absorbed into his skin. He smiled and said, "You're still a magician, doctor."

"Just good Chinese medicine. Magic costs extra. Now what can I do for you?"

Kats pulled on his shirt and said, "I may need a bit of that magic. I need something that will incapacitate a very strong man."

Han looked him in the eye, "Incapacitate?" he said, weighing the word. "For how long? A minute? An hour? Forever?" he asked flatly.

"Nothing fatal, doctor. I'm actually trying to help this person. But he may not see it that way. I need something that will work quickly. How long it lasts is less important."

Han walked behind the counter, looking thoughtful. "If you need quick, it can't be ingested. If we're not going lethal, it will take too long." He turned to look at the wall of containers, his gaze sweeping across them. "I believe something inhaled will work. But dosing this man will require you to be very close. Is that acceptable?"

"It will have to be."

Han nodded. "Give me two hours. Go have some dim sum." Han turned back toward the wall of ingredients behind him and began to think. Kats stood and exited the shop.

By the time Kats left Chinatown more than two hours later, he was comfortably stuffed with dim sum and had a box of leftovers for Molly. He also had two small wooden tubes that looked like thick, five-inch straws. Capped with wax at both ends, each tube contained what Dr. Han called "Two-Step Powder," meaning that after getting a lungful, you'd take two steps before falling unconscious. He estimated a man would be out for a good hour. He did warn Kats to be careful of blowback because the powder didn't differentiate friend from foe. "Noted," said Kats, and he paid the doctor despite his protestations. All part of the ritual.

When he arrived home, he found Molly in the kitchen, finishing a sandwich. "Is that dim sum?" she asked excitedly.

"From that new place on Powell, Yank Sing. Really good," Kats replied as he handed her the box. Molly cooed with delight and pushed aside what remained of a baloney sandwich. Kats sat down and watched as she attacked the dim sum.

"I'm still worried about tonight," he began. She nodded, her mouth full of pork shumai, and waved her hands. "I know it's only recon," Kats continued, "but the Hei Long are bastards. They're the most ruthless of the Tong. I understand why John hates them."

Molly put a hand over his, "Honey, think of this as a job interview. Lola and I will be fine. She knows that guy Stiles and said this was like the first time around. There's a process they need to explain to the girls to get the results they're looking for." Kats nodded but still looked unconvinced. "And if we find something that can be used to shut down this new operation, won't that also shut down the Hei Long?" she asked. *There was that possibility*, he thought.

"Yeah, OK. But you know I'm going to be outside waiting for you two to come out."

"I'd expect nothing less," she said, planting a kiss on him.

CHAPTER 18

Across town, in the dilapidated hangar that was their base of operations, Larry Thorne strode into Hauser's office. He stood there a moment while Hauser pretended to ignore him in favor of the report on his desk. Feeling the man's eyes boring into the top of his skull, Hauser cleared his throat and looked up. "Can I help you, captain?"

"My men are bored, Colonel Hauser."

"I think there are some cards in the mess," Hauser replied sardonically.

"Cards aren't the answer," Thorne replied, not being baited by the man's sarcasm. "There's only so much ... how shall I say ... cleaning one's own rifle that a man can do. And with no sign of our quarry, there's nothing else to do."

"So you're requesting ..."

"A night out. Let them get a bit of exercise."

Hauser knew that there was a kind of anxiousness that overtook even the best trained soldiers when there was no fighting to keep them focused. A thought entered his mind, and he realized he could kill two birds with one stone. He nodded knowingly to Thorne and said, "Of course. Your team had been on call for weeks before arriving. I believe I have a solution." Thorne smiled and gestured for him to continue.

"One of our partners, a local concern, has a delivery of weapons owed to them. They're located in Chinatown at a night club that they say has the best entertainment, drinks, and whores in the city. Perhaps your team might deliver the package to them tonight and then stay and reconnoiter the operation?" Hauser gave him a sideways smile that Thorne returned.

"Fine," Thorne said, "but make sure some of your grunts come along to do the heavy lifting."

At 7 pm Molly came downstairs into the kitchen wearing a pretty green dress that would have looked more appropriate at church than at a bordello. "You look nice," Kats said, "but shouldn't you look a bit more ..." he struggled to find the words.

"A bit tartier?" she asked with a laugh. "Remember that I'm not going for that business, just to get the story on the drug operation. Plus, I don't want them to get any other ideas on this trip inside."

Thirty minutes later they stood at the corner of Jackson and Grant as the evening sky was beginning to turn reddish and the lights of Chinatown started to flicker on. Looking east down Jackson he could see the club. Its front doors were open but showing none of the signs of life it exhibited during the night. Kats checked his watch. "She's late," he said absently.

Molly put a hand on his chest, in part to reassure him but also to calm herself. Talking about a reconnaissance mission inside a Tong brothel was one thing. Actually doing it was a bit more stressful. Looking over Kats' shoulder, she saw Lola walking down Grant Avenue toward them. Lola smiled and gave a small wave as she approached. She wore a stylish blue dress. It was a bit more flirty than Molly's, but that fit her personality. Her hair was pulled back and, as usual, her makeup was flawless. Kats pulled them around the corner, out of sight from the front of the club just in case anyone came out.

"I'm going to be out front until you come out," he began.

"There are a couple of restaurants and a tea shop across from the entrance, and I can keep an eye out for you."

"What about if you have to pee or get a drink?" Lola asked.

"I'll hold it. Army training," he replied, and Molly laughed.

"All that tea?" she smiled. "You can pee in the woods, but you can't pee in a restaurant booth or in front of a shop," Molly said. Kats grunted and nodded.

"That's why I called Shig. He's going to meet me after he closes City Lights. I can wait till then."

"That's my guy," Molly said with a laugh and a slap on his back.

"Back to business. There's a rear entrance and a fire escape on the other side of the building. But if all goes according to plan, you should come out the front door." They both nodded.

"Piece of cake," Lola said with more confidence than she felt. She pulled a compact from her purse to check her still perfect makeup. Kats put a hand on Molly's elbow, turning her toward him.

"Take this and put it in your purse," he said as he held out a six-inch-long wooden cylinder that was stained a dark color. She recognized the *yawara* stick from their training together. Kats had shown her how to use the stick against pressure points by focusing its end into those sensitive spots. She'd learned a few of the tricks with it, and of course it made for a formidable cudgel when used like a hammer. She slipped it into her purse and gave him a nod. "In and out," he said with a tight-lipped smile.

She nodded, gave him a kiss, and took Lola by the arm. Together they walked toward the club. Kats watched from down the block as they stopped, adjusted their hair and dresses, and then entered the building. Now the wait.

Even midweek and still early evening, the club was already busy as day drunks shifted to their evening posture and the employees prepped for the coming crowd. There was no band playing yet, but somewhere a jukebox was playing, and Miles Davis' *Porgy and Bess* filled the hall. They were directed to the back staircase Molly had observed on their last visit. No Tong guards this time. They climbed up two flights of stairs to the third floor. The first two floors were the public-facing portion of the Hong Kong Club. Dance floor, ballroom, and bar on the first; and private rooms that were more like opera boxes on the second, along with another bar that didn't water down its drinks. The upper two floors were for more 'specialized' services.

They stood in a long hallway that was draped with heavy red velvet curtains. Incense burned from multiple sconces, and Molly noted that each door was emblazoned with a Chinese character that she couldn't read. It looked like an over-the-top designer's caricature of what a brothel would look like. Standing in the hall were half a dozen Asian girls— Chinese, Molly assumed—along with two older women, who must be the madams. The girls looked tired and a bit glassy eyed. Molly looked over at Lola, who leaned over to Molly's ear and whispered, "Drugged." Molly nodded, and then she noticed traces of a sickly sweet smell that she recognized. *Opium.* Just then, two men came walking down from the fourth floor. She immediately recognized Stiles, but the younger man was new.

Stiles gave Lola a nod and raised his hands to get their attention. The two madams clapped their hands like grade schoolteachers, and the girls turned toward Stiles. "OK, so we have a lot to go over with you all," Stiles began, "but the best place to start is upstairs because we can't use these rooms," he gestured down the hall. He turned and walked up the stairs with the retinue of girls following.

The fourth floor was darker and more ominous than the ones below. The smell of opium was much stronger here, and Molly noted that attendants were moving in and out of the curtained doorways down one end of the hall. *An opium den,* she thought. *Of course, it would make sense for the Hei Long to offer all kinds of pleasures in their club.* Lola raised her eyebrows at Molly but said nothing. Stiles led them down toward the other end of the hallway. There was a red lacquered door with a dragon inlay that looked like ivory. Stiles' assistant held open the door, and they passed into a lavish bedroom. Velvet curtains covered the walls, and a huge four-poster bed was on the left, covered in pillows and silk sheets. Behind it, set at a slight downward angle toward the bed, was a large mirror. There were two floor lamps, with colored silk draped over them to create what some might call 'mood' lighting. A credenza held several bottles of liquor and a number of glasses. On the other wall was another mirror. *Classy*, thought Molly sardonically.

Stiles then began what turned out to be a lengthy description about the great service the girls were doing for science and for America. The two madams provided translation, but Molly could tell that the girls couldn't care less about science or patriotism. They just wanted their next meal or maybe their next fix. Stiles explained that the girls had to get the guys to drink from the 'special' glass. They needed to be careful not to mix them up, or they'd dose themselves. They were told what to expect, but Molly noted that Lola looked skeptical at the benign description Stiles told of the drug's effects. Then he walked to the wall beside the mirror. He pulled back the curtain, revealing a wooden panel. He pushed a spot on the upper-right side, and a hidden door clicked open. This made the girls perk up a bit. Stiles smiled like he was Harry Houdini and led them through the door into the hidden rooms behind the wall. There they saw the one-way mirror, which the girls marveled at, as well as the movie camera. Molly noted the back room with its boxes and what looked a bit like a chemistry set on a table. She also saw two shotguns on a rack.

Molly spoke up, "So, what do we do if one of these guys has a bad reaction?" She already knew but wanted to hear it from Stiles.

"There will always be trained personnel back here, and if there's an emergency, we'll intervene." He looked at Lola and said, "We've learned that lesson." Molly marveled at Lola's composure.

"The last thing we need to go over is how to pick the clients," Stiles said as he exited the back room into the bedroom. "We need you to pick guys who are alone. Ones who won't be missed by friends. This is key." He waited for the translation and for the nodding of heads. Just then the outer door opened, and in walked a Chinese man who was dressed in a black silk suit. Molly noted the man's face, specifically his bright blue left eye that at first glance she thought was made of glass. *Dragon Eye*, thought Molly, as she remembered Kats' description of the Hei Long's ruthless leader. Two more of his men followed into the room, which now seemed cramped.

Stiles gave a deferential nod to Wen, who wasn't looking at him but rather at Molly and Lola. He walked closer and turned his 'dragon eye' first toward Lola and then toward

Molly. He appraised her up and down, and Molly felt like a horse being evaluated by a buyer. She did her best to hold his gaze as he stared at her and surprised herself by doing so. Wen twisted his mouth and spun toward Stiles.

"What are these two doing here?" he asked angrily.

"Um, we thought that a bit of variety might be good for the program," Stiles said.

"You and Hauser?" Wen pressed.

"Well, I ..." Stiles began, but Wen cut him off with a curt hand gesture.

"No outsiders. We agreed to use only Hei Long girls. We control. These *gwaipo* aren't our girls."

Stiles was trying to come up with a response when Molly stepped forward and said, "Hey, fine with us. We don't need this crazy shit." She grabbed Lola's arm to go.

"They've seen things?" Wen asked Stiles, who could only nod.

Wen shook his head and then turned to his men and said something in Chinese. The two men stepped forward and grabbed Molly and Lola. As a hand closed on her arm, Molly's hand found her purse, and she gripped the *yawara* stick. She raised her hand high and brought its bullet-ended point down hard on the man's shoulder. He howled in pain, and Molly gave him a push. It wasn't a push like you might give a door, but the powerful, percussive push that came from lowering the hips and exploding through the target as Kats had taught her. The man flew backward and slammed into the wall. She was about to turn when she felt a hand in her hair. *Wen*, she thought, and was pulled backward and down, landing hard on the floor beside him. He put his foot on her chest and smiled. "Fire, like your hair," he said. "We will make you into one of our girls." Several more men entered the room and pulled her to her feet. "Introduce these two to the dragon's breath," he said, and the men dragged Lola and Molly down the hallway.

They entered one of the curtained dens, and two men held each of them while two of the small attendants busied themselves at the table. A minute later they turned toward Molly and Lola, each holding what looked like a two-headed ceramic pipe. There was a bowl with two stems extending from it. In the bowl was a sticky-looking black substance that Molly could smell from across the room. Black tar opium. The first attendant held a candle beneath the bowl, and a sweet smoke began to rise from the pipe. He approached Lola, who tried to twist and turn her head away, but powerful hands held her. They twisted her face forward, and the small attendant placed one end of the pipe in front of her face. Then he placed the other end in his own mouth, puffed, and blew a stream of smoke into Lola's face. She coughed, gasped for air, and coughed again. He quickly repeated the process, and this time Lola barely twisted as the smoke hit her face. Molly saw that Lola's head tilted forward and her body went slack. The men holding her moved her over to a bed, and she collapsed there bonelessly. Then they turned to Molly.

Molly struggled against the hands holding her as the man approached with the pipe. She kicked her feet toward him, and he made a gesture with his head. The man on her right drove a fist into her stomach that doubled her over. As she rose up gasping for air, the sickly sweet cloud hit her directly in the face. She felt herself swoon. *No!* she thought. But then a strange lassitude came over her, and she felt like she was floating. Another wave of the sweet smoke washed over her, and by the time the cloud fully passed her by, she was out.

CHAPTER 19

The delivery truck crawled slowly down the alley toward the Hong Kong Club. It might have been a food or beer delivery but for the late hour. It stopped when two black-garbed members of the Hei Long signaled for it to halt. The driver, a sergeant by day but tonight in civilian garb, rolled down the window. "We got your goods," he said, and the Hei Long looked in the cabin, noting the blond man sitting in the passenger seat, calmly smoking a cigarette.

"Open the back," said the Tong, and the driver exited the vehicle. Taking the keys, he unlocked the back and opened the doors to reveal several unmarked wooden crates and three more men. The small Hispanic man gave them a smile as he jumped down from his seat on the oblong crates. The other two followed.

Larry Thorne joined his men at the back of the truck as two more of the Tong appeared from the doorway. The Black Dragon pointed to the crates and said, "Inside."

Thorne looked at the man and then at the crates that contained the guns and said to his men, "The sooner we dump these inside, the sooner we get to the bar. Let's go." They moved the crates into the building, and several more of the Hei Long appeared and began carrying the crates up the stairs, two men per crate. The Hispanic soldier, Esteban, and the French mercenary, Zapek, grabbed one crate. Collins, the Black soldier, smiled and hefted a crate over his shoulder and followed the others up the back stairwell.

"Very good, gentlemen. I shall be with you momentarily," Thorne said. He turned to the driver, smiled, and said, "Don't wait up for us."

"But, sir, I was told to stay and drive you all back to the base," the sergeant protested.

"These men have found their way home from far more dangerous places than this," Thorne gestured with his hands. "We'll be fine. Go," he said with a shooing motion. The sergeant turned and headed back to the truck as Thorne entered the door and mounted the steps, taking them two at a time.

By 9 pm Kats had eaten twice, barely tasting his food, and read the latest editions of the *San Francisco Chronicle* and the *Examiner*. By 10 pm when Shig arrived after closing City Lights early, he was inwardly climbing the walls while trying to keep calm. "Hey, man," Shig said, pulling up a chair at the window-side table. Across the street, the Hong Kong Club was brightly illuminated with neon lights. Kats looked across the table at his friend.

"Thanks for coming," he said, returning his gaze toward the street.

"How long have they been inside?" Shig asked.

"Going on three hours."

The waitress came by, and Shig ordered a Coke and pork lo mein. Turning back to Kats, he said, "OK. That's not too long, is it?"

"This was supposed to be a training day for them. Three hours is about as long as I'd expect."

"So, what are you thinking?"

"I'm thinking I need to go back in there." As Kats said this, Shig noted the dark look that passed over his face.

"Man, you gotta give them more time. Just have some more tea, and let's see what happens." The waitress returned with Shig's Coke and noodles, which he eagerly dug into.

Between bites, he asked, "So, what happened at the wizard's place?"

Kats, happy to be thinking of something else, explained the visit to Han and pulled the two wooden tubes from his front jacket pocket. "He calls it, Two-Step Powder," Kats said with a wry grin. "Breathe this in, and you're unconscious in two steps."

"Is that his professional opinion?" Shig asked with a smile. Kats nodded.

"You should try it," Shig said.

"How am I going to try it?"

"I don't know. Maybe on a monkey or something."

"No monkeys to be found," Kats said and rose from the table. "Gotta hit the latrine. Keep an eye on the club." Shig nodded.

Eleven o'clock came and went, and the two men sat in

silence watching and waiting. Shig looked at his watch. "This place is gonna close at midnight," he said.

Kats stared out and said, "I'm going in."

"And do what? That place is full of Black Dragon goons."

"I've gotten Molly out of other places as bad."

"Yeah, but you had a plan then. You had equipment and backup."

"I've got to do something, Shig. This is making me crazy."

"Hey, you need to slow down. Breathe and find that place of stillness," Shig said.

Kats looked at him. "Are you quoting me to me?"

"Yeah, I am. You've told me many times that waiting is a secret weapon that most people don't think about. You need to listen to yourself."

Kats made a tight-lipped grimace and balled his fists on top of the table. "*Kuso*," he said under his breath.

"I know it's shit, but you'd need a commando raid to take down that place," Shig said.

Kats looked sharply at his friend, his mind racing. "A raid," he said to Shig. "A raid!" He stood and slapped Shig on the shoulder. "Come on."

Officer Elliot Blackstone was getting ready for bed when his phone began ringing. He quickly answered it so as not to wake up his already sleeping wife. "Blackstone," he said.

"Elliot, it's Kats Takemoto."

"Kats, hey. Bit late, isn't it?"

"I'm sorry, Elliot, but I have a situation and I need a favor."

Blackstone sat down, rubbing his tired eyes. "How did you get this number?"

"I'm a detective, remember? But please, I need your help."

"OK. What do you need?"

"A raid."

"A what?"

"I need a vice raid on the Hong Kong Club in Chinatown."

Blackstone was wide awake now. "OK, Kats. Two things. One, that's a Tong operation. I know they have some bad stuff going on there, but we've been told to leave them and most of those operations in Chinatown alone. Two, I need a crime to authorize a raid."

"What about this whole Tong war stuff?" Kats pressed. "Think of this as a way to preemptively stop them from something much worse."

"Law enforcement doesn't work like that. I have to have a crime."

"How about kidnapping? Two women," Kats said. "Two White women."

"That shouldn't matter," Blackstone replied.

"But we know it does, Elliot," Kats said.

"Are you saying the Tong kidnapped these two women?"

"Well, not exactly. They went into the club tonight and haven't come out."

"They voluntarily went into the club?"

"Yes, they were sort of on a reconnaissance mission."

"So they've been gone a few hours?"

"Yes."

"Kats, there's no way I can authorize a raid on that. They might just be in there having a great time. Maybe they got drunk, or maybe they slipped out the side door. We can only go in if there's clear evidence of a crime or some other emergency."

"Yeah, I thought that might be the case. What about a fight?"

"Like a bar fight? That's what bouncers are for."

"What about a big fight, between rival Tong? You saw the headlines about the 'Tong War' the papers think is going on. Shouldn't the police be interested in stopping that kind of violence? Bad for the city."

"Is this fight going on right now?"

"No, but if you can get your men in place in the next ninety minutes, I can pretty much guarantee there will be a disturbance in the club."

"Kats ..." Blackstone began, and Kats finished for him.

"I know this isn't how law enforcement works. But someone I care deeply about is in there and in trouble. Plus, we both know that there's a ton of bad stuff going on in there. You can say that the police were responding to the fight and discovered the drugs, the gambling, the prostitution ... who knows the extent of the operation. Please, Elliot."

Blackstone took a deep breath, thinking back on the times that Kats had helped him, had helped the police department with information and leads on some very bad actors. Kats wasn't one to remind him of those favors. He knew it was his own job to remember. "All right, Kats. What do you need?"

After hanging up with Elliot, Kats dropped more coins into the pay phone. After two rings, it connected. "*Wéi.*"

"This is Kats Takemoto. I need to speak with Lin Tai Lo immediately." Kats knew that John wasn't likely at the Hop Sing Tong headquarters, but he had to start somewhere. A few moments later, a familiar voice came on the line.

"Hello, Kats," said Lin Tai Lo.

"John! I didn't think you would be there, but I'm glad you are."

"Lately it feels like I'm always here. What can I do for you? Do you have something on my cousin's killer?"

"Not exactly, but I do have something on the Hei Long and people behind the operation Mai was involved in. I can explain later, but right now I need your help."

"I'm listening," John replied.

"We have sent two women, my ... partner, Molly, and another woman inside the Hong Kong Club to learn more about the drug operation. But I fear things may have gone bad. They are well overdue to come out, and I can't storm in there alone. I need a diversion. I need the Hop Sing Tong."

Kats went on to explain the rough plan he'd hastily sketched out to get the police to raid the Hong Kong Club in response to a 'disturbance' inside the club. The Hop Sing Tong would start an altercation that the police would respond to, allowing Kats the diversion to find Molly and Lola. "So, that's what I need," Kats finished.

There was silence on the end of the line, and Kats momentarily wondered if they'd been cut off. "John? Are you there?"

"I am," he replied. Kats heard him draw a deep breath before he said, "The Hop Sing Tong can't help you."

"John, please ..."

"There's been an official peace between the Tong since before the war. Father Sun has made preserving that peace a priority, and even if I disagree with that, I'm honor bound to not allow Hop Sing soldiers to break that peace." Kats felt his heart sink along with the only option he could currently see. "However, I'm free to have a drink with an old friend in any club in Chinatown. Even the Hei Long stronghold. That's part of the peace."

Kats began to see where John was going. "And if you were to have a drink with an old friend, such as me ..."

"And that old friend said something that offended my

honor, I'd be perfectly justified in fighting him, no matter where we happened to be," John finished.

"Can you meet me outside the club in an hour?" Kats asked.

"See you there."

Thorne and his men had started with drinks at the bar on the first floor. Esteban favored tequila, while Zapek and Collins stuck with whiskey. Thorne slowly drank his beer. After several rounds there, they'd been invited by Dragon Eye Wen to his second-floor court, where they overlooked the three-quarters-filled club. Wen quickly assessed that Thorne was the leader of this crew, and he peppered the man with questions about Hauser and the operation he now housed upstairs but didn't fully understand.

"I know nothing about drugs and prostitutes save that I have a taste for both," Thorne replied with a smirk and a raised glass. "Speaking of which, I think my men and I would like to visit your rooms upstairs." Wen nodded, and with a wave of his hand had one of his men lead Thorne's men up the stairs. Before Thorne could follow, Wen raised his hand and stepped forward.

"Mr. Thorne, a moment please." Collins looked back at Thorne, a silent conversation between the two men. Thorne nodded, and Collins turned and walked up the stairs. Wen gestured for Thorne to sit and then followed suit.

"What do you know about the Tong, Mr. Thorne?" Wen asked.

Thorne shrugged, "More than most, less than some."

"That's a very Chinese answer, Mr. Thorne," Wen smiled.

"Just 'Thorne.' The 'mister' makes me nervous," Thorne said, sipping his beer.

"Yes, Thorne. But that isn't your real name, is it?" Wen grinned. "You don't seem like a Larry to me."

"It's a name. I've had many, and they're just like any other uniform I've worn."

"Yes, you have the look of a man who's seen battle. A man who has led men in battle." Thorne gave a noncommittal shrug, and Wen continued. "Do you think that the Tong could rule this city?" Wen asked. "There are more than a dozen Tong, some bigger, some smaller. But all together, we would have over a thousand soldiers if we could unite under one leader. That's more than all the police officers in San Francisco."

"The mafia and some of the other gangs might have something to say about your takeover plans," Thorne replied.

"Ha. The mafia family here was attacked a year ago and still hasn't recovered. The low-level street gangs of the Blacks and the Hispanics fight for neighborhoods. I want to bring organization to the underworld here. I want to be what the Triads are in Hong Kong. I want to be *the* power in San Francisco."

"Well, the guns should help," Thorne said, getting up. "Good luck."

"We could use a combat leader," Wen pressed. "Someone who knows how to not only use those guns but deploy the men carrying them. I think you might be that man, Thorne."

Thorne was slowly shaking his head as Wen said, "How does it end for a man like you otherwise, Thorne? A soldier, moving from battleground to battleground. Maybe you're the lucky one to get to old age, but most likely you'll die in some far-off place, just a pawn in some government operation. But say you do make it through. You have what? A pension? A few medals? The gratitude of your country?" Wen laughed bitterly. "I can offer you money and power and a way to enjoy life. Here and now, not at the end of your days when your body is used up and broken down."

Thorne stood still, looking downward, his expression unreadable. Finally, he said, "You make an interesting case. I shall consider it," he said carefully. "But tonight I'll partake of more earthly pleasures." Wen smiled and made a gesture to the door.

"Of course. Please enjoy the bounty of our house."

Kats looked at his watch. Just after 1 am. He stood up the block from the Hong Kong Club, Shig by his side, looking nervously up and down the street. "Hey, relax. Your part in this is pretty simple."

"Yeah, I know. Just anxious to get started," Shig replied.

"Me too, but Elliot and his men won't be in place for at least thirty more minutes." Looking up the still busy street, Kats caught sight of a tall figure in a lightweight jacket, a white shirt, and chinos. "There's John," he said to Shig. The powerfully built man approached and nodded to Kats and Shig.

"Thanks for coming," Kats said. "This is my friend Shig Murao ..."

"From the bookstore. Yes, I read about you," John said, causing Shig to blush and smile. He extended a hand, which John shook.

"Shig is coming in with us. We need him to make this work. Normally bouncers break up a bar fight. Once we start our 'fight,' he'll run out of the club, yelling for the police, which will be their signal to come into the club." John nodded.

"Can you two guys make a big enough diversion?" Shig

asked.

Kats and John looked at each other, remembering their sparring sessions back in college, where they'd pushed each other to their limits. "We should be able to make a good show of it," Kats said with a sly grin at John. Kats looked at his watch and said, "Let's go. We can get into place."

They walked to the other end of the block, and as they approached the entrance, the doorman, who seemed bored, stared at John with a look of recognition. John simply ignored him and walked into the headquarters of his blood enemies. "I think they recognized you, John," Kats said quietly as they moved toward the main bar.

"As they should. But under the terms of the peace agreement, I'm free to be here. They'll watch us, though."

"That should work to our advantage," Kats said as they found a table near the bar. As they sat down, a Chinese man dressed in a tuxedo came to the table and gave a small bow.

"Welcome, Mr. Lin. A pleasure to have you with us tonight." John gave a small nod of his head. "Please enjoy a round of drinks on the house," the man said as a pretty waitress in a black *cheongsam* dress came to their table, smiled a tired smile, and asked for their drink order.

"In that case, I'll have a Brandy Alexander," Shig said, getting the evil eye from Kats.

"I'll have a beer," Kats said, and John nodded as well.

"Actually, change mine to a Coke please," Shig added.

John looked around the busy club, noting the mix of Asian faces, with some Black but mostly White patrons. All the staff were Asian, though not all were Chinese. "Too many of our people serving drinks and not enough of them having drinks," John said with sigh.

"Lin Tai Lo. Welcome!" said Dragon Eye Wen as he approached their table. "You honor us with your presence," he said with a slight bow of the head.

"Good evening, Wen Tsui Shen," John said as he remained seated but turned slightly in his chair and returned the gesture.

"To what do we owe the pleasure?" Wen asked with false hospitality.

"Catching up with some old friends," John gestured to Kats and Shig. "They'd heard about the club and wanted to see for themselves."

Wen barely glanced at Kats and Shig, still trying to understand why his primary competition for control of Chinatown was sitting in his club.

"If your friends would like to partake of our many other pleasures, they're most welcome. As are you, Lin Tai Lo," he said with a slight smirk. John stared straight ahead, and Kats could tell he was striving for self-control. Wen continued.

"There's no reason why you and I shouldn't be friends. We're the next generation of leadership in Chinatown. As allies, as partners, there's much we could do. You should consider it." John's face was icy, and Kats worried that his iron control was being tested at that moment.

Just then their drinks arrived, and Kats relaxed a bit as John thanked the waitress and took a sip of his beer. Wen stared a moment and then turned and retreated back across the bar. "Clearly, he was happy to see you," Kats said sarcastically.

"He has much ambition," John said, taking another sip of his beer. "But he thinks far too much of himself and not enough about our people."

Shig's fingers nervously twiddled on the table. "So, how are you guys going to start this?" Shig asked. "I mean, it has to look convincing."

"We'll make it look convincing," Kats said, looking at his watch. "We just need to wait another ten minutes or so to make sure the police are in place outside."

Shig nodded, took a sip of his Coke, and looked between the two men. "So, how did you guys meet?"

"We met in college. San Francisco University," Kats said with a smile. "I used the GI Bill to go to school. We met in a philosophy class."

"Yes," John continued, "we argued about Plato and the romantic ideal. Rubbish."

"He tried to explain that Nietzsche wasn't a nihilistic ego-maniac," Kats countered.

"Still with the relativism, Katsuhiro," John said with a grimace.

"The real trouble started when he introduced me to his cousin Gracie," Kats said.

"The Tiger Lady!" Shig said with a smile, recalling their meeting with the black-market queen of Chinatown the previous year as they were acquiring some special supplies for the confrontation with the Lanza crime family. "She was a little scary."

"Back then she was a journalism major," Kats said. "We all spent a lot of time together."

"What happened to you guys?" Shig asked, sensing the tension between these two old friends.

"Family obligations," John said.

"Tong obligations," Kats countered.

"For me they're one and the same," John said and finished his beer. "You didn't understand that then, and you still don't."

"You were the first one in your family to go to college.

You could have been so much more than a ..." Kats caught himself.

"Than a what, Katsuhiro? A Tong? A gang member? A criminal?" John said, anger now coming into his voice. "That's always how you've seen the Hop Sing Tong. Admit it."

"I admit that it makes me sad thinking about what might have been," Kats said.

"So, I could have been more like you, Takemoto? A man disconnected from his family? You can't even talk to your father about who you really are!"

Now Shig could see anger crossing Kats' face. He'd rarely seen his friend truly angry, but the flush in his face now wasn't from the alcohol. "Ahhh guys ..." Shig said as the two men glared across the table from each other.

"It was a good thing my cousin ended things with you," John said, "I told her that our family wouldn't accept a Japanese." John poked the old wound in Kats.

"So you were part of that whole deal with her? She said it was her family, but I didn't think you were part of that. I thought we were friends!"

"We may have been friends, but that doesn't mean you were good enough for my cousin," John said, leaning forward and staring into Kats' face.

Kats felt his face flush, and he stood up, pushing his chair backward. John stood as well, and with his right hand, he tossed the table aside and let out a blood-curdling "*Kiaaaiii!*" as he launched himself at Kats. In an instant the two men were locked in combat.

Shig stood for a second, thinking he should pull them apart. Then he remembered the plan. He looked around and saw the nearby patrons pull back. Then some began to cheer at the new entertainment. From the corners of the bar he could see several men, bouncers, rush forward. He stepped back and headed quickly toward the door. As he reached the atrium, the sound of crashing glass filled the room.

CHAPTER 20

Kats felt John's powerful hands slide up his chest toward his face. *He's trying to control my head*, he thought, and twisted to bring his arm over top of John's outstretched hands. Dropping his weight, he cleared John's hands and used his forward momentum to push him into the bar. As he followed, hoping to take this momentary advantage, John fired a back kick that caught Kats in the midsection. With a grunt, he fell backward, rolled, and came up just as John stepped forward and grabbed him. Kats felt himself lifted off his center, a bad position to be in. John could have flipped him and driven him into the floor, but to his surprise Kats found himself lifted and then airborne over the bar, crashing into the wall of bottles and glass behind the bar.

Glass and liquor showered down on him, and as he stood, Kats saw that two large bouncers had reached John. The first tried to wrap his arms around him from behind. John dropped to one knee, pulled the bouncer's arm forward and over his shoulder, and then flipped him to the floor, where he landed with an audible thud. The second bouncer tried to deliver a straight punch to John's head but was surprised when his target slid under the blow. He was even more surprised when John's open palm found his chin, knocking him up and backward. Kats smiled, thinking *nice move*. He could see several more bouncers approaching as he hopped over the bar and squared off against John again.

Shig ran out into the cool night air, the neon lights of

Chinatown swirling around him. "Help!" he yelled. "Help! There's a riot inside! Help! Call the police!" he screamed into the night. People on the street turned to look. Behind him he saw the doorman rush inside, and as he turned to look across the street, he saw uniformed San Francisco policemen rushing around the corner toward the door. He jumped up and down, pointing inside, "Riot! Inside, there's a riot!"

John and Kats looked into each other's eyes, but in their peripheral vision they could see the approaching men. Their training let them feel the approach, and they exchanged a slight nod, which launched them into action. To an outside observer it looked as if they'd charged each other and missed, instead hitting the approaching men. Kats swept a leg, taking a man down as he twisted and redirected a charging guard into one of his compatriots. Over his shoulder he saw three men clinging to John, trying to bring him down. He was about to intervene when a shout came from the front of the club. "*Jingcha!*" Police.

At the shout of *jingcha,* panic erupted in the club as the patrons and employees scurried like roaches when a light is turned on. The bouncers released John and rushed toward the stairs in the back. Kats looked up to the second-floor balcony and caught a glimpse of Dragon Eye Wen shouting at his men. He pointed toward the stairs and said to John, "Let's go!"

As he ran up the stairs, Kats could hear the shouting behind him as the police yelled for people to stop. As he hit the second-floor landing, four Black Dragons, armed with clubs, charged him. The first approached, and Kats knocked the lead man back into the others. Kats twisted the fallen man's arm, wrenching the club away, which fell to the ground.

Kats deftly put his foot under the fallen weapon and popped it upward into the hand of John, who stormed up the steps behind him. He gave a swing that took down another man. Then he dropped down to backhand the next man across his knee. The man fell, howling in pain. "Go, I've got them," John said, and Kats took off up the stairs, his heart racing and his eyes searching for Molly.

In a candlelit room on the third floor, Lauri Törni, aka Larry Thorne, sat bolt upright in the large bed, almost throwing the tiny Chinese girl off of him. She had been exuberant if not highly skilled, but even her vigorous movements astride him couldn't turn off Thorne's battle instincts. The noise came up from below, and he knew something was happening. Pushing the girl aside, he went to the door and stuck his head out. Men were running down the hall, and from below he heard shouts and what had to be fighting. Across the hall, another door opened, and Leroy Collins stepped out into the hallway, completely naked with a huge erection. His dark skin glistened like he'd been working out, which, Thorne surmised, he had been.

"Trouble, boss?" Collins said, and Thorne nodded.

"Best we make an exit," Thorne replied. "Where are Zapek and Esteban?"

"I left them at the bar a while ago."

"*Paska*," Thorne swore, reverting to Finnish. "They'll have to find their own way out. Get some clothes on. We're going up and out the fourth floor." Ten seconds later, both men had on their clothes and headed up the stairs as the cries from below grew louder.

On the fourth floor, Dragon Eye Wen snarled at his men,

"Slow down the police!" and he pointed down the stairs. At least a dozen men charged down the stairs toward the conflict with the police. Wen pointed to several more men, "Take the weapons down the fire escape and to the hospital." The men nodded and raced into the storeroom. Wen turned to see Hauser's man, Stiles, approaching him.

"What the hell is going on?" Stiles asked. Wen stepped forward and punched him in the face, dropping Stiles to the floor as he grasped his nose.

"This is your doing!" Wen spat at the prostrate man. "You bring the police, the *gwaipo* women," he kicked Stiles. *The White women*, he thought. *Chinese girls wouldn't talk, but the White women could be a problem.* He shouted to one of his men who was racing down the hall.

"Li! Come here!" The young Black Dragon came running.

"There are two *gwaipo* in the den down the hall. They're under the dragon's breath. We must get them out of the building. Take them down the fire escape and to the hospital."

"The hospital, *sifu?*" the young man asked, not comprehending.

"Down Cooper Alley," Wen said, pushing the young man down the hallway. "Quickly!" As they raced down the hall, Wen saw Thorne and his Black companion come up the stairs.

"This a regular occurrence, Wen?" Thorne snorted.

"*Jingcha*," Wen replied. "Police. Come. We exit down here," and he pushed past them.

At the end of the hallway, Wen threw open a door and signaled for his man to enter. Thorne looked into the small room and saw two women splayed out on the twin couches. A sickly sweet smell hit his nose. Opium. And judging from their state, these two were deep in the poppy. "The police can't find these women here," Wen said. "Bring them," he ordered.

"Not our fucking problem," Thorne replied, watching the young Tong struggle to pick up the blond woman.

"You're Hauser's man, so yes, it *is* your fucking problem!" Wen shouted.

Dammit, thought Thorne. He looked at Collins and nodded. The ex-marine strode inside and grabbed the blond woman from Li's arms and tossed her over his shoulder like a fireman carrying a small child. Thorne moved in behind him and pulled the other woman, a redhead, up by the arms. He got her in a seated position and was about to hoist her up when he saw her eyes open, unfocused at first, then blinking quickly. He started to pull her up, but she went rigid and pushed back from him.

"No time for this," he said, hitting the woman in the stomach. Once the air left her lungs, she collapsed forward into his arms, and he hoisted her up and moved out of the room. He followed Wen to the end of the hall, which led to a metal landing outside a large window. In a moment, they were out the window, onto the fire escape, and headed down into the dark alley.

Kats raced up and down the third-floor hallway, looking into bedrooms at several women in various stages of undress. Clients were throwing on clothes and heading for the stairs. A few Black Dragons raced past him on their way downstairs to confront the police. Kats looked like a confused john in the chaos. He turned and raced up to the fourth floor. To his left as he reached the landing he saw a man struggling to get up. It was the man Lola had identified. Stiles. Kats ran toward him as he stood up on wobbly legs. Then he grabbed the man by his shirt front and slammed him into the wall.

"Where is she?" he shouted into the man's pained and bloody face.

Stiles shook his head, "Who?" he breathed, which brought Kats' fist into his belly, and he collapsed forward. Kats held him up and slammed him against the wall again.

"The redhead and the blond. Where are they?" Stiles weakly raised his hand and pointed down the hall. Kats released him, and the man fell to the floor. Running to the end of the hall, Kats saw the open window and the landing of the fire escape. He turned and looked into the small room with the open door. Two couches. Empty. And that smell. He knew that smell. Opium.

Kats heard a door open behind him. Turning, he saw two Hei Long soldiers stride toward him. Each held a hatchet in hand. "*Jingcha!*" yelled the bald one as he charged, followed by his partner. All thoughts of restraint had left Kats, and where he might have had some mercy on soldiers caught up in a fight bigger than themselves, tonight he didn't have time. He squared up on the charging man, and as the man rushed in, Kats dove forward, tucking into a tight roll that took the lead man's legs out. He fell over Kats with an ungraceful thud. The second man had a moment to halt his charge, which gave Kats the opening he needed. From the ground, he spun and swung his right leg low, catching the Tong below the knees, knocking him off his feet. Kats was on him in a flash, driving his elbow into the man's face. He felt bone and cartilage give way. Kats rolled off him as the first man was struggling to his feet.

The bald Tong twirled his hatchet in a show of intimidation, not realizing he couldn't intimidate this opponent.

With a shout he sprung forward, swinging the ax in a deadly arc. Kats stepped inside the arc and caught the man's right arm in his left hand. Then he used the man's momentum to continue forward, now under Kats' control. With a slight step and a pivot, Kats drove the man, shoulder first, into the floor. The man screamed as his collarbone broke and his hatchet fell from numb fingers. Kats rolled him on his back, placing his knee on the man's heaving chest.

"Where are the girls?" Kats demanded.

Through bloody lips, the man laughed, "Girls are everywhere. Take pick."

"The White girls? The redhead?"

"Fucking *gwaipo*," said the man. Then he spit at Kats.

In *budo*, the Japanese martial arts, some techniques are quietly taught. Some of these techniques kill, some maim, and some cause excruciating pain. Even though Kats' father was, by Western standards, a pacifist, he knew these techniques. When Kats had grown into an athletic teen, his father had begun to teach him these skills, but always with the caution of when to use them—only in great need and self-defense. Kats had been an apt pupil and had learned well.

Kats leaned forward and found the pressure point on the right side of the man's neck, below the ear. The *koppo* technique used only his left thumb to apply pressure on that nerve cluster. The man felt heat at first, radiating from his neck, into his shoulder, down his arm, and then upward into the base of his skull. It felt like liquid fire filling a balloon. The man screamed.

"Where?" asked Kats in a flat voice he didn't recognize. The balloon kept filling. The man screamed again and tried to twist out of the viselike grip that held him.

"Where?!" Kats shouted.

"Kats!" Elliot Blackstone yelled as he came racing down the hall, followed by another officer.

"Cooper ... Cooper Alley" cried the man, and Kats released him.

"My God, Kats. You're better than that!" Blackstone said.

"Not tonight, Elliot. There's too much at stake." He turned and went out the window that opened onto the fire escape. From the dark alley below he heard sounds but couldn't make out who was down there. He looked out toward the lit street and saw several people exiting the alley. Some looked to be carrying boxes, and others appeared to be carrying—"Molly!" he said out loud. He flew down the metal steps.

Zapek and Esteban stood at the bar, laughing as the club exploded into chaos around them. As the bartenders rushed to get clear of the oncoming police, Zapek reached over the bar and liberated a nearly full bottle of Jack Daniels. Smiling, he showed it to Esteban, "Zis is the good stuff," he said in his thick French accent. He poured shots for the two of them, which they quickly downed and refilled.

Esteban looked serious for a moment. "Should we see about Thorne and Collins?" he asked.

"*Non*," said Zapek. "They probably won't even stop with their exercise for the *gendarmes*." He toasted, "To *les belles filles!*" As Esteban joined him, two uniformed officers carrying nightsticks approached them.

"All right, you two," said the older cop, "turn around and put your hands on the bar."

He gestured with the nightstick, and Esteban and Zapek broke out in drunken laughter.

"*Pourquoi?*" asked the Frenchman. "We're only drinking,

mon ami. Is this not what one is supposed to do in a bar?" he winked at the man.

"Tell it to the judge," said the younger cop, not used to having orders questioned. He stepped forward and pointed to the bar, "Hands on the bar," he said as he grabbed the smaller Esteban by the shoulder. Instead of turning toward the bar, Esteban stepped forward and headbutted the young officer, the crown of his head finding the soft center of the man's face. The officer collapsed backward, blood spurting from a broken nose.

Shock, then anger, registered on the face of the older officer. He stepped forward and raised his club toward Esteban. In that moment, Zapek's right foot came slicing upward, catching the officer on the side of the head. He fell like a tree. Esteban looked at his compatriot, who smiled.

"*Savate,*" he said. "The French art of fighting with the feet."

"Fucking French," Esteban said with a shake of his head. "You fight with your feet and make love with your faces."

"Jealous?" Zapek said with a grin as he took the bottle of whiskey from the bar.

"Come on. Let's get out of here before some idiot starts shooting," Esteban said, and they headed toward the door with the last of the fleeing patrons.

CHAPTER 21

As they cleared the alley behind the Hong Kong Club, the Black Dragons headed up to Jackson and then turned right, moving away from the club. Wen directed his men, looking back to see if any police had followed. He pointed down the sidewalk where a narrow cut-through, barely an alley, divided the clusters of buildings. Cooper Alley wasn't for tourists, and even the locals avoided it. Deep in the recesses of the buildings, the local brothels had set up what they loosely called, 'The Hospital,' where girls from the various houses were sent for medical treatment. This ranged from treatment for the clap, to stiches when overzealous clients got out of hand, to literal back-alley abortions. Wen led them down the dark alley to a set of stairs that ran down into a basement space below. As they entered, a middle-aged man, dressed in a dark gray *hanfu,* stepped forward. He bowed, recognizing Wen.

"*Sifu,* Wen," he said. "This ..." he gestured to the men, the crates, and the unconscious White women, "this is most unusual."

The Hei Long—in fact, all of the Tong—were welcome there, but only if it was related to their women. Showing up here with guns and captives was against the rules, but Wen didn't care. He turned to the man and said, "Find a place for them," he gestured toward Thorne and Collins, who carried the two women. The gray-suited man bowed and escorted Thorne and Collins deeper inside the cave-like basement. Wen stood, inwardly seething at the invasion of his base. He had paid off the appropriate people in the police department. He should have gotten a warning. Someone would pay for this. He wondered if the appearance of Lin Tai Lo from the hated Hop Sing Tong was connected. The girls and the liquor could be replaced. He had the guns. *This only delayed the plans*, he told himself.

Molly imagined she was riding a horse. A weirdly shaped, uncomfortable horse. The world seemed to sway every time she moved her head, and she felt like she could throw up. When the uncomfortable horse ride stopped, she found herself on a bed, in a dimly lit room, surrounded by other beds. She felt like her head was stuffed with cotton, and she had to blink multiple times to get her eyes to focus. As she looked up, she saw a strange face looking down at her. A blond man, handsome in a hard way, sat on her bedside. She tried to talk but could only hear malformed sounds coming from her mouth. Then she remembered. The pipe, the smoke, the opium!

The blond man gave her a smile and said something that she thought might have been, "Low dead." He sounded far away. She rose onto an elbow and gave a slight shake of her head. "What?" formed in her mouth.

"Hello, red," the blond man repeated.

She blinked and mouthed, "Where?"

"I have no fucking idea. Chinatown is like another world. Around every corner is something hidden and secret. I just wanted a drink tonight. Maybe a little company."

Molly felt more of herself returning as she looked over the man's shoulder to the bed next to her. Lola lay there, still unconscious. Her focus returned to the blond man when she realized he had his hand on her stomach.

"Sorry about the jab earlier," he said, giving her belly a pat. "Had to get you out of there, you know." It seemed like he was talking to another person, but his closeness was all she could feel. "What was a lovely girl like you doing in a place like that?"

Her brain sluggishly tried to process that question when shouts came from far away and the blond man's head snapped around. A moment later he was gone, and Molly wondered if she'd imagined him.

As Kats emerged from the end of the alley onto Jackson Street, he looked up the street and heard a shout.

"Kats!" Shig yelled as he jumped up and down at the corner. He waved at him as Kats ran forward. "That way!" he pointed down the street. "They went up an alley in the middle of the block." Crossing over to the next block, Kats raced forward with Shig on his heels. They came to the tiny entrance of Cooper Alley. Kats held an arm out, stopping Shig short of running in.

"This must be where they turned in," Shig said excitedly. Kats nodded and then squatted down before easing his head around the corner. Shig hunkered down beside him.

"Recon trick," Kats said as he peered down the alley. "Don't put your head where they expect it. Too easy to get shot."

"Good to know," Shig quipped. "See anything?"

"Some lights down deep in the alley, and I think I saw some movement a second ago."

"What's the plan?" Shig asked. "Get the cops?"

"No," Kats said firmly. "We go get them."

"Is this your professional opinion?"[10]

"Follow me." He was up and moving quickly before Shig could object. Kats stayed to the right side of the narrow alley, mostly avoiding the small pools of light that barely illuminated the way forward. Shig tried his best to follow quietly. Shig could sense more than see the end of the alley and the open doorways into a basement. Dim lights appeared below, and Shig could hear voices and movement. Kats turned to him and signaled for him to stop with an upheld palm. Kats leaned toward him and whispered in his ear.

"Wait until you hear them coming after me, and then slip in and find Molly and Lola." Kats' eyes looked huge in the near darkness, and Shig gave a nod. Kats thumped him on the shoulder and turned toward the stairs. In a swift, silent movement, he was down them and into the basement below.

Kats' sharp eyes adjusted to the candlelight that filled the basement. As he reached the bottom of the stairs he saw a large, open room that extended far back below the buildings above. The ceiling was low and made of thick wooden timbers and open pipework, making him think this had been built as a service area but now appeared to be some kind of flophouse. Beds and cots lined the walls, and there had to be a dozen or so people ... women, he now realized ... stretched out on them. Several older women moved about tending to them. It reminded him of the field hospitals during the war, and then he realized that's exactly what this was: a clinic of some kind treating these women. No one was paying attention to him as they watched the Tong soldiers who were moving a number of wooden crates against the far wall. There, directing the work, stood Dragon Eye Wen. Kats moved forward, taking cover behind one of the many thick columns that marked the expanse. As he stood behind the column, trying to decide his next move, a shout came from the darkness.

"Aaayaaa! What you doing there?" screamed a tiny old woman who carried a basin of water. At the shout, the eyes across the room turned toward Kats' hiding place, and he knew he had to move. With a "Go for Broke" move that the 442nd Regimental Combat Team had made famous, he charged forward toward the group of men.

The momentary shock of seeing a single man charge out of the shadows from across the room passed quickly among the experienced Tong fighters. By the time Kats reached them, they were ready, eight against one. As he approached the first man, Kats gave a great "*Kiiaaiii!*" which momentarily froze them, and then to their surprise, he ran back toward the shadows.

Wen screamed at his men, "Get him!" and they charged after him. Kats jumped over an occupied bed and then tossed a chair toward the men, tripping the leader, and slowing the rest of them down. Thus began an almost comic chase scene as Kats used the columns, the beds, the nurses, and the pursuing men themselves as obstacles in what appeared to be an adult game of tag. That's how it looked to Shig, who was creeping down the opposite wall as this Marx Brothers–like spectacle played out.

Shig headed deeper into the recesses of the basement, peering into a couple of supply closets, and then going down a dimly lit corridor. Behind him he heard a huge crash that he imagined wasn't a good sign for Kats, but he kept to his mission. Ahead of him, he saw movement and the outline of a man. Then another appeared. The men rushed forward, and Shig pressed himself to the wall and saw a blond White man followed by a big Black man move down the corridor. Shig braced himself for a blow that didn't come, as they weren't interested in him. They moved back toward the action and toward Kats. Shig fought a sinking feeling and pressed forward. At the end of the corridor, the basement opened up to another large room, but this one had a series of small doors that separated the space. The first door on his right was slightly ajar, and candlelight could be seen from within. He cautiously pushed the door open.

"Molly!" he shouted. He raced to her bedside where she sat, clearly dazed. He raised her face to look at her eyes and could tell she was drugged. She blinked, and he heard her say, "Shig?"

"Molly, we're here. We're gonna get you out." She nodded, forcing herself to sit up.

"Help Lola," she said, pointing to the adjacent bed, where the blond woman was lying unconscious. Shig turned to her and gave a shake, which elicited a groan, but her eyes remained closed.

"I can't carry both of you," Shig said desperately. "I promised Kats I'd get you out."

"Help me up. I can walk," she said, not actually sure she could. Shig pulled her up, and she fought the nausea and the dizziness. She took a deep breath and gave Shig a thumbs up. "Get her," she said.

With surprising strength, Shig lifted Lola and carried her in his arms out the door and back through the corridor. Molly placed a hand on his shoulder to steady herself, and the three of them moved back toward the light.

Kats was running out of time and moves. He'd successfully evaded the pursuing men as he leaped, rolled, twisted, and cartwheeled around the dimly lit space. Along the way, he'd managed to land several blows, and two of the men were down, but he was tiring, and the remaining men were now more cautious and not getting in each other's way as much as before. From the side, Wen shouted, "Get him, you fools!" Next to him stood two men who looked out of place: a lean blond man and a solidly built Black man. Kats had no time to ponder their connection to this because the Tong were now advancing in a broad formation, hoping to contain Kats. In a novel move, Kats charged to his left, toward the oncoming men. He then leaped onto an empty bed that sprung him over the outstretched arms of a surprised man. Kats landed and rolled forward, but as he started to rise, one of the downed men, not entirely unconscious, reached and grabbed his leg, which was just enough to slow him down, and the group of men pounced. As hands tried to grasp Kats, he twisted, kicked, and bit, but the sheer weight of them eventually brought him down.

As they stood him up, Wen approached, looking at Kats

with recognition. "You," he said, "you were with Lin Tai Lo. What's the meaning of this?" He stepped forward and drove his fist into Kats' stomach. Even braced for the blow, Kats doubled over.

From the dark corridor, Shig and Molly watched with horror as Kats fell to the Tong. Molly cried out, but Shig held her back. "You can't do anything," he whispered to her. "Stay here with Lola."

"What are you gonna do?"

"What Kats would do. Go for broke." He gave her a nod and, taking a deep breath, he charged out of the darkness.

As Wen grabbed Kats by the hair, turning his face upward, the room filled with a shout, *"Banzai!"* Faces turned toward the sounds, and from the darkness a man charged forward, arms raised and face defiant. The sheer audacity and stupidity of the attack momentarily froze all of them, which is all that Kats needed. He twisted loose, firing quick punches to the left and right, and then throwing the man who was behind him forward, into the surprised Wen. As the Tong turned toward the onrushing Shig, Kats clipped two of them from behind with elbows that dropped them to the floor. Reaching Shig, they turned shoulder to shoulder as the Tong regrouped and advanced.

"This is a bit more than I was hoping for tonight," Thorne said to Collins as they watched the strange battle before them. "Time to go," he said, and Collins gave a grunt of approval. They skirted the periphery of the conflict and moved toward the stairs that would take them up to the alley. As they approached the stairs, someone came charging down the stairs and, reaching the basement floor, the man bellowed, "Wen!"

The men approaching Kats and Shig stopped at the shout behind them, and all eyes turned toward Lin Tai Lo, who stood there, his shirt ripped and a cut on his left cheek, but his eyes blazing with intensity as he searched the room for the rival Tong leader. "Dragon Eye, face me. I challenge you to personal combat. Face me if you have any honor!"

Behind the man, Thorne stopped short and held Collins back, "Wait. This just got interesting," he said, and they stepped back into the shadows.

John stepped forward toward the circle of men and pointed toward Wen. "You see yourself as the next leader of Chinatown. Let's settle that question right now, without the bloodshed of our men. You and me for the future of Chinatown." All eyes moved between this newcomer and the Hei Long leader. Wen seethed with anger and the fear of being humiliated in front of all these people. He knew he was a skilled fighter, but he also knew Lin Tai Lo had been the main enforcer for the Hop Sing. He considered ordering his men to attack, knowing they would do so, but word would spread throughout the Hei Long and then to all of Chinatown. He ground his teeth and sneered at John.

"Hop Sing dog! I will parade your broken body through Chinatown," he pointed, stepping forward and removing his outer coat. John stepped forward, and a circle formed in the heart of the basement.

Momentarily forgotten, Shig whispered to Kats, "The girls are in the corridor there," he pointed to the darkened recess of the room. Kats rushed forward, slipping into the darkness, and there, leaning against the back wall, Molly stood with an arm around Lola.

"God, are you OK?" Kats asked as his hands found her shoulders and he looked into her eyes. She nodded, seemingly a bit drunk.

"Opium," she said, with a slight slur to her speech. He nodded as Shig appeared at his shoulder.

"Can you carry Lola?" he asked, and Shig stepped forward and lifted the blond woman. Kats pulled Molly up and put her arm over his shoulder, and they moved forward to the stairs.

No one paid them any heed as John and Dragon Eye stood at opposite sides of the circle. Reaching the stairs, the foursome struggled upward into the darkened alley. As they reached the top, Molly tapped Kats on the shoulder.

"What about John?" she said, her voice stronger now. "You can't leave him alone."

"I've got to get you and Lola out of here," he said and moved to pull them forward.

"I can walk," she said. "Apparently the Irish can handle their whiskey and opium better than most. We can get to the street."

"Cops should still be there," Shig offered, lifting Lola, whose eyes were fluttering. "I got them," he said to Kats. "Help John."

"I can't interfere with his fight. John's honor wouldn't permit it, and if an outsider intervened, everything could go to hell."

"You can't leave John alone," Molly said fiercely. "Shig, let's go," and she started down the alley. She met Kats' eyes and gave him a firm nod, which he returned. Then he headed back down into the basement as sounds of combat rose to his ears.

When two masters from a similar martial discipline square off, there's a subtlety to their interaction that may seem odd to an outside observer. As Kats watched, Wen and John moved slowly around each other, each in a similar stance favored by kung-fu practitioners. Their weight slightly back, front leg lightly pointed toward the opponent. Their arms were raised, and their open hands moved like blades back and forth. Each step was a measurement, a test of the other, and a search for an opening. Kats was familiar with kung-fu, having observed several different styles of the Chinese martial art over the years. He'd trained with John back in college and understood the rudimentary positions well enough to see that, like John, Wen was a master. John was younger and looked bigger and stronger, but those advantages were no guarantee of victory.

Wen hopped forward and, with blinding speed, flicked his extended fingers toward John's eyes. John expertly deflected the blow, countering with a lightning-fast strike of his own to Wen's face that was similarly turned aside. Wen swept his front leg forward in a low kick toward John's groin. John twisted slightly and raised his knee to block the blow. Wen's men began to shout encouragement to their leader. Somewhere a drum was being rhythmically pounded.

It was John who initiated the next attack that followed with another rapid-fire exchange of blows and blocks, but this one ended with an elbow strike to the side of Wen's head that pushed the Hei Long leader backward. John tried to maintain the advantage, but Kats saw that it had been a ruse by Wen to bring John inside. As the distance between them closed, the bone hard side of Wen's left hand struck John near his liver. John winced and spun sideways, putting distance between the two of them. Wen now seized the initiative.

He stepped forward, again firing toward John's eyes, but this time it was a feint to raise John's defenses, and Wen followed with a low stomp kick to John's front leg, staggering him. Wen initiated a flurry of strikes that John barely deflected until a blow landed on his cheek, again causing him to back away.

This isn't good, Kats thought. Wen is faster, and his style of kung-fu was cutting through John's defenses. Another flurry, again ending with a sharp blow to the face that sent John reeling back as he spit blood from his mouth. Wen turned to the crowd, raising his arms and urging them on. He faced John again, smiling malevolently, and waved for him to come forward.

Kats gritted his teeth, wanting to help his friend and attack Wen himself but knowing he couldn't. Then he recalled an argument he'd had with John years ago about boxing. Specifically, it was about the boxers Sugar Ray Robinson, one of the fastest and most skilled fighters of his generation, and the one man who gave Robinson fits: the tough brawler Jake LaMotta. Kats and John had argued about the merits of each fighter and whether skill or an iron jaw was the greater asset.

Kats yelled into the ring, "Jake LaMotta!"

As the two men circled each other again, Wen smiling cruelly as he saw John slightly drag his right foot. Kats noticed it too and was worried that John hadn't heard him until Wen advanced with another flurry aimed at his opponent's head. Unlike previous exchanges where parries and counters bounced back and forth, this time John covered like a boxer, his arms and hands in front of his face, and absorbed the blows as he rocked backward. Wen growled and attacked again, ferociously trying to reach the soft parts of John's head and torso. Again, he covered like a boxer in the corner, letting Wen expend massive amounts of energy. Then, just like Jake LaMotta, who was famous for his ability to absorb punishment to bring his opponent inside and then viciously counter, John pulled Wen in and threw a right cross that connected, followed by a left to the stomach that doubled Wen over and he reeled back, gasping for air. John stood hunched forward, chin low, and hands extended like a boxer, and now he waved for Wen to come forward.

Wen responded with a furious series of arm gestures, common in kung-fu and used to intimidate and confuse an opponent. John simply stood his ground, bobbing up and down on the balls of his feet. Wen charged forward, feinting high with his hands and thrusting a foot forward toward John's center. John caught the foot in his gut, a grunt escaping his lips, but he now had Wen in close range, and he threw a series of body shots to Wen that caused him to reel and pull back. As Wen staggered, feeling broken ribs moving, he felt John press forward. He caught John on the side of the head, but John's momentum carried him forward, driving Wen into the wall behind him. There John pinned him like a boxer pins another to the ropes, and he worked Wen's damaged body with a series of blows that made all watching wince in pain. John finished the flurry with a right uppercut that connected squarely with Wen's cheek, sending the man to the stone floor.

Kats raised his hands and shouted "Yes!" as the Hei Long looked on in astonishment. John staggered back, wiping the blood and sweat from his face. Unbelievably, Wen was struggling to stand, and even Kats was impressed with the man's strength. Kats saw Wen holding his stomach, thinking him holding broken ribs. Then, as he rose, Kats saw a glint of metal in his right hand. "Look out!" he shouted, but Wen was already moving forward.

John saw the man coming forward and covered again like a boxer would. This time as the blows landed, John felt a stinging up and down his left arm. Then, as Wen slashed his hand across John's legs, he felt the blade across his thigh. Wen was holding a 'push knife,' also known as a 'punch knife,' a short blade attached to a handle you held in your fist so that the blade protruded between your knuckles. *It must have been in his belt buckle,* John thought as he felt blood flow down his left arm from the holes Wen had punched into him. John backed up now, watching the deadly right hand with cautious eyes.

Wen stood. His left 'dragon eye' was swollen shut, and blood flowed from his cheek. He aimed the tiny dagger at John and stepped forward. Both men were tired, but Wen remained the faster of the two, and he threw his right hand forward, followed by a left kick that caught John's leg, opening him up for a follow-up from the knife that sunk into John's shoulder. John cried out in pain and, with a massive shove, threw Wen back into the arms of his men. Kats stepped forward, but John caught his gaze and gave a single violent shake of his head. *No!* John was telling him.

The two men now slowly circled each other, the Hei Long cheering their leader, despite his clear breach of honor. Kats tensed, knowing that he would not, could not, allow John to die, and if that meant disobeying his friend's orders, so be it. But Kats and John also knew something. They'd discussed it in their training and their musings on martial arts. People with weapons, even experienced fighters, often become fixated on the weapon, forgetting that they have other options and other less obvious weapons at their command. Kats saw John taking in the knife held before him. He also saw Wen licking his lips, twisting the knife back and forth, clearly fixed on the weapon. There was another lesson they'd discussed as well. The armed person didn't expect the unarmed person to attack, and John used that surprise to his advantage.

John had timed his charge so that Wen was caught between steps. That tiny gap was all he needed. He came in low and deflected toward Wen's left knowing that Wen would favor the blade in his right hand to counter. John's weight hit him on his left side as the right-hand blade swung over John's shoulder. Before Wen could pull back, John wrapped him up, lifting him off the ground, and then tipped forward, piledriving Wen into the hard stone floor. Kats saw the blade clatter into the darkness as Wen's semi-conscious hands opened involuntarily. John swung upon him, his fist raised to deliver a killing blow.

"John, no!" Kats yelled, stepping forward into the circle of light. "He's beaten, and everyone will know it." He took another step forward. John seemed to sway atop Wen, and Kats thought his friend might actually deliver the coup de grace, but John lowered his fist and sat back. Kats rushed to his side and helped him off Wen. He saw that John's left side was soaked in blood, and he looked for something to staunch the bleeding.

"Police! Everyone freeze!" came the shout from across the room. Kats looked up to see uniformed men flowing down the stairs. They fanned out, but people were scattering, fleeing deeper into the basement and other side exits. In the confusion, the Hei Long dragged the semi-conscious Wen into the darkness at the rear of the basement.

Coming down the stairs, Kats saw two familiar faces. First was Elliot Blackstone, and right behind him, Shig's anxious face searched the room for Kats. Seeing his friend,

Shig smiled and rushed over to them.

"You OK, man?" he asked Kats, who nodded.

"Help me with John. He needs medical attention."

"There's an ambulance back at the club," Shig said, and they lifted John under the arms. As they stood, Elliot came up to Kats.

"I'm going to have a hell of a time explaining all this, Kats," he said, and Kats laughed.

"Elliot, you're swearing,"

"Damn right I am," Blackstone continued. Then he smiled, "But it looks like we put a hurt on the Black Dragons. Thanks for the tip."

Kats nodded and said, "Thanks for trusting me." They turned and moved up the stairs and out to the main street, where two ambulances sat with lights flashing. Sitting in the back of one, Kats saw Molly, a medic looking her over. She saw Kats approach, smiled, and pushed the medic aside to exit the vehicle. Kats sat John down as the other medics came forward, and he rushed to his redheaded girl. She threw herself at him, and they embraced. They both felt tears on their cheeks as the fear and tension of the night finally gave way to relief. He held her close, whispering in her ear, "I've got you. I've always got you."

She said, "I knew you'd come for us. Shig, too," she smiled and looked over at the smiling bookseller, yet again an unlikely hero. "Is your friend OK?" she asked about John.

"I think so," he replied and looked over at John, who was on a stretcher being attended to by two medics. Kats and Molly walked over, his arm still around her, not wanting to let her go. He knelt beside John, whose eyes opened, and he gave a slight smile. "Jake LaMotta," John said with a wheeze and a smile.

"Jake LaMotta," Kats laughed but then turned serious. "Thank you for your help. I couldn't ... we ..." he struggled to find the words. John closed his eyes and nodded.

"Katsuhiro, I'm sorry about the words I said about your family. I was trying to get you fired up. I have no right to question another man's relationship with his family. Especially with his father." John reached out and clasped Kats' hand. Kats squeezed his hand back.

"We've got to get him to the hospital," said the medic. "He needs stitches to close these wounds." They lifted John's stretcher and moved him into the ambulance.

"See you soon," Kats said as they closed the door. Turning back to Molly and Shig who stood there watching, Kats felt a surge of emotion, and he reached out to embrace both of them. Hot tears filled his eyes, but laughter came from his mouth. He hugged them both fiercely. "I love you guys," he said and hugged them even tighter. They hugged him back, but after a few moments, Shig pulled back, a strange look on his face.

"What is it?" Kats asked. "You look like you're trying to do math in your head."

"This is gonna sound crazy," he said as he looked back down the street and then around the area like he was searching for someone, "but I think I saw our guy," he said.

"Our guy?" Kats asked.

"Steven Epps," Shig said.

CHAPTER 22

There's an anonymity to big cities. Thousands of people pass each other every day, with little thought or recognition. Going to a small town invites attention. People notice strangers in a small town, but in a big city like San Francisco, one can hide in plain sight. There's also something about the urban hustle and bustle. Epps found the city's pulse and constant noise oddly calming. When things were too quiet, the demons came. The city was like background noise, just enough to drown out the unkind voices in his head.

He liked to walk the city at night. More accurately, he *needed* to walk the city at night. Despite daily labors at construction sites or warehouses or the wharf, he still had too much energy to sleep. He found himself wandering the streets, often until 2 or 3 am, before returning to his bed and finding sleep. During those walks, he let his mind drift, and he took in the sights, the sounds, the smells of the city. One of his favorite places to walk had always been Chinatown, with its bright lights, colorful buildings, and busy streets. Even deep into the night, he found it soothing. But since the incident at the Jefferson Hotel, he'd been reluctant to venture there, lest that Chinese gang spot him again. Tonight, as he skirted the edge of Chinatown, he noticed sirens and people headed toward a brightly lit block. His natural curiosity drew him in. He raised the collar of his jacket and lowered the brim of his baseball cap as he approached the chaotic scene on Jackson Street.

As he watched from half a block away, he saw the Hong

Kong Club ringed by people and at least a dozen police officers. There were two paddy wagons parked out front. Closer to him were two ambulances that seemed to be treating cuts and bruises, but nothing too serious as far as he could tell. His eyes caught sight of an Asian man emerging from a narrow alley across the street, carrying a woman who appeared unconscious. Just behind him, another woman staggered, holding onto the wall, as she tried to move forward. Most every eye was focused up the street, so no one moved to help them. Epps crossed the street, reaching the trailing woman. He pulled her upward, supporting her as they walked toward the ambulances. She seemed to acknowledge him, but her eyes were a bit glassy, and she seemed to be drunk. She was lovely, he noticed, with long, red hair and pale, white skin.

Epps followed the Asian man as he delivered his armload to a medic, who immediately checked the woman, a pretty blond, for a pulse, nodded, and moved her into the ambulance. He led the woman forward, and then the Asian man turned to him, taking the redhead, and brought her to the ambulance. The Asian man turned to him, saying, "Thanks, man." Epps nodded and turned away.

He moved on through the night, heading west. He'd thought that camping in the hills above the city would be a temporary thing, but he found that he enjoyed it. When he was finally ready for sleep, the forest ground and the makeshift cave were as familiar as any bed. Perhaps he'd eventually find another room or an apartment, but for the summer at least, he was quite content sleeping among the tall eucalyptus trees. It took him nearly an hour to reach the west side of Twin Peaks tunnel. He stood still in the shadow of a building, making sure there were no eyes on him. Satisfied that the night was his alone, he stepped toward the line of trees and entered the hidden trail he'd come to know well, day or night. With little light, most people would have been utterly lost, but years of training and navigation let him move up the pathway like a wolf. Twenty minutes later he arrived at his small campsite in the hollow of a rock face near the top of Mount Sutro. He sat down, finally relaxing enough that he felt sleep might come. He took a Baby Ruth candy bar out of his coat pocket and quietly ate, thinking about how pretty that redhead had been.

"Where? Where did you see him?" Kats implored, looking around as well.

"Um, well," Shig stuttered, "I think he carried Molly to the ambulance."

"What?!" Kats and Molly said together.

"It was like how you remember something from a dream, you know? I was focused on getting Molly and Lola to the medics, and this guy came up to help as we cleared Cooper Alley. I barely looked at him. Just saw that he was a White guy, so not a Tong. Sorry, man," Shig said contritely.

Kats put a hand on his shoulder, "Nothing to apologize for," he said. "You got the girls out, and you kind of saved my bacon back there as well with that well-timed '*Banzai.*'"

Shig looked a bit surprised and then smiled broadly, "I guess I did save you!" he laughed as Molly kissed him on the cheek.

As they turned back toward the medics, a police officer approached them. Kats waved to him, "Elliot," he said as the tired-looking man approached.

"Molly, Shig, this is Officer Elliot Blackstone," Kats said as he shook Elliot's hand. "The man I owe a big debt of gratitude to for bringing the police into this. Thank you."

Blackstone shook his hand and smiled, "I think we owe you a thank-you for the heads-up on this one. We arrested two dozen Tong. We also recovered a dozen rifles and some machine guns and pistols and put a dent in the prostitution operations of all the Tong. This was a good night." Kats smiled in agreement.

"What about the girls?" Molly asked as she looked over at a dozen or so scared young women who had been in the so-called "hospital."

Blackstone followed her gaze and gave a sigh. "We'll do our best to find them legitimate work and safe places to live. There are a couple of organizations here that help these women."

"God will provide," Kats said without irony, and Blackstone slapped him on the shoulder.

"He always does," Elliot said, and he returned to his operation.

Kats wanted Molly and the now awake Lola to go to the hospital to get checked out, but both of them insisted they were fine. Lola did admit to still feeling "fuzzy." They all agreed to go to Kats' house so that they could get some rest and hopefully sleep off any lingering effects of the opium. They put Lola in the guest room, Shig took the couch in Kats' office, and Molly was soon asleep in Kats' bed. He held her there, tired but unable to fall asleep. He thought about the confrontation with John and his words about not being able to really talk to his father. They stung because he knew there was truth in them. Now wasn't the time to delve into that particular pool. Instead, his mind flowed to the near-contact with Steven Epps. If it was Epps, and he still wasn't convinced it was, then helping a stranger out of danger was a very normal, sane thing to do. Perhaps Epps wasn't the crazed, wild man he had been. He wished he could discuss it with Dominic. He looked at the clock. 4:22 am. He felt Molly nestle further into the crook of his right arm and closed his eyes. Sleep came quickly.

Conrad Hauser wasn't known for his laughter. But he'd laughed out loud that morning when Stiles had called, his one phone call, to explain what had happened and asking Hauser to bail him out of jail. That unfamiliar sound of his boss laughing was the last thing Stiles heard before the line clicked closed. Now Hauser sat in his makeshift office, the morning paper on his desk. 'Chinatown Raid' read the headline. The timing of it made him wonder, but fortunately they had little reinvested in the Hong Kong Club operation up to this point except time.

Time was the element that Hauser felt most challenged by. He could arrange for yet another safe house and set up the drug testing again. The director demanded results. He was more concerned with the loose end that Steven Epps represented. He held the outside hope that they could recover Epps and turn him into something useful. A CIA-run tool, ideally under his operational authority. He thought of the things that such a tool could do, but the possibility of that seemed to grow more remote each day the man remained at large, and his patience was running low. He had only to contact their resources in the police department to turn Epps into a fugitive and the most wanted man in the Bay Area. Instead, he picked up the phone and dialed the operator. "Yes, get me the JAG office." He waited and was connected.

"Yes, this is Colonel Hauser from Special Services," he said, using his cover. "I need one of your team to bail out an idiot."

Turier sat in the commissary reading the morning paper with his coffee. He scanned the story about the Chinatown Raid for the second time. As he did, he saw Thorne approach and sit down heavily across the table from him. The man was uncharacteristically disheveled, unshaven, and bleary eyed as he sipped his coffee.

"You look like shit," Turier said.

"Matches how I feel, doctor," Thorne replied quietly and took another drink of his coffee.

"Did I hear you and your men were in Chinatown last night?" Turier asked. Thorne gave a slight nod of his head.

"Did you see this?" he asked and held up the headline for Thorne to read.

"Actually, doctor, we were in the raid," he said. Turier was about to ask for details when a corporal approached them.

"Colonel Hauser wants you two in his office immediately."

"You think he's in the woods, doctor?" Hauser said after hearing the latest theory from the Frenchman. "You had thought the day labor market last week."

"I still think he's involved in the day labor markets, but I believe he's staying or will gravitate toward the woods and the high ground of the city since the Tong found him at the SRO."[11]

Hauser looked at Thorne, who shrugged his shoulders. "The city has a fair number of hills," he said. "Where do you suggest we start?"

"I thought of this while on my morning run the other day. Golden Gate Park seemed too busy for someone trying to hide, but maybe Buena Vista Park would be a good option.

It's steep, dense, and located in the midst of the city."

"Very well, doctor, but time is running out on this operation. Bring me some results, or this goes to the local authorities." He turned his gaze to Thorne. "When can your team be ready to begin?"

"Oh, almost immediately," Thorne lied.

CHAPTER 23

The front door to his office opened, and Naoko Harada stepped inside. *"Irashaimase,"* Kats said quietly as he walked down the stairs from the second-floor kitchen. Mrs. Harada, his elderly neighbor from up the street, smiled and held up a covered dish to him. He smiled, "Thank you, *obatchan.*" Grandmother. He really had come to think of her like a grandmother figure since she'd made it her mission to take care of him after his parents had returned to Japan. That meant cooking, cleaning, and even doing his laundry. He knew that telling her to stop would be useless because the bonds of familial friendship as well as the time-honored Japanese traditions of honor and obligation were all part of the complex dynamic. Telling her to stop would shame her and embarrass his parents five thousand miles away. Plus, she was a really good cook.

"Thank you for coming," he said with a small bow. "Molly and a friend of ours are recovering from a bit too much excitement last night," he said cautiously.

Her head bobbed up and down, and she smiled. "Young people," she said knowingly.

"What is it that you have brought?" he asked as he took the covered dish, thinking it might be one of her many Japanese specialties.

"Apple pie," she said, making him laugh out loud.

By early afternoon, Kats had made his way to the western end of the Twin Peaks Tunnel and parked his car a block off the main drag, Laguna Honda. He walked to the streetcar station and looked down the two-mile-long tunnel that ran underneath Twin Peaks hills and exited at Market Street. The tunnel opened in 1917 after three years of construction, and to Kats it still seemed like a marvel of engineering. He stood on the platform, imagining himself exiting the streetcar and heading out into the neighborhood. He looked up at Mount Sutro, completely visible today with no fog. He walked down the street toward the trailhead he knew was a short distance down the road on his right. Behind street-fronting buildings, he could see the eucalyptus forest rising up the hill. He slowly walked the couple of hundred yards down the road and turned into the trailhead on the right. He watched as a couple exited the trail, likely returning from a walk into the forest preserve that former Mayor Adolph Sutro had gifted to the city. Kats touched the front pocket of his jacket, feeling the wooden tubes there, and then walked slowly onto the forest trail.

As soon as he entered the trail, he was surrounded by eucalyptus trees, many well over a hundred feet tall. The sunlight was diffuse in the undergrowth, and the smell of the eucalyptus was powerful. Kats walked for several minutes, and two more hikers came marching down the mountain on the trail. *This is too busy*, he thought. *Way too many people.* He looked up the trail, noticing a switchback ahead. He continued to climb and emerged at a crossing where the walking trail crossed a gravel service road. He stopped and looked at the road, seeing signs of fresh tire tracks. He turned and followed the service road upward as it wound around the hill.

Kats continued to march upward, noting that he was getting near the top of the mountain. Rounding a curve, he looked up the road to see an army jeep parked across the way and two soldiers leaning against the vehicle. Seeing him, they straightened themselves, and Kats saw that they both lifted their rifles to a casual but not completely unthreatening posture. Kats smiled, raised his hands, and walked forward.

One of the soldiers, a corporal, Kats noted, stepped forward as well, raising a hand to stop Kats. "I'm sorry, sir, but this is a restricted area."

"Sorry, no problem," Kats replied, still coming forward. "What's going on up there?" he pointed.

"Just some routine maintenance on one of our buildings, but we can't let folks up there while they're working."

"Sure, sure," Kats sympathized. "Is that the missile building I read about?" he pressed, recalling what Shig had told him. The two soldiers looked at each other, and the corporal answered.

"This is just a radar outpost," he said as he gave a subtle but noticeable lift of his rifle. "We do need you to head back down, sir."

"Of course. Have a good day," Kats said and turned back down the mountain. As he walked back, he tried to remember the last time he'd seen armed guards for a construction site.

By the time Thorne, his team, and the support personnel they required were ready to depart, it was nearly noon. Not long after that, Dominic Turier decided he didn't have what it might take to be a spy. The ongoing pretense was exhausting, as was his internal conflict regarding Steven Epps. He was concerned about his patient, but he also feared what might happen if Epps was left untreated and at large in the city. He had a duty to the man and a duty to society.

He had led Thorne and his men to the park as planned. What he hadn't realized was that there would be two dozen more support personnel stationed around the park in unmarked vehicles. The radio waves crackled with their constant updates and notifications of being in or out of position. Each car had a walkie-talkie, and each of Thorne's men carried one as well. Because they couldn't openly carry rifles around the park, the team except for Thorne carried long backpacks that held their disassembled rifles. Turier knew that those rifles could be out and assembled in moments after watching Collins field strip his firearm. But it wasn't the intense level of operational procedure that wore on him. It was the relentless subterfuge of having to pretend to look around every corner and high hideaway that was exhausting.

Thorne and Zapek were the expert trackers, and they'd split up, with Thorne bringing Collins and Turier with him. Collins quietly walked point twenty yards in front of them, and Turier watched as Thorne would pause, look at something, and bend and touch the trail or the grass to the side, parsing some hidden message that only he could see. Turier had the disquieting thought that he wouldn't want Larry Thorne searching for him.

Over the next three hours, they ranged up the hill, discovering a small campsite that held four older hobos, who were startled to look up from their drink to see men peering at them from the foliage. They also came upon a young couple in a hidden grove, partially dressed and deep in the throes of their passion. Thorne and Collins stopped to watch for a few moments. Then Thorne silently turned and raised a finger to his lips as he looked at Turier and they withdrew.

As they made their way down the park, they spotted Zapek and Esteban approaching from the other side of the hill. They made a slashing gesture across their necks to indicate they hadn't had any luck. Thorne looked at his watch and at the late-afternoon sun. He extended the antenna of the device and raised his walkie-talkie to his face. "This is Thorne. We have nothing here. Break it down and head back to base." He slammed the antenna down, and his men looked at him. "Back to the base, gentlemen. Perhaps not such a late night tonight, and we try again tomorrow." They nodded and marched down the trail, but Thorne stayed still, his eyes ranging over the park and the hill above.

"Perhaps you were wrong, doctor," he said, not looking at Turier. "Is there anything you want to tell me?" Turier felt his stomach tighten.

"I've told you and Hauser my theory about where Steven would seek refuge. Just because he's not here doesn't mean my theory is wrong."

Thorne nodded, still not looking directly at Turier. "Yes, you said that Epps had training as an alpine soldier, a Montagnard. And that would lead him to the parks, to the high ground, the mountains."

"*Oui*, I still believe that."

"Well *that*," Thorne emphasized as he pointed to the south, "looks a hell of a lot more like a mountain than this oversized hill." Turier's eyes followed the line from Thorne's fingertip that pointed directly at Mount Sutro.

Kats returned to the streetcar station. This time, he recalled the historic map and the Indian trails that crossed over the mountain. He walked slowly down the street and then took an alleyway to the back of the buildings where the forest began. Now his eyes searched for something different, something subtle. He recalled walking the forests in eastern France, searching for German units and encampments. Most of the time, the enemy wasn't clever, but occasionally it took a different eye to find them. Sometimes it was as subtle as how the wind blew the trees, exposing an otherwise unseen pathway or water running down a hillside ... you just had to ... there!

As Kats gently touched a lush, low branch, he saw the hint of an opening. He stepped into the tree line and then looked up. These trees had been here for decades, and the forefathers of these trees had been here more than a century ago when those old maps had been made. As the footfalls had disappeared over the years and the undergrowth slowly took back the trail, the legacy of the trail was still marked above. As he looked up, he could see the tiny break in the tree canopy that represented the old scar on the forest floor where no trees grew. His eyes adjusted to the diffuse light, and he looked for any small sign of human passage. There it was! Not broken twigs of trampled grass, but the slight push of leaves that accompanied careful steps. *Let's see where this goes*, he thought.

He went slowly, deliberately, so as not to mark his own passing. He moved upward, but the trail seemed to follow the natural curves of the mountain in an almost organic pathway. It made Kats think of how in tune the first inhabitants of San Francisco had been with their natural environment. He stopped taking in the contours of the hill and let himself think like a lone soldier in the wilderness. Above him was a large rock formation, and the trail moved to his right and around it. He scanned to his left and saw the barest hint of recent passage through what would look to most like solid underbrush. He carefully stepped into the underbrush, not wanting to disturb anything in case he was correct. A dozen steps up and away from the Indian trail, a smaller pathway rose up to the opposite side of the rocks above. This must be where Epps moved off the path for extra security.

Kats followed the tiny trail and found himself on the backside of the rocks that overlooked the city. A shallow cave, perhaps ten feet deep, was hidden in the crevice of the rocks that rose another fifty feet above it. He saw a sleeping bag, the remnants of a campfire, some stacked K-rations, and a bucket filled with what he thought was rainwater. There was also an old footlocker, probably purchased at the Army Navy store. Kats felt strangely reticent to open it. His days in a barracks with dozens of other men and almost no privacy except one's own thoughts and each man's footlocker meant you didn't mess with another soldier's footlocker. He did note two paperback books atop it: Dashielle Hammett's *The Thin Man*, made popular again by the recent NBC TV series, and a surprising copy of *The Way of Zen* by Alan Watts. That book had come out a couple of years before and was required reading among the young and artistic, at least according to Shig. Kats had read it and found Watt's introduction of Zen to the west a good read. But he recalled an appropriate parable, or *koan* as the Zen mind-bending problems were properly called: Reading about Zen is like trying to scratch your foot through your shoe.[12]

The small campsite was neat, functional, and, to Kats, tremendously sad. This was a fellow soldier reduced to living out in the woods, isolated, and in fact hunted for things that had been done to him while in service to his country. Kats wondered if he'd not met Dominic, whether he would've ended up in a similar situation. He felt a renewed sense of purpose in finding Epps and making sure that he got the help he needed.

Standing there, he realized he could hear the sounds of construction. He turned and tried to get a bearing on the source. He moved to the end of the rock face, and from there he could see, between the eucalyptus trees, movement and what appeared to be a bulldozer scraping an adjacent hilltop some seventy-five yards away. The radar site. Kats now had to decide how to proceed. He was nearly certain that the campsite belonged to Epps, but he had to admit that it might be some other homeless man, down on his luck. He considered staying there and waiting for Epps or whoever to return. But as skittish as the man was, Kats feared that without the familiar face of Dominic, Epps would bolt again, and they might never find him. Worse, if Epps took Kats as a threat, he knew that his only chance to stop him was the 'Two-Step Powder' he carried, and that meant a dangerous confrontation with the freakishly strong soldier. *Plan B*, he thought, and turned to head back down the mountain.

High above the campsite in the rocks above, a shadow detached itself and slowly peered over the edge of the precipice as the man below retreated. The shadow waited a full minute before rising, silently climbing down to the camp, and then following the man down the trail.

Moving carefully down, Kats emerged thirty minutes later from the tree line near Laguna Honda station. He crossed the street and walked the block to his car. He looked at his watch. Just after 4 pm. If Epps was at a worksite, he'd likely be returning here in the next couple of hours. Recon training said to confirm before initiating action, so Kats got in his car and moved it to a space across the street from the streetcar station and in the line of sight of both the main trailhead and the hidden trail entrance. Now for the main part of his profession: the wait.

CHAPTER 24

Kats shifted on the front bench seat of his blue-and-white 1955 Chevy Bel Air as he looked out across the busy street. He couldn't have afforded the car four years ago, but a client had offered it to him after he successfully found her missing husband. The 'missing' man had been in Los Angeles with his young secretary and a large bag of client money when the police had arrived at their hotel, following a tip from an anonymous source. The Bel Air had been a planned gift for the young secretary, but the police arrested the man before he could do further damage.

In the aftermath of all that, his client, the outraged wife, wanted to move on and offered him the car at a ridiculously low price. The V8 was powerful, the car handled like a dream, and it was well suited for stakeouts, though he still preferred the nimble freedom of his motorcycle. Putting Molly on the back of his bike and riding out to the Great Highway, with her arms wrapped tightly around him, was a pleasure like no other. His thoughts drifted to her, and he wanted to find a pay phone and call to check on her and Lola, but self-discipline told him no. That same self-discipline was being tested in the warmth of the late afternoon, as the past several days of effort weighed on his mind and body. He shifted and rolled his head to fight the fatigue that was threatening to overcome him.

Out of the corner of his eye, he caught a shadow cross behind the car in the rearview mirror. A moment later, he was startled when a hand knocked on his passenger side window. His first thought was a police officer. Had he parked in a loading zone? He looked over at the window as the figure crouched down and felt his heart lurch as Steven Epps peered into his window. He froze, momentarily unsure of what to do as Epps held his gaze with steady, unblinking eyes. Kats heard the door open, and Epps climbed into the front seat across from him.

Kats was conscious of his hands on the steering wheel as Epps looked discerningly at him as if trying to place his face. Kats was about to speak when Epps broke the silence.

"I seem to remember you," he said and paused. "You were at the parking garage with the Chinese gang." Kats nodded, keeping his hands on the wheel.

"Yes, but I wasn't with them. I was trying to find you, but I couldn't let you kill those men."

Epps tilted his head slightly, "Why not? They were trying to kill me."

Kats didn't have an immediately ready response to that,

so he changed the topic. "My name is Katsuhiro Takemoto. I was a solider like you, and now I'm a private detective. This is my card," he said as he started to reach his right hand into his front jacket pocket. Epps' hand moved like a blur, catching his wrist and holding it there with a viselike grip. Kats knew he couldn't outmuscle the man, and there was no way to outmaneuver him in the confines of the car, so he relaxed and opened his hands in a gesture of surrender. Epps held Kats' arm for a couple more seconds before releasing him.

"I just want to show you who I am," Kats said and delicately removed one of his cards from his pocket and handed it to Epps, who glanced at it and then stuffed it in his jacket pocket. "Dr. Dominic Turier asked me to help find you. Do you remember him?"

Epps' eyes narrowed at the mention of Turier's name, but he gave a slight nod, "The Frenchman. From the hospital."

"Yes."

"I hated it there," Epps said.

"I get it, but Dominic is worried about you out here, and he wants to help. He helped me years ago during the war, and I think he can help you too."

Epps sat back, stretched his neck, and looked out the windshield at the people passing by. "I just want to stop the voices and the red," Epps said.

"The red?" Kats asked.

"Something happens to me when I'm angry or when I'm attacked. The world goes red, and I become something else. I lose time and then wake up not knowing where I am or what happened."

"Is that what happened to you when you went with the Chinese girl to her place? Something happened there, and people were killed. Do you remember any of that?"

"I remember a pretty girl and going to her apartment. I remember ... her and then the red." Epps paused, trying to remember.

"I woke up in Golden Gate Park, half dressed, with a bullet wound across my ribs. I don't remember any guns, but I've been shot enough to know what the wound looks like."

"Yeah, me too," Kats said quietly.

"I read about the killings in the paper, put two and two together, and realized they must have dosed me," he said. "I didn't mean to kill those people."

"Dominic told me that you didn't kill the girl. It was some kind of accident." Epps gave a wan smile as Kats continued. "They didn't know about your ..." Kats paused, also looking for the words.

"My condition?" Epps said flatly. "I don't even know how to describe it myself. Turier said it was 'battlefield stress' and a treatable condition."

"He's very good at what he does. He helped me through a bad time in Europe during the war," Kats shared. "And he's very worried about you. The government wants you back, but he says that if they can't find you soon, they're going to report you to the local authorities as the killer of those two people."

"Then I'll leave town," Epps said.

"They'll turn your photo over to the police, and it'll be all over the news. Everyone in California will be looking for you." Epps shrugged his shoulders. "You'll be running until someone recognizes you and an overzealous deputy shoots you."

"I'm not going back to that hospital," Epps said fiercely, the first time showing any emotion. "I'd rather die than let them take me back there."

"I thought Turier helped you?" Kats asked, now confused.

"Not Turier, but those other fucking doctors. They were shooting me up with stuff, shooting electric current through my head, poking, prodding, even forcing me to kill."

"What?" Kats asked, shocked at the accusation.

"They forced me to fight other guys. Prisoners maybe, or criminals. I don't know. They'd toss us into a cage and give them clubs, knives, chains, shit like that, just to see what I'd do. I didn't even break a sweat against the first few they sent, but the time they sent four guys, I remember thinking these guys were different, that they had training and that they were killers. I don't remember much of the actual fight because I went red. Woke up the next day with cuts and bruises on my knuckles but nothing else." Epps went quiet and stared out the front windshield.

Kats was horrified. They were trying to trigger Epps, to understand how his chemistry might be replicated and weaponized. He was a lab rat to them. He knew he couldn't let this man, this soldier, fall back into the government's hands. "What if they thought you were dead?" Kats asked. "We could get you out, and they'd never come looking for you again."

"You have a plan?" Epps asked.

"Not really, but I think Dominic can help us. I just need to find a way to contact him."

"Well, I guess we could go ask him and his buddy over there," Epps said with a nod toward the station. Kats looked over, and stepping out of a car was Dominic Turier. Beside him was a lean, blond man who had the carriage of a soldier. Perhaps this is the man Dominic mentioned, the dangerous one named Thorne.

"What are they doing here?" Kats asked out loud. "He wasn't supposed to be here yet."

"Yet?" Epps asked. Kats explained Turier's theory that Epps would find high ground in the hills and how Kats was supposed to scout out the locations before the government came in. Clearly, something had forced the issue. They watched as the two men walked to the trailhead and disappeared into the forest.

Turier followed Thorne's long strides up the trail, looking back and forth, illogically afraid that he might see Epps or Kats or both. But he knew that Thorne was like a hound with a scent now and feared that they might find something. Fifteen minutes up the trail, they'd passed two other hikers coming down before reaching the service road that led up the mountain to their left and down toward the street on their right. Thorne paused, listening. Turier heard it then too. It was a vehicle, a truck, rumbling down the road. The truck, an army M35 two-and-a-half-ton six-wheeled truck, rounded the curve above, and they saw the army markings on it. Thorne stepped into the middle of the road, pulling out his military police badge, and the truck slowed to a halt.

Thorne moved to the driver side of the truck. Two men sat up front, and four more were squatting in the open truck bed, tools spread out before them. Thorne noted the Army Corps of Engineers insignia all of them wore. He smiled at the driver and put on his odd southern drawl again.

"Howdy, boys," he said. "I'm Captain Thomas, with the military police."

"What can I do for you, sir?" said the passenger seat occupant, a sergeant, and seemingly the leader.

"Well," Thorne continued, "we're following a lead about a deserter who might be hiding out in the hills up here. Have you seen anything up there?"

"We've been working up here for the past couple of weeks and can't say we've seen much except the worksite," said the foreman, a sergeant major. "Lot of places to hide up here. But, come to think of it, a couple of my guys did claim they seen something up in the hills a few days ago. Joked it was Big Foot."[13]

Thorne looked at Turier and raised an eyebrow. *Non*, thought Turier, *this is too soon*, but he tried to keep his face calm.

"What are you guys working on up there? Anything interesting?" Thorne asked the sergeant with a laugh.

"Updating a missile command site. The army is installing the Nike Hercules missiles to replace the old Ajax versions. Can't be too secret. Even the press knows about it."

Thorne nodded and waved them through. "Thanks for your help," he said, and the sergeant gave a salute as they continued down the road. Thorne pulled his backpack off his shoulder and pulled out the walkie-talkie.

"What are you going to do?" Turier asked. Thorne ignored him, pulling the antenna out and raising the device to his ear. "Zorro, this is Left Turn. Do you copy? Zorro, come in." A moment later came a reply.

"Zorro here." Turier recognized Zapek's French accent. "Go ahead, Left Turn."

"Get your asses to Mount Sutro. We have a lead on the target."

"Shit," Kats said as he watched Turier and the man emerge from the deep undergrowth just a few steps off the pathway. He couldn't hear what was said, but as soon as he saw the walkie-talkie, he knew that something bad had happened. Behind him, Epps squatted in silence. Kats' mind was racing now. He needed to get to Dominic. He felt Epps tap him on the shoulder, and he turned. Epps pointed at the man, made a slash across his throat, and Kats shook his head forcefully. *No!* Kats raised an open palm to Epps and pointed to the ground. *Wait here.* Epps nodded.

Kats reached over and took Epps' ball cap and pulled it low over his eyes. Then he delved into his jacket pocket, taking out the folded map and one of the small wooden tubes containing the 'Two-Step Powder.' He removed the wax seals, leaving only the thin paper membrane that held the powder in place. He placed the tube in his hand with the map and, from a distance, it looked like a pencil. He hoped.

Kats stepped out onto the pathway, adjusted his jacket, and then loudly began to walk up the trail. Hearing him, Turier and the blond man turned toward him. Dominic's eyes widened a moment later with recognition, but before he could act, Kats spoke.

"Oh, hey, guys," he said in a loud, friendly voice as he raised the map up in his hand. "I'm a bit lost here. Do either of you know how to read a map?"

Turier stood silent, his mouth working but not finding words. The blond man smiled and waved him over, but Kats noticed his right hand dip into his right pocket. *Gun,* he thought. Kats awkwardly moved over, shifting the map to and fro as he did. "I'm trying to find the trail that leads to Twin Peaks, but this darn map ..." The blond man stepped closer as if to look.

Kats raised the 'pen' to mark something on the map. As he did so, he brought the end to his lips and, in one quick breath, a cloud of yellow dust hit the man full in the face. Kats pushed Dominic to the left and followed him with a roll just as the gun cleared Thorne's pocket. Muscle memory raised the arm, but the cloud of chemicals short-circuited any further thought as Thorne slumped to the ground.

"Kats! *Mon Dieu*, you're here," Turier gaped as he helped Kats to his feet. "How did you find us?"

"We saw you arrive down the hill."

"We?" Turier asked with a wrinkle of his forehead.

"We," said Kats as he pointed to the man walking up the trail toward them.

"Steven!" Turier shouted and rushed forward. Kats thought he was going to embrace the soldier, but he stopped short, looking him up and down.

"Hello, doctor," Epps said quietly.

"How ... How did you two ..." Turier couldn't find the words.

"No time for the backstory," Kats said. "What was that radio communication?"

"Thorne," Turier gestured to the prone man, "called for the team to come here."

"I was afraid of that," Kats said.

"Is he dead?" Turier asked.

"No, just unconscious for an hour or two, but we'd better move him off the road," Kats said, and Epps picked up the man easily and placed him behind a tree, making him invisible from the road and the trail.

Kats looked down the trail in the fading light, then up toward the top of the hill. "How many men on Thorne's team?" he asked.

"Three other specialists, but they had a whole squad of soldiers backing them up earlier today," Turier responded. "What are you thinking?"

"I'm thinking they may already be moving into position

at the base of the mountain."

"Can we cut across the forest and escape that way?" Turier asked.

"Possibly, but then they'll do what you were worried about and turn this over to the police. The manhunt for our friend here would be massive," Kats said, and Turier nodded dejectedly.

"We could fight," Epps said flatly. "I'll finish the one in the bushes now, and we can wait for the rest." Kats shook his head, and Turier looked troubled.

"*Non*, Steven, please. You can't kill that man in cold blood. Yes, he's a killer, but ..." Turier struggled to articulate the complexity that was Larry Thorne. He didn't think they'd understand his view of Thorne; he wasn't sure he fully understood it himself. Then he recalled something Thorne had said, and it seemed appropriate, "He's what the world made him. Please don't kill him."

Epps looked back and forth, gave a shrug, and asked, "Then what do we do?"

"We need to get off this mountain," Kats said, looking around. "There are guards up the road and probably at the main access points."

"We should go back down the hidden trail we came up," Epps said. "When we get close to the bottom, I know another way out near the station."

Kats looked back and forth between the two men and then nodded. "OK, lead on," he said to Epps, who hesitated and looked up the hill toward where his camp was located.

"I need to get something first," he said and headed up the trail. Kats and Turier followed.

CHAPTER 25

Minutes later they arrived at the bare campsite Epps had established for himself. Turier looked about in dismay as Kats watched Epps go over to the small footlocker and open it. He pushed aside a couple of shirts and pulled out a notebook and a small leather pouch. He stuffed those in the breast pocket of his jacket and turned to the two men. "Ready," he said.

Epps led them down the trail. Turier followed, and Kats brought up the rear. As they walked, Turier quietly asked, "How long have you been here?"

"A week, I think," Epps replied. "I'd been staying at a cheap hotel in the Tenderloin, but some gang spotted me. Couldn't go back after that. I'm not even sure what I did to piss them off."

"A girl was killed, and they think you did it. But Steven, you didn't." Epps stopped, and both he and Kats turned toward Turier.

"How can you know that?" Epps asked.

"Because I've seen the film of the whole incident. Steven, you defended yourself from the other man, and that man shot the girl while trying to kill you."

"They covered up that bit," Kats said, "and I'm sure that they won't release that footage because it incriminates the government for the whole operation."

Epps took a deep breath. "At least I didn't kill her."

"Steven, you're not responsible for these deaths. What was done to you in Korea was inhuman. You aren't the monster here."

"Dominic, you haven't been told the whole story," Kats said, looking back and forth at the two other men. "There has been more done to him over here. Just as bad. No, actually even worse."

Turier looked confused. Kats said to Epps, "He needs to know." Kats walked a way down the trail to allow them to talk. As the next five minutes unfolded, Kats could see the shock, pain, and outrage on his friend's face as Dominic's faith in humanity was put to the ultimate test. As Epps finished the story, Turier had hot tears in his eyes, and his face was flush with anger.

"*Putain de merde*," he said hotly. "They used me. Steven, I am so very sorry," he said and laid a hand on Epps' shoulder.

"I never thought you were part of that, doctor," Epps said. "But I won't let them take me back there. Or anywhere. I'll die first."

"Let's hope it doesn't come to that," Kats said.

As they approached the bottom of the trail, Epps pointed to a slight incline on their left. "If we follow that hill, it takes us around to the back of the streetcar station. Gets muddy, so I tried to avoid it."

"OK," Kats said. "Give me a couple of minutes' head start. I'll go down this path, then up the road to my car. You two go around to the station and then come out the main exit like you were on the train. I'll pick you up. Blue-and-white Chevy Bel Air." Turier looked confused, and Kats realized he didn't know American cars. "Blue and white. I'll find you." They both nodded, and Kats turned and headed down the trail.

Ten minutes later, Turier and Epps stepped out of the station with a late-day crowd that had exited the streetcar.

Kats waved from the curb, and the two men crossed the sidewalk and jumped into the car, Epps in the backseat. Kats looked into his mirror and hissed, "Get down!"

As the two men hunkered down, an unmarked gray truck rumbled past them and down the street. Kats watched it slow and turn into the service road by the trailhead. "You're clear," he said, and Turier and Epps peered down the street as another gray truck came up the road and turned into the service area.

"Time to go," Kats said, and he turned into the other lane, taking them away from the mountain.

Thorne's eyes fluttered. He heard voices. Then he smelled gunpowder and oil. *Stalingrad! I'm in Stalingrad*, his mind shouted as he tried to focus his eyes. He saw a face leaning over his and instinctively struck out.

"*Enculé!*" spat Zapek as he held his nose while Thorne struggled to sit up. He looked wildly around, seeing his team and several more men fanned out around him. Hauser stood nearby, eyeing him coldly.

"How does a psychiatrist get the drop on you?" Hauser said accusingly. Thorne blew out his cheeks, and Zapek pulled him to his feet. He gave a shake of his head, like a dog shaking off the rain.

"It wasn't Turier. He had some help. Another man, an Asian guy who kind of looked familiar. He hit me with some kind of drug."

"Asian? Japanese maybe?" Hauser said. "Thirties, fit?"

"Sounds about right."

"I know who helped him. It was that man from the hospital, his old friend, the private eye. So Turier betrayed us," Hauser said matter of factly.

"It would appear so."

Hauser looked around the hillside, thinking. "There can't be many Japanese private eyes in San Francisco. We can track him down." He turned to Thorne and made a circling gesture with his hand above his head. The men turned and headed back down the service road.

Thorne walked beside Hauser, rubbing his head as if to shake something loose. "I'm remembering him now too. He was there in the basement in Chinatown. He was fighting the Tong. And there was another man."

"Where?" Hauser said.

"There was an Asian man in the basement in Chinatown. I ran past him."

"An Asian man in Chinatown?" Hauser said sarcastically. "Shocking." Thorne ignored the jibe.

"I saw him before. At the bookstore Turier wanted to go to. They chatted for a few moments about something. Didn't seem important then, but I'm pretty sure it was the same guy."

"Another lead then," Hauser said as they moved down the hill toward the waiting trucks.

"Hello," Molly said into the phone.

"Hey, it's me. You feeling OK?" Kats asked.

"Yeah, I'm good. Mostly mad at getting caught like that."

"Give yourself a break. What you did was very brave. And we put a stop to the Black Dragon operation." Kats said. "How's Lola?"

"She went home a few hours ago. I tried to get her to stay, but she was having none of it either. I sent Shig home too, but I presume he's at City Lights."

"OK. So I have some news. "

"Did you find something?" she asked, her mood brightening at the prospect.

"Actually, I found someone. More accurately, he found me."

"What? Epps found you?"

"Yes, he ..."

"Are you OK?"

"I'm fine. We're all fine."

"Umm, OK. Who all are you talking about?"

"Dominic is with us."

"Jesus, you've been busy!"

"Yeah, and I'll explain everything, but right now we need a place to lay low for a bit."

"Not here, I take it?"

"No. I think they'll find me soon enough."

"Who is they?"

"Maybe the government, the army, the Hei Long Tong. That's why you need to get out of my place too."

"Where then?" she asked.

"For the moment, I was hoping we could go to your place."

An hour later, Molly turned the lock on her front door and entered the small apartment on the second floor of a four-story building in Hayes Valley. She dropped the bag of supplies Kats had asked for on the floor as she moved into the space, self-consciously straightening up as she did. A few minutes later there was a soft knock on the door, which she opened to find Kats and two men, one of whom she immediately recognized from the photograph they'd been showing around town. They quickly entered, and as the door closed, Molly fiercely embraced Kats.

He squeezed her back, relief filling his heart. He kissed

her and then turned to introduce the other two men. "Molly, this is Dominic, my old friend from France."

"Very happy to finally meet you, Dominic," she smiled.

"My pleasure *mademoiselle*," Turier said as he kissed her hand. Molly actually giggled at that. Turier turned toward Epps and said, "This is Steven." Epps stood still, his dark eyes taking everything in.

Molly smiled and quietly said, "Hi, Steven." Epps raised his eyes momentarily and met hers. He gave a tiny nod.

"I remember you," he said quietly. Molly looked back and forth at Kats and Turier, not sure how to respond.

"Did we meet somewhere?" she asked, and he gave a nod.

"The night before, in Chinatown. I helped you to the ambulance." Molly looked intently at Epps for a moment. Then she smiled and shook her head.

"I'm sorry. I was out of it. There was a lot going on. But thank you, Steven," she said, and Epps gave a small smile. Kats silently nodded his thanks as well.

"I'm putting on a pot of coffee, and I want to hear everything," she said, turning to Kats.

An hour and several cups of coffee later, the three of them huddled in the living room as Epps sat by the window, watching the street play out below them. Molly turned the conversation back to the immediate challenge at hand. "We can stay here tonight, but it's too small for very long. Where can we go?"

"They'll find me soon enough," Kats said. "I was there in Menlo Park when I met Dominic. They'll find my PI license. That means my place is going to be watched."

"Do either of you have family nearby?" Turier asked.

"No, neither of us has family here in town," Molly said.

"Well," Kats said, pursing his lips, "I kinda do." Molly

looked confused. "Mrs. Harada, my neighbor down the street. She and her daughter are like family." Molly smiled at that.

"Could that work?" Dominic asked.

"She has a house down the street from me. It's far enough away to be safe but actually close enough that we could watch my house for surveillance. There's a back-alley entrance too. I hate to ask her for this favor, but we're pretty limited on options at the moment." He stood up, "Let me call her," and he headed into the kitchen for the phone.

Molly and Dominic watched him go and then turned toward each other.

"So, you're the doctor," she said quietly.

"And you're the girlfriend," he said with a smile. "Kats speaks very highly of you."

Molly blushed a bit in the dimly lit room.

"He also speaks well of you. He said you saved his life," she said, looking deeply into his face. "I've only known him for a year and a half, but I can't imagine him being that ..." she trailed off, looking for the words.

"Broken?" he said quietly. "I can understand that. He's a soldier. No, more than a soldier. He's a classic warrior. He's one of the strongest people I've ever met. But even such strength can be useless when the thing we battle is ourselves."

"Himself?" Molly asked, as she settled into the couch across from Turier. "What do you mean?"

"When a man such as Kats goes through a traumatic event, the mind and body will go to extreme lengths to protect themselves from further injury."

"Injuries like him being shot?"

"That was part of it, but the real injuries he suffered in France were to his sense of self. The battle forced him to confront a side of himself that was shocking to his mind, to that sense of self."

"He's told me some of the story, but I know there's more."

Turier smiled gently. "Well, it's not my story to tell, but I'll say that in my experience, it's often our own image of ourselves that can be the most difficult to reconcile." Molly still looked confused.

"We all have an image of ourselves in our mind. Freud calls it our Ego. Others call it the Self. I prefer to think of it as our 'essential' self. The 'real' self. Well, war and extreme trauma can shock that real self by revealing some things we didn't know were there, or things that we'd hidden from our consciousness. That revelation can unmoor the mind and body, sending us into deep and unfamiliar waters."

"And that's what happened to Kats?" Molly asked, her heart aching as she did.

"It happened to many men," he replied, not wanting to cross an ethical boundary.

"But he's good now, right?" she asked hopefully. "You treated him?"

"I did. I think he's very good, very centered. And he tells me he's very happy, especially with you." Molly smiled with relief and gratitude. "But you need to understand that with men like Kats," Turier nodded toward Epps, who sat at the window looking out into the night, "and Steven, there's no cure. For them it's an ongoing struggle to contain themselves and cope with those things that stress and trigger them. That's what I taught to Kats and tried to teach to Steven." Turier looked at the man across the room. "Some results have been better than others."

They turned as Kats came back from the small kitchen with a smile on his face.

"What is it?" Molly asked. "Is she OK with our plan?"

"Not only that, but she asked what we wanted to eat!"

CHAPTER 26

The rear door of the Imperial Dragon Restaurant slammed shut behind them as two men dragged an older man inside and then toward the stairs in the back. A third man followed, carrying a satchel. The eyes in the kitchen looked away, knowing it was better not to know what might be going on upstairs.

At the top of the stairs, they entered a long hallway that contained two more *hanfu*-clad men. Red silk emblazoned their cuffs, and they opened the heavy door to allow the group to pass. Inside the room, a plush couch that once resided in the foyer of the restaurant now contained a prone man, whose face was bruised and swollen, his left eye completely shut. His shirt was off, and his chest bore scrapes and several bruises. The Tong pulled the old man forward and stood him up in front of their leader. Dragon Eye Wen slowly raised himself to a sitting position, clearly in pain.

"Wen Tsui Shen," said the old man with a small bow that was the minimum amount necessary to be polite.

"Dr. Han," Wen replied with a slight slur of his speech. "I am in need of your services."

"I can see. You need only come to my shop. I would be happy to treat you there."

"Impossible at the moment, doctor. The police and the damned Hop Sing are searching for me. You will treat me here." At that command, Wen's man with the satchel stepped forward and handed the bag to Han.

Han stood still, holding the bag. "If I do this for you, Wen Tsui Shen ..." he began.

"You'll do this, Han," Dragon Eye Wen declared, "or I'll have your precious shop turned to ashes." Wen then tacked like a sailboat in the wind. Managing a painful looking smile, he said, "But let us not speak of such things. You will be well paid for your time. And once I come to power, you will have a favored position in the new order."

"You seem very sure of yourself for a man who was just bested by Lin Tai Lo," Han said, knowing this truth would anger Wen.

"That is why you must first heal me, doctor," Wen said confidently. "Then we'll discuss how your other talents can help me take hold of Chinatown."

"My other talents?" Han asked.

"They say you're a magician." Wen leaned forward, and Han looked impassively back at him. "I want your blackest magic."

"You found him?" Shig asked excitedly into the phone. The customers in City Lights cast a glance at him and then continued on their literary explorations.

"Yeah, he's here with us now."

"How is that? I mean, that guy is kind of scary, right?"

"He seems fine," Kats said quietly into Molly's phone in the tiny kitchen. "He's very quiet, but I've seen other vets who were far worse than he appears to be."

"Just don't get him angry," Shig said cautiously.

"Obviously," Kats replied. "Hey, by the way, you were right. He was there in Chinatown the other night. He recognized Molly and said he helped her to the ambulance."

"Ha! I told you, man!" Shig said as he jumped to his feet in the store. "I'm getting good at this private eye stuff!"

"You actually are, Shig," Kats said earnestly. "We appreciate it."

"Aw, shucks," Shig laughed. "So, what's the plan now?"

"Well, we can't go back to my place because they'll identify me soon enough, so we're at Molly's right now."

"Bit tight?"

"Yeah. That's why we're going to move tomorrow. Mrs. Harada has agreed to let us use her house while we figure out an actual plan."

"Nice. Smart," Shig said. "And she'll probably feed you like kings."

"She already said she'll make *tonkatsu* tomorrow night. And yes, you're invited."

Japanese pork chops! Shig thought, and did a little dance behind the counter before he calmly said, "See you tomorrow."

Across town at 137 Waverly Place in Chinatown, the green building was brightly illuminated by the many street-lights and wax paper lanterns that stretched across the street and lit the neighborhood. The sign above the main entrance read 'Hop Sing Benevolent Association,' but the Chinese characters to the side of the entrance representing a roof, over a mouth above the land, marked it clearly as Tong. From across the street, two men dressed as workers slowly moved boxes and wooden pallets in the alley. Their work was slow because they weren't doing anything other than watching the entrance to the building. In the past forty-five minutes they'd seen two groups enter and one man leave. Though it looked like no one was guarding the entrance, they noted that as soon as someone reached the door, several men appeared in the foyer to meet them. They also noted the regular appearance of faces on the balconies above. These men would peer over the walls, walk from side to side, and then disappear from view. So they knew that eyes were watching above and below.

Just as they were about to wrap up and head back to their leader, they saw a small pickup truck, at least twenty years old, rusted, with one headlight missing, pull up next to the Green Palace, the small restaurant next door to the Hop Sing Tong. An old man exited the driver's side, and another man, younger but not young, joined him at the back of the pickup. There they lowered a metal barrel that was at least three feet high from the group of barrels in the back. On the side of the barrel, they could read 'Cooking Oil' stenciled in English. They put the drum onto a dolly and walked to the front of the closed restaurant. They knocked, and a moment later, the door opened and they entered. The men in the alley noted that the guards in the Hop Sing Benevolent Association made no move or took no notice of the truck.

Three minutes later the restaurant door opened again and the men returned dragging a different barrel, one that looked well used, out of the restaurant. They maneuvered it to the rear of the truck and, with practiced effort, lifted the barrel of used cooking oil onto the bed of the truck. They wiped their hands, got in the truck, and continued down the block. The men noted that they stopped at the end of the block and appeared to repeat the process at a different restaurant up the way. They knew their leader would find this most interesting.

In a room, four stories above the street, Lin Tai Lo shifted uncomfortably on the bed inside the apartment that took up half of the upper floor. Their leader, Father Sun, had used the apartment for years, but as his family grew and his grandchildren grew in number, Sun preferred to spend time at his home in Pacific Heights. He'd also purchased several homes for his children nearby as a way to keep them and the beloved grandchildren close. That left the apartment to John, who now lamented the fourth-floor walk up because his side still ached from the wounds he received in his battle with Dragon Eye Wen.

His men had celebrated once news of his victory raced across Chinatown, as gossip so often did. They'd brought him here instead of the hospital, knowing their doctors could tend to him and he'd be safe in their headquarters. Now John felt restless as the wounds began to heal, but the consequences of the battle were yet to be determined. He was pleased that his men lauded his victory over the hated Hei Long Tong, but officially, John had broken the peace that had held all the Chinatown Tong in place for decades. He'd received a curt phone call from Father Sun asking about his health. "I'll recover soon," he'd said, and was prepared to try to explain himself, but Sun had simply grunted and hung up. Now he wondered what the repercussions of his independent actions might hold for his future with the Hop Sing.

He slowly walked to the kitchen, where he began to make a pot of tea, when there was a knock at the back door. Before he could respond, the door opened, and in walked Father Sun, the venerable leader of the Hop Sing Tong. John turned and gave a deep bow. "Father Sun," he said, "I wasn't expecting you."

Sun, dressed in a well-cut business suit, leaned on his ebony-handled cane and looked around the kitchen. "I always liked this kitchen," he said, walking inside.

"May I offer you some tea?" John asked.

"Tea would be most welcome," Sun said and sat down at the kitchen table. John pulled two delicate porcelain cups from the shelf and brought them and the pot to the table. He set them down with a small bow, and Sun gestured for him to sit.

John eased himself down into the chair, with Sun noting the tightening of the younger man's face as he did so. Once seated, John poured tea for the man who'd been like a father to him for many years. They drank in silence.

"Sir, I must apologize for ..." John began, but Sun held up his hand and gave a somber nod of his head.

"I've heard what the Hei Long were doing to those girls," he said quietly. "Of course, there was talk before, but I didn't want to believe." He took another sip of tea. "I'm an old man now, Tai Lo. My stomach for battle has grown small."

John was surprised by this admission from his revered elder. He eased into the waters, saying, "You've become wiser, *Sun Zi*." Great Master. John leaned a bit forward and continued.

"My taste for battle has diminished as well. To lead in war is in some ways simple compared to the complexities of leading in peace," John said, and Sun gave a weary shake of his head.

"I recall you saying, years ago when I asked you about the Boxer Rebellion, about the futility of fighting the English with their guns and you with your fists." John continued, "I asked about it because it was a conflict doomed to fail. Do you recall what you told me then?"

"No."

"You said that there's a peace that can only be found on the other side of war. Even a war that's lost."

"Words," Sun said and sat back in his chair.

"Good words. I see now that there must be peace among the Tong if we're to lift our people up. But the Hei Long won't permit that, so there must be a fight before we can find that peace. I'd hoped that if I defeated Wen, we might avoid the risk to so many more men, but he escaped."

"Yes, but word of your victory has spread all over Chinatown," Sun said, smiling at him for the first time. "They know him as a coward, and your stature has only grown. I'm very proud of you, my son," he said, and John felt his throat tighten and his eyes well up. He bowed his head and stammered to say thank you. Sun reached over and lay his weathered hand on the man's shoulder.

"I think that once you're well and we've finally settled this matter with the Hei Long," he said, "it's time for you to assume the mantle of leadership." John looked up, blinking back tears and letting that information sink in. "You're ready to lead, and I'm ready to just be a grandfather. You'll take our people into a new decade. But first we must put an end to the Black Dragons."

It was just after 10 pm, and City Lights Bookstore was closing. A few stragglers had to be shooed out as usual. The bookstore had become a hangout and a cheap date for young Beats out on the town, so Shig was used to this routine. Scanning the shelves, he spotted one last patron.

"Hey, man, we're closing up," Shig said to the back of the man in the history section. As the man turned and walked toward the counter, Shig's heart thundered as he recognized the man from the basement in Chinatown and his previous visit to the store with the doctor. Thorne smiled as he approached, and Shig did his best to act casually.

"Do you remember me? My name is Thorne. I came in a few days ago with a friend of mine. You sold us a copy of *Doctor Zhivago*," Thorne said.

"Oh, yeah. Sure. The Communist thing. Umm, how can I help you?"

"I seem to have lost my friend, and I think you might be able to help me find him," Thorne said with an unpleasant smile.

"I have no idea what you're talking about, man."

Thorne leaned onto the counter, bringing him unnervingly close to Shig. "I also seem to recall we were in Chinatown together a couple nights ago. I never forget a face, Mr. Murao." Thorne waved his hand, and two other men entered: a small Hispanic man, and a broad Black man who flanked Shig as he stood up.

"Please come quietly, or there will be consequences." Shig nodded as the two escorted him out of the store and into a waiting car. Thorne walked over to a display and removed a book, placing it on the stool that Shig was perpetually ensconced upon. Then he walked to the door, flipped the sign over to 'Closed,' turned off the lights, and shut the door. A moment later, he was in the car and gone.

CHAPTER 27

As midnight approached, Epps began to exhibit signs of stress. He rose and walked the small apartment, going to the window, back to the kitchen, sitting for a few minutes, and then repeating the process. Dominic took him into the kitchen, and Kats and Molly could hear the Frenchman speaking in a low but urgent voice but couldn't make out the words. Occasionally they heard Epps' voice but not the content of his response.

"Sounds like a therapy session," Molly said, and Kats nodded.

"I remember nights back in the hospital in France when I couldn't sleep. Too much noise in my head."

"How did you deal with that?" Molly asked cautiously.

"There were some meditation techniques that helped, at least a bit. Thorazine is pretty effective, but I don't think of it as a long-term solution." She gave a grim smile at his attempt at humor and pressed onward.

"What did Dominic do that helped?"

"He got me active again. We started to run together, and as my body recovered, my head kind of followed. We would talk, usually after the runs, but nothing was forced. In hindsight I realize it was therapy, but it didn't feel like therapy."

She slid closer to him on the couch and took his hand in hers. "You know, you can always talk to me," she said, looking into his eyes. He smiled and nodded his head as he always did when things got serious. "Kats, really. I mean it. I want us to be able to share, *really* share, what's going on with us now, what happened to us in the past, and hopefully support each other."

This time he looked into her hazel eyes, seeing she really was trying to coax him into a conversation. He took a deep breath and squeezed her hand. "I think I'd like that," he said. "Thank you, Molly." She smiled, leaned over, and kissed him.

"So, tell me this," she began. "How did you feel about helping another soldier?"

He paused, letting the question sink in before he replied. "It feels important," he said. "It feels like something I have to do." He looked over her shoulder into the kitchen. "There's a connection that soldiers share. It's like a brotherhood, but even that doesn't fully describe it. There's a recognition that we share, even if we didn't serve in the same unit or even the same war." He thought of one-armed Cyril back in the library and the connection, unspoken, but clearly there. He thought of his friend Tak who'd pulled him out of that bunker in France and about how he was willing to help and protect Steven Epps when he sat down in his car today.

"In Japanese culture, there are twin concepts of *on* and *giri*. They're both about honor and obligation, but they're very different. *On* is that which is voluntarily accepted and taken as one might agree to do a favor for a friend. *Giri* is different. It's the obligation that arises out of family, duty, and responsibility. *Giri* is heavy, and it can be difficult, but it's a matter of honor. The connection we soldiers feel, at least for me, touches on both of these ideas. Does that make sense?"

"I think so," she said.

"It also means I should try to help Dominic now," he said as he stood up. Molly watched him go into the kitchen. She could hear them speaking in low voices as she closed her eyes and laid her head on the couch pillows.

She hadn't intended to fall asleep, but she jerked awake

as Kats sat down beside her and stroked her arm. Turier and Epps stood by the door wearing their jackets. He pulled the small blanket up to cover her shoulders and kissed her forehead.

"Are you going somewhere?" she asked in a sleepy voice.

"We're going for a walk. It will help Steven relax. Apparently, he does it every night, and it relieves his stress."

She sat up and looked at the three of them. "You two should put on hats," she said, looking at the Frenchman and the soldier. "You can find a couple of baseball caps in that closet."

"Thanks," said Kats. "We should be back in a couple hours."

Shig sat in a starkly lit conference room. The table was surrounded by eight chairs, and a water cooler was in the corner near the locked door. He'd been in the room for well over an hour but had lost his sense of time, along with his watch and the contents of his pockets. At first he'd been terrified, riding in the back of the unmarked car, flanked by two silent men. The man he knew to be Thorne sat up front with the driver, but no one spoke. Shig watched as the car rolled through town, and shortly after he realized that they were headed out onto the Presidio.

As they slowed at the entrance gate, the large Black man next to him put his arm around Shig's shoulder, and the smaller Hispanic man put his hand on Shig's knee, squeezing. The driver flashed some credential, and the guard gave a salute as the gate opened. They rolled past Chrissy Field to an old hangar building. Shig was hustled inside and moved to a locked conference room.

After that initial rush of fear and adrenaline, Shig now

found himself tired. He had paced around and was thinking of climbing on top of the conference table for a nap when he heard a key in the door. A moment later it opened. A thickset White man, in his forties with thinning brown hair and a mustache, entered first, followed by the lean predator that was Thorne. Shig unconsciously stepped back but did his best to keep a calm face.

The mustache spoke first. "Mr. Murao, please sit down," Hauser gestured to the chair at the end of the conference table.

"What the hell is this, man?" Shig said, forcing his voice to sound more authoritative than he felt. "You can't just grab an American citizen off the street."

"We can do far more than that, Mr. Murao. Sit down please." Hauser pointed to the chair, and Shig looked at Thorne, who gave him a wink and nodded toward the chair. Shig sat.

"Shigeyoshi Murao," Hauser began. "Born December 8, 1926, in Seattle, Washington. Son of Shigekata and Ume. Army veteran. Served with the Military Intelligence Service[14] during the war. Stationed in Japan as a translator during the Occupation. Attended Roosevelt College in Chicago but didn't complete a degree. Currently the manager of City Lights Bookstore. Arrested on obscenity charges in 1957 for the sale of a book of poetry. Last seen in a Chinatown basement two nights ago."

"I also play the flute,"[15] Shig said with a tight-lipped smile. Hauser ignored the retort.

"Mr. Murao ..."

"Call me Shig. Everybody calls me Shig."

"Shig it is. Shig, you're in a shitload of trouble. You see, you and your friend, the private detective, have involved yourselves in an important government project. If you thought federal obscenity charges were serious, this is a whole other can of worms. Do you have any idea of the trouble you and your friend are in?"

"I've heard that drug dealers don't like it when you mess with their operation, but this is my first time, so I'm still learning."

"We're doing vital research, and yes, there are drugs involved. But the purpose is to protect the country. You were a soldier. Don't you want to protect your country?"

"My country and I have a complex relationship. I fight for her, but she's been a bit of an indifferent bitch to me and folks who look like me. So maybe save the King and Country pitch."

Thorne actually smiled at that, and Hauser glowered. "I know you and the detective have been working with the Frenchman, Turier. We need to locate him as well as a certain missing soldier that you must know about."

"Steven Epps," Shig said. "Yeah, just saw him the other night." Hauser spun around at that and leaned over Shig.

"You saw Epps?" Shig nodded with a smile. "Where?"

"Chinatown actually," Shig looked at Thorne. "Saw you there too." Thorne and Hauser exchanged looks, and then Hauser pressed on.

"Do you know where Epps is?" Hauser asked.

"I have no damn idea," Shig said confidently. "Epps was there in the crowd but slipped away. I ain't seen him since," he said truthfully.

"What about the Frenchman and your friend, the private eye?"

"I don't know the French guy. He's an old friend of Kats. Heard he was actually working for you," he said, looking up at Hauser.

"Where are they?"

"Did you try Kats' house in Japantown?"

"We're watching it."

Shig gave a shrug and spread his empty hands as if to say, *that's all I've got.* Hauser didn't believe him. "Mr. Murao ..."

"Shig."

"Yes, Shig. I want to believe you, but I'm just not sure," Hauser said with feigned sympathy.

"You gonna bust out the thumbscrews and rubber hoses?" Shig asked far more casually than he felt.

"Nothing so primitive. No, you'll actually get to help us in our experiments." Hauser walked to the door and opened it to allow two men, clad in white lab coats, to enter. The one carried a metal box that he set on the table in front of Shig. Once it was open, Shig could see a hypodermic needle and a vial of clear liquid sitting in the padded foam interior.

"What the hell is that?" Shig asked, his eyes growing wide.

"Lysergic Acid Diethylamide. LSD, but with some of our special additives. Think of it as truth serum." Hauser nodded, and Thorne and the other white-clad man gripped Shig from behind, pinning him to the chair. He swayed back and forth but couldn't get any leverage while seated. He saw the medical technician fill the syringe with the clear liquid and jerked his head. Hauser ordered the man to proceed. Shig's mind raced, but the men who held him were too strong. As the needle entered his arm, he gritted his teeth and thought, *What would Kats do?*

Two in the morning came and went, and Epps still continued his relentless pace up and down the hills of San Francisco. Turier and Kats would occasionally talk, but Epps remained silent. They wound their way north on Divisadero to the bay, then east along the water, passing Fort Mason to the Embarcadero. They followed that around the edge of the city, the light of the near full moon on the dark water. The salt air mixed with the smell of oil and gasoline from the working boats and trucks that called the waterfront home. Even at this late hour, many late-night revelers and third-shift workers were bringing the city to life. As they approached the Ferry Building, they could see the massive Embarcadero Highway construction that had begun and soon would connect downtown San Francisco to all the bridges and bring the car to the forefront of city design.

"What's this building called?" Turier asked as they paused along the water, looking up at the clocktower. 2:45 am, it declared.

"The Ferry Building," Kats replied. "One of the busiest transit centers in the world. At least, it used to be until they opened that bridge," he pointed to the illuminated Bay Bridge, "and everybody started traveling by car."

"This is beautiful," Turier said. "You see the French Beaux-Arts style in the design."

Epps looked over at the highway construction that would soon block the view of the building, "Seems wrong to put something that ugly next to something this pretty," he said. Kats and Turier turned toward him, nodding in agreement.

They headed inland on Mission back toward Hayes Valley. Walking in companionable silence, Epps was in the lead. Passing a service alley on their right, a voice came out of the darkness, "Hey, you gotta smoke?" The three of them stopped, as a shape, then another, moved out of the darkness into the pool of a streetlight. Two tattered-looking men emerged from the alley, and in the hand of the lead man was the glint of steel. A gun. Kats cursed himself for the lapse in attention as they stopped.

The man with the gun pushed it forward, his clothes dirty and worn. He and his friend looked as though they'd been sleeping in that alley for days. "Gimme your wallets," he said with a slight waver in his voice, like he wasn't sure that was what he wanted to say. His friend stood at his side, desperation in his eyes as well. Kats knew that desperate men could be very dangerous, so he slowly reached for his wallet, and holding it in front of him, he stepped forward in front of Dominic. The Frenchman pulled some cash from his front pocket and held it before him as well. From the corners of their eyes, they were also watching Epps, silently willing him to remain calm.

The unarmed man reached forward, grabbing at the extended money in Turier's hands, and then turned toward Kats. At the same time, the gunman turned the barrel in Epps' direction, "You too. Wallet," he said with a shake of the gun. Epps stood motionless, his eyes focused on the gunman. The gunman shook the gun again and took a half step toward him when Epps moved like a mongoose. One second he was there motionless, and the next was a blur. He slapped the gun out of the man's hand and threw him over his hip, bringing the man down hard upon his back. His friend's eyes went wide, and in that second, Kats moved forward with a shoulder strike that propelled the man backward into the wall. With an audible grunt, the friend collapsed forward onto his knees. Kats looked at Turier, who gave a nod that he was OK. The two of them turned toward Epps, who squatted beside the prone man, looking into his pained eyes with an unwavering stare. Epps slowly tilted his head back and forth like a cat regarding its captured mouse.

"Steven?" Turier said quietly, "can you hear me?" Epps showed no sign that he could. "Steven, these are poor, desperate men. They don't deserve to die. Please, they're not the enemy."

Epps leaned close to the frightened man, looking closely at him, smelling him. The dirt, the sweat, and the booze filled his nose. "Were you a soldier?" he asked the man, who frantically nodded.

"Yeah. Yeah, I was in the army. Served in Italy," he said, looking up at Epps.

"Then be a soldier. Be better than this," Epps said to him. "We're supposed to protect people, fight for them. Remember that?" The man stared back at Epps, and a moment later, he blinked and slowly nodded his head. Then, to Kats' surprise, the man began to cry. Epps laid a hand on the man's shoulder. Then he reached into his own pocket and pulled out a handful of cash and handed it over to the man, who looked even more surprised than before. Epps helped the man to his feet. "You can still be a soldier," he said to the man, who was wiping his eyes. "Go." The man turned and grabbed his friend, and they disappeared up the alley.

"Steven, that was amazing," Turier said, coming forward. "You were calm, and the gun didn't affect you." Epps looked at Turier and gave him a small smile. Then he caught Kats' eye. The two men stared for a moment, Epps knowing that Kats understood how close he'd come to killing that man, and Kats knowing how much effort it had taken Epps to reign in that savage instinct.

"Woooaaahhhh!" Shig yelled as he stood on top of the conference table, laughing and staring intently at the coffee cup in his hand. "This is so cool!" He then sank down onto

PETER KAGEYAMA | 275

the table, sitting cross-legged and holding the cup like a baby bird. The two men, one a trained nurse and the other a newly minted agent fresh from Washington, DC, looked at each other. For the past hour, they'd observed the increasingly animated Shig move from a dreamy state to the manic happiness that was now on full display. The nurse moved to take the coffee cup from Shig, who released it with a huge smile. "Be free," he whispered. The young agent snapped his fingers, trying to get Shig to focus.

"Mr. Murao, do you know where this man is?" he asked, holding up a photo of Turier. "This is Dominic Turier. We need to find him. Do you know where he is?" Shig's eyes widened momentarily and then seemed to focus on the photo. He smiled.

"Can I have a Coke?" he asked, looking back and forth at the two increasingly impatient men.

"Tell us where this man is," he shook the photo, "and I'll get you a Coke."

"I want a Coke now!" Shig yelled as he took the photo from the man's hand. As the man tried to grab the photo back, Shig held it away from him, playing adult keep-away as he laughed.

"Coke! Coke! Coke!" he sang, and then he rolled backward onto the table, lying flat, looking up at the ceiling.

"Get him a fucking Coke," the agent said to the nurse.

Ten minutes and two bottles of Coke later, they were no closer to the answers they sought, as Shig sat contentedly at the table, singing softly to himself. The door to the conference room opened, and Hauser stepped inside, glowering at the scene before him.

"What the hell is going on here?" Hauser demanded.

"Sir," the nurse said, "he's had an unusual reaction to the injection ..."

"Hey, man!" Shig waved at Hauser and then let out a huge belch. He raised an empty Coke bottle and asked, "Do you want a Coke?" Hauser shook his head, looking at the two men. He balled up his fist and made a punching gesture.

"Sir, I don't think that would have any effect," said the nurse. "He's in a euphoric state, and a punch in the face probably wouldn't even register as anything like pain. More like a new sensation." Hauser looked like he wanted to punch the nurse, but instead he turned and pulled up a chair to sit in front of Shig.

"Mr. Murao," he began.

"Call me Shig," he replied with a grin, pointing toward his face. His eyes followed the finger, and he laughed again.

"Shig, your friends called. Katsuhiro and Dominic ..."

"Kats!" Shig said.

"Cats?" Hauser looked confused.

"Call him Kats, man." Shig winked at Hauser.

"Yes, Kats and Dominic want you to meet them."

"Really? OK, cool. Let's go," he started to stand, but Hauser put up a hand.

"But where should we go? Where are they?" Hauser asked. Shig's eyes seemed to go in and out of focus as he screwed up his face thinking. "Where are they?" Hauser repeated.

"Pork chops!" Shig yelled. "We're gonna have pork chops!"

"He said something about pork chops earlier, sir," the young agent interjected. Hauser looked back at Shig and smiled and nodded his head, which made Shig smile and nod with him.

"I like pork chops too," he said. "Where are the pork-chops?"

"*Tonkatsu,* dummy," Shig laughed. "We call them *tonkatsu!*"

Hauser smiled and nodded at Shig. He stood and turned to the two men, "Japantown," he said. "Find out who Takemoto's friends are in that neighborhood."

CHAPTER 28

Kats awoke next to Molly in her bed. The sunlight was creeping into the windows at an angle that he knew made it early. He quietly rose, letting her sleep. He closed the bedroom door and walked into the living room. Turier was asleep on the couch, but the pillow and blanket Epps had taken for his bed were empty below the front windows. Kats turned and walked to the kitchen, where he found Epps sitting at Molly's small dining table. He was drawing in the notebook and looked up as Kats entered.

"Good morning," Kats said, and Epps nodded. "Did you get any sleep?" he asked.

Epps smiled, "A bit. I don't need much sleep anymore since the ..." he trailed off. Kats went to the counter and started making coffee. As he worked, he glanced over at Epps.

"What are you drawing?" he asked casually. Epps looked down at the page he'd been working on and turned it so Kats could see. There in a series of graceful pencil strokes, Dominic Turier's face looked back from the page. Kats nodded appreciatively.

"He had me start drawing a while ago, but they would only give me crayons back at the hospital. Drawing helps," he said with a shrug.

"Tell me something," Kats asked. "Dominic has said that when you become stressed or angry, your body produces hormones and chemicals that make you stronger and faster than normal men." Kats caught himself, "Sorry, not normal. I mean like average men." Epps nodded. "I saw that myself when we first met in that parking garage." The coffee pot began to boil, and Kats poured them both cups of black coffee. He sat down opposite Epps.

"But yesterday, with those two guys in the alley and in my car, you moved faster than I've ever seen anybody move. And you didn't seem stressed or angry. So ..." Kats let the thought hang there. Epps took a sip of his coffee.

"I'm faster and stronger than I ever thought possible. I don't need to be in that manic state for it to happen, I'm just like that all the time," Epps said, taking another sip of coffee.

"Amazing," Kats said.

"But I still worry about entering that crazy state. It happened in that garage with the fight with that gang. When I become like that, I can't control myself. People died then, and I might have killed you," he said to Kats.

"Do you remember much?"

"I remember what led up to it, and then after that things went red. I get flashes of faces, events, like remembering a crazy dream."

Kats nodded, thinking about the implications for Epps. "It seems like you're gaining more control of yourself and what might trigger you. Some might say that you have superpowers now."

Epps looked into his coffee cup. "Maybe. Doesn't feel too super, and I don't think it'll last."

"What do you mean?" Kats asked.

"I can't explain it, but I feel like a candle that's burning down. Like all this power is using up my body."

"We should tell Dominic and get you to some real doctors."

"No fucking way," Epps said with a snort. "I've had it with the doctors, the prodding, the tests, the needles ... Never again."

Kats nodded, trying to understand this man's experience and respecting his perspective. He stood up and went to make a cup of coffee for Molly. "Cream and two sugars," he said to Epps. "I like bringing her coffee in bed."

"You're lucky to have someone like that," Epps said.

"Yes, I am."

By midmorning they'd packed up and driven to Japantown. Kats parked in a public lot a block away from Mrs. Harada's home, and they walked up the alley to the back entrance of her house on Buchanan. A quiet knock, and the tiny, smiling, gray-haired lady welcomed them inside. Kats motioned to the men, "Take off your shoes," and he pointed to the row of slippers that were atop the small *getabako*, the shoe box for outside footwear. Mrs. Harada welcomed Molly with a hug and turned to look at the two strangers with them.

"*Obatchan*," Kats used the polite term for grandmother, "these are my friends Dominic and Steven." The two men made small bows to the tiny woman, who smiled up at them and gestured for them to come inside. Mrs. Harada had doted upon Kats for years since his parents had returned to Japan, but when her only daughter, Emiko, had moved out into her own place late last year, Kats felt that she needed somewhere to direct her energies. Now she had a whole houseful to take care of. Within minutes of their arrival at their new hideout, she served them tea along with sweet *mochi* from Benkyodo Bakery just up the street.

Later that afternoon, Kats pulled Molly aside and, in a serious tone, he asked, "OK, are you ready for this?" Molly adjusted the scarf on her head that all but covered her red hair. She pulled on a pair of stylish sunglasses as well, and the disguise was complete.

"Kats, we're going to the grocery store," she said in a low voice, trying to be serious.

"You're on a reconnaissance mission," he said, as he adjusted the scarf. "OK, you're good," he said, and she kissed him. Mrs. Harada moved to the front door with her small pull cart that she used to go to the local market. She and Molly put on their shoes and left, walking down Buchanan Street toward Post. At the corner they looked east, to their left, and saw Kats' home at 1664 Post. The three-story Victorian was one of many. They crossed Post and walked up the street toward the small grocery that the Shinjo family owned. Mrs. Harada walked at Molly's side, with the cart rolling behind her. Molly took advantage of the slow pace to look around, searching for signs that Kats' home was being watched.

The street was busy as usual during the late afternoon, but as they walked up the street, Molly noticed a dark sedan parked on their side of the road, a few car lengths past 1664. There were two men in the front seat, and Molly noted cigarette smoke coming out of the open windows. They walked past them, and Molly made a pretense of leaning in toward Mrs. Harada to bend down a bit and look in the window. Two White men, dressed in suits and wearing dark glasses, sat in the car. One was reading a newspaper as the other had his head turned toward Kats' home. Molly then stood upright, and they continued their way to the corner store. Mrs. Harada shopped for the evening meal as Molly stood inside the storefront peering out the front window. As she scanned the street scene, she noted a second car at the far corner, also with two men sitting inside.

As Molly stepped forward to pull the cart for her, Mrs. Harada looked up at the tall woman and asked, "Do you see anything?"

Molly nodded, "At least two cars are watching his house," she said, and Mrs. Harada nodded. Molly was silently impressed with the older woman's calm acceptance of the extraordinary circumstances she found herself in. As they walked home, Molly ventured a question.

"Doesn't all of this worry you?"

Mrs. Harada walked a few steps and then looked up at Molly, "I know Katsuhiro is a good boy. A good man. I not worry so much about him now. I worry more when he was in war."

"Were you in the same camp as Kats' family?"

"No, we were sent to Topaz[16] in Utah. But I write to Yaeko, Katsuhiro's mother, all the time. We both worry so much about our sons."

"Was your son in the 442nd as well?" Molly asked, referring to the famed nisei army unit that Kats belonged to.

"No. My son, Seiji, didn't serve. Seiji was one of the 'No No Boys,'" she said.

"I don't know what that means," Molly said.

"During war, the government say that nisei boys could fight. But to be able to fight, all nisei had to swear loyalty to America first. Most all did. Katsuhiro did. My son Seiji and some others would not. They say they fight, but not swear oath. Say German or Italian boys not have to swear oath, so it was wrong for nisei boys to have to say. They call them 'No No Boys' because they answer 'no' on two boxes in enlistment papers."[17]

"I had no idea," Molly said. They continued walking.

"The government take Seiji away to Tule Lake Camp in northern California. They put all the No No Boys and the ones they think most disloyal in that camp. It was very bad."

"I'm so sorry that happened to you, to all of you," Molly said, not knowing what else to say.

"It all work out. Seiji took that experience, and it make him go to law school. He is lawyer in Chicago now."

"What did Kats think of Seiji's decision?" Mrs. Harada shrugged her shoulders.

"He respect decision, and they still friends. Seiji always say he is very proud of Katsuhiro's service. Katsuhiro was groomsman in Seiji's wedding."

"Wow," was all Molly could say.

As they arrived back home, Molly saw that Kats was on the phone. "Message service," he said as they came into the kitchen. It had been two days since he'd checked in, and there were a couple of inquiries and a message from John with a number to reach him. Kats still wasn't sure how to explain Epps to John, so he decided that call could wait. But he did need to update Shig on where they were and make sure he was coming to dinner, so he dialed the number for City Lights. Ten minutes later, he came into Mrs. Harada's living room, where they all sat watching TV. Molly looked up and saw concern on Kats' face.

"What's wrong?" she asked.

"Shig is missing," he replied.

"What do you mean, missing?"

"He was supposed to be at the store this afternoon but didn't show up. They sent a guy to look for him at the usual haunts, Caffe Trieste, Washington Square Park, Vesuvio. Then they tried Shig's place, called Ginsberg and some of the other writers he hangs out with ... nothing."

"No note, no message anywhere?" Molly asked as the others listened with concern.

"They said the morning person found a copy of *Doctor*

Zhivago placed on the stool up front that he usually perches himself upon.

"*Doctor Zhivago?*" Turier exclaimed. "Oh, Kats. I fear I know what that means." He explained to them the trip to City Lights with Thorne and the book reference. "They wanted us to find that. It must mean they want to talk."

"No," Kats said, "it means they want to trade."

"Trade?" Turier asked.

"Yeah. You for Shig," Kats replied.

"Me? I thought they would want Steven."

"They do, but they don't know he's with us. They must think he's still at large."

"*Mon Dieu*, you're right! Can we use that?"

"I hope so," Kats said, the beginnings of a plan forming in his head.

Shig sat in an overstuffed chair in the kitchen of the converted hangar that had become the base of operations for Hauser's team. He took a swig of Coke from the bottle in front of him and laughed. "You rate James Joyce over Ernest Hemingway? I can't even keep up with the stream of conscious musing in *Ulysses*."

Thorne shrugged his shoulders and took a sip of his coffee. "Perhaps because I have a more European perspective to their work. Hemingway, despite his cosmopolitan airs, is an American cowboy at heart. All the guns, the hunting, the bullfighting. Joyce was an artist with his words."

"Hemingway is absolutely an artist with his words! A minimalist artist, and that's what makes him remarkable. Think about what he doesn't write!" Thorne laughed out loud at that and went to pour himself another cup of coffee from the pot. Shig's eyes followed him. He knew he was still technically a prisoner in this building, but when he'd awoken earlier in the day, a bit fuzzy headed and wildly hungry, Thorne had come to escort him to the kitchen. Shig knew he couldn't outrun and certainly couldn't outfight this man, so he accepted the situation as best he could. As he ate, their conversation eventually came around to books, and Shig was surprised to find out how well read this soldier was. For the past two hours they'd gone back and forth on various literary topics, and Shig found that Thorne had insightful opinions on all of it. He'd been particularly interested in Shig's experience with Allen Ginsberg's *Howl* and the obscenity trial that followed.

"It shocks me that your country," Thorne said, "with its freedom of speech, would be so fearful of something like a poem."

"Words, art, can be more powerful than guns. And people fear change," Shig said.

"It's beneath you," Thorne said. "Actually, it's beneath us," he finished emphatically.

"You're an American citizen?"

"For several years now. In return for my service."

"So, you work for an asshole like Hauser?" Shig deadpanned.

"I'm a soldier. Working for assholes is part of the job description."

"You're not what I expected," Shig said to him. Thorne gave a slight side-to-side motion of his head as he poured his coffee. "Don't you want to be something more than a soldier? You're clearly a smart guy. You could be lots of other things."

Thorne sat down, "At some point, you've been something so long, you don't know how to be anything else."

"Tell you what. Get me out of here, and I'll get you a job

at City Lights. Pay isn't so great, but you get a 20% discount on books."

"Let me think about it," Thorne said with a wry grin.

CHAPTER 29

After twenty-four hours of sitting in the heat of the sun and the chill of the San Francisco night, the two surveillance teams were tired, unshaven, irritable, and ready to be anywhere else. The senior agent—Harrison was his name—got out of the car and walked stiffly to the coffee shop at the end of the street. He passed through the lunch crowd and headed to the back of the shop, where he used the restroom and then went to the pay phone by the back door and dialed a familiar number. Thirty seconds and two transfers later, Hauser picked up. "Status?" he asked.

"No change, sir. The place is quiet as a tomb," Harrison said. "I think he's too smart to come back, sir," he ventured, almost hearing his boss's jaw clenching through the phone.

"Stay on-site," Hauser said and hung up the phone. *Time to escalate*, he thought as he opened his notebook to search for a phone number.

Despite being exceptionally well fed for the past twenty-four hours, Kats and his friends were becoming restless, especially Epps. It had taken a toll on him not to go out walking during the night. It required a marathon session of Gin Rummy with Kats and Turier to distract him. The following morning, Kats invited him to join for calisthenics in the basement. The hour-long session had left Kats and Turier astounded at Epps' strength and endurance as he rattled off a hundred push-ups like they were nothing. But they all worked up a sweat and a bit of an appetite that Mrs. Harada was happy to accommodate. Kats had called his message service several times hoping that Hauser might use that method to contact them regarding Shig. Nothing. After the evening meal, a dish from southern Japan called *okonomiyaki*, a savory pancake of meat, vegetables, and seafood, the group sullenly watched TV while Kats and Epps cleaned up after dinner. 'KP,' Kats had called it, and Epps happily joined him in washing dishes. As they were finishing up, Molly yelled from the living room.

"Kats, get in here quick!" she shouted, and they came into the room, lit by the evening news on the television set. There on the screen, Kats saw his own face, the picture from his P.I. license that was on file with the city.

"We repeat, if you've seen this man, identified as Katsuhiro Takeemoto," the male voice mispronounced his name, "please contact the San Francisco Police Department. He's wanted for questioning in connection with the double murder in the Tenderloin two weeks ago. He's believed to have two associates, a dark-skinned Frenchman and a redheaded woman. The suspect may be somewhere in Japantown, and there's a reward for information leading to his arrest."

"Shit," Molly said, still looking at the screen. Turier shook his head, while Epps returned to the kitchen to finish cleaning up.

"I'm not entirely surprised," Kats said. "They're getting desperate to find you, Dominic."

Molly looked worried but said nothing. Kats continued, "We were wondering if Hauser was going to reach out to us, and that's exactly what he did. He thinks he can get to you by finding me."

"We were already laying low. Now the whole city is going to be looking for us," Molly said. "We can't stay here, can we Kats?"

"No, we can't."

"Then where?" Turier asked.

"I think we need the Hop Sing Tong, but I have to talk to John before we can accept his help."

"Because he still believes Steven killed his cousin," Turier said.

"Yeah, we can't take Steven to John if he still thinks him responsible for Mai's death."

"And if he doesn't believe you?" Molly asked.

"Let's not jump off that bridge until we have to," Kats said and headed toward the phone.

John wasn't surprised by the phone call from Kats. His men had transferred the call up to the apartment, where he was slowly recovering. On the third ring, he picked it up, "*Wei*," he said casually into the mouthpiece.

"It's Kats," said the familiar voice on the other end. "I need your help."

"I imagine you do. That photo on the TV ... you look so young. The perfect, clean-cut Oriental boy." Kats ignored the jibe, setting long-standing arguments aside.

"The people behind all of this are getting desperate, which is why they're trying to bring me in. They think I can lead them to the people they seek."

"Can you?" John asked pointedly.

"It's more complicated than I can go into right now. I need to meet you in person before we can move forward, and time is getting tight because the police could start going door to door in J-town."

"How are you going to get out?"

"I have a little grocery list for your men to deliver. Once I get that stuff, I should be able to slip out and meet you."

"Tell me what you need," John said, sitting down at the desk.

Three hours later there was a knock at the front door of Mrs. Harada's home. Kats nodded to the group, and Mrs. Harada went forward to answer the door. There stood a young Chinese man, wearing a lightweight jacket over a food-stained t-shirt. His jacket read 'Delivery,' and he carried two large bags marked Green Palace Restaurant. Mrs. Harada ushered him inside, and he placed the bags on the dining room table. The man looked nervously about as Kats and the others entered the room. When his eyes found Molly, they went wide with surprise.

She looked curiously at him for a moment and then nodded in recognition. He was the cocky young Tong who'd grabbed her ass. As Kats was opening the bags, he noticed the strange interplay between the two and asked, "Do you know each other?"

"Haoyu, right?" she asked with a sly smile. The young man nodded. "Yeah. We met last week. He was with Shan in Chinatown. Thanks for bringing this," she nodded toward the bags.

Haoyu nodded in reply, smiled, and gave Molly a bow. Kats continued removing containers that clearly didn't contain food. He opened several of them, taking inventory, nodding, and pressing on.

He turned to Haoyu, "Looks good, thank you. Please tell Lin Tai Lo that I'll be there as soon as possible."

Epps was observing the exchange. "Is there anything to eat in there?" he asked expectantly. Haoyu nodded and reached into the bottom of a bag and pulled out a container marked "Egg rolls."

Kats looked at the container and grunted. "John knows I

hate egg rolls," he said to Molly, who found John's sense of humor quite funny.

Kats adjusted the fedora, pulling it down over the gray wig that covered his head. The gray mustache was secured via a small bottle of spirit gum, and the rumpled pants and suit jacket completed the ensemble. Earlier Molly had applied a bit of the stage makeup to his face, but she was surprised when Kats had taken over with practiced hands.

"Part of being a private eye," he said as he applied pancake, then a darker layer, some powder, and finally some darkened lines in the creases of his face. In minutes, his smooth thirty-something face looked sixty.

He'd wrapped a small pillow to his waist and secured it with bandages. Once covered in a shirt, it gave him an old man's belly. The jacket and hat completed the costume. He added the remaining tube of 'Two-Step Powder' to his breast pocket as a precaution. Molly stared at him.

"Well? How do I look?" Kats asked, turning around in the small bathroom.

"I don't like you in hats," Molly frowned, "but I suppose that's not the point. You don't look like you."

"That's the point," he smiled. "Now to get in character."

"What do you mean?" she asked as they returned to the living room. Everyone nodded their approval. Kats stopped and closed his eyes for a moment. As they watched, a miraculous transformation occurred right in front of them. Kats seemed to shrink a bit, and the clothes hung looser around him. He started to walk, but not his normal athletic stride. Instead, it was a slower, slightly pained walk of a man twice his age, whose bones and joints didn't work the same as a young man. Kats stooped to pick up a small bag, and again, the movement was that of an old man.

"You're a superb actor," Dominic said with a nod of his head.

"Another part of being a private detective," Kats replied, in a raspy, deeper voice. Molly laughed out loud.

It took Kats nearly an hour of slow, purposeful walking to make his way from Japantown to the Hop Sing Tong Benevolent Association building in Chinatown. He was just another old man walking the streets of San Francisco, no one giving him a second glance. Twice, police cars had driven past him, but he didn't alter has gaze or his gait, and they continued on their way. He walked into the first-floor entrance of the building which, despite the late hour, was still lit and busy. As he opened the door, two young Tong approached him, while two more eyed him from across the lobby.

"*Old man,*" said the one in Chinese, and Kats waved his hand in front of his face indicating he didn't understand.

"Old man," repeated the guard in English, "what's your business this late?"

"I'm here to see Lin Tai Lo," Kats answered in his old-man voice and gave a slight bow. The guards eyed him suspiciously.

"Lin Tai Lo isn't here," he lied, "but I'll take a message."

Kats smiled a weary smile, bobbed his head again, and said, "He's expecting me. Tell him his great-uncle is here." The men looked back and forth at each other. Then one nodded and went into a darkened office next to the lobby. Inside, he picked up a phone and dialed.

John answered on the first ring. "Sir, there's an old man here who says he's your great-uncle and wishes to see you."

"Yes, bring him up," John said with a half-grin.

"Sir, I'm not sure he can climb all the stairs," stammered the guard.

"He can climb them," John said and hung up the phone.

The knock was followed by a voice inside the room, "Come in," it said. The guard opened the door, and the old man stepped inside. The guard looked expectantly at John, who waved him away. "Go," he said.

Kats shuffled forward, still in character, and John gave him an appraising look. "I knew that semester of theater you took would come in useful," John said.

Kats stood up straight, twisting his shoulders back and forth, "It's hard to stay focused like that for long periods of time. Thanks for sending the supplies," he said. "How's the side?"

It was John's turn to grimace a bit as he stretched his left side. "Stiff, and it itches," he said and gestured for them to sit. On the coffee table was a pot of tea and some rice crackers.

John poured the tea and they drank. Kats had to hold his mustache to the side a couple of times before he figured out how to safely sip his tea. "You have some news, I take it?" he asked.

Kats nodded, carefully choosing his next words. "The man you think killed your cousin didn't do it. There was a confrontation, but your cousin was accidentally killed by one of the men she was working for."

John eyed him over the rim of his teacup as he took a sip. "And you know this how?"

"There's a film of the incident. My friend has seen it and confirmed that Mai's death was unintentional, but she was part of something terrible." Kats went on to explain the LSD experiments that were being conducted and Mai's tragic role in the operation.

John's face was a mask of control. Kats continued, "The man you thought killed her is named Steven Epps. He was a soldier and a prisoner of war. The Koreans and the Chinese experimented on him, and when Mai dosed him with the LSD, it triggered him. It made him violent. The government man was trying to stop Epps and accidentally shot your cousin."

John nodded, taking in this news. "There's more," Kats pressed on.

"I found the man, Epps." John's knuckles went white on the sides of his chair, and he sat forward. Kats put up a placating hand. "Please, let me finish."

"Epps was brought back to the US to be treated by doctors and psychiatrists. In fact, his psychiatrist is an old friend of mine from France. We worked together in the war. Epps was a very special case. So special that elements of the military and the government continued to experiment on him once he came back here. Horrible experiments."

"Your friend was part of that?" John asked sharply.

"No, Dominic knew nothing about that. But those experiments made Epps more dangerous, and when he escaped months ago, they thought he'd left the city. They didn't know who or what he was when Mai brought him back to that apartment in the Tenderloin. The drugs they gave him interacted with his unique system and caused the death of your cousin."

"What about the incident with my men in the parking garage?" John said.

"When they attacked Epps, his system reacted and triggered this crazy combination of drugs and hormones. He becomes stronger, faster, and more dangerous than an ordinary man. He reacted, and unfortunately your men were ..."

"Killed!" John exclaimed as he stood. "Three more dead, and one will never walk right again." He started to pace the room, wringing his hands.

"I know. I was there, remember?" Kats said calmly. "Epps is a killer, but he's not a murderer. His response was provoked." John started to say something but then snapped his jaw shut, eyes blazing at Kats.

"Katsuhiro," John strained as he spoke, "I must do something. My family and my Tong brothers have been killed." Kats nodded.

"What if I told you the man most responsible for putting your cousin in that room with Epps and triggering this whole chain of events is here in San Francisco? He continues to pull the strings, and he has my friend Shig captive somewhere." John slowly nodded.

"You also need to know that he's been supporting the Hei Long Tong. The Black Dragons have been supplying drugs and girls and space for this man's operation." Now Kats knew he had John's attention.

"I know this is hard, John. I really do. But leaders need to see beyond the emotions and look at the bigger picture. Epps isn't your enemy. The Hei Long and this man Hauser are. Can you see that?" Kats looked at him.

"Just two nights ago, Father Sun and I sat up here talking," John said. "He anointed me as his successor and the next leader of the Hop Sing Tong." Kats nodded. "He told me I was ready to lead. I thought that was true, but now this makes me doubt my own resolve."

"Leadership is about doing the hard thing," Kats said, "and I know you're strong enough to do that. Sounds like Father Sun knows that too. You just have to believe it."

John continued to pace, looking absently at the walls. He walked over to the chair he had sat in and put his powerful hands on the chair back. Kats could see the veins swell as he gripped it tightly, but in a firm, controlled voice he said, "I will show the Hop Sing Tong who our real enemies are."

"I have your word?" Kats asked, staring into his eyes.

"You do." Kats nodded, knowing John's word was iron-clad.

"Then we need to figure out how to get Epps and his doctor here."

"Here?" John asked, a bit surprised.

"They're being pursued by the police, the military, and the government. I can't just put them in a hotel. You can provide them the protection they need until we can get them out of the country."

"You have a plan for that?" John asked.

"More like a concept of how it would work. The plan is still ..." Kats waved his hand side to side. John snorted.

"Then let's arrange a cab and get them here," John said.

"I'm afraid it's not that easy. The police and government are looking for me, hence the disguise." John nodded. "They know I'm from Japantown, so they have that whole area staked out. Even before the police were alerted to me being a person of interest, we noted surveillance in the neighbor-hood."

"They're in Japantown?"

"Yes, along with Molly, my girlfriend."

"What about the bookseller?" John asked.

"We think they have Shig, and he might have been co-erced into giving up our location. We need to move them out of J-town. Fast." John seemed to be thinking as Kats spoke.

"My cousin," he said, "owns a tour bus that he drives

around the city giving tours that include the authentic 'Oriental' experience. Benedict Shen Tours. We could use that."

"Benedict Shen?" Kats asked, making a face. "Sounds kind of familiar ..."

"Everybody calls him 'Egg' because of his first name."

CHAPTER 30

Two gray unmarked trucks rolled out of the Presidio gates as the morning sky turned to orange in anticipation of the sun. Riding in the passenger seat of the lead truck, Thorne eyed the roads coldly as he smoked a cigarette. In the covered rear of the truck, his team along with two of Hauser's agents, all in civilian dress, rode in silence. They headed out of the base and toward their destination in Japantown.

For the past two days, surveillance had reported no signs of Takemoto, but Hauser knew today would be different. Having leaned on his police connections, he knew that a sweep of Japantown by the police was coming. Knocking door to door and making a visible presence, they hoped to find Takemoto. Hauser knew the man was clever and anticipated that he could slip through their net, which is why his men would be in place to snare the detective when he was flushed. Hauser rode in the passenger seat of the second truck with three more agents in the back. As a bit of added insurance, the second truck also held a grumpy Shig in the back. Thorne had watched Shig being placed in the back of the second truck and quietly asked Hauser, "Why are we bringing the bookseller?"

"Because he's Takemoto's best friend. If we need some leverage, he's right here," Hauser replied as he mounted the truck. Thorne watched him for a moment before returning to his vehicle.

The trucks rolled into a parking lot several blocks from Japantown. There they rechecked their radios, their maps, and their weapons. They knew the police sweep was coming later in the morning, so they had time to get into place. The trucks moved to their designated locations, the lead truck with Hauser's men to the south and west of Japantown on Fillmore and Thorne's team to the north of Japantown, just off Buchanan Avenue, near the heart of the neighborhood. As the city awoke around them, the teams moved into place.

Around that same time, Kats was wrapping up his phone call with Molly.

"We'll be ready," she said.

"Make sure there's no evidence connecting us to Mrs. Harada," Kats warned. "We don't want any trouble for her."

"Roger that," Molly said, which made Kats smile.

Just after 9 a.m., Kats and John walked out of the Hop Sing Tong Benevolent Association as a small bus rolled slowly up Waverly Place. The bus was old but brightly painted with primary Chinese colors—red, gold, and a prominent swatch of Hop Sing green down the side. "Benedict Shen Tours" was emblazoned with stylized lettering. The bus stopped, and the passenger door opened. A somewhat crazed-looking driver jumped out of the bus and approached John. He was small, and Kats estimated him to be in his forties, thinning hair, with the archetypal 'Fu Manchu' beard. He also had a slightly odd eye that further gave him a wild appearance.

"Hey, cousin!" said the man as he shook John's hand.

"Hello, Benedict. Thank you for helping me out," John replied.

"Of course, of course," said the small man. "Who's the old man?" he asked as he looked at Kats, still in his disguise.

"This my old friend Goto," John said with a smile. "Goto, this is my cousin Benedict Shen."

Kats extended his hand, which Shen heartily shook.

"Egg. Everybody calls me Egg. Nice to meet you," he smiled. "I hear we're going to Japantown."

"Yes," Kats said cautiously. "John explained we're collecting some friends ..."

"Discretely," Shen finished.

"Yes," John said. "You were going to provide some 'tourists' as part of the ruse," he gestured to the empty bus.

"We're gonna pick them up now!" Shen laughed as he headed back into the bus.

"We'll be expecting you," John said to Kats, who nodded and jumped onto the bus.

"Welcome, welcome!" Shen smiled as he ushered a dozen tourists onto his bus at Portsmouth Square. Kats sat in the front seat next to the door, keeping his head down a bit, just in case a sharp-eyed visitor might see through his disguise. No one gave him a second look as they took their seats and excitedly looked around, waiting for the tour to begin. Shen jumped spryly onto the bus and faced the group.

"Welcome to Benedict Shen's tour of exotic San Francisco. I'm Benedict Shen, your humble tour guide, driver, and sherpa through the secret Oriental side of this great city. We'll be stopping at a few places, so I hope you have on your walking shoes, ladies," he said, clapped his hands, and started the engine.

Over the next forty-five minutes, Shen drove slowly around the Chinatown neighborhood, constantly talking. He filled the tourists with half-truths, a few actual facts, and some wild stories that had Kats fighting not to laugh. They drove through North Beach, and Shen told them to be on the lookout for Beatniks and then excitedly pointed to a man walking down the street wearing a black turtleneck as authentic Beatnik. To Kats he looked like a local who knew summers in San Francisco were often cold, but the entire bus moved to the sidewalk side and attempted to take pictures of the confused man.

Kats knew their rough itinerary, but he still anxiously checked his watch. The bus had headed west and then south toward the Fillmore District, which bordered Japantown. They were planning on a stop there, and while the group looked at the theater, Kats would do a quick look around. The bus rattled down Fillmore, approaching the theater on their right. As the bus stopped at a red light, Kats caught something to his right on Geary Boulevard. A gray truck, with a canvas-covered bed, was parked half a dozen cars up the street. He'd seen those trucks the other day at Mount Sutro and knew they were from the army base. Now on high alert, Kats stared intently at the truck. Just before the bus began to move with the green light, a man in civilian clothes pushed back the rear flap of the truck and climbed down to the street. As he did, the morning sunlight shown in the back of the vehicle, and sitting there like the Buddha was Shig!

The bus crossed Geary and pulled up in front of the Fillmore Auditorium. "Folks, we're going to take a look at this lovely theater, the Fillmore. It's owned by Charles Sullivan and is a fantastic venue for bands visiting the Bay Area." Kats exited first and stood looking at the truck down the street as the tour group shuffled off the bus. He scanned the area, looking for another truck or men in a car. He walked back across the street, making a point of not staring at the truck, but taking in the entire scene. He saw the man return to the back of the truck carrying a small bag. As he stepped into the back, Kats noted another set of arms that helped him inside and the shape of Shig sitting further back. At least two guards, he realized.

Taking a chance, he walked his old man walk down the street. He moved closer to the truck as he shambled past. Just as he passed the truck bed, he heard the unmistakable buzz of a push-to-talk trigger being engaged on a walkie-talkie. He heard voices muffled behind the canvas cover but couldn't make out the words. Kats proceeded up the block, crossed the street, and returned to the Fillmore Auditorium as Shen was bringing the tour group back onto the bus. He caught Shen's eye and gestured for him to come closer.

"Slight change of plan," Kats said. "You still head to Japantown and the stop as we planned, but I've got to take care of that truck over my shoulder." Shen's eyes flicked past his, and then he nodded.

"We should be at the stop in ten minutes, give another ten for them to go in and come back out," Shen said. Kats looked at his watch.

"We'll try to be there, but if not, don't wait." Kats said.

"We?" Shen asked, but Kats was already on the move.

The residents of Japantown watched with a mixture of fascination and unease as six patrol cars parked at the edges of the neighborhood. Pairs of officers began walking the streets, holding pictures of the two suspects, Kats and the Frenchman, asking those who passed by if they'd seen either of them. The officers walked into shops and restaurants and were met with averted eyes and shaking heads. Most of them knew Kats; he and his family were long-time residents of the neighborhood. Many of them had solicited his services over the years and felt a sense of obligation to him. Moreover, most of the Japanese community didn't trust the police department. Those old enough to remember the war also remembered that the police had been part of the roundup of the Japanese community here and all over the west coast. They were respectful of the police but didn't wholly trust them. All of this Officer Elliot Blackstone knew, which was why he'd specifically requested this assignment.

Blackstone walked down Post, passing in front of Kats' house at 1664. He looked up at the second-floor window, thinking about sitting there in the kitchen, eating dinner and talking about all manner of things. He knew Kats had nothing to do with the killings in the Tenderloin and had told his superiors as much when the orders to sweep Japantown had come down. Despite these assurances, his captain shrugged and told him that the orders were coming from higher up and they had no choice. That was when Blackstone had insisted on being part of the detail. Now as he walked the streets of J-town, he hoped Kats was far away from this charade.

Thorne stood at the entrance to the alley running behind Post, holding the radio at his side, his eyes sweeping the street out of habit. Across the street he saw Esteban walking down the block. He'd seen two of Hauser's agents several minutes before, and he knew that Collins was in the coffee shop around the block with Zapek, watching the street from the window. The police had arrived some thirty minutes earlier, and he watched their clumsy efforts with disgust. He thought the whole exercise a long shot at best. He knew that the private eye was a soldier with significant field experience. He put himself in the man's shoes and wouldn't be anywhere near his home neighborhood, but Thorne was well versed in following ill-conceived orders.

There was a buzz on the radio, followed by the metallic voice of Hauser. "All positions report," the voice said. Several clicks overlapped each other, and Thorne made a face. Slowly they sorted themselves, and all reported the same thing: no sign of the targets. The handset clicked again, "Thorne? Recommendations?" Hauser asked.

Thorne did his best to sound professional, "I think our men should begin a moving sweep through the alleys," he said. It was a remote possibility, but it was the one area that might result in a hit.

Hauser clicked in, "Let's do it. Thorne, your teams move west. The rest of you move east."

As Elliot Blackstone stood on the corner, he saw a man standing in the alley and was surprised to see the man raise a radio handset to his ear and speak into the device. He recognized the PR6 walkie-talkie, which had replaced the cumbersome devices he'd seen during World War II. The SFPD had some of those, but few officers or field units used them. The man pushed the antenna down and stepped onto the sidewalk, turning toward Blackstone. As he looked up, he caught sight of the officer watching him, and his eyes widened just enough for Elliot to place his hand on the butt of his service revolver.

"Excuse me, sir," Blackstone said, holding up his left hand for Thorne to stop. "That's a bit of unusual hardware you've got there. Mind telling me what you're doing here?" His right hand rested on his holstered gun. Thorne eyed him up and down, disappointed in himself for his own sloppiness in being seen. He thought about the pistol in his shoulder holster and the small piece strapped to his leg but instead turned on a smile.

"Hey, officer," he said in his southern accent, "I think we're on the same team here." He raised his hands. "May I reach for my badge?" he asked.

"Slowly," Blackstone said as Thorne reached into his front-left lapel and pulled out the Military Police badge he'd used before. He showed it to Blackstone, who said, "What's an MP doing here?"

"Orders from army brass to back you guys up. The Frenchman you're looking for works for us, so they sent my team here," Thorne said with an 'aw shucks' shrug of his shoulders.

"I wish they'd let SFPD know. We could be stepping all over each other."

"Above my pay grade," Thorne said sympathetically, and Blackstone waved for him to follow. Thorne fell into step just behind Blackstone. In a smooth, nonchalant motion, he returned his badge to his breast pocket and, unseen by the police officer, slid the gun from the shoulder holster and into his waistband under his jacket. The two men walked back into J-town.

"All right, get ready for a real Oriental treat," Shen said in a loud voice as the bus rolled down Buchanan Street. The bus stopped just past Sutter Street and parked in a loading zone. "Here we are, folks, the famous Japanese bakery, Benkyodo." Shen stepped off the bus, and the others followed as they congregated outside the small shop. "This bakery has been here since just after the great earthquake and fire of 1906.[18] Every day they serve hundreds of Japanese confections, such as *mochi* and *manju*. They usually sell out by lunch time, so come on inside for a taste of authentic Japan!" he said, opening the door.

"Man, I gotta pee," Shig whined to the two agents in the back of the truck. They ignored him, glancing repeatedly at their watches. The bigger one, though they were both much bigger than Shig, held the radio and was the one who reported in every five minutes or so.

"Shut up or we'll put the gag back on," they warned. Shig rolled his eyes but held his tongue and tried not to think about his bladder.

Kats had made a purposeful walk back up the block, pausing to sit on a bus bench while he eyed the truck. He pulled the wooden tube out of his jacket and carefully removed the outer seals, leaving only the thin wax closures to hold the potent powder in place. He placed the tube behind his right ear like it was a cigarette and adjusted his hat to ensure he could easily grasp it. Satisfied, he crossed the street and now walked slowly toward the front of the truck. The sidewalk was busy, and late-morning traffic on Geary made him just another small element of the urban scene. He approached the truck, noting the rope ties that held the canvas tarp in place over the rear of the truck. There was just enough space for what he had in mind. Spotting a small gap in the tarp, Kats pulled the tube from behind his ear, and just before putting its end to his lips he shouted in Japanese, *"Bookseller! Hold your breath!"*

Inside the truck, Shig's eyes went wide at the shout. The two other men looked confused and then shocked as a cloud of yellow powder billowed into the enclosed space. Shig snapped his eyes and mouth closed as he heard the men grunt and sputter. Then with a thud, they were silent. A second later, the front tarp whipped back, and sunlight streamed into the back as Shig opened his eyes. He blinked furiously through the cloud, seeing a human shape standing at the foot of the truck.

"Shig, it's me! Jump down, but don't breathe that stuff," said an old man who held a hat in front of his face. Thinking this the better option than staying, Shig bolted forward and made an awkward jump out of the truck. The old man caught him with arms that were much stronger than he would have expected. Shig looked into the old man's face, who smiled back at him. Something in that smile he recognized.

"Kats?" he laughed. "Holy shit! It's you!"

"Yeah, it's me. Hold on a second." Kats put the hat in front of his face again as he reached up into the truck and then pulled his hand back, holding the radio. He and Shig headed north up Fillmore and then crossed the street and took a narrow alley that headed east toward Japantown.

"Hold up a second," Shig hissed as he stood facing a stack of crates in the dirty alley. "I told those guys I had to pee!" Despite the danger, Kats had to laugh.

They made their way through the alley that connected to another one that ran parallel to Buchanan and behind

Benkyodo. The two men peered out from behind the corner.

"What's the plan?" Shig asked.

"We have a ride, but we need to time this just right. You stay here. I'm going to the corner to see where they're at. If I wave you up, walk with me and join in the group that's getting on the bus. Keep your face down."

"Roger that," Shig said. Kats looked at him. "What? Isn't that what all you guys say?"

"The things people pick up on," Kats said with a grin, and he stepped into the alley. He walked up to the corner, looked back at Shig, and then proceeded toward the front of the store.

Three doors down from Benkyodo, Molly stared out the window at the parked bus in front of the bakery. It had been there about five minutes, and she was waiting to see the tourists start to reboard the bus. Turier and Epps stood by the front door waiting for the signal. They both wore baseball caps and had their jacket collars turned upward. Molly's hair was wrapped in a scarf again. Mrs. Harada stood next to her and reached over to take Molly's hand. She looked down at the smaller woman, who held a look of determination in her eyes. Molly squeezed her hand, "Thank you for all you've done for us," she said. Mrs. Harada smiled and gave a simple bow of her head.

"They're starting to come out," Molly said. "Let's move."

Kats approached the Japanese bakery and peered through its large front windows. Inside, several people sat at their coffee counter, but nearly a dozen stood in line, ordering from the counter. Egg Shen stood by the front door and, after a moment, he saw Kats through the glass. He gave a small nod that Kats returned. From outside, Kats could see Shen gesturing and waving his charges toward the waiting bus. Kats moved back toward the alley. *Now to move them out of position.* He raised the radio to his ear, clicked the handset several times, and in an out-of-breath voice said into the receiver, "Attention! Murao has escaped! Headed west on Geary. In pursuit. Repeat, escape ... west ... Geary!"

As the radio exploded with clicks and confusion, Kats waved Shig up the way, and together they casually walked toward the front of Benkyodo. As they rounded the corner, the last of the tourists were climbing on board Shen's bus, most clutching a small bag of confections from the bakery. Kats pushed Shig in front of him and onto the bus. As he did so, he looked over Shen's shoulder at three more people coming toward the bus. Two men, hats pulled low over their faces, approached, and Shen waved them in. They smiled at Kats as they jumped on the bus. Two steps behind came Molly, her eyes locked on Kats. She gave a huge grin as he gallantly gestured for her to board the bus. Kats followed, and the two of them found a seat up front next to Shen, who jumped on board and started the bus. The old bus complained for a moment as Shen struggled to put her in gear, but then they were slowly rolling down the street.

Relief filled Molly's heart as she kissed the old man, who looked like he could be her grandfather. As they sat next to the passenger window, Molly looked out as they passed Mrs. Harada's home. The old woman stood on her front porch watching them. Instinctually, Molly raised her hand to wave, and Mrs. Harada returned the gesture and gave a small smile.

Thorne's radio had suddenly exploded as he and Blackstone approached the corner of Post and Buchanan. He heard

"Murao" and "escape" and shook his head. He noticed a couple of Hauser's agents begin to run west toward Fillmore. "Excuse me, officer," he said as he picked up his pace and tried to get a clear message amid all the cross talk. As he stood on the corner trying to assess the situation, his eyes were drawn to movement on the right. He looked up the street at a colorful bus pulling out into traffic. Red, yellow, and bright green. Seemed a bit out of place for here. Then his keen eyes saw something else that was unusual. An old woman, Japanese he guessed, stood on her porch, also looking at the bus. Then, as the bus passed, she raised her hand and waved. Thorne watched the bus approach him. 'Benedict Shen Tours,' he read, and noted a dozen or so people in the back. He watched it roll down the street and turn left on the next block.

He started to walk up the street toward the old woman's house. The radio squawked. "Thorne, where the hell are you?" Hauser's voice barked. Thorne ignored him and stood in front of the home. The old woman had gone inside. He raised the radio to his mouth.

"Meet me at 1523 Buchanan," he said flatly and walked to the front door. He knocked. A moment later, the old woman opened the door and stared defiantly up at him. Thorne made a slight bow, almost apologetically, and then pushed his way inside. The woman was forced back but could do nothing, so she stoically stood aside.

"Shoes," she said in a firm voice, pointing to Thorne's shoes. Thorne looked surprised and then gave a smile and removed his boots. He stepped inside and began to look around. Naoko Harada prided herself on her clean house, and though four others had been staying there for several days, she knew there would be no sign of them. No dishes in the sink, no dirty clothes, nothing. Thorne went upstairs, and she could hear him moving around. Another *hakujin* came bounding up the steps. He was bigger, heavier, and breathing heavily as he arrived.

"Shoes," she repeated firmly, but Hauser brushed past her, looking for Thorne.

"*Iteki,*" she said quietly. Barbarian.

"Thorne!" Hauser shouted. "What do you have?" Thorne came down the stairs, still looking intently as if he couldn't quite put his finger on something. He walked into the kitchen, and Hauser followed. He looked in the sink and opened the cupboards and drawers while Hauser watched. Thorne's eyes noted a piece of paper on the table with a pencil drawing of the old woman. It was simple but quite good.

"What the hell are you looking for?" Hauser asked. Thorne walked past him and opened the refrigerator. Inside he noted a surprising amount of leftovers. Far more than a tiny Japanese woman could eat.

"They were here. I'm sure of it," Thorne finally said.

"How did they get away?"

"They had help. A tour bus. We can look it up."

"Bring the old woman," Hauser said. At that moment, there was a voice at the front.

"San Francisco Police," Blackstone said from the entrance. "Everything all right here?" He peered into the home and noted the elderly Japanese woman who seemed to be a bit shaken.

Thorne shook his head at Hauser. "No need to bring her. I think I know where to go."

"Where?" Hauser asked.

Thorne walked over to the trash can and pulled several containers out of the bin. They were marked 'Green Palace Restaurant.'

CHAPTER 31

The bus stopped on Waverly outside the Hop Sing Tong Benevolent Association after returning the happy but somewhat confused tourists to Portsmouth Square. Kats clapped Shen on the back. "Thank you, Benedict," he said, "that was a very enlightening tour of our city." Shen smiled.

"Anytime," he said. "I also do Bat Mitzvahs."

Several of the Hop Sing soldiers approached the bus and made a line leading into the building. As Kats stepped out of the bus, he saw John slowly coming out the door toward them. Shen jumped out and stood with Kats as the others shuffled off the bus. John looked from Kats, then to the others, his eyes lingering on Epps. Then he turned to his cousin.

He put his hand on Shen's small shoulder and handed him a thick envelope that Shen expertly pocketed. "I think you and the bus should get out of town for a few days. Go visit the redwoods. See some nature," John said.

Shen let out a cackle, patting the bulge in his jacket, "Redwoods? I'm headed to Vegas!" He gave Kats a punch in the shoulder, turned to the others, and gave a dramatic bow before leaping onto the bus and motoring down the street.

From the fourth-floor window of an old residential building, just down the street from the Hop Sing headquarters, a curtain rustled as a pair of eyes, aided by binoculars, observed the unusual drop-off in front of the building. He said something in Chinese, and the second man, seated in the room, hastily scratched notes onto a pad of paper.

John drew a measured breath, "We should go inside." Kats nodded, and the others followed. As they entered the building, Kats reached up and slowly peeled the mustache from his face.

"That itched like crazy," he said, wiggling his nose. He noticed again that John was staring at Epps, who returned the gaze impassively. Kats raised his hands and pointed to an empty community room across the lobby. "We should all talk," he said, leaning on John to come with him. They moved quietly into the room, and Kats flipped on the lights. John gestured to his men, who were ready to follow.

"Wait here," he said and closed the door. He turned and looked coldly at Epps.

"John, you know my friends Molly and Shig," Kats gestured to them as they sat down. "These two men are also my friends. Dominic Turier," he turned to the Frenchman, "and Steven Epps."

Turier extended his hand to John, "Thank you for your help," he said, and John looked at his hand. Slowly he reached out and shook it. Turier continued. "I know you were led to believe that he," Turier gestured toward Epps, "that Steven hurt your family ..."

"He did hurt my family," John said coldly.

"Please understand," Turier explained, "that he was drugged, and it caused a terrible reaction. But Steven didn't kill your cousin. I've seen the film."

"Not just Mai," John said, "my Tong family. My brothers. Three of them dead at his hand. More if not for Takemoto's intervention."

"John, you know they were supposed to wait for me. They acted rashly and ..." Kats trailed off, knowing this was cold comfort to John.

Epps had been strangely quiet since boarding the bus back in Japantown. He'd smiled a bit when Dominic had clapped him on the shoulder, saying they were going to safety. But Kats had been watching him, quietly worried that this might be stressing the man out. Kats feared something might push him over the edge, though they'd spoken at length the evening before about the family connection the Tong leader had to the girl who was killed. Epps nodded that he understood but said nothing more. Now Kats was worried that perhaps Epps didn't truly understand.

"I'm sorry about your cousin," Epps said quietly. The whole room went silent. "She didn't deserve that. I actually don't remember what happened, but Dr. Turier explained it all to me." Kats looked at John, seeing his jaw clenching. Epps stepped forward.

"I'm not sorry about your men," Epps said matter of factly. "They came after me. I defended myself."

"You remember that?" John asked with a thick voice.

Epps nodded. "Most of it." John turned away from the man, wringing his hands and trying to find his center again.

He turned back again, looking at Epps, but said to Kats, "This is very hard."

"I know, John. But you'll be the leader of the Hop Sing Tong. You have to be able to do the hard thing." John's head dropped forward and then rose again.

"For what it's worth," Epps said, "I *am* sorry for the pain this has caused you and your family." He looked squarely at John, who returned the gaze. After a long moment, John nodded, and Epps did the same.

On the other side of Chinatown, Dragon Eye Wen stretched and tested his recovering body. The herbs and ointments Dr. Han had provided seemed to have done their work. His strength was returning, and his battered face now merely showed the dark outlines of fading bruises. It was the battered reputation that now occupied Wen's thoughts.

His defeat at the hands of Lin Tai Lo had been news all through Chinatown within hours of the fight. The other Tong were quietly relieved that Wen's power had been diminished, but his hold over the Hei Long Tong remained like a vise. Wen had purposefully weeded out other aspirants to his throne, leaving only loyal, if somewhat dull, soldiers who lionized the man, even in defeat. They'd even helped to create a counter story, saying that Wen had succumbed to the treacherous attack of the Japanese private detective who had aided Lin Tai Lo. It provided just enough plausibility that Wen could save some face and, in turn, show his own face in Chinatown.

Descending the stairs from his temporary apartment, Wen was met by three of his soldiers in the back of the Imperial Dragon Restaurant. From there they exited and made their way to Ross Alley and the small, dark wooden door of Dr. Han. As Wen strode inside, a customer, chatting at the counter, made a quick bow to the doctor followed by a hasty retreat from the store. Wen smiled at the retreating man, taking pleasure in the fear he still could inspire.

Dr. Han looked impassively at Wen, though he noted the elixirs he'd given him were certainly working. Physically, Wen looked well enough, but Han feared the man's mind was slipping. Always an egotist, the recent defeat has sent his world into flux. He'd convinced his men and apparently himself that he'd been cheated in the fight, that he was robbed of the rightful victory, though the story Han had heard through the pervasive Chinese grapevine told exactly the opposite story. Han's denial of reality had gone from self-delusion to compulsion.

"You have something to show me, doctor," Wen said, making the question a statement. Han nodded and walked to the far side of the store. A large worktable of weathered wood, polished smooth by years of use, sat empty in expectation of Wen's arrival. The area around the table had been cleared of its usual clutter as well, giving it a sterile, isolated look in the otherwise crowded apothecary. From a small shelf, Han pulled down a clear glass vial that contained granules of gray-black material. As first glance, one would think it coarse gunpower except that as the light struck them, they looked metallic. Han placed a sheet of rice paper on the empty table. Then he poured a thin layer of granules onto the paper.

"It looks like gunpowder," Wen said petulantly.

"This is to gunpowder what opium is to curry spice," Han replied. "Step back."

Han lit a match and lit the edge of the paper beneath the grains. He stepped quickly back. The paper blackened, and fire licked toward the grains. At the moment the flame reached the first grains, they erupted into a ball of blue flame. The heat washed over both men, and Wen laughed out loud. A moment later, a thick cloud of blue-black smoke filled the room, causing Wen to cough and blink. Han opened a window and then stood impassively.

"What is this magic, doctor?" Wen asked with an evil smile.

"A mix of nitric and sulfuric acid and my own special mixture of additives," Han said, both pleased with himself and fearful of what this man would do with his work.

"Can it be mixed with gasoline?" Wen asked, and Han reluctantly nodded.

"Effect?"

"Frightening."

"Excellent work, doctor."

"They saw us coming a mile away," Thorne said. The rest of his team, Stiles, and Hauser sat around the conference table back at the Presidio hangar. "Those 'unmarked' trucks fool no one. There was way too much going on with the police and the other agents who lost Murao." Hauser frowned but said nothing.

"They had help from Chinatown. Mr. Stiles, do you have something for us?" Thorne asked, and Stiles nodded as he read from his notes.

"The Green Palace Restaurant is on Waverly in Chinatown. It's located next to the headquarters of the Hop Sing Tong. In fact, the restaurant is owned by the Hop Sing Tong," Stiles said.

"Anything else?" Thorne said, watching Hauser the entire time, quietly enjoying the man's discomfort.

"We traced the vehicle, the bus. Motor vehicle records show it's registered to one Benedict Shen. Also believed to be a member of the Tong from some old police records."

Thorne turned to Hauser, "So it really does look like a Tong war after all." He looked around the table. "We need to get eyes on that building immediately. They're likely there, but for how long ..." he trailed off.

"What do you propose, Thorne?" Hauser asked. "Just walk through their front door?"

Thorne looked at Hauser and then made deliberate eye contact with each of his men. A wolflike shine came to all their eyes, and Thorne smiled at Hauser and said, "Actually, yes."

The third floor of the Benevolent Association held a set of dorm rooms for men and women, each with a set of showers and facilities. Molly enjoyed the whole space to herself as the men retreated to the showers. They'd all been wearing the same clothes for several days, so they welcomed the opportunity to change. Each now wore the traditional black Chinese *hanfu*. The frog-buttoned jackets and loose pants were functional and comfortable, though finding a size big enough for Epps was a challenge. The emerald-green cuffs and collars marked them as Hop Sing uniforms. Shig admired himself in the mirror.

"I look good!" he smiled.

"What's next?" Turier asked Kats.

"John has resources and means of moving people and goods in and out of San Francisco. We need to lay low for a bit and then get you and Epps on a boat. Have you thought about where you might go?" Kats asked.

Turier looked at Epps and then said, "I'd thought perhaps back to France, but I don't believe Steven would be safe there."

"Mexico," Epps said quietly. "I've always wanted to see Mexico." Kats nodded.

"I'd like to come with you, Steven," Turier said. "I feel a certain responsibility to make sure you're ..."

"Not a danger to people?" Epps asked flatly.

"*Non, non,* Steven. I want to make sure you're safe and in a good place for you to continue to get better. I'm so very impressed with what you've accomplished here. I ..." he trailed off, searching for the words. "I still would like to help you if you'll let me."

Epps gave a shrug of his shoulders, "I don't think I have that much time, but you're welcome to join me." Turier looked quizzically at the soldier.

"What do you mean?"

Epps looked at Kats, who gave him a nod. "I feel like I'm a candle burning down to the wax. Whatever was done to me gave me all this strength, but it feels like it's using me up."

Turier looked concerned, nodding his head in understanding, "We can find you better doctors," but Epps cut him off.

"Never again," he said, and Turier knew the truth of that from the hardness in his eyes. "If the end comes, it will be on my terms."

"Let's go up and talk to John about getting you to Mexico," Kats said. They stood and walked into the outer hall, just as Molly was coming out of the women's dormitory. The men stopped short.

Molly had been given an emerald-green *cheongsam* dress. High necked, short sleeved, and cut well up her shapely leg, the dress clung to her like a second skin. She'd casually piled her long red hair atop her head, which further accentuated her long neck. She noted the stares of everyone and looked self-consciously at herself, wondering if something was wrong.

"Wow!" Shig said with a laugh and clap of his hands.

"*Très jolie*," Turier added, and Epps gave an appreciative nod.

Kats gaped openly. She was stunning. This mix of East and West made his chest pound.

"Thank you, boys," Molly smiled and walked toward Kats. As she did, she wiggled a bit and tugged at the dress. "It's a little tight. Do you like it?" she asked Kats.

"You look amazing." She beamed, and her face blushed. "That dress ..." he started.

"Yeah?" she said.

"You're keeping that dress." She kissed him.

CHAPTER 32

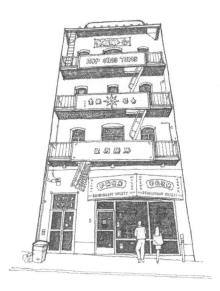

The long twilight of summer held Chinatown in the gloaming as Dragon Eye Wen paced the upper floor room overlooking Waverly Place. Three of his most trusted men and the two observers who'd been stationed there the past several days crowded into the small space. The wheels of the plan were now in motion, and Wen looked at the clock on the table, comparing it to his own watch yet again. Next to the clock, three dark bottles corked with lengths of cloth stood at the ready.

Earlier that day, Dr. Han had provided a large porcelain container for the Hei Long. Most of the coarse granules had been carefully poured into a 30-gallon steel drum filled with gasoline. The drum was old and rusty, so it matched perfectly with two others that held thick cooking oil that had been collected from restaurants around Chinatown. They sat in the bed of an old truck with one headlight. Finding the truck that had made the weekly collection at the Green Palace Restaurant hadn't been very hard. Nor had purchasing the decrepit old vehicle from its owner at a price affording him a newer, if not new, truck. When asked to sell their old work overalls, they were surprised, but they agreed to it. The only pushback from the old man and his son had come when the Hei Long had told him that they'd be making the deliveries to the restaurants on Waverly Place. The old man mouthed a protest, but Wen turned his 'dragon eye' on the man, who made a hurried bow followed by a hurried retreat.

From the fourth-floor window, Wen could see down the street to the front of the Hop Sing headquarters. The street was still busy. Cars rolled past, and people still walked the sidewalks. But as the sun set, this street would grow quieter save for a few businesses that remained open late. The streetlights had flickered on minutes ago, and darkness was coming.

Wen looked across the street at the four-story building where two more of his men waited on the opposite roof. They'd moved up there several hours ago and were waiting for the sign. The building between them and the Hop Sing Tong was also four stories, but some *gweilo* architect had added a peaked roof in what they no doubt thought was an 'Oriental' style. Wen knew his men could be over it and at the Hop Sing rooftop in seconds. Each carried a bottle identical to the ones on the table. Leaning against the table were two Thompson submachine guns, oiled, loaded, and waiting.

Wen leaned against the wall and pulled the heavy .45 caliber pistol from his belt. He hefted it and rechecked it with a familiarity that may have surprised some. While not the favored weapons of the Tong, Wen had realized long ago that superior weapons meant quicker victories, so he'd become adept in the use of such weapons. *No art, no style,* he thought. But effective. The phone on the desk rang, and the room jumped with expectation. The nearest man picked up the handset. "*Wei?*" Then he nodded as he held the phone out for Wen.

"Speak," Wen said.

"The truck is preparing to leave. It should be on-site in ten minutes. We'll be following at a safe distance," the man said.

"Excellent," Wen said, hanging up the phone. Inside he felt his heart flutter with anticipation. He knew that his future, not just the future of the Hei Long, was going to be written over the next hour.

A postal delivery truck sat quietly on the corner of Stockton and Clay, one block to the south and west of the Hop Sing headquarters. It looked only slightly out of place because of the late hour and its darkened windows. It had taken two phone calls from Hauser to have one delivered to the Presidio. Now in the back, lit by the overhead work light, he sat with Thorne, Collins, and Zapek. Esteban, the small, Hispanic soldier, had taken his gear, loaded into a mail bag, and was enroute to his destination atop a nearby building. Waiting in silence, Thorne's men checked and rechecked their weapons: the modified carbine rifles that now shot tranquilizer darts and their sidearms, the heavy .45 caliber pistols. Hauser had a .38 service revolver holstered at his side.

Thorne sat with his legs extended, crossed at the ankles, like he was waiting for a bus. Beside him, his left hand rested on a leather satchel that bulged ominously.

Thorne's plan was simple, bold, and aggressive - characteristics that had served the man well in two official wars and many other conflicts around the world. Once confidence was high that their targets were still inside the building, Thorne's team would move through the front door, heavily armed, brandishing their military police identification and demanding the surrender of Takemoto and the French doctor. They knew that the Tong were organized and quasi-criminal in their orientation, but they weren't likely to be disciplined in the aggressive face of guns and badges. They might have some guns of their own, but pulling them on apparent law enforcement wasn't likely. Or so they calculated. If they did fight, Thorne and his men were veterans of bloody building-to-building, room-to-room combat that would end in the same bad result for the Tong. The bag of gas grenades at Thorne's side was insurance.

The walkie-talkie chirped at Thorne. He casually picked it up, clicking back. From the tiny speaker, Esteban's voice came through metallically. "In position," he said. "Building looks busy enough. Lights on every floor. I just saw two Tong enter and one woman leave."

"What about the top floor and the roof?" Thorne replied.

Esteban paused as he peered through binoculars from the nearby rooftop. "Movement on the roof. Looks like two guards up top." Another pause. "Shadows moving on the fourth floor, but no clear line of sight on people." Thorne looked at his watch. 9:15 pm.

"Give us fifteen more minutes of overwatch," he said, and then he turned to Hauser. "Have your men move to their perimeter."

Hauser nodded, picked up his radio, and quietly moved his men into position. If targets were flushed, they'd be responsible for containing them. They were also far enough away so as not to attract attention. Hauser felt his stomach tighten. He'd spent time in the field, but years of behind-the-scenes maneuvers and desk work left him out of practice for this type of wet work. But he'd insisted on coming along and couldn't back out now. He saw Thorne looking at him and forced a calm to his face. Thorne gave him a raised eyebrow and a half smile. *The man looked like he could take a fucking nap*, Hauser thought.

The handset chirped. *Click.* Thorne picked up the radio. "Go."

"There are more lights on in the fourth floor. I can confirm movement through the windows, but all these guys wear the same damn outfits," Esteban complained. He stared through the binoculars into the upper floor windows. His angle made for limited sightlines, but they had no time to pick out a better roost. He saw a door swing open. Movement in the upper hallway. "Hold on," he said into the radio. His eyes swept up to a dusky colored man with a beard and mustache.

"I've got eyes on the doc," he said. "Couple other guys. Maybe our private detective. And a woman. Red hair ... nice set on her."

Thorne spoke into the radio. "Good work. If the doctor is there, the private investigator is likely there as well. Get back down here. We go in ten."

"Roger that," Esteban replied and lowered the binoculars from his face. As he did so, he saw an old truck coming down the street. He watched it slow as it neared the Hop Sing building. He clicked back to Thorne.

"Boss, hold a second. We got something incoming," Esteban said. Sitting in the rear of the postal truck, Thorne looked at Hauser and his men. He was about to respond when Esteban's voice came through again.

"Looks like a delivery truck to the restaurant next door. Give it a minute to clear ..." The radio clicked. "Shit!" Esteban hissed. "Boss, we got a situation ..." Esteban's voice was lost to the nearby and unmistakable sound of an explosion.

The old truck chugged along the dark streets, moving cautiously toward the target. They believed the contents in the back were safe enough to transport, but human nature made them drive slowly, unconsciously holding their breath after encountering a pothole.

Moving slowly down Waverly, the truck pulled to a stop in front of the Green Palace Restaurant, just past the entrance to the Hop Sing building. The passenger opened the door and made a few steps toward the restaurant. As he did, he pulled a dark colored tube from his jacket pocket, and the glint of a lighter flashed in his other hand. He flicked the lighter, a flame appearing that he touched to the wick that extended from the tube. As he did so, the driver threw the truck into reverse, cutting the wheel so that the back of the truck banked over the low curb and crashed into the entrance of the Tong headquarters. The driver opened his door and ran from the truck as the other man tossed the sparking stick into the bed of the truck that now blocked the doorway of the building. He turned and ran.

The four young Tong soldiers in the lobby of their headquarters looked up at the truck that slowed in front of their door. Recognizing the old delivery vehicle, they returned to their mahjong game. Just as the next tile was about to be placed, they heard the screech of tires and looked up to see the old truck backing into the doorway. It stopped with a crash, the door pushed inward and the front windows broken. Thinking 'that old fool of a driver,' they rushed forward.

They had a brief moment where they saw a white flash of light, sensed a massive change in atmospheric pressure, then, mercifully, nothing.

The truck exploded in two steps. The stick of dynamite went first, rending the entire truck, igniting the old gas tank. Shrapnel sprayed in every direction. The doorway and second-floor landing above it disappeared. The second step was the massive fireball of bluish flame that arose from the drum of doctored gasoline. The wave of fire climbed up the front of the building. It seemed to cling to every exposed surface, spreading its flame impossibly fast up the entire face of the building. Within a handful of seconds, the entire front of the building seemed to be ablaze.

After the explosion, the two Hei Long on the rooftop grabbed their satchels and leaped onto the adjacent building. They scrambled up the faux Oriental peak roof and slid down the other side. They didn't need to worry about noise because the screams from below filled the night. The two guards on their rooftop looked over the front edge of the building even as flames raced up toward them. They never saw the Hei Long. A flick of a lighter, and two bottles sailed onto the rooftop: one toward the back, the other toward the front. The one aimed at the front landed right behind the two guards. When it exploded, a gout of blue flame mushroomed, and the Hei Long had to avert their eyes for a moment. When they looked back, they saw the two men on fire. Brief, shrill screams ended quickly.

From his vantage point down the street, Wen laughed with delight, the fire brighter and hotter than he'd even hoped. He signaled his men, who grabbed their weapons and raced down the stairs toward the pyre. Wen took another satisfied look at the headquarters of his hated enemies, turned, and grabbed the one remaining bottle from the table and walked out the door.

"What the hell was that?" Hauser shouted. Thorne held the walkie-talkie, trying to raise Esteban.

"Car bomb," he said to Hauser. He jerked his head toward the rear door. Collins and Zapek pushed it open.

Esteban's voice came through the radio, "Bomb in the back of that truck," he shouted. "The building's on fire!"

"Get back here," Thorne said into the radio. Hauser picked up his handset.

"Belay that," he barked. "Move in."

"What are you doing?" Thorne asked. "This isn't our job."

"The doctor won't stay in a burning building," Hauser replied, "Go get him." Thorne looked at his men, who waited for his order. He barked into the radio to Esteban.

"We're moving in." He leaped from the back of the truck, tucked the radio under his arm, and the men ran toward the chaos.

Rounding the corner, Thorne was shocked to see how far the flames had already engulfed the building. He'd seen car bombs before, but this looked like someone had hit the entire front of the building with a flamethrower. As soon as they emerged from around the corner, a wave of heat hit them. People were screaming and pouring into the street as they retreated from the flames. The overturned wreckage of what had been a truck burned in the middle of the street. Then he heard the gunshots.

Instinct took over, and Thorne, Zapek, and Collins crouched and moved toward the cover of a row of parked cars. More shots, but not in their direction. They peered over the cars and saw several men standing outside the building in the street. Two of them held machine guns. Just then a man ran from the burning doorway, and the guns turned toward him, gunning him down. Thorne saw several more bodies lying in the entranceway. Having tried to escape one hell, they ran headlong into another one.

"What the fuck are they doing?" Collins growled.

"Tong," Thorne said, recognizing the blood-red markings of the Hei Long Tong. "They're taking out their rivals."

"By burning down the whole damn neighborhood," Zapek finished. "Orders, captain?"

Thorne paused, looking at the carnage, the people running past them to get away from the fire, the bullets. He knew this place; he'd seen it too many times. He heard a shout from the street and looked over the tailfin of the car. He recognized the man in front of the building who was waving a pistol and shouting orders. Dragon Eye Wen.

Collins leaned over to Thorne. "That's the asshole from the club. The one with the crazy eye. That means those guns came from us," Collins said plaintively. Thorne silently nodded. "That's fucked up, captain."

The radio squawked, and Hauser's voice cut through the night. "Thorne, report!" The sound reached the ears of the closest Hei Long Tong, who turned, looking in their direction. He saw shapes crouching behind the cars across the street. In the heightened state of adrenaline and fear, the man raised his gun and fired several shots into the car.

Before Thorne could even give the order, battlefield instincts kicked in. Zapek rolled forward. Coming up in one smooth motion, he raised his pistol and returned fire. Collins moved to the rear of the car, drawing his gun but holding his fire until Zapek completed his burst. Small-squad tactics in an urban environment. Fire, cover, move. Repeat. Your team members shouldn't be on the same step; that way you fire while they move, giving them cover.

Thorne reached into the satchel at his side. Removing a tear gas grenade, he pulled the pin and lobbed it over the cars in Wen's direction. He repeated this, and they heard two muffled pops as the cannisters detonated. Acrid white smoke was mixed with the dark smoke and backlit by the growing fire.

Thorne slung the radio over his shoulder and moved forward past Zapek, keeping low behind the row of parked cars. His eyes searched for Wen. He heard the distinct 'pop' of the .45 caliber pistols his men carried, then the 'budda, budda, budda' of the Thompsons. He looked up to see Esteban round the far corner and come into the street, his pistol extended before him. Esteban fired, and a black-clad Tong fell. This brought several more guns to bear on Esteban, who dove into a doorway and didn't move. Thorne sighted along his arm, firing in two triple bursts. Two more Tong fell. He was about to shout an order to his men when a spinning object sailed above the cars. His eyes reflexively followed the arc, seeing flame licking at one end. It landed just behind them, as Thorne dove forward, out of cover but out of the splatter of the Molotov cocktail that exploded on the sidewalk. Immense heat washed over him even before his eyes saw it. He heard a scream behind him.

Thorne spun to see Zapek on fire. The liquid had splashed up his legs and back, which poured blue fire. He screamed, trying to pull off his jacket and wildly spinning about. Thorne sprinted forward, tackling the man, taking them out of the radius of fire. He covered Zapek with his own body and began to roll, trying to extinguish the fire. But these flames refused to die easily. It took a few seconds before the flames extinguished. Thorne looked at Zapek, his clothes smoldering. He could see pink flesh in places, and the man's hands were raw and already blistering. Zapek's eyes were closed, but he was breathing. He heard a gun in front of him, Collins returning fire. Bullets whined above him. *I'm in a firefight in fucking California*, he thought ironically.

Wen smiled as the bottle arced over the cars and exploded in a burst of blue flame. He laughed out loud at seeing the man on fire. He didn't even realize it was the same group of men who'd come to his club with Hauser until the flames were licking about them. *Gweilo* bastards like Hauser. The white smoke burned his eyes and nose, but he shouted to his men, "Kill them!" as he pointed to the flaming cars. Six of his men moved forward, sending bullets into the burning metal. Three moved left, two moved right, and Wen stood back waiting for them to be flushed out.

"I'm low," Collins said from the rear bumper as his eyes saw the Tong slowly approaching from both sides. Thorne raised a small .38 caliber revolver that had been strapped to his ankle.

"I've got six," he said to Collins.

"Make 'em count," came the reply.

As the two men on his right approached the cars, Wen

saw a Black man slide out on one knee, minimal silhouette, and fire. A spurt of blood and a cry spun the lead man to the ground as the other charged forward, firing. Metallic flashes appeared around the car, and a grunt could be heard. As his man rounded the car, he was suddenly forced back by the charging Black man, and they rolled to the ground.

Collins felt the blood running down his arm, making it weak, but he wrapped the Tong in a tackle that would have done his high school football team proud. He drove the man to the ground, sweeping the gun hand away. Using his superior size and strength to push the man down, he brought his head forward into the man's nose, which flattened with a satisfying crunch to Collins' ear. As his eyes found the next danger, he saw Wen pointing a machine gun in his direction. He rolled back, pulling the Tong on top of him as the bullets from the machine gun jerked and hammered the body. A pause. Collins looked around the lolling head of his human shield to see Wen reloading the drum of the Thompson submachine gun. With a grunt, he threw the body aside and charged toward Wen, whose eyes went wide just before the lowered shoulder crashed into him. The gun went sailing, and Wen found himself in the grip of arms that were like pythons. They squeezed him, and he felt the air pushed from his lungs. Desperately, he clawed at the arms that held him, his hand finding a warm wetness. Savagely, he pressed his fingers deep into the gunshot in the man's upper arm. Collins hissed and then screamed as the pain radiated up his arm, but still he wouldn't release him. He felt Wen begin to fade, unconsciousness just moments away. Just then the butt of a rifle crashed into the back of Collins' head, sending him sprawling. His eyes wouldn't focus, and he couldn't feel the ground under his palms, but still he struggled to rise. The second blow rained down on his head, sending him into darkness.

Thorne lay on the ground, looking underneath the cars. He could see two sets of feet moving his way. He extended his arm low and fired, and he was rewarded with a scream. He fired again in the direction of the second set of feet, but no scream came back. Now he had to move. He slid further under the car, scurrying like a lizard. He pulled himself out the other side and noticed a Tong sitting on the ground, clutching a shattered ankle. He spent one more bullet into the man's head before spinning to see the other Tong leaping across the car at him. His gun roared again before the man's weight came crashing down on top of him. Thorne heard footsteps approach his head. Then he felt a kick to his side that he was sure cracked some ribs, followed by another to his knee that made him cry out. He tried to roll free but was pressed down by the man on top of him as the others circled him, kicking and stomping where they could find an opening. When a foot clipped the side of his head, Thorne's vision narrowed, and he fought a wave of blackness. His right hand found the groin of the man on top of him. He grabbed and twisted, eliciting a scream as the man lurched off him.

Thorne dragged himself to one knee, turning the gun toward the Tong. He fired once, and a man fell backward. As he was turning, a metal spike magically appeared in the back of his gun hand. The pain was exquisite, and Thorne's fingers nervelessly dropped the gun. He spun to his left as a hatchet passed by his face, and he rolled to the ground. Pulling the metal spike from the back of his right hand, he hefted it in his left. *Haven't tried this in a while,* he thought. As the hatchet man turned to attack again, Thorne threw the spike in one smooth motion. This time it magically appeared in the man's right eye. The Tong screamed, clutching his face as he fell to the ground.

The remaining man retreated back toward Wen and a second soldier, who stood over the prone body of Collins. Thorne tried to stand, but his knee buckled and gave way as he fell. He watched as Wen said something to his men. Then they left at a gallop, Wen hoisting the machine gun before him. A shout drew Wen's attention. It was in Chinese, but Thorne understood the tone.

"Dragon Eye! They're escaping out the back of the building," shouted the Hei Long lieutenant as he pointed to the corner. They turned and ran to the corner. Wen reloaded the drum of the machine gun and followed.

Thorne lay back, his leg throbbing. He took a deep breath and then forced himself up and over to Collins. He felt for a pulse and found it. Strong and steady. *The man had a head like stone*, he thought with the grimace of a smile. He looked around the battlefield, planning his next move. Two of his men injured, probably three. His leg, useless. Sirens in the distance indicated firetrucks, but he knew the Tong headquarters was beyond saving. They would have to fight to keep the block from going up. Retreat and regroup is what experience told him. But the irrational part of him, the feral part of him that had served him so well over the years, blazed hot at the thought of Wen winning. He forced himself up and began searching the ground for the .45 he'd lost. Finding it, he did a quick check of the magazine. Half. He slammed the clip back into the gun, cocked it, and took an unsteady, painful step in the direction Wen had disappeared.

Hauser had been shouting into the walkie-talkie for over

a minute, getting nothing but static in response. He could hear the gunshots and knew that something was amiss. He opened the rear door of the postal truck and stepped out onto the street. He could hear the shouts, the distant sirens, and the gunshots clearly now.

Hauser wasn't a coward. Far from it. He'd faced mortal danger numerous times over the course of his service. But he was ultimately a pragmatist. What was the risk? What was the reward? That calculus was ultimately what moved him. The cold rationality of his process had served him well as a field officer in the OSS, then the CIA. Now he thought about the possibility of capturing the French doctor. They would reward him for the capture of a traitor, though he wondered if Turier could be considered a traitor since he wasn't American. *Details*, he dismissed. But there was the remote possibility that Turier could lead to Epps. That thought justified the personal risk, and he focused on that outcome as he circled the block, planning to come up the far side of the building.

CHAPTER 33

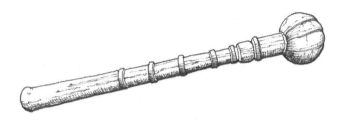

Kats had seen fire during the war. He'd been both in and around burning buildings, even as recently as last year on the waterfront. He wasn't a stranger to conflagration. He knew that the key to dealing with fire was not to let the primal human fear of it overcome one's thinking. Fire moved in mostly predictable ways. It obeyed fundamental laws of physics and chemistry. But this fire was something more, something different. It was as if someone had doused the building in lighter fluid before tossing in a match. The flames moved faster and burned hotter than they should have, and there was a dark, foul-smelling smoke that he'd never experienced before. Stepping back from the windows and the open balcony, he yelled, "The front of the building is covered in fire, and it looks like the entrance has collapsed."

Epps looked up at the ceiling, noting it was beginning to sag in places and the paint was darkening with heat. "The roof too," he said flatly.

"Can't go up," Kats said, "so down it is."

John waved them toward the door and the hallway outside. "There's a back exit into the alleys. Follow me." Even as they stepped into the fourth-floor hallway, smoke, blacker and thicker than it should have been, was rising from below and darkening the air. As they moved down the stairs to the third floor, they heard a rumbling sound and a crash from below.

"What the hell was that?" Shig shouted from the collar of his jacket that he held in front of his mouth.

"I think the front entrance is now completely gone," John said with a cough.

The third floor was hotter and the smoke thicker. Kats looked about for signs of others when he heard a shout from the front of the building. "Help! Help!" came a female voice.

John moved forward and Kats started to follow. Then Kats quickly turned to the others, "Get downstairs and out the back. We'll be right behind you!" Molly's eyes locked on Kats for a heartbeat. She gave him a nod and mouthed the word, "Go."

He ran forward to catch John, who pushed open a thick door to reveal the front room where a large office had been. The windows that once had opened onto the balcony were gone, the outer wall blown inward. Fire covered the balcony, and smoke nearly filled the room. Two people were in the room. A woman, middle aged, Chinese, her hair wild and her face dirty, was trying to pull a man from the smoldering ruins of the wall. The man lay on his stomach, and Kats noted his hands and arms moving, though there was blood on the side of his head. John stooped to pull the man up, and Kats moved to help him.

From somewhere outside another explosion rocked the building. The floor shook, and the woman fell backward as the floor below her opened up. With a wide-eyed scream, she fell even as John reached for her with a grasping hand. He teetered on the edge of the flames, looking down into an inferno.

"John!" Kats yelled, "we've got to move him." John's face was tight as he helped Kats stand the injured man up and begin slowly moving back toward the rear of the building. As they reached the rear stairway, the smoke was becoming truly dangerous. Kats felt his lungs burning and could barely draw a full breath. He saw that John was in a similar state. He motioned for them to duck down. As they crawled forward, the air was a bit clearer, and they could breathe again, but now they were on their hands and knees, laboriously moving forward, dragging the unconscious man.

They reached the staircase landing, where John motioned for Kats to go first. There wasn't enough room for three abreast, so Kats nodded and took a deep breath before heading down the stairs into an even thicker cloud of smoke. Behind him, John hoisted the man over his broad shoulder and followed. Kats hit the bottom of the stairs. He could feel the heat on his exposed skin and in his eyes. He heard the entire building groan and creak like a great wooden ship in a storm. He turned to look back at John.

Moving deliberately, step by step, John was halfway down the stairs when a loud crack emanated from the floor, the stairs collapsing beneath them, followed by a stream of falling wood, bricks, and smoke that pushed Kats back and momentarily blinded him. Kats shook the hot embers from his clothes and his hair. Looking up, he was horrified to see that the whole stairwell had collapsed from above but hadn't broken through to the floor below. He saw a pair of legs extended from the debris. John!

He crawled forward, moving debris off the legs to reveal the two men. John lay on his back, his legs slowly moving. *Alive*, Kats thought. As he moved upward, he saw a terrible wound in John's chest. A metal bracing bar, exposed in the collapse, protruded from his upper-right chest, blood covering the sharp, exposed edge. John's head moved from side to side, his eyes blinking, trying to focus. Kats looked to the other man. A sharp piece of wood pierced the man's neck, and blood had already soaked the area beneath him.

John coughed, blood speckling his lips. Kats made a battlefield assessment of the wound. Two inches of metal, clean through the chest, but not too close to the heart. The bar itself prevented too much bleeding, but once removed, John would bleed badly. Maybe bleed out before a medic could be reached. John's eyes fixed on Kats.

"Go on, get out," he rasped.

"I'm not going anywhere," Kats said more calmly than he felt.

When they reached the second floor, Molly saw the staircase down was completely engulfed in flames. The smoke was so thick that they had to move bent over to see and breathe.

Epps had taken the point and looked as though he might risk running through the pyre. He might make it through the flames with his speed and endurance, but the others wouldn't. He looked back toward the rear of the building. There was less smoke there, and less heat.

"This way," he said, and led them back toward a few moments of respite. They entered a large room that seemed ceremonial. Scrolls and tapestries lined three of the walls. The fourth wall was covered in martial arts weapons. Spears, swords, knives, and many things that Molly didn't recognize.

They staggered inside, coughing.

Turier looked around, taking in the room as Shig came over to Molly. She gave him a thumbs up and wiped the sweat from her face. From above they heard more of the building collapsing. Their collective eyes scanned the ceiling, wondering how long it might hold. Epps stood and went to the door, and to their surprise, darted back outside. Turier looked after him and then said to Molly and Shig, "Stay here. I'll bring him back." He took two deep breaths and then moved after Epps at a low run.

Twenty feet down the hallway, smoke nearly blinding him, he ran into Epps, who stood looking upward. There was a hole in the ceiling, where a large beam had fallen from above and broken through the floor. Turier looked up, sensing what Epps was thinking.

"We need to get up there," he coughed, "but I don't think I can jump that far." Epps looked up and then hoisted the doctor upward, lifting him like a small child. Turier moved his foot upward, and Epps caught it. Then with a small dip, he thrust upward, and Turier was hoisted into the ceiling. He found a handhold above and pulled himself through the hole. Turning on his stomach, he looked down at Epps' upturned face.

"Move!" Epps shouted and waved his hand. Turier pulled his head back as Epps launched himself upward. On near-superhuman legs, he cleared the edge of the hole with his upper body. He caught himself, and in one fluid motion, rolled on the floor. Epps was on his feet in a flash and pulled Turier up. They blinked and looked down the hallway, searching for a sign of Kats and John. They stepped forward into the smoke.

Kats felt underneath where John lay, hoping that the metal that impaled his friend could be moved. He found that the other end was embedded in a remnant of the wall it had once anchored. Kats knew he'd have to pull John off the shard and then hope to quickly get him to medical attention. *First things first*, he thought, and braced himself for the excruciating maneuver to come.

"I've got to lift you off this spike," he said to John, who looked at him and then the spike and nodded. "This is gonna hurt," Kats said. John smiled, blood coloring his teeth. He stood and straddled John's chest and reached down to grab both shoulders, knowing it would take one smooth, strong pull to lift the man. He wiped his hands on his pants and moved over to John.

"Ready?" he said, looking into the man's eyes. John gave a single nod.

"Kats!" he heard from behind. He looked and saw Epps and Turier come through the smoke and kneel at his side. They looked at John, and both men's eyes went wide.

"That looks bad," Turier said and ran his hands over the bar and then underneath John. "That piece is what's keeping him from bleeding out," he said.

"What else can we do?" Kats said with a cough, feeling the air getting even worse.

"Can we lift the whole piece out there?" Turier asked.

"It's embedded in a piece of the wall," Kats said. Epps looked back and forth.

"Let me try," he said, and Kats gave way for Epps. John looked up at the soldier with pain-filled eyes but said nothing. Epps reached one hand below John, the other on top of the bar that extended from the Tong leader's chest. He spread his feet wide and pulled. Kats could see the man's shoulders hunch with the effort. Epps' jaw clenched, and his eyes closed.

He rocked back and forth, trying to loosen the bar. John screamed, writhing in pain. Kats leaned forward, grasping John's free hand and trying to keep him from moving. Epps exhaled and released the still-embedded bar.

"Damn," he said.

"Try again, Steven. You can do it," Turier said.

Epps looked again at John, who gave him a slow shake of his head. "Go. I'm done."

"The hell with that," Epps spat. "I owe you for your cousin." He grabbed the bar again, and Kats grabbed John to brace him. Epps' shoulders hunched, his legs trembled, and the cords in his neck stood out like rope. He raised his face upward and let out a roar, "Aaarrhhh!"

There was a crack and then another, and with a final heave, the bar came free of its anchor. John rolled onto his left side, seemingly losing consciousness.

Turier pointed down the hall, "There's a hole to the next floor," he said. "Come!" Kats and Epps lifted John, the steel bar moving along with them. They looked down the hole. Kats jumped down, landing lithely, and then looked up.

"Dominic, come down, and you can help me with John!"

Turier leaned over the edge and then dropped onto the next level, thankful he'd kept fit with his running. They looked upward, and Epps lowered John by his left arm. He dangled there unconscious, and Kats and Turier were able to lower him to the floor. Epps followed with a casual drop through the hole. He picked John up and carried him in front of him as they followed Turier back to the weapons room.

They collapsed inside, the room more smoke free than the rest of the building, but for how long? They lay John on the floor, who groaned but didn't open his eyes. Molly ran to Kats, and he told her, "I'm OK, but John's in bad shape." She looked down at him, her eyes seeing but her mind not fully comprehending the metal piece that bisected the man's upper chest. She thought of her own experience of being shot and her breath caught in her chest, not just because of the smoke. She had to turn away, her face buried in Kats' shoulder.

"Is there another way out of this room?" Kats asked Shig, who knelt nearby.

"Just back the way you came," he said. "The windows ..." he pointed to narrow slits, designed for a bit of light but not egress. Fire licked outside them. Shig started to say something when he was cut off as the electric lights, which had been working, flickered and then went out. They found themselves in a darkened room, lit only by the fires outside that were in the process of coming in.

Kats looked around furiously, his mind racing. He could hear the fire. He could hear sections of the building surrendering to its heat. He looked at Molly, then Shig, then Turier. He felt helpless in that moment, like he'd failed all of them. Hot tears of pain, frustration, and rage welled up in his eyes. He was about to say what was in his heart at that moment—*I love you. I'm sorry*—when John groaned something. His attention came back to the moment.

"What did you say," he asked John, leaning close.

"There's a tunnel in the basement. Out through there," John rasped.

"A tunnel?" Shig said. "Great, but how do we get down there?"

Kats' eyes moved to the wall, which included all manner of Chinese martial arts weapons: swords, knives, iron fans, and chain whips. He was proficient with many of these, but they weren't suited to what he was now thinking. But there on the makeshift altar in front of the wall, crossed in ceremonial repose, were two steel-bladed hatchets that the Tong soldiers favored. Kats moved over to them. Taking one in each hand, he turned back to the rear of the room. He crossed the wooden floor, stomping down, searching for something.

"What are you thinking?" Turier asked, coming to his side.

"I'm trying to find the space between the beams." He stomped again, searching for the hollow sound between the massive wooden struts. He brought his foot down again. "Here," he said. Kats handed the second hatchet to Turier. Then in one powerful overhand blow, Kats brought his ax downward into the polished wood floor. The hatchet bit into the wood, and Kats began to chop away. Turier followed suit next to him. Molly looked up from tending John, and Shig ran to the wall, grabbing a spear. He stood nearby, jabbing the point into the expanding wound in the floor as Kats and Turier stopped, gasping in the bad air and changing hands as they continued to attack the floor.

Epps watched for a moment and then turned to the wall of weapons, his eyes scanning. His eyes landed on a large iron mace. It was nearly five feet long, with a steel reinforced handle that led up to a round metal head, ridged on the sides. The *chui* was an ancient Chinese weapon that required immense strength to wield, making it impractical for most marital arts practitioners. They existed mostly as ceremonial arms, like giant battle axes in European armories. Epps pulled the mace off the wall, hefting it in one hand. He turned to where Kats and Turier had begun to splinter the wood floor. "Let me," he said. They rolled out of the way as Epps raised the massive weapon and then brought it down on the wood with a rending crash. Wood splintered, and the floor shuddered. Epps pulled the weapon back, raising it above his head with two hands. Kats saw the man's eyes flash wide as he brought the cudgel down again. This time it buried deep into the floor. Epps twisted it free, and Kats could see light coming from below. He raised his hand for Epps to hold and worked the hole with his hatchet, moved his foot over the hole, and stomped downward. His foot crashed through, and below he saw the floor. No fire. Yet.

Coughing, Kats motioned for Turier to squeeze through. He held Turier's arm and lowered him through the hole and then dropped him below. Epps dropped the mace through the hole and then followed in one smooth jump. John looked at Kats, wiped his left hand across his sweaty brow, and motioned for Molly to help him sit up. They moved John over the hole and dropped his feet first. Then they moved his upper body, holding onto his left arm, to the waiting arms of Epps below. Kats lowered Molly through the hole and jumped down after her into what was the first-floor kitchen in the back of the building.

For a moment, they caught their breath in the relative quiet of the kitchen. The room was dark, illuminated only by the light coming through the hole in the ceiling and by two windows that overlooked the sinks and out the rear of the building. A thick metal door leading to the alley was bolted shut. Outside, Kats could hear sirens and the unmistakable pop of gunshots. Epps heard the shots as well, his head cocked sharply as Kats eyed him. Turier noticed also.

Shig stood up and crossed the room toward the door. "We can get out through the alley," he said.

"Shig, stay down!" Kats yelled as his friend crossed in front of the dimly illuminated windows. A shot rang out, then another and another. The glass in one of the windows shattered, and Kats heard a bullet ricochet off the interior wall. Shig dove to the floor, glass raining down behind him.

"Shig! You OK?" Kats asked.

"Yeah," he said with a nod of his head. Kats knelt next to his friend, who looked up at him. "Next time I complain about working a double shift at the store, kick me right in the nuts, OK?"

"Will do," Kats grunted. Behind him, Kats heard Turier speaking.

"Steven," he said in a calm voice, "take a deep breath." Epps took a deep, somewhat ragged breath and then nodded to the Frenchman.

From his position on the floor, John pointed to a small door that looked like a pantry. "The tunnel is there," he said. Their eyes followed. Then, to their surprise, the door began to open into the kitchen. Kats grabbed the hatchet from the floor beside him and moved toward the door. As it opened, the shape of a man stepped through.

"Wait!" yelled Molly, recognizing the young man's face. Haoyu looked wide-eyed into the kitchen and then gave a start as he saw the hatchet in Kats' hand. His eyes then moved to John, and he rushed forward to his captain.

"Lin Tai Lo!" he gasped, seeing the impaling metal.

"Haoyu," John managed with a grimace, "what are you doing here?"

"I led our people out through tunnel. I came back to see if more need help," the young man said in his accented English. John gave a nod and closed his eyes.

"What happened?" Kats asked.

"Hei Long attack. They explode a bomb in front of the building. The fire spread fast. Many trapped here inside. They shoot us as we escape. Then I remember the tunnel."

"OK, good work," Kats said. "We need to get John," Kats caught himself, "Lin Tai Lo, out of here and to a doctor." Haoyu nodded.

"Tunnel is narrow and come out in basement across street," Haoyu said. "Follow." Kats nodded, but as he turned toward the group, the remaining windows exploded inward, and bullets peppered the room.

CHAPTER 34

D ragon Eye Wen raced around the block to find his three men firing shots into the back of the building. The men, seeing Wen approach, turned to him. One said, "*We saw movement in the windows.*" Wen cocked the machine gun, raised it, and sent a fusillade of bullets into the rear of the building, shattering the glass windows. He laughed as the drum emptied.

Inside the kitchen, everyone had hit the floor. Kats positioned himself over top of John, keeping the flying glass off of him. As the shots subsided, Haoyu moved to the door of the tunnel as Molly, followed by Shig, crawled across the glass-strewn floor. Together they pulled John, who groaned in semi-consciousness, into the tiny stairway that led into the bowels of Chinatown. The young Tong hissed at the rest of them, "Come!" Kats looked up to see Turier on one knee, facing Epps, whose back was to Kats. Epps was on his hands and knees, but his breathing seemed labored, and his back arched upward like a cat.

"Steven!" Turier said plaintively, trying to find the man's face. "It's all right. You must breathe, Steven. Please, look at me!" he said. For a moment, his eyes found Kats', and they were wide with fear. *Not good*, thought Kats.

Epps raised his head and looked into Turier's face. The Frenchman forced a smile and said, "Easy, easy. Come with me." Then he took Epps' hand. The man looked into Turier's eyes, holding his gaze. In his head he saw the color red at the edges of his vision. But he heard the doctor's voice, like a foghorn in a thick mist. "Come with me," Turier repeated. Epps took a deep breath, and with a supreme effort of will, gave a slow nod at Turier. Kats saw the doctor's face relax. Then the room exploded with bullets again.

Kats hit the floor as bullets pinged into the kitchen. They pounded into the wooden cabinets behind them and ricocheted off the iron stove and refrigerator. He heard Turier shout in pain. Looking up, he saw the doctor recoil, clutching his face. Kats could see blood coming from between his fingers. Kats now saw Epps clench his fists, his shoulders shaking. *He's losing it*, Kats thought. If Epps was triggered, he might run. He might try to kill them. Turier saw it too. He raised his hands, now covered in blood from his left cheek, which was in tatters.

Kats looked across the floor, covered in glass and debris. He knew he was no match for Epps, but then his eyes landed on the long shape of the *chiu*, the huge iron mace that Epps had used to smash through the floor. Kats reached over and pulled it to him. It was shockingly heavy, yet Epps had hefted it like a baton. Using both hands, he hoisted it in front of him as Turier pleaded with Epps. Kats drew it back, taking careful aim, and swung it forward like a sledgehammer. The iron head crashed into Epps' upper back. The impact slammed him forward, and he dropped to his hands and knees. Epps swayed back and forth, and a low groan escaped his lips. Turier moved forward toward Epps when Kats yelled, "Dominic, get back!" as he swung the bludgeon at Epps' head, careful not to strike him too hard. This time Epps went down and didn't move.

"*Mon Dieu!*" Turier shouted as he knelt by Epps. He checked for a pulse. Kats eyed him, unconsciously holding his breath. Turier nodded his head, looking at Kats, "He's alive. But we need to get him out of here." There was an apparent break in the gunfire, so they moved to the tunnel, with Turier below and Kats lowering the unconscious soldier down the stairs.

Hauser rounded the corner, hearing the chugging sound of the machine gun. There at the rear of the building, in the fire-illuminated alley, he saw Dragon Eye Wen, with three other armed men. Wen had sprayed the rear doorway of the building with bullets, shattering all the glass. Hauser could see flames licking inside the building, moving toward the rear. Wen was reloading the drum of the Thompson as Hauser drew his pistol and fired. The first shot found the nearest Tong, who fell forward, dead before hitting the ground. The others spun around, looking for the source of the shot. Hauser moved forward, gun in front of him, sighting the other rifles, knowing they were the immediate danger. He fired again, then again. Another fell, but the third man's rifle came up firing. Hauser felt the bullet pass just to his side as he dove to his left. He brought the gun up again. This time he fired twice, both rounds finding the center of the Tong. Now he turned his attention to Wen ...

The Thompson burped steel, and Hauser felt the hot fire across his legs, knowing he'd been hit. He tried to roll forward, but his muscles refused to comply. Instead, he flopped onto his chest, gun extended forward. He looked up, trying to draw a sighting on Wen. A foot came down on his gun hand. He cried out, the hand releasing the weapon. A foot swept the pistol into the darkness. Then a kick slammed into his head as he sprawled onto his back. As his vision cleared, he saw Wen standing above him, the barrel of the machine gun pointing at his chest. He raised his hands slowly.

Wen stared down savagely at him. "Fucking *gweilo.* I told you I'd rule Chinatown."

"I believe you," Hauser said, trying to sound calm. "I can still help you. If you ..."

"No!" Wen shouted and thrust the gun forward. "You brought the police and the Hop Sing to my operation. You cost me the respect of Chinatown!"

Hauser looked up at Dragon Eye. The flames from the building behind him made him appear like a demon in the night. He said as calmly as he could, "You were right. I'm CIA. I can get you whatever you want. Just ask."

"I want my honor back, and I'll get it too. With your fucking head!" The gun roared again, and a dozen bullets thundered into Hauser's chest. His eyes went wide and then closed. The blood splattered upward, spraying Wen's clothes and face, making him look truly demonic. He stared down hard at the carcass below him, his heart still racing and his mind whirling. Then he remembered the movement in the back of the Hop Sing building. Flames were moving in, but he turned, strode to the door, and kicked it in. There he found a kitchen, filled with shattered glass and debris. He was about to turn and leave when his eyes noted a small door, slightly ajar. He stepped forward and used the barrel of the gun to push it further open. He could make out stairs going down. He knew there were tunnels under Chinatown, and this must be how the Hop Sing were escaping. He stepped through the doorway, his bloodlust leading him forward.

The tunnel was narrow and smelled of oil and decay. Barely wider that a broad-shouldered man, the rock and clay walls were lined with planks that precariously held the works together. Kats had no energy to worry about the engineering as he struggled forward, Epps draped over his shoulder. In front of him, Turier held the small oil lamp that had been left at the foot of the stairs. They moved purposely forward. Above, perhaps no more than fifteen feet, they could hear sirens and the low rumble of trucks moving into position. They had gone what felt like nearly a block when they noticed the tunnel start to slope slightly upward. They saw another light at the end, and from somewhere above a woman's voice yelled, "Kats!" It was Molly.

At the end of the tunnel, a wooden ladder led upward into a room. Molly and Shig peered down from above and then helped pull Turier through the hole. Kats positioned the unconscious Epps at the bottom of the stairs while Shig came partway down the ladder and grabbed the man by the collar. In tandem, one pushing, one pulling, they moved his two hundred pounds up the ladder and into what appeared to be a storage closet. Kats climbed up the ladder and rolled onto the floor, his breath coming in gulps, sweat running down his face. He opened his eyes to see Molly's face over his. "Nice work, soldier," she said. He smiled and managed a nod in return.

Kats managed to sit up, taking in the scene. The storage room contained crates of canned food, bags of rice, tea, and other sundries. "Where are we?" he asked.

"Restaurant across the street," Shig said. "We can get out the alley there," he pointed. "A couple of their guys are moving John now." Kats nodded, relieved.

"Kats," Turier said, "we need to get Steven to a doctor as well." Turier held Epps' eyelids up and was looking at the man's pupils. "I fear he has a concussion, maybe worse."

"If we take him to a hospital, they'll arrest him, Dominic," Kats replied. "I don't think he'd want that." He met the

Frenchman's worried gaze.

Shig looked back and forth at the two men, "He needs a doctor, right?" They both nodded. "What about the wizard?"

"The wizard?" Turier asked.

"Chinese medicine man," Kats said. "And close by." He thumped Shig on the shoulder. "Let's go."

Wen climbed down into the darkness. Within half a dozen steps the light from where he came had all but disappeared and he found himself stumbling forward, one hand extended before him, sliding along the rough walls. He could hear the city above, and he thought perhaps voices coming from in front of him. He kept going and saw the hint of light ahead. Moving closer, he could see a pool of light that came from above and then shadows moving across it. He moved cautiously forward, seeing a ladder. Listening, he heard nothing above. Hefting the machine gun, he began to climb.

Molly and Shig held the door open as Kats and Turier lifted Epps between them, each with one of the man's arms over their shoulders. To their left was the street, brightly lit from the nearby streetlights, but they turned right and moved deeper into the alley, deeper into the dark, and away from the fire trucks, police, and gawkers that had flooded the next block over.

Wen emerged into the storeroom and saw the open rear door. He peered around the doorframe and, to his right, he saw several men clad in the black-and-green uniforms of the Hop Sing. He smiled, cocked the machine gun, and raced down the alley. Drawing closer, he fired a short burst into the air, causing the men to stop and turn. Wen lev-

eled the gun toward them and smiled. "Hop Sing dogs!
You die tonight!" he shouted. All eyes turned to see Wen.

Kats had twisted and spun, hearing the gunshots. He
shifted Epps onto Turier, but Wen was twenty feet from
him. It was too far to cross before the gun would empty its
lethal payload toward them. His eyes swept the alley floor,
searching for a weapon but finding none. Wen smiled, his
blood-covered face a nightmare sight, and prepared to fire.
"Hop Sing dogs," he repeated. Bang!

A red plume of blood erupted from Wen's forehead, followed by the gray thinking matter that had once dreamed of
ruling the city. The body, not sure of its next move, took a
beat before collapsing to the ground like a curtain falling to
reveal Larry Thorne holding an outstretched pistol.

All eyes moved to Thorne as he slowly limped toward
them, the gun before him. Turier shook his head, "*Incroyable*,"
he breathed. Kats started to step forward when Turier's hand
pulled his shoulder and the doctor said, "Thorne, please. I
know you're an honorable man. Please, don't let that bastard
Hauser win."

"Hauser's dead. That prick killed him," he indicated Wen's
body with the pistol.

"All the more reason to walk away," Turier pleaded.

"I'm a soldier, doctor, I have my orders."

"Is there not a code among soldiers? Is there not an hon-
or among men like you and him?" Turier said, pointing to
Epps. "If soldiers like you all are merely tools for assholes
like Hauser, then you're all easily disposed of, replaced. Make
them see you as men. Not tools."

Thorne paused, looking back and forth to Kats and Turier. Kats tensed, unable to read Thorne's face.

From beside him, Kats saw Shig come forward. "Larry, I was serious about the job offer. You can be something else, man," Shig said, and Thorne gave a wry smile.

"Thorne, please," Turier said. "He is what the world has made him. Please, let me take him away from all those men who would use his pain for their gain."

Thorne looked over the end of his pistol, his eyes unwavering. Kats braced for a last-ditch movement to push Dominic aside and try to reach Thorne before the gun could track him. He didn't like the odds.

The shot he feared coming never rang out. Thorne lowered the pistol and stared at them. Then he gave a nod.

"As you say, doctor. They made us all. And tonight, I'm tired." He then stood up straight, tucked the pistol into his belt, and made a crisp salute at them. He turned and walked back toward the light.

CHAPTER 35

I n the dark confusion that swirled in Chinatown that night, Kats and Turier brought the unconscious Epps to Dr. Han's storefront in Ross Alley. The normally placid old man had seemed shaken by the news of the fire and the fight at the Hop Sing Tong headquarters. He moved them inside and promised to look after Turier and Epps and keep them safe. Kats had promised to pay him, but Han adamantly refused.

As Kats turned to leave, Turier asked, "Where are you going now?"

"To turn myself in to the police," he said with a half-smile.

"*Non, mon ami.* Why must you do this?"

"I'm still wanted for questioning, but we know they have nothing on me. You and Steven are the ones they're still looking for, and to the best of my knowledge, both of you perished in that fire." Turier blinked, trying to fully comprehend.

"Dominic, you said it yourself that the government will be after him as long as he's alive. Even if Hauser's dead, there's always another one like him in the wings. If they think you and Epps are dead, they'll stop looking. And, sadly, we know there are going to be many burned bodies back in the building. They'll never know."

"Thank you," Dominic said, and he hugged Kats, who fiercely hugged him back.

"Thank you for what you did for me," Kats said, "and for Steven."

Kats headed to Shig's place in North Beach, where he and Molly were waiting. They had cleaned up and changed clothes. Molly's hair was wet, and she wore one of Shig's t-shirts. He asked, "What's the word on John?"

"They took him to the hospital," Shig said. "One of their guys called an hour ago and said he was in surgery and that they'd call with any news." Kats nodded, allowing himself to relax a bit more. He sat down, and Molly brought him a glass of water.

"Our friends are ..." she began.

"Safe with Dr. Han. He was insistent on helping them."

Molly sat down next to him. She sniffed and wrinkled her nose. "You smell like a bonfire." He smiled.

"Shower, then sleep," he said wearily. "Tomorrow I'll go to the police." She and Shig looked concerned. "It'll be fine. I'll call my friend Elliott on the force and arrange everything. I'll be out by dinner time," he said reassuringly.

He was out two days later. The police and the press were on high alert after a firebomb in Chinatown resulted in half a block being burned down and over a dozen people killed in the blaze. The press also reported gunfire between local Tong gangs, resulting in additional deaths including known Hei Long leader Wen Tsui Shen and a colonel in the US Army, Conrad Hauser, who apparently tried to help and was in the wrong place at the wrong time.

Questioning had been intense, but Kats repeated his story that he was working for John Lin on an investigation and that unfortunately he'd been in the building when the bomb went off. He'd helped Lin escape the blaze through a service tunnel under the building. The others had perished in the fire. It had the ring of truth. John had successfully come out of surgery and, when questioned in the hospital, confirmed Kats' version of the story.

When word came that there were no charges being filed against Kats, Elliott Blackstone came to the holding cell in the Hall of Justice, carrying a cup of coffee for him. "They're processing your release now," he said, handing the cup to Kats, who took it gratefully.

"Someday, you're gonna tell me what really happened, right?" he said to Kats.

"Someday," Kats smiled. "But just know that the good guys won and justice was actually done."

"Fair enough," Blackstone replied.

As he exited the rear doors of the Hall of Justice, avoiding the press out front who'd been alerted to his release, he saw Molly waiting for him. "This is becoming a regular thing for us," she smiled.

"God, I hope not," he laughed.

That afternoon they headed over to St. Francis Memorial Hospital where John was recovering. There were no police guards outside his third-floor room, but they did note several black-clad Hop Sing soldiers seated in the hallway. As Kats and Molly approached, a tall, black-clad man stood before them. He left arm was in a plaster cast up to the elbow and carried in a sling in front of his chest. His hair was cropped short. Shan, the Red Pole enforcer of the Hop Sing Tong, looked squarely at Kats, who returned his gaze. Shan then gave a deep bow to Kats. Molly squeezed Kats' arm.

Shan rose and said, "I thank you for saving the life of Lin Tai Lo. And I thank you for saving my life as well. I'm in your debt." Kats nodded, knowing how important it was for Shan to express that obligation. Westerners would brush it off, saying not to worry about it, but Easterners knew that doing so would be rude. Kats gave a solemn nod.

"I like the haircut," Kats said with a smile. Shan smiled as well.

"A lesson learned," he said. Molly caught his eyes, and they also exchanged a smile.

John was propped up in his bed, a tube draining from his upper chest. He had a sizable hole punched in him, and that simply couldn't be stitched up. It had to be allowed to heal from the inside out. This meant a prolonged stay in the hospital.

He opened his eyes as they approached. He raised his left hand, which Kats took, and the two men looked at each other. It was wordless communication between men not used to expressing their emotions. Molly watched and smiled.

"My family thanks you," John said in a tight, formal voice. "Mai has justice." Both men were quiet.

Kats finally said, "We should hang out more. It's been too long since we did anything like that."

"I too would like that," John said, "But I'll be here for a bit," he looked at the tube coming out of his chest. *These guys are terrible at this,* Molly thought. She nudged Kats.

"Of course, when you're feeling better," Kats nodded, his mind searching, "I have season tickets to the Giants. Do you like baseball?"

"No."

"That's OK. The hotdogs are great."

EPILOGUE

Kats drove the Chevy Bel Air north across the Golden Gate. Molly sat beside him, and Shig rode in the back and tapped Kats on the shoulder. "Hey, man. Change this old man station to KOBY. Better music."

He rolled the radio dial to KOBY, and Elvis Presley's "A Big Hunk O' Love" filled the car. Shig snapped his fingers, "I'm tellin' you, man. Elvis is gonna be bigger than Sinatra ever was." Kats wrinkled his nose at that idea. He still preferred Sinatra, but he knew Molly liked Presley, so he said nothing.

Kats said to Molly, "So she really just quit?"

"Yeah. Called me this morning. She said she was done with San Francisco," Molly said.

"Who quit?" Shig asked.

"Lola," Molly replied. "She said she needed a fresh start, and a friend of hers from England invited her to come over there. She said she was moving to Soho and wanted to find a nice English boy."

"Awww," Shig said, "she deserves to be happy. I hope she finds it."

They exited just over the bridge and headed toward the waterfront town of Sausalito. Tucked into Richardson Bay, Sausalito had been a community of shipbuilding and maritime businesses. Since the war, more artists and retirees were moving there, turning it into a wealthier residential community, and though it was only a few miles from San

Francisco, it seemed like another world.

They drove through downtown and circled the edge of the town on Bridgeway. Passing a waterfront park, they turned right onto an outcropping of land that showed rows of docks, many with houseboats moored next to them. They arrived at a large parcel of land, dominated by a warehouse, that looked surprisingly new. Behind the warehouse, two long docks stretched into the bay. Kats parked, and the three of them walked around to the dock. A wooden sailboat, some forty feet long with a single elegant mast, was nestled next to the dock. As they approached, a young, sandy-haired man came up from below deck and, seeing the trio, waved them over.

Anton Vello, the youngest son of master boat builder Carlo Vello and now co-owner of the recently renamed Vello Brothers Boats, strode off the boat, beaming at them, and gave Molly a big hug. Shig and Kats waited their turns to shake Anton's hand, smiling the whole time. Anton's father had passed away a year and a half before, and the events surrounding their family shipyard near the Hunters Point Naval Base had brought Anton and his brother Gianni over to Sausalito.

"You look good, Anton," Kats said. "Shipbuilding seems to agree with you."

"It actually does," he laughed. "I still find some time for poetry, and I've even been writing a bit lately."

"A novel?" Shig asked with a grin.

"Maybe," Anton said. "Probably too soon to tell. But this beauty," he turned and looked at the boat, "is the first boat designed and built by Gianni and me, without our father."

They all looked appreciatively at the sailboat, knowing that Anton's father, Carlo, had been a master of his craft.

The sons seemed to have inherited his talent.

"Your dad would be so proud of you," Molly said.

Anton nodded, feeling his emotions well up. Molly squeezed his hand.

Kats let the moment sink in before he said, "Thank you for helping our friends. This is really above and beyond."

Anton's handsome face turned to Kats, "Of course, we'd help you. Besides, she needs a good shakedown cruise," he laughed. They watched as three more of Anton's men emerged from below deck, readying the boat for the journey.

Just then a taxicab pulled up in front of the Vello Brothers warehouse, and two figures emerged. They walked down the dock, each carrying a small suitcase. Turier and Epps.

In the three weeks since the fire in Chinatown, they'd been in the care of Dr. Han. Besides being an incredible herbalist and apothecary, Han proved to be a competent medical doctor and a very good cook. He'd treated Steven Epps for a concussion and a subdural hematoma—some bleeding in the brain from the blow Kats had delivered with the mace. His shoulder blade had been cracked as well, so Han had immobilized his arm, giving it time to heal. Epps wore a pair of sunglasses and moved slowly, but otherwise he seemed whole. Turier smiled at them. He'd shaved his beard and mustache, making him look much younger and nothing like the photo that had been circulated of him in the press. He now bore a 'dueling scar' on his left cheek. Most everyone thought he'd perished in the fire along with the suspect in the blackmail house killings. John had carefully dropped that last tidbit during his questioning with the police. No one was looking for them, but they needed a quiet way out of the country.

That's where Anton and his men came in. The new boat

needed a sea test, and a trip to Mexico and back would be ideal. Turier and Epps could get off in the port of their choice.

"*Bonjour!*" Turier said with a wave. Epps gave a nod as well. Turier gave the customary double-cheeked kisses to Molly. Kats turned toward Anton and made the introductions all around. They chatted a bit about the journey, the travel time, and the weather.

Anton said, "My men are ready to go whenever you two are. We're loaded with supplies, including some good French wine," he smiled at Turier. "I'll let you all say your farewells."

"Thanks, Anton," Kats said. He turned to Turier and extended his hand. "Dominic, it's been great to see you again, and I'm so glad we could help." Turier laughed and moved in to embrace Kats.

"Thank you, Kats," he said squeezing him hard. "You've become an amazing man. I'm so very proud of you." Kats smiled and felt his face flush at that. Turier turned to Molly, "Take good care of him, Molly."

"I will, Dominic," she replied.

"I'll eventually find my way back to France. I'll let you know, and you two must come visit me. Have you been to Paris, Molly?"

"Never."

"You'll love it," he smiled. *I bet I will*, she thought.

Kats turned to see Epps and Shig laughing as Shig patted him on the shoulder. Shig had given him a copy of *Doctor Zhivago*, "Something to read on the trip," he said. Kats and Molly walked over to Epps.

She handed him a brown paper-wrapped package. He took it, looking curiously at it. "It's a new sketchbook and some good pencils." He smiled.

"Thank you," he said quietly. Then he looked at Kats.

"I'm sorry about having to knock you out," Kats said earnestly.

"I've had worse," Epps said quietly, "Besides, you had to do it. You did us all a favor." Epps extended his hand to Kats, who shook it.

"I hope you find some peace in whatever time you have left. You deserve it," Kats said.

"We both do," he replied. "But I may have more time than I thought."

"Really?" Kats replied.

"Yeah, your friend Dr. Han is kind of amazing with all those herbs and things. He said my body was way out of alignment and unbalanced. He did some acupuncture on me and gave me this horrible-tasting medicine for the past couple of weeks. He said it would help me."

"So you don't feel ..." Kats began.

"Like a clock winding down? No, not anymore. I don't know if it'll last, but he gave me this special tea," he hefted a porcelain container from his pocket, "and wrote this message in Chinese. He said I could get more of this in any Chinatown in the world." Epps shrugged his shoulders. "I guess we'll see."

"None of us really knows how much time we have," Kats said. "Just makes you like the rest of us."

"I like that," Epps said with a smile.

Kats, Molly, Shig, and Anton stood on the dock as the boat cast off. They watched as it slowly drifted into the bay before the sails unfurled and caught the light afternoon wind. The boat seemed to leap with excitement at the chance to run. "She really is beautiful," Shig said admiringly.

"Yes, she is," Kats said, and Molly saw he was looking at her when he said it.

Two weeks later, on July 22, 1959, Kats, Molly, and Shig took John to his first baseball game at Seals Stadium. He didn't understand the game, but he did love the hotdogs.

The Giants beat the Cardinals, 6-1.

Kats, Molly, and Shig will return.

FURTHER READING

No-No Boy by **John Okada.** Published in 1956, this book got little critical attention and very little love from the Japanese American community at the time. Perhaps the wounds were too fresh for some to embrace a story about nisei voices of dissent during the war. Today it reads differently and should be seen in that light as a chronicle of that time and work about conscientious protest.

The Good Asian by **Pornsak Pichetshote.** Outstanding graphic novel about a fictional Chinese American police detective in 1936 San Francisco. Classic noir tale meets a fresh perspective and great artwork. I learned about the 'chop suey circuit' of Chinese owned night clubs such as Forbidden City, after which the Hong Kong Club is inspired.

Last Night at the Telegraph Club by **Malinda Lo.** The intimate story of a young girl coming of age in Chinatown in the 1950's. A totally different perspective on the city and that time period.

Evergreen by **Naomi Hirahara.** Aki, the protagonist from *Clark and Division* returns in this mystery set in Los Angeles after WWII. Many Japanese Americans did not return to the west coast after the war, but some did, and Hirahara chronicles the challenges they faced into this second installment of the Japantown Mystery series.

ENDNOTES

1   Elliot Blackstone was a real police officer in San Francisco. He was an early pioneer of what we would call 'community policing' today. In 1962 he was designated the first police officer to officially coordinate with the gay community. A deeply religious and straight man, he became a beloved champion of the LGBTQ+ community, even presiding as the Grand Marshall of the 2006 Gay Pride Parade.

2   MKUltra was a top secret CIA operation that ran from 1953 to 1973. They did use hospitals, prisons, universities and pharmaceutical companies as front operations to conduct these mind control experiments. In the 1973 CIA Director Richard Helms ordered all documentation relating to MKUltra be destroyed. The truth of the operation only became known following a Freedom of Information Act request that found some 20,000 documents relating to MKUltra that had been misfiled and thus escaped the CIA's attempt to cover up the entire operation.

3   Midnight Climax really was a CIA operation in San Francisco and New York City. The operation began in 1954 and ran for over a decade. I first learned about this from a story my friend and San Francisco chronicler Gary Kamiya wrote about this crazy episode in American history. The original story can be found here:

https://www.sfchronicle.com/chronicle_vault/article When-the-CIA-ran-a-LSD-sex-house-in-San-Francis-co-7223346.php

4   Ken Kesey will become known as one of America's great writers with the 1962 publication of *One Flew Over the Cuckoo's Nest*. In 1959 he was a graduate student at Stanford University and worked as an orderly at Menlo Park Hospital. While there he voluntarily participated in the government sponsored LSD experiments. Kesey also becomes a significant figure in the 1960's counter cultural movement. He famously credits the US government for getting him high for years.

5   Lauri Törni was a real soldier and a commissioned officer in the German SS. After the war, he was recruited under the auspices of the Lodge-Philbin Act of 1950 that authorized the US military to engage highly trained foreign nationals as soldiers. In return for their service, these men were eventually granted citizenship. Larry Thorne was the name he was given in the US. Thorne served in the US Special Forces until he was killed in action in Vietnam in 1965. Today there is a Special Forces award bearing his name that is given out every year. There is also a command building at Fort Carson, Colorado that is named after him. In 2011 he was inducted into the United States Special Operational Command (USSOCOM) Commando Hall of Honor.

6   Blum's really was known for its Coffee Crunch Cake. You can find the actual recipe here: https:// www.facebook.com/LostSanFrancisco/photos

/a.414325578625750/824946214230349/

7   The company was founded by Adolph "Adi" Dassler af-
      ter World War I. The company would go on to become
      Addidas after the Second World War.

8   With apologies to all indigenous peoples, especially those
      connected to Northern California, at that time in history,
      Indian was the term that these men would have used.
      For Kats' generation as well, the term Oriental was still
      commonly used.

9   Hakujin is the term primarily used by Japanese Ameri-
      cans for White people. It's not seen as derogatory.

10   Shig famously used that quote, "Is that your professional
      opinion?" as a way to tease and wind up his friends and
      colleagues. Here it is more of a nervous response to stress.

11   SRO refers to single-room occupancy. Downtown San
      Francicso has a large number of these cheap, multitenant
      buildings. They were an important part of the city's early
      boom periods providing necessary housing mostly to
      single men. Many of them are now historically protect-
      ed and look much like they did a century ago. Efforts to
      modernize them or in some cases eliminate them in favor
      of modern affordable housing have been mostly stymied,
      contributing to the housing crisis in the Bay Area.

12   As a young man, I read Watt's *The Way of Zen*. I remem-
      ber carrying it around in junior high school, and I look

back at it now as part of my quest to understand my Asian heritage, which was something of a challenge growing up in Akron, Ohio.

13 Legends of wild men and humanoid creatures in the woods had been part of the lore of the Pacific Northwest for centuries. But in the fall of 1958, members of a logging crew in Humbolt County, California, claimed to have found a series of giant footprints in the northern California woods. Stories of incidents involving the mysterious creature led to the men calling it "Big Foot." The story got picked up by the national media, with the New York Times and the Los Angeles Times running pictures of the huge plaster casts of the forest dweller's footprints.

14 The Military Intelligence Service was the language training school that the military established shortly before the attack on Pearl Harbor. The military realized they needed translators to intercept radio communications, read captured documents and interrogate captured Japanese prisoners. They recruited nisei men who were familiar with the language from birth. The first school was located on the Presidio but in 1942, after Roosevelt signed the executive order creating the west coast exclusionary zone, they had to move the school to Minnesota. Over 5,000 men went through the program including Shig Murao and my father, Paul Kageyama. My father and Shig were born about one month apart making them eligible for enlistment right around the same time. I do not know if for a fact, but it is very possible that my dad and Shig were at the language school at the same time and may very well have known each other then. I'd like to believe

that their paths did cross.

15   Shig did take up the shakuhachi, the Japanese wooden flute and by accounts from friends, became a good player.

16   My family was sent to the Topaz Internment Camp in Utah.

17   The "No No Boys" were so named because they answered "No" to the last two questions on the loyalty oath that all persons of Japanese ancestry were required to sign before being allowed to serve in the military for men, or in the support services such as nursing for women. The vast majority of nisei signed the oath but some objected to the unfair singling out of Japanese Americans. German and Italian Americans did not have to sign any such oath. This caused a significant schism in the Japanese American community that would take years to be reconciled. I have in mind a future story that will address this schism.

18   Benkyodo was a real Japanese bakery on Buchanan. It opened just after the 1906 earthquake and was a fixture in Japantown and the city as a whole for more than a hundred years. Benkyodo closed in March of 2022. My father, Paul Kageyama, just like Kats, loved the green tea mochi.

About the Author

Peter Kageyama is a sansei, a third generation Japanese American. Born in Akron, Ohio, he attended The Ohio State University, receiving a B.A. in Political Science, and Case Western University School of Law for his J.D. He practiced law for a couple of years but describes himself as a 'recovering attorney'.

Peter is the author of four nonfiction books on cities and urban affairs. His first book, *For the Love of Cities*, was recognized as a Top 10 Book in Urban Planning and Development. He speaks all over the world about better placemaking that emphasizes small, inexpensive, and fun approaches to city building. He was a Senior Advisor to the Alliance for Innovation, a national network of city leaders, and is a special advisor to America in Bloom.

In his spare time Peter is an avid board gamer, comic book geek and classic rock nerd. He lives in downtown St. Petersburg, Florida with his wife, award winning architect Lisa Wannemacher, and their dog Dobby.

www.peterkageyama.com